George Mivart

On the Genesis of Species

Anatiposi

George Mivart

On the Genesis of Species

Reprint of the original, first published in 1871.

1st Edition 2023 | ISBN: 978-3-38211-523-4

Anatiposi Verlag is an imprint of Outlook Verlagsgesellschaft mbH.

Verlag (Publisher): Outlook Verlag GmbH, Zeilweg 44, 60439 Frankfurt, Deutschland
Vertretungsberechtigt (Authorized to represent): E. Roepke, Zeilweg 44, 60439 Frankfurt, Deutschland
Druck (Print): Books on Demand GmbH, In de Tarpen 42, 22848 Norderstedt, Deutschland

ON THE GENESIS OF SPECIES.

THE AARD-VARK (ORYCTEROPUS).

ON

THE GENESIS OF SPECIES.

BY

ST. GEORGE MIVART, F.R.S.

WITH NUMEROUS ILLUSTRATIONS.

SECOND EDITION.

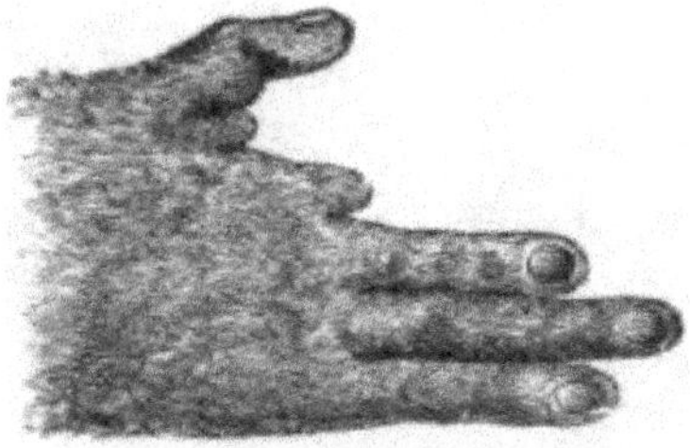

HAND OF THE POTTO (PERODICTICUS), FROM LIFE.

London and New York:
MACMILLAN AND CO.
1871.

TO

SIR HENRY HOLLAND, BART., M.D.,
F.R.S., D.C.L., ETC. ETC.

MY DEAR SIR HENRY,

IN giving myself the pleasure to dedicate, as I now do, this work to you, it is not my intention to identify you with any views of my own advocated in it.

I simply avail myself of an opportunity of paying a tribute of esteem and regard to my earliest scientific friend—the first to encourage me in pursuing the study of nature.

I remain,

MY DEAR SIR HENRY,

Ever faithfully yours,

ST. GEORGE MIVART.

7, NORTH BANK, REGENT'S PARK,
December 8, 1870.

CONTENTS.

CHAPTER I.

INTRODUCTORY.

CHAPTER II.

THE INCOMPETENCY OF "NATURAL SELECTION" TO ACCOUNT FOR THE INCIPIENT STAGES OF USEFUL STRUCTURES.

CHAPTER V.

AS TO SPECIFIC STABILITY.

CHAPTER VI.

SPECIES AND TIME.

CHAPTER VII.

SPECIES AND SPACE.

CHAPTER VIII.

HOMOLOGIES

CHAPTER IX.

EVOLUTION AND ETHICS.

CHAPTER XII.

THEOLOGY AND EVOLUTION.

LIST OF ILLUSTRATIONS.

THE GENESIS OF SPECIES.

CHAPTER I.

INTRODUCTORY.

The problem of the genesis of species stated.—Nature of its probable solution.—Importance of the question.—Position here defended.—Statement of the DARWINIAN THEORY.—Its applicability to details of geographical distribution; to rudimentary structures; to homology; to mimicry, &c.—Consequent utility of the theory.—Its wide acceptance.—Reasons for this, other than, and in addition to, its scientific value.—Its simplicity.—Its bearing on religious questions.—*Odium theologicum* and *odium antitheologicum*.—The antagonism supposed by many to exist between it and theology neither necessary nor universal.—Christian authorities in favour of evolution.—Mr. Darwin's "Animals and Plants under Domestication."—Difficulties of the Darwinian theory enumerated.

THE great problem which has so long exercised the minds of naturalists, namely, that concerning the origin of different kinds of animals and plants, seems at last to be fairly on the road to receive—perhaps at no very distant future—as satisfactory a solution as it can well have.

But the problem presents peculiar difficulties. The birth of a "species" has often been compared with that of an "individual." The origin, however, of even an individual animal or plant (that which determines an embryo to

evolve itself,—as, *e.g.*, a spider rather than
rose-plant rather than a pear) is shrouded in o
A fortiori must this be the case with the orig
a "species."

Moreover, the analogy between a "species" and an "individual" is a very incomplete one. The word "individual" denotes a concrete whole with a real, separate, and distinct existence. The word "species," on the other hand, denotes a peculiar congeries of characters, innate powers and qualities, and a certain nature realized indeed in individuals, but having no separate existence, except ideally as a thought in some mind.

Thus the birth of a "species" can only be compared metaphorically, and very imperfectly, with that of an "individual."

Individuals *as individuals*, actually and directly produce and bring forth other individuals; but no "congeries of characters," no "common nature" *as such*, can directly bring forth another "common nature," because, *per se*, it has no existence (other than ideal) apart from the individuals in which it is manifested.

The problem then is, "by what combination of natural laws does a new 'common nature' appear upon the scene of realized existence?" *i.e.* how is an individual embodying such new characters produced?

For the approximation we have of late made towards the solution of this problem, we are mainly indebted to the invaluable labours and active brains of Charles Darwin and Alfred Wallace.

Nevertheless, important as have been the impulse and direction given by those writers to both our observations and speculations, the solution will not (if the views here advocated are correct) ultimately present that aspect and character with which it has issued from the hands of those writers.

Neither, most certainly, will that solution agree in appearance or substance with the more or less crude conceptions which have been put forth by most of the opponents of Messrs. Darwin and Wallace.

Rather, judging from the more recent manifestations of thought on opposite sides, we may expect the development of some *tertium quid*—the resultant of forces coming from different quarters, and not coinciding in direction with any one of them.

As error is almost always partial truth, and so consists in the exaggeration or distortion of one verity by the suppression of another which qualifies and modifies the former, we may hope, by the synthesis of the truths contended for by various advocates, to arrive at the one conciliating reality.

Signs of this conciliation are not wanting: opposite scientific views, opposite philosophical conceptions and opposite religious beliefs, are rapidly tending by their vigorous conflict to evolve such a systematic and comprehensive view of the genesis of species as will completely harmonize with the teachings of science, philosophy and religion.

To endeavour to add one stone to this temple of concord, to try and remove a few of the misconceptions and mutual misunderstandings which oppose harmonious action, is the aim and endeavour of the present work. This aim it is hoped to attain, not by shirking difficulties, but analysing them, and by endeavouring to dig down to the common root which supports and unites diverging stems of truth.

It cannot but be a gain when the labourers in the three fields above mentioned, namely, science, philosophy and religion, shall fully recognize this harmony. Then the energy too often spent in futile controversy, or withheld through prejudice, may be profitably and reciprocally exercised for the mutual benefit of all.

Remarkable is the rapidity with which an interest in the question of specific origination has spread. But a few years ago it scarcely occupied the minds of any but naturalists. Then the crude theory put forth by Lamarck, and by his English interpreter, the author of the "Vestiges of Creation," had rather discredited than helped on a belief in organic evolution—a belief, that is, in new kinds being produced from older ones by the ordinary and constant operation of natural laws. Now, however, this notion is widely diffused. Indeed, there are few drawing-rooms where it is not the subject of occasional discussion, and artisans and schoolboys have their views as to the permanence of organic forms. Moreover, the reception of this doctrine tends actually, though by no means necessarily, to be accompanied by certain beliefs with regard to quite distinct and very momentous subject-matter. So that the question of the "Genesis of Species" is not only one of great interest, but also of much consequence.

But though the calm and thorough consideration of this matter is at the present moment exceedingly desirable, yet the actual importance of the question itself as to its consequences in the domain of theology has been strangely exaggerated by many, both of its opponents and supporters. This is especially the case with that form of the evolution theory which is associated with the name of Mr. Darwin; and yet neither the refutation nor the demonstration of that doctrine would be necessarily accompanied by the results which are hoped for by one party and dreaded by another.

The general theory of evolution has indeed for some time past steadily gained ground, and it may be safely predicted that the number of facts which can be brought forward in its support will, in a few years, be vastly augmented. But the prevalence of this theory need alarm no one, for it is, without any doubt, perfectly consistent with strictest and most orthodox Christian theology. Moreover, it is not altogether without obscurities, and cannot yet be considered as fully demonstrated.

The special Darwinian hypothesis, however, is beset with certain scientific difficulties, which must by no means be ignored, and some of which, the author ventures to think, are absolutely insuperable. What Darwinism or "Natural Selection" is, will be shortly explained; but before doing so, it may be well to state the object of this book, and the view taken up and defended in it. Its object is to maintain the position that "Natural Selection" acts, and indeed must act; but that still, in order to account for the production of known kinds of animals and plants, it requires to be supplemented by the action of some other natural law or laws as yet undiscovered.[1] Also, that the consequences which have been drawn from Evolution, whether exclusively Darwinian or not, to the prejudice of religion, by no means follow from it, and are in fact illegitimate.

[1] In the last edition of the "Origin of Species" (1869) Mr. Darwin himself admits that "Natural Selection" has not been the exclusive means of modification, though he still contends it has been the most important one.

The Darwinian theory of "Natural Selection" may be shortly stated thus:[1]—

Every kind of animal and plant tends to increase in numbers in a geometrical progression.

Every kind of animal and plant transmits a general likeness, with individual differences, to its offspring.

Every individual may present minute variations of any kind and in any direction.

Past time has been practically infinite.

Every individual has to maintain a very severe struggle for existence, owing to the tendency to geometrical increase of all kinds of animals and plants, while (from the constancy of physical conditions acting as a continual check on such increase) the total amount of animal and vegetable population (man and his agency excepted) remains almost stationary from year to year.

Thus, every variation of a sort tending to save the life of the individual possessing it, or to enable it more surely to propagate its kind, will in the long run be preserved, and the organism that has it will transmit its favourable peculiarity to some of its offspring, which peculiarity will thus become intensified till it reaches the maximum degree of utility. On the other hand, individuals presenting unfavourable peculiarities will be ruthlessly destroyed. The action of this law of "Natural Selection" may thus be well represented by the convenient expression "survival of the fittest."[2]

Now this conception of Mr. Darwin is perhaps the

[1] See Mr. Wallace's recent work, entitled "Contributions to the Theory of Natural Selection," where, at p. 302, it is very well and shortly stated.

[2] "Natural Selection" is happily so termed by Mr. Herbert Spencer in his "Principles of Biology."

most interesting theory, in relation to natural science, which has been promulgated during the present century. Remarkable indeed is the way in which it groups together so vast and varied a series of biological[1] facts, and even paradoxes, which it appears more or less clearly to explain, as the following instances will show.

By this theory of "Natural Selection," light is thrown on the more singular facts relating to the geographical distribution of animals and plants; for example, on the resemblance between the past and present inhabitants of different parts of the earth's surface. Thus in Australia remains have been found of creatures closely allied to kangaroos and other kinds of pouched beasts, which in the present day exist nowhere but in the Australian region. Similarly in South America, and nowhere else, are found sloths and armadillos, and in that same part of the world have been discovered bones of animals different indeed from existing sloths and armadillos, but much more nearly related to them than to any other kinds whatever. Such coincidences between the existing and antecedent geographical distribution of forms are numerous. Again, "Natural Selection" serves to explain the circumstance that often in adjacent islands we find animals closely resembling, and appearing to represent, each other; while if certain of these islands show signs (by depth of surrounding sea or what not) of more ancient separation, the animals inhabiting them exhibit a corresponding divergence.[2] The explanation consists in representing the forms inhabiting the islands as being the modified

[1] Biology is the science of life. It contains zoology, or the science of animals, and botany, or that of plants.

[2] For very interesting examples, see Mr. Wallace's "Malay Archipelago."

descendants of a common stock, the modification being greatest where the separation has been the most prolonged.

"Rudimentary structures" also receive an explanation by means of this theory. These structures are parts which are apparently functionless and useless where they occur, but which represent similar parts of large size and functional importance in other animals. Examples of such "rudimentary structures" are the fœtal teeth of whales, and those of the front part of the upper jaw of ruminating quadrupeds. These fœtal structures are minute in size, and never cut the gum, but are re-absorbed without ever coming into use, while no other teeth succeed or represent them in the adult condition of those animals. The mammary glands of all male beasts constitute another example, as also does the wing of the apteryx—a New Zealand bird utterly incapable of flight, and with the wing in a quite rudimentary condition (whence the name of the animal). Yet this rudimentary wing contains bones which are miniature representatives of the ordinary wing-bones of birds of flight. Now, the presence of these useless bones and teeth is explained if they may be considered as actually being the inherited diminished representatives of parts of large size and functional importance in the remote ancestors of these various animals.

Again, the singular facts of homology are similarly capable of deeper explanation by "Natural Selection." "Homology" is the name applied to the investigation of those resemblances which have so often been found to underlie superficial differences between animals of very different form and habit. Thus man, the horse, the whale, and the bat, all have the pectoral limb, whether it be the arm, or fore-leg, or paddle, or wing, formed on essentially the same type, though the number and proportion of parts may more or less differ. Again, the butterfly and the shrimp, different as they are in appearance and mode of life, are yet constructed on one common plan, of which they constitute diverging manifestations. No *a priori* reason is conceivable why such similarities should be necessary, but they are readily explicable on the assumption of a genetic relationship and affinity between the animals in question, assuming, that is, that they are the modified descendants of some ancient form—their common ancestor.

That remarkable series of changes which animals undergo before they attain their adult condition, which is called their process of development, and during which they more or less closely resemble other animals during the early stages of the same process, has also great light thrown on it from the same source. The question as to the singularly complex resemblances borne by every adult animal and plant to a certain number of other animals and plants—resemblances by means of which the adopted zoological and botanical systems of classification have been possible—finds its solution through the same hypothesis, classification becoming the expression of a genealogical relationship. Finally, by this theory—and as yet by this alone—can any explanation be given of that extraordinary phenomenon which is metaphorically termed *mimicry*. Mimicry is a close and striking, yet superficial resemblance borne by some animal or plant to some other, perhaps very different, animal or plant. The "walking leaf" (an insect belonging to the grasshopper and cricket order) is a well-known and conspicuous instance of the assumption by an animal of the appearance of a vegetable structure (see illustration on p. 40);

and the bee, fly, and spider orchids are familiar examples of a converse resemblance. Birds, butterflies, reptiles, and even fish, seem to bear in certain instances a similarly striking resemblance to other birds, butterflies, reptiles and fish, of altogether distinct kinds. The explanation of this matter which "Natural Selection" offers, as to animals, is that certain varieties of one kind have found exemption from persecution in consequence of an accidental resemblance which such varieties have exhibited to animals of another kind, or to plants; and that they were thus preserved, and the degree of resemblance was continually augmented in their descendants. As to plants, the explanation offered by this theory might perhaps be that varieties of plants which presented a certain superficial resemblance in their flowers to insects, have thereby attracted such insects, and have so been helped to propagate their kind, the visit of certain insects being useful or indispensable to the fertilization of many flowers.

We have thus a whole series of important facts which "Natural Selection" helps us to understand and co-ordinate. And not only are all these diverse facts strung together, as it were, by the theory in question; not only does it explain the development of the complex instincts of the beaver, the cuckoo, the bee, and the ant, as also the dazzling brilliancy of the humming-bird, the glowing tail and neck of the peacock, and the melody of the nightingale; the perfume of the rose and the violet, the brilliancy of the tulip and the sweetness of the nectar of flowers; not only does it help us to understand all these, but it also serves as a basis of future research and of inference from the known to the unknown, and guides the investigator to the discovery of new facts which, when ascertained, it seems also able to co-ordinate.[1] Nay, "Natural Selection" seems capable of application not only to the building up of the smallest and most insignificant organisms, but even of extension beyond the biological domain altogether, so as possibly to have relation to the stable equilibrium of the solar system itself, and even of the whole sidereal universe. Thus, whether this theory be true or false, all lovers of natural science should acknowledge a deep debt of gratitude to Messrs. Darwin and Wallace, on account of its practical utility. But the utility of a theory by no means implies its truth. What do we not owe, for example, to the labours of the Alchemists? The emission theory of light, again, has been pregnant with valuable results, as still is the Atomic theory, and others which will readily suggest themselves.

With regard to Mr. Darwin (with whose name, on account of the noble self-abnegation of Mr. Wallace, the theory is in general exclusively associated), his friends may heartily congratulate him on the fact that he is one of the few exceptions to the rule respecting the non-appreciation of a prophet in his own country. It would be difficult to name another living labourer in the field of physical science who has excited an interest so wide-spread, and given rise to so much praise, gathering round him, as he has done, a chorus of more or less completely acquiescing disciples, themselves masters in science and each the representative of a crowd of enthusiastic followers.

[1] See Müller's work, "Für Darwin," lately translated into English by Mr. Dallas. Mr. Wallace also predicts the discovery, in Madagascar, of a hawk-moth with an enormously long proboscis, and he does this on account of the discovery there of an orchid with a nectary from ten to fourteen inches in length. See *Quarterly Journal of Science*, October 1867, and "Natural Selection," p. 275.

Such is the Darwinian theory of "Natural Selection," such are the more remarkable facts which it is potent to explain, and such is the reception it has met with in the world. A few words now as to the reasons for the very wide-spread interest it has awakened, and the keenness with which the theory has been both advocated and combated.

The important bearing it has on such an extensive range of scientific facts, its utility, and the vast knowledge and great ingenuity of its promulgator, are enough to account for the heartiness of its reception by those learned in natural history. But quite other causes have concurred to produce the general and higher degree of interest felt in the theory beside the readiness with which it harmonizes with biological facts. These latter could only be appreciated by physiologists, zoologists, and botanists; whereas the Darwinian theory, so novel and so startling, has found a cloud of advocates and opponents beyond and outside the world of physical science.

In the first place, it was inevitable that very many half-educated men and shallow thinkers should accept with eagerness the theory of "Natural Selection," or rather what they think to be such (for few things are more remarkable than the manner in which it has been misunderstood), on account of a certain characteristic it has in common with other theories which should not be mentioned in the same breath with it, except, as now, with the accompaniment of protest and apology. We refer to its remarkable simplicity and the ready way in which phenomena the most complex appear explicable by a cause for the comprehension of which laborious and persevering efforts are not required, but which may be represented by the simple phrase "survival of the fittest." With nothing more than this, can, on the Darwinian theory, all the most intricate facts of distribution and affinity, form, and colour, be accounted for; as well as the most complex instincts and the most admirable adjustments, such as those of the human eye and ear. It is in great measure then, owing to this supposed simplicity, and to a belief in its being yet easier and more simple than it is, that Darwinism, however imperfectly understood, has become a subject for general conversation and has been able thus widely to increase a certain knowledge of biological matters: and this excitation of interest in quarters where otherwise it would have been entirely wanting, is an additional motive for gratitude on the part of naturalists to the authors of the new theory. At the same time it must be admitted that a similar "simplicity"—the apparently easy explanation of complex phenomena—also constitutes the charm of such matters as hydropathy and phrenology, in the eyes of the unlearned or half-educated public. It is indeed *the* charm of all those seeming "short cuts" to knowledge, by which the labour of mastering scientific details is spared to those who believe that without such labour they can yet attain all the most valuable results of scientific research. It is not, of course, meant to imply that its "simplicity" tells at all against "Natural Selection," but only that the actual or supposed possession of that quality is a strong reason for the wide and somewhat hasty acceptance of the theory, whether it be true or not.

In the second place, it was inevitable that a theory appearing to have very grave relations with questions of the ast importance and interest to man, that is, with questions of religious belief, should call up an army of assailants and defenders. Nor have the supporters of the theory much reason, in many cases, to blame the more or less unskilful and hasty attacks of adversaries, seeing that those attacks have been in great part due to the unskilful and perverse advocacy of the cause on the part of some of its adherents. If the *odium theologicum* has inspired some of its opponents, it is undeniable that the *odium antitheologicum* has possessed not a few of its supporters. It is true (and in appreciating some of Mr. Darwin's expressions it should never be forgotten) that the theory has been both at its first promulgation and since vehemently attacked and denounced as unchristian, nay, as necessarily atheistic; but it is not less true that it has been made use of as a weapon of offence by irreligious writers, and has been again and again, especially in continental Europe, thrown, as it were, in the face of believers, with sneers and contumely. When we recollect the warmth with which what he thought was Darwinism was advocated by such a writer as Professor Vogt, one cause of his zeal was not far to seek —a zeal, by the way, certainly not "according to knowledge;" for few conceptions could have been more conflicting with true Darwinism than the theory he formerly maintained, but has since abandoned, viz. that the men of the Old World were descended from African and Asiatic apes, while, similarly, the American apes were the progenitors of the human beings of the New World. The cause of this palpable error in a too eager disciple, one might hope, was not anxiety to snatch up all or any arms available against Christianity, were it not for the tone unhappily adopted by him. But it is unfortunately quite impossible to mistake his meaning and intention, for he is a writer whose offensiveness is gross, while it is sometimes almost surpassed by an amazing shallowness. Of course, as might be expected, he adopts and reproduces the absurdly irrelevant objections to absolute morality drawn from differences in national customs.[1] And he seems to have as little conception of the distinction between "formally" moral actions and those which are only "materially" moral, as of that between the *verbum mentale* and the *verbum oris*. As an example of the onesidedness of his views, it may be remarked that he compares the skulls of the American monkeys (*Cebus apella* and *C. albifrons*) with the intention of showing that man is of several distinct species, because skulls of different men are less alike than those of these two monkeys; and he does this regardless of how the skulls of domestic animals (with which it is far more legitimate to compare races of men than with wild kinds), *e.g.* of different dogs or pigeons, tell precisely in the opposite direction—regardless also of the fact that perhaps no genus of monkeys is in a more unsatisfactory state as to the determination of its different kinds than the genus chosen by him for illustration. This is so much the case that J. A. Wagner (in his supplement to Schreber's great work on Beasts) at first included all the kinds in a single species.

As to the strength of his prejudice and his regrettable coarseness, one quotation will be enough to display both. Speaking of certain early Christian missionaries, he says:[2] "It is not so very improbable that the new religion, before which the flourishing Roman civilization relapsed into a state of barbarism, should have been introduced by people in whose skulls the anatomist finds simious characters so

[1] "Lectures on Man," translated by the Anthropological Society, 1864, p. 229.
[2] Ibid. p. 378.

well developed, and in which the phrenologist finds the organ of veneration so much enlarged. I shall, in the meanwhile, call these simious narrow skulls of Switzerland 'Apostle skulls,' as I imagine that in life they must have resembled the type of Peter, the Apostle, as represented in Byzantine-Nazarene art."

In encountering such a spirit, can it be wondered at that disputants have grown warm? Moreover, in estimating the vehemence of the opposition which has been offered, it should be borne in mind that the views defended by religious writers are, or should be, all-important in their eyes. They could not be expected to view with equanimity the destruction in many minds of "theology, natural and revealed, psychology, and metaphysics;" nor to weigh with calm and frigid impartiality arguments which seemed to them to be fraught with results of the highest moment to mankind, and, therefore, imposing on their consciences strenuous opposition as a first duty. Cool judicial impartiality in them would have been a sign perhaps of intellectual power, but also of a grievous deficiency of generous emotion.

It is easy to complain of onesidedness in the views of many who oppose Darwinism in the interest of orthodoxy; but not at all less patent is the intolerance and narrow-mindedness of some of those who advocate it, avowedly or covertly, in the interest of heterodoxy. This hastiness of rejection or acceptance, determined by ulterior consequences believed to attach to "Natural Selection," is unfortunately in part to be accounted for by some expressions and a certain tone to be found in Mr. Darwin's writings. That his expressions, however, are not always to be construed literally is manifest. His frequent use metaphorically of the theistic expressions, "contrivance," for example, and "purpose," has elicited, from the Duke of Argyll and others, criticisms which fail to tell against their opponent, solely because such expressions are, in Mr. Darwin's writings, merely figurative—metaphors, and nothing more.

It may be hoped, then, that a similar looseness of expression will account for passages of a directly opposite tendency to that of his theistic metaphors.

Moreover, it must not be forgotten that he frequently uses that absolutely theological term, "the Creator," and that he has retained in all the editions of his "Origin of Species" an expression which has been much criticised: he speaks "of life, with its several powers, having been originally breathed by the Creator into a few forms, or into one."[1] This is mentioned in justice to Mr. Darwin only, and by no means because it is a position which this book is intended to support. For, from Mr. Darwin's usual mode of speaking, it appears that by such Divine action he means a supernatural intervention, whereas it is here contended that throughout the whole process of physical evolution—the first manifestation of life included—*supernatural* action is assuredly not to be looked for.

Again, in justice to Mr. Darwin, it may be observed that he is addressing the general public, and opposing the ordinary and common objections of popular religionists, who have inveighed against "Evolution" and "Natural Selection" as atheistic, impious, and directly conflicting with the dogma of creation.

[1] See Fifth Edition, 1869, p. 579. In his recent work, "The Descent of Man," vol ii. p. 396, Mr. Darwin also says, "The birth both of the species and of the individual are equally parts of that grand sequence of events which our minds refuse to accept as the result of blind chance."

Still, in so important a matter, it is to be regretted that he did not take the trouble to distinguish between such merely popular notions and those which repose upon some more venerable authority. Mr. John Stuart Mill has replied to similar critics, by endeavouring to show that there is no foundation for the assertion that his philosophy is irreconcilable with theism; and it would have been better if Mr. Darwin had dealt in the same manner with some of his assailants, and shown the futility of certain of their objections when viewed from a more elevated religious standpoint. Instead of so doing, he seems to adopt the narrowest notions of his opponents, and, far from endeavouring to expand them, appears to wish to endorse them and to lend to them the weight of his authority. It is thus that Mr. Darwin seems to admit and assume that the idea of "creation" necessitates a belief in an interference with, or dispensation of, natural laws, and that "creation" must be accompanied by arbitrary and unorderly phenomena. None but the crudest conceptions are placed by him to the credit of supporters of the dogma of creation, and it is constantly asserted that they, to be consistent, must offer "creative fiats" as explanations of physical phenomena, and be guilty of numerous other such absurdities. It is impossible, therefore, to acquit Mr. Darwin of at least a certain carelessness in this matter; and the result is, he has the appearance of opposing ideas which he gives no clear evidence of having ever fully appreciated. He is far from being alone in this, and perhaps merely takes up and reiterates, without much consideration, assertions previously put forth by others. Nothing could be further from Mr. Darwin's mind than any, however small, intentional misrepresentation; and it is therefore the more unfortunate that he should not have shown any appreciation of a position opposed to his own other than that gross and crude one which he combats so superfluously—that he should appear, even for a moment, to be one of those, of whom there are far too many, who first misrepresent their adversary's view, and then elaborately refute it; who, in fact, erect a doll utterly incapable of self-defence, and then, with a flourish of trumpets and many vigorous strokes, overthrow the helpless dummy they have previously raised.

This is what many do who more or less distinctly oppose theism in the interests, as they believe, of physical science; and they often represent, amongst other things, a gross and narrow anthropomorphism as the necessary consequence of views opposed to those which they themselves advocate. Mr. Darwin and others may perhaps be excused if they have not devoted much time to the study of Christian philosophy; but they have no right to assume or accept without careful examination, as an unquestioned fact, that in that philosophy there is a necessary antagonism between the two ideas, "creation" and "evolution," as applied to organic forms.

It is notorious and patent to all who choose to seek, that many distinguished Christian thinkers have accepted and do accept both ideas, *i.e.* both "creation" and "evolution."

As much as ten years ago, an eminently Christian writer observed: "The creationist theory does not necessitate the perpetual search after manifestations of miraculous powers and perpetual 'catastrophes.' Creation is not a miraculous interference with the laws of nature, but the very institution of those laws. Law and regularity, not arbitrary intervention, was the patristic ideal of creation. With this notion, they admitted without difficulty the most surprising origin of living creatures, provided it took place by *law*. They held that when God said, 'Let the waters produce,' 'Let the earth produce,' He conferred forces on the elements of earth and water, which enabled them naturally to produce the various species of organic beings. This power, they thought, remains attached to the elements throughout all time."[1] The same writer quotes St. Augustine and St. Thomas Aquinas, to the effect that, "in the institution of nature, we do not look for miracles, but for the laws of nature."[2] And, again, St. Basil,[3] speaks of the continued operation of natural laws in the production of all organisms.[4]

So much for writers of early and mediæval times. As to the present day, the Author can confidently affirm that there are many as well versed in theology as Mr. Darwin is in his own department of natural knowledge, who would not be disturbed by the thorough demonstration of his theory. Nay, they would not even be in the least painfully affected at witnessing the generation of animals of complex organization by the skilful artificial arrangement of natural forces, and the production, in the future, of a fish, by means analogous to those by which we now produce urea.

And this because they know that the possibility of such

[1] *The Rambler*, March 1860, vol. xii. p. 372.

[2] "In primâ institutione naturæ non quæritur miraculum, sed quid natura rerum habeat, ut Augustinus dicit, lib. ii. sup. Gen. ad lit. c. 1." (St. Thomas, Sum. I^æ. lxvii. 4, ad 3.)

[3] "Hexaem." Hom. ix. p. 81.

[4] Since the first edition of this work appeared, the notice given of it in the *Dublin Review* for April 1871, demonstrates how great a mistake those make who think that the strictest orthodoxy is necessarily unfriendly to advanced physical science.

phenomena, though by no means actually foreseen, has yet been fully provided for in the old philosophy centuries before Darwin, or even centuries before Bacon, and that their place in the system can be at once assigned them without even disturbing its order or marring its harmony.

Moreover, the old tradition in this respect has never been abandoned, however much it may have been ignored or neglected by some modern writers. In proof of this it may be observed that perhaps no post-mediæval theologian has a wider reception amongst Christians throughout the world than Suarez, who has a separate section[1] in opposition to those who maintain the distinct creation of the various kinds—or substantial forms—of organic life.

But the consideration of this matter must be deferred for the present, and the question of evolution, whether Darwinian or other, be first gone into. It is proposed, after that has been done, to return to this subject (here merely referred to), and to consider at some length the bearing of "Evolution," whether Darwinian or non-Darwinian, upon "Creation and Theism."

Now we will revert simply to the consideration of the theory of "Natural Selection" itself.

Whatever may have hitherto been the amount of acceptance that this theory has met with, all, I think, anticipated that the appearance of Mr. Darwin's large and careful work on "Animals and Plants under Domestication" could but further increase that acceptance. It is, however, somewhat problematical how far such anticipations will be realized. The newer book seems to add but very little in support of the theory, and to leave most, if not all, its

1 Suarez, Metaphysica. Edition Vivés. Paris, 1868. Vol. I. Disputatio xv. § 2.

difficulties exactly where they were. It is a question, also, whether the hypothesis of "Pangenesis"[1] may not be found rather to encumber than to support the theory it is intended to subserve. However, the work in question treats only of domestic animals, and probably the next instalment will address itself more vigorously and directly to the difficulties which seem to us yet to bar the way to a complete acceptance of the doctrine.[2]

If the theory of Natural Selection can be shown to be quite insufficient to explain any considerable number of important phenomena connected with the origin of species, that theory, as *the* explanation, must be considered as so far discredited.

If other causes than Natural (including sexual) Selection can be proved to have acted—if variation can in any cases be proved to be subject to certain determinations in special directions by different means than Natural Selection, it then becomes antecedently probable that it is so in other cases, and that Natural Selection depends upon, and only supplements, such means; which conception is opposed to the pure Darwinian position.

Now it is certain, *a priori*, that variation is obedient to some law, and therefore that "Natural Selection" itself

[1] "Pangenesis" is the name of the new theory proposed by Mr. Darwin, in order to account for various obscure physiological facts, such, *e.g.*, as the occasional reproduction, by individuals, of parts which they have lost; the appearance in offspring of parental, and sometimes of remote ancestral, characters, &c. It accounts for these phenomena by supposing that every creature possesses countless indefinitely-minute organic atoms, termed "gemmules," which atoms are supposed to be generated in every part of every organ, to be in constant circulation about the body, and to have the power of reproduction. Moreover, atoms from every part are supposed to be stored in the generative products.

[2] These anticipations of the Author have not been fully realized in Mr. Darwin's most recent work, "The Descent of Man."

must be capable of being subsumed into some higher law; and, the Author believes, it is evident *a posteriori*, that "Natural Selection" is, at the very least, aided and supplemented by some other agency.

Admitting, then, organic and other evolution, and that new forms of animals and plants (new species, genera, &c.) have from time to time been evolved from preceding animals and plants, it follows, if the views here advocated are true, that this evolution has not taken place by the action of "Natural Selection" *alone*, but through it (amongst other influences) aided by the concurrent action of some other natural law or laws, at present undiscovered. It is probable also that the genesis of species takes place partly, perhaps mainly, through laws which may be most conveniently spoken of as special powers and tendencies existing in each organism; and partly through influences exerted on each such organism by surrounding conditions and agencies organic and inorganic, terrestrial and cosmical, among which the "survival of the fittest" plays a certain but subordinate part.

The theory of "Natural Selection" may (though it need not) be understood in such a way as to lead men to consider the present organic world to be formed, so to speak, *accidentally*, beautiful and wonderful as is confessedly the hap-hazard result. The same may perhaps be said with regard to the system advocated by Mr. Herbert Spencer, who, however, also degrades "Natural Selection" to a subordinate office. The view here advocated, on the other hand, exhibits the whole organic world as arising and going forward in one harmonious development similar to that which displays itself in the growth and action of each separate individual organism. It also regards each such separate organism as the expression of powers and tendencies not to be accounted for by "Natural Selection" alone, or even by that together with merely the direct influence of surrounding conditions.

The difficulties which appear to oppose themselves to the reception of "Natural Selection" or "the survival of the fittest," as the one explanation of the origin of species, have no doubt been already considered by Mr. Darwin. Nevertheless, it may be worth while to enumerate them, and to state the considerations which appear to give them weight; and there is no doubt but that a naturalist so candid and careful as the author of the theory in question, will feel obliged, rather than the reverse, by the suggestion of all the difficulties which can be brought against it.

What is to be brought forward may be summed up as follows:—

That "Natural Selection" is incompetent to account for the incipient stages of useful structures.

That it does not harmonize with the co-existence of closely similar structures of diverse origin.

That there are grounds for thinking that specific differences may be developed suddenly instead of gradually.

That the opinion that species have definite though very different limits to their variability is still tenable.

That certain fossil transitional forms are absent, which might have been expected to be present.

That some facts of geographical distribution intensify other difficulties.

That the objection drawn from the physiological difference between "species" and "races" still exists unrefuted.

That there are many remarkable phenomena in organic forms upon which "Natural Selection" throws no light whatever, but the explanations of which, if they could be attained, might throw light upon specific origination.

Besides these objections to the sufficiency of "Natural Selection," others may be brought against the hypothesis of "Pangenesis," which, professing as it does to explain great difficulties, seems to do so by presenting others not less great—in fact almost to be the explanation of *obscurum per obscurius*.

CHAPTER II.

THE INCOMPETENCY OF "NATURAL SELECTION" TO ACCOUNT FOR THE INCIPIENT STAGES OF USEFUL STRUCTURES.

Mr. Darwin supposes that Natural Selection acts by slight variations.—These must be useful at once.—Difficulties as to the giraffe; as to mimicry; as to the heads of flat-fishes; as to the origin and constancy of the vertebrate limbs; as to whalebone; as to the young kangaroo; as to sea-urchins; as to certain processes of metamorphosis; as to the mammary gland; as to certain ape characters; as to the rattlesnake and cobra; as to the process of formation of the eye and ear; as to the fully developed condition of the eye and ear; as to the voice; as to shell-fish; as to orchids; as to ants.—The necessity for the simultaneous modification of many individuals.—Summary and conclusion.

"Natural Selection," simply and by itself, is potent to explain the maintenance or the further extension and development of favourable variations, which are at once sufficiently considerable to be useful from the first to the individual possessing them. But Natural Selection utterly fails to account for the conservation and development of the minute and rudimentary beginnings, the slight and insignificant commencements of structures, however useful those structures may afterwards become.

Now, it is distinctly enunciated by Mr. Darwin, that the spontaneous variations upon which his theory depends are individually slight, minute, and insensible. He says,[1]

[1] "Animals and Plants under Domestication," vol. ii. p. 192.

"Slight individual differences, however, suffice for the work, and are probably the sole differences which are effective in the production of new species." And again, after mentioning the frequent sudden appearances of domestic varieties, he speaks of "the false belief as to the similarity of natural species in this respect."[1] In his work on the "Origin of Species," he also observes, "Natural Selection acts only by the preservation and accumulation of small inherited modifications."[2] And "Natural Selection, if it be a true principle, will banish the belief . . . of any great and sudden modification in their structure."[3] Finally, he adds, "If it could be demonstrated that any complex organ existed, which could not possibly have been formed by numerous, successive, slight modifications, my theory would absolutely break down."[4]

Now the conservation of minute variations in many instances is, of course, plain and intelligible enough; such, *e.g.*, as those which tend to promote the destructive faculties of beasts of prey on the one hand, or to facilitate the flight or concealment of the animals pursued on the other; provided always that these minute beginnings are of such a kind as really to have a certain efficiency, however small, in favour of the conservation of the individual possessing them; and also provided that no unfavourable peculiarity in any other direction accompanies and neutralizes, in the struggle for life, the minute favourable variation.

1 "Animals and Plants under Domestication," vol. ii. p. 414.

2 "Origin of Species," 5th edit., 1869, p. 110.

3 Ibid. p. 111.

4 Ibid. p. 227. Even in his recently published work, Mr. Darwin observes, "Slight fluctuating differences in the individual suffice for the work of natural selection." See "Descent of Man," vol. ii. p. 387.

But some of the cases which have been brought forward, and which have met with very general acceptance, seem less satisfactory when carefully analysed than they at first appear to be. Amongst these we may mention "the neck of the giraffe."

At first sight it would seem as though a better example in support of "Natural Selection" could hardly have been chosen. Let the fact of the occurrence of occasional, severe droughts in the country which that animal has inhabited be granted. In that case, when the ground vegetation has been consumed, and the trees alone remain, it is plain that at such times only those individuals (of what we assume to be the nascent giraffe species) which were able to reach high up would be preserved, and would become the parents of the following generation, some individuals of which would, of course, inherit that high-reaching power which alone preserved their parents. Only the high-reaching issue of these high-reaching individuals would again, *cæteris paribus*, be preserved at the next drought, and would again transmit to their offspring their still loftier stature; and so on, from period to period, through æons of time, all the individuals tending to revert to the ancient shorter type of body, being ruthlessly destroyed at the occurrence of each drought.

(1.) But against this it may be said, in the first place, that the argument proves too much; for, on this supposition, many species must have tended to undergo a similar modification, and we ought to have at least several forms, similar to the giraffe, developed from different Ungulata.[1]

[1] The order *Ungulata* contains the hoofed beasts; that is, all oxen, deer, antelopes, sheep, goats, camels, hogs, the hippopotamus, the different kinds of rhinoceros, the tapirs, horses, asses, zebras, quaggas, &c.

A careful observer of animal life who has long resided in South Africa, explored the interior, and lived in the giraffe country, has assured the Author that the giraffe has powers of locomotion and endurance fully equal to those possessed by any of the other Ungulata of that continent. It would seem, therefore, that some of these other Ungulates ought to have developed in a similar manner as to the neck, under pain of being starved, when the long neck of the giraffe was in its incipient stage.

To this criticism it has been objected that different kinds of animals are preserved, in the struggle for life, in very different ways, and even that "high-reaching" may be attained in more modes than one—as, for example, by the trunk of the elephant. This is indeed true, but then none of the African Ungulata[1] have, nor do they appear ever to have had, any proboscis whatsoever; nor have they acquired such a development as to allow them to rise on their hind limbs and graze on trees in kangaroo-attitude, nor a power of climbing, nor, as far as known, any other modification tending to compensate for the comparative shortness of the neck. Again, it may perhaps be said that leaf-eating forms are exceptional, and that therefore the struggle to attain high branches would not affect many Ungulates. But surely, when these severe droughts necessary for the theory occur, the ground vegetation is supposed to be exhausted; and, indeed, the giraffe is quite capable of feeding from off the ground. So that, in these cases, the other Ungulata *must* have taken to leaf-eating or have starved, and thus must have had any accidental long-necked varieties favoured and preserved exactly as the long-necked vari-

[1] The elephants of Africa and India, with their extinct allies, constitute the order *Proboscidea*, and do not belong to the Ungulata.

ties of the giraffe are supposed to have been favoured and preserved.

The argument as to the different modes of preservation has been very well put by Mr. Wallace,[1] in reply to the objection that "colour, being dangerous, should not exist in nature." This objection appears similar to the one here urged; as it is here said that a giraffe neck being needful, there should be many animals with it, while the objector noticed by Mr. Wallace says, "A dull colour being needful, all animals should be so coloured." And Mr. Wallace shows in reply how porcupines, tortoises and mussels, very hard-coated bombardier beetles, stinging insects and nauseous-tasted caterpillars, can afford to be brilliant by the various means of active defence or passive protection they possess, other than obscure coloration. He says, "The attitudes of some insects may also protect them, as the habit of turning up the tail by the harmless rove-beetles (Staphylinidæ) no doubt leads other animals, besides children, to the belief that they can sting. The curious attitude assumed by sphinx caterpillars is probably a safeguard, as well as the blood-red tentacles which can suddenly be thrown out from the neck by the caterpillars of all the true swallow-tailed butterflies."

But, because many different kinds of animals can elude the observation or defy the attack of enemies in a great variety of ways, it by no means follows that there are any similar number and variety of ways for attaining vegetable food in a country where all such food, other than the lofty branches of trees, has been for a time destroyed. In such a country we have a number of vegetable-feeding Ungulates, all of which present minute variations as to the

[1] See "Natural Selection," pp. 60—75.

length of the neck. If, as Mr. Darwin contends, the natural selection of these favourable variations has alone lengthened the neck of the giraffe by preserving long-necked individuals during droughts; similar variations, in other similarly-feeding forms, ought similarly to have been preserved, and so have lengthened the neck of such other Ungulates by similarly preserving them during the same droughts.

(2.) It may be also objected, that the power of reaching upwards, acquired by the lengthening of the neck and legs, must have necessitated a considerable increase in the entire size and mass of the body (larger bones requiring stronger and more voluminous muscles and tendons, and these again necessitating larger nerves, more capacious blood-vessels, &c.), and it is very problematical whether the disadvantages thence arising would not, in times of scarcity, more than counterbalance the advantages. For a considerable increase in the supply of food would be requisite on account of this increase in size and mass, while at the same time there would be a certain decrease in strength; since, as Mr. Herbert Spencer says:[1] "It is demonstrable that the excess of absorbed over expended nutriment must, other things equal, become less as the size of an animal becomes greater. In similarly-shaped bodies, the masses vary as the cubes of the dimensions; whereas the strengths vary as the squares of the dimensions." .... "Supposing a creature which a year ago was one foot high, has now become two feet high, while it is unchanged in proportions and structure—what are the necessary concomitant changes that have taken place in it? It is eight times as heavy; that is to say, it has to resist eight times the strain which gravitation puts on its struc-

[1] "Principles of Biology," vol. i. p. 122.

ture; and in producing, as well as in arresting, every one of its movements, it has to overcome eight times the inertia. Meanwhile, the muscles and bones have severally increased their contractile and resisting powers, in proportion to the areas of their transverse sections; and hence are severally but four times as strong as they were. Thus, while the creature has doubled in height, and while its ability to overcome forces has quadrupled, the forces it has to overcome have grown eight times as great. Hence, to raise its body through a given space, its muscles have to be contracted with twice the intensity, at a double cost of matter expended." Again, as to the cost at which nutriment is distributed through the body, and effete matters removed from it, "Each increment of growth being added at the periphery of an organism, the force expended in the transfer of matter must increase in a rapid progression—a progression more rapid than that of the mass."

There is yet another point. Vast as may have been the time during which the process of evolution has continued, it is nevertheless not infinite. Yet, as every kind, on the Darwinian hypothesis, varies slightly but indefinitely in every organ and every part of every organ, how very generally must favourable variations as to the length of the neck have been accompanied by some unfavourable variation in some other part, neutralizing the action of the favourable one, the latter, moreover, only taking effect during these periods of drought! How often must individuals, favoured by a slightly increased length of neck, have failed to enjoy the elevated foliage which they had not strength or endurance to attain; while other individuals, exceptionally robust, could struggle on yet further till they arrived at vegetation within their reach.

However, allowing this example to pass, many other instances will be found to present great difficulties.

Let us take the cases of mimicry amongst Lepidoptera and other insects. Of this subject Mr. Wallace has given a most interesting and complete account,[1] showing in how many and strange instances this superficial resemblance by one creature to some other quite distinct creature acts as a safeguard to the first. One or two instances must here suffice. In South America there is a family of butterflies, termed *Heliconidæ*, which is very conspicuously coloured and slow in flight, and yet the individuals abound in prodigious numbers, and take no precautions to conceal themselves, even when at rest during the night. Mr. Bates (the author of the very interesting work "The Naturalist on the River Amazons," and the discoverer of "Mimicry") found that these conspicuous butterflies had a very strong and disagreeable odour; so much so that any one handling them and squeezing them, as a collector must do, has his fingers stained and so infected by the smell as to require time and much trouble to remove it.

It is suggested that this unpleasant quality is the cause of the abundance of the Heliconidæ; Mr. Bates and other observers reporting that they have never seen them attacked by the birds, reptiles, or insects which prey upon other Lepidoptera.

Now it is a curious fact that very different South American butterflies put on, as it were, the exact dress of these offensive beauties and mimic them even in their mode of flight.

In explaining the mode of action of this protecting re-

[1] See "Natural Selection," chap. iii. p. 45.

semblance Mr. Wallace observes:[1] "Tropical insectivorous birds very frequently sit on dead branches of a lofty tree, or on those which overhang forest paths, gazing intently around, and darting off at intervals to seize an insect at a considerable distance, with which they generally return to their station to devour. If a bird began by capturing the slow-flying conspicuous Heliconidæ, and found them always so disagreeable that it could not eat them, it would after a very few trials leave off catching them at all; and their whole appearance, form, colouring, and mode of flight is so peculiar, that there can be little doubt birds would soon learn to distinguish them at a long distance, and never waste any time in pursuit of them. Under these circumstances, it is evident that any other butterfly of a group which birds were accustomed to devour, would be almost equally well protected by closely resembling a Heliconia externally, as if it acquired also the disagreeable odour; always supposing that there were only a few of them among a great number of Heliconias.

"The approach in colour and form to the Heliconidæ, however, would be at the first a positive, though perhaps a slight, advantage; for although at short distances this variety would be easily distinguished and devoured, yet at a longer distance it might be mistaken for one of the uneatable group, and so be passed by and gain another day's life, which might in many cases be sufficient for it to lay a quantity of eggs and leave a numerous progeny, many of which would inherit the peculiarity which had been the safeguard of their parent."

As a complete example of mimicry Mr. Wallace refers to a common Indian butterfly. He says:[2] "But the

[1] Loc. cit. p. 80. [2] Ibid. p. 59.

most wonderful and undoubted case of protective resem-

LEAF BUTTERFLY IN FLIGHT AND REPOSE.

blance in a butterfly which I have ever seen, is that of the common Indian *Kallima inachis,* and its Malayan ally, *Kallima paralekta*. The upper surface of these is very striking and showy, as they are of a large size, and are adorned with a broad band of rich orange on a deep bluish ground. The under-side is very variable in colour, so that out of fifty specimens no two can be found exactly alike, but every one of them will be of some shade of ash, or brown, or ochre, such as are found among dead, dry, or decaying leaves. The apex of the upper wings is produced into an acute point, a very common form in the leaves of tropical shrubs and trees, and the lower wings are also produced into a short narrow tail. Between these two points runs a dark curved line exactly representing the midrib of a leaf, and from this radiate on each side a few oblique lines, which serve to indicate the lateral veins of a leaf. These marks are more clearly seen on the outer portion of the base of the wings, and on the inner side towards the middle and apex; and it is very curious to observe how the usual marginal and transverse striæ of the group are here modified and strengthened so as to become adapted for an imitation of the venation of a leaf." . . . "But this resemblance, close as it is, would be of little use if the habits of the insect did not accord with it. If the butterfly sat upon leaves or upon flowers, or opened its wings so as to expose the upper surface, or exposed and moved its head and antennæ as many other butterflies do, its disguise would be of little avail. We might be sure, however, from the analogy of many other cases, that the habits of the insect are such as still further to aid its deceptive garb; but we are not obliged to make any such supposition, since I myself had the good fortune to observe scores of *Kallima paralekta* in Sumatra, and to capture many of them, and can vouch for the accuracy of the following details. These butterflies frequent dry forests, and fly very swiftly. They were seen to settle on a flower or a green leaf, but were many times lost sight of in a bush or tree of dead leaves. On such occasions they were generally searched for in vain, for while gazing intently at the very spot where one had disappeared, it would often suddenly dart out, and again vanish twenty or fifty yards further on. On one or two occasions the insect was detected reposing, and it could then be seen how completely it assimilates itself to the surrounding leaves. It sits on a nearly upright twig, the wings fitting closely back to back, concealing the antennæ and head, which are drawn up between their bases. The little tails of the hind wing touch the branch, and form a perfect stalk to the leaf, which is supported in its place by the claws of the middle pair of feet, which are slender and inconspicuous. The irregular outline of the wings gives exactly the perspective effect of a shrivelled leaf. We thus have size, colour, form, markings, and habits, all combining together to produce a disguise which may be said to be absolutely perfect; and the protection which it affords is sufficiently indicated by the abundance of the individuals that possess it."

Beetles also imitate bees and wasps, as do some Lepidoptera; and objects the most bizarre and unexpected are simulated, such as dung and drops of dew. Certain insects, called bamboo and walking-stick insects, have a most remarkable resemblance to pieces of bamboo, to twigs and branches. Of these latter insects Mr. Wallace says:[1] "Some of these are a foot long and as thick as one's finger, and their whole colouring, form, rugosity, and the arrange-

[1] Loc. cit. p. 64.

ment of the head, legs and antennæ, are such as to render them absolutely identical in appearance with dry sticks. They hang loosely about shrubs in the forest, and have the extraordinary habit of stretching out their legs unsymmetrically, so as to render the deception more complete." Now let us suppose that the ancestors of these various animals were all destitute of the very special protections they at present possess, as on the Darwinian hypothesis we must do. Let it also be conceded that small deviations from the antecedent colouring or form would tend to make some of their ancestors escape destruction by causing them more or less frequently to be passed over, or mistaken by their persecutors. Yet the deviation must, as the event has shown, in each case be in some definite direction, whether it be towards some other animal or plant, or towards some dead or inorganic matter. But as, according to Mr. Darwin's theory, there is a constant tendency to indefinite variation, and as the minute incipient variations will be in *all directions*, they must tend to neutralize each other, and at first to form such unstable modifications that it is difficult, if not impossible, to see how such indefinite oscillations of insignificant beginnings can ever build up a sufficiently appreciable resemblance to a leaf, bamboo, or other object, for "Natural Selection" to seize upon and perpetuate. This difficulty is augmented when we consider—a point to be dwelt upon hereafter—how necessary it is that many individuals should be similarly modified simultaneously. This has been insisted on in an able article in the *North British Review* for June 1867, p. 286, and the consideration of the article has occasioned Mr. Darwin to make an important modification in his views.[1]

[1] "Origin of Species," 5th edit. p. 104.

In these cases of mimicry it seems difficult indeed to imagine a reason why variations tending in a *minute degree* in any special direction should be preserved. All variations would be preserved which tended to obscure the perception of an animal by its enemies, whatever direction those variations might take, and the common preservation of conflicting tendencies would greatly favour their mutual neutralization and obliteration if we may rely on the many cases recently brought forward by Mr. Darwin with regard to domestic animals.

Mr. Darwin explains the imitation of some species by others more or less nearly allied to them, by the common origin of both the mimic and the mimicked species, and the consequent possession by both (according to the theory of "Pangenesis") of gemmules tending to reproduce ancestral characters, which characters the mimic must be assumed first to have lost and then to have recovered. Mr. Darwin says,[1] "Varieties of one species frequently mock distinct species, a fact in perfect harmony with the foregoing cases, and explicable *only on the theory of descent.*" But this at the best is but a partial and very incomplete explanation. It is one, moreover, which Mr. Wallace does not accept.[2] It is very incomplete, because it has no bearing on some of the most striking cases, and of course Mr. Darwin does not pretend that it has. We should have to go back far indeed to reach the common ancestor of the mimicking walking-leaf insect and of the real leaf it mimics, or the original progenitor of both the bamboo insect and the bamboo itself.

As these last most remarkable cases have certainly

[1] "Animals and Plants under Domestication," vol. ii. p. 351.

[2] Loc. cit. pp. 109, 110.

nothing to do with heredity,[1] it is unwarrantable to make use of that explanation for other protective resemblances, seeing that its inapplicability, in certain instances, is so manifest.

Again, at the other end of the process it is as difficult to account for the last touches of perfection in the mimicry.

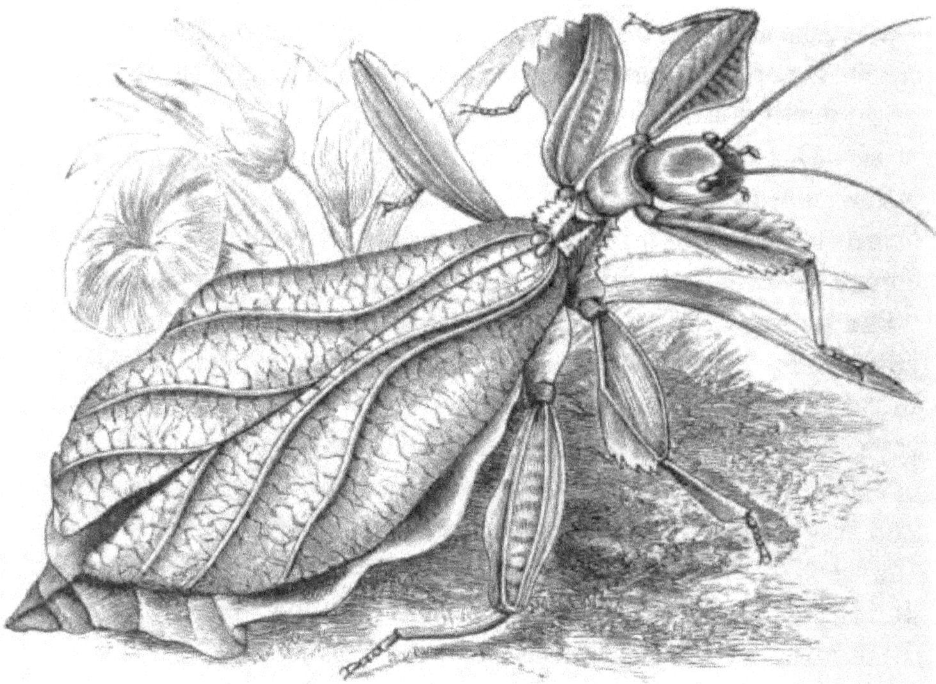

THE WALKING-LEAF INSECT.

Some insects which imitate leaves extend the imitation even to the very injuries on those leaves made by the attacks of insects or of fungi. Thus, speaking of one of the walking-stick insects, Mr. Wallace says:[2] "One of

[1] Heredity is the term used to denote the tendency which there is in offspring to reproduce parental features.

[2] Loc. cit. p. 64.

these creatures obtained by myself in Borneo (*Ceroxylus laceratus*) was covered over with foliaceous excrescences of a clear olive-green colour, so as exactly to resemble a stick grown over by a creeping moss or jungermannia. The Dyak who brought it me assured me it was grown over with moss although alive, and it was only after a most minute examination that I could convince myself it was not so." Again, as to the leaf butterfly, he says:[1] "We come to a still more extraordinary part of the imitation, for we find representations of leaves in every stage of decay, variously blotched, and mildewed, and pierced with holes, and in many cases irregularly covered with powdery black dots, gathered into patches and spots, so closely resembling the various kinds of minute fungi that grow on dead leaves, that it is impossible to avoid thinking at first sight that the butterflies themselves have been attacked by real fungi."

Here imitation has attained a development which seems utterly beyond the power of the mere "survival of the fittest" to produce. How this double mimicry can importantly aid in the struggle for life seems puzzling indeed, but much more so how the first faint beginnings of the imitation of such injuries in the leaf can be developed in the animal into such a complete representation of them—*a fortiori* how simultaneous and similar first beginnings of imitations of such injuries could ever have been developed in several individuals, out of utterly indifferent and indeterminate minute variations in all conceivable directions.

Another instance which may be cited is the asymmetrical condition of the heads of the flat-fishes (Pleuronectidæ), such as the sole, the flounder, the brill, the turbot, &c. In

[1] Loc. cit. p. 60.

all these fishes the two eyes, which in the young are situated as usual one on each side, come to be placed, in the adult, both on the same side of the head. If this condition had appeared at once, if in the hypothetically fortunate common ancestor of these fishes an eye had suddenly become thus transferred, then the perpetuation of such a transformation by the action of "Natural Selection" is conceivable enough. Such sudden changes, however, are not those favoured by the Darwinian theory, and indeed the accidental occurrence of such a spontaneous

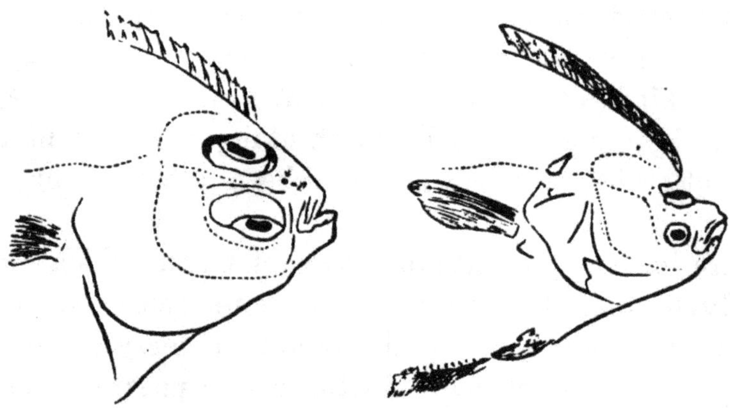

PLEURONECTIDÆ, WITH THE PECULIARLY PLACED EYE IN DIFFERENT POSITIONS.

transformation is far from probable. But if this is not so, if the transit was gradual, then how such transit of one eye a minute fraction of the journey towards the other side of the head could benefit the individual is indeed far from clear. It seems, even, that such an incipient transformation must rather have been injurious. Another point with regard to these flat-fishes is that they appear to be in all probability of recent origin—*i.e.* geologically speaking. There is, of course, no great stress to be laid on the mere absence of their remains from the secondary strata; nevertheless that absence is noteworthy, seeing that existing fish families, *e.g.* sharks (Squalidæ), have been found abundantly even down so far as the carboniferous rocks, and traces of them in the Upper Silurian.

Another difficulty seems to be the first formation of the limbs of the higher animals. The lowest Vertebrata[1] are perfectly limbless; and if, as most Darwinians would probably assume, the primeval vertebrate creature was also apodal, how are the preservation and development of the first rudiments of limbs to be accounted for—such rudiments being, on the hypothesis in question, minute and functionless?

In reply to this it has been suggested that a mere flattening of the end of the body has been useful, such, *e.g.*, as we see in sea-snakes,[2] and that this flattening might have thus constituted the rudiment of a tail formed strictly to aid in swimming. Also that a mere *roughness* of the skin might be useful to a swimming animal by holding the water better, that thus minute processes might be selected and preserved, and that, in the same way, these might be gradually increased into limbs. But it is, to say the least, very questionable whether a roughness of the skin, or minute processes, would be useful to a swimming animal; the motion of which they would as much impede as aid, unless they were at once capable of a suitable and appro-

[1] The term "Vertebrata" denotes that large group of animals which are characterized by the possession of a spinal column, commonly known as the "backbone." Such animals are ourselves, together with all beasts, birds, reptiles, frogs, toads, and efts, and also fishes.

[2] It is hardly necessary to observe that these "sea-snakes" have no relation to the often-talked-of "sea-serpent." They are small, venomous reptiles, which abound in the Indian seas.

priate action, which is against the hypothesis. Again, the change from mere indefinite and accidental processes to two regular pairs of symmetrical limbs, as the result of merely fortuitous favouring variations, is a step the feasibility of which hardly commends itself to the reason, seeing the very different positions assumed by the ventral fins in different fishes. If the above suggestion made in opposition to the views here asserted be true, then the general constancy of position of the limbs of the Vertebrata may be considered as due to the position assumed by the primitive rugosities from which those limbs were generated. Clearly only two pairs of rugosities were so preserved and developed, and all limbs (on this view) are descendants of the same two pairs, as all have so similar a fundamental structure. Yet we find in many fishes the pair of fins, which correspond to the hinder limbs of other animals, placed so far forwards as to be either on the same level with, or actually in front of, the normally anterior pair of limbs; and such fishes are from this circumstance called "thoracic" or "jugular" fishes respectively, as the weaver fishes and the cod. This is a wonderful contrast to the fixity of position of vertebrate limbs generally. If then such a change can have taken place in the comparatively short time occupied by the evolution of these special fish forms, we might certainly expect that other and far more bizarre structures would (did not some law forbid) have been developed, from other rugosities, in the manifold exigencies of the multitudinous organisms which must (on the Darwinian hypothesis) have been gradually evolved during the enormous period intervening between the first appearance of vertebrate life and the present day. Yet, with these exceptions, the position of the limbs is constant from the lower fishes up to man, there being always an anterior pectoral pair placed in front of a posterior or pelvic pair when both are present, and in no single instance are there more than these two pairs.

The development of whalebone (baleen) in the mouth of the whale is another difficulty. A whale's mouth is fur-

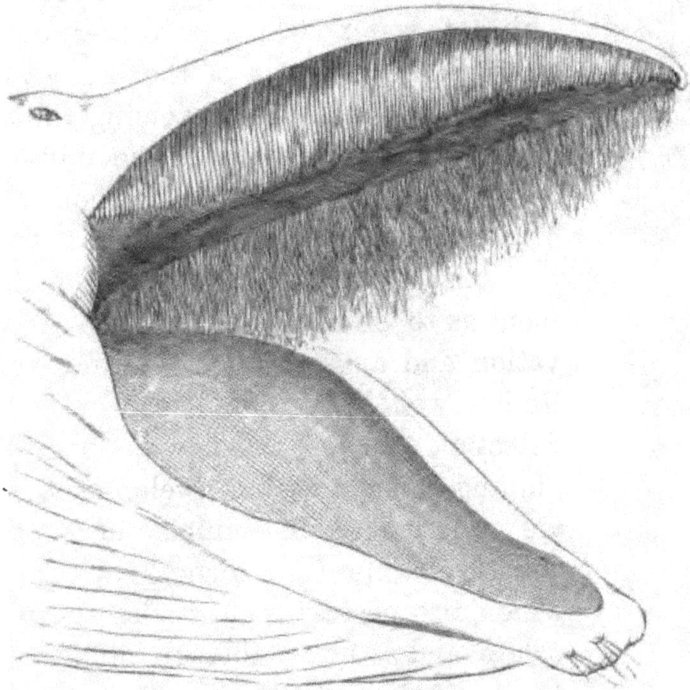

MOUTH OF A WHALE.

nished with very numerous horny plates, which hang down from the palate along each side of the mouth. They thus form two longitudinal series, each plate of which is placed transversely to the long axis of the body, and all are very close together. On depressing the lower lip the free outer edges of these plates come into view. Their inner edges are furnished with numerous coarse hair-like processes, consisting of some of the constituent fibres of the horny plates—which, as it were, fray out, and the mouth is thus lined, except below, by a network of countless fibres formed by the inner edges of the two series of plates. This network acts as a sort of sieve. When the whale feeds it takes into its mouth a great gulp of water, which it drives out again through the intervals of the horny plates of baleen, the fluid thus traversing the sieve of horny fibres, which retains the minute creatures on which these marine monsters subsist. Now it is obvious, that if this baleen had once attained such a size and development as to be at all useful, then its preservation and augmentation within serviceable limits would be promoted by "Natural Selection" alone. But how to obtain the beginning of such useful development? There are indeed certain animals of exclusively aquatic habits (the dugong and manatee) which also possess more or less horn on the palate, and at first sight this might be taken as a mitigation of the difficulty; but it is not so, and the fact does not help us one step further along the road: for, in the first place, these latter animals differ so materially in structure from whales and porpoises that they form an altogether distinct order, and cannot be thought to approximate to the whale's progenitors. They are vegetarians; the whales feed on animals; the former never have the ribs articulated in the mode in which they are in some of the latter; the former

FOUR PLATES OF BALEEN SEEN OBLIQUELY FROM WITHIN.

have pectoral mammæ, and the latter are provided with two inguinal mammary glands, and have the nostrils enlarged into blowers, which the former have not. The former thus constitute the order Sirenia, while the latter belong to the Cetacea. In the second place, the horny matter on the

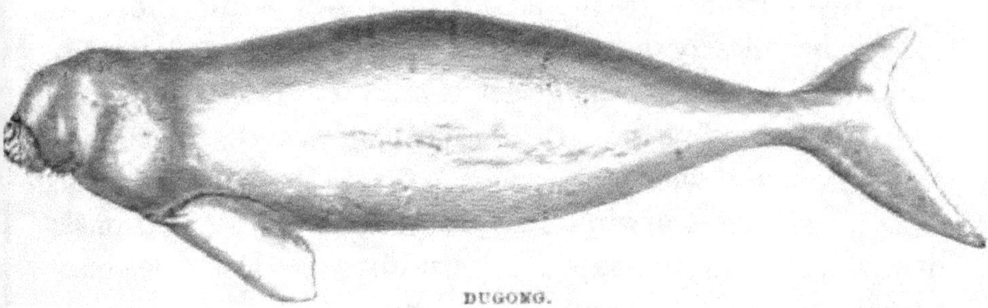

DUGONG.

palates of the dugong and manatee has not, even initially, that "strainer" action which is the characteristic function of the Cetacean "baleen."

There is another very curious structure, the origin or the disappearance of which it seems impossible to account for on the hypothesis of minute indefinite variations. It is that of the mouth of the young kangaroo. In all mammals, as in ourselves, the air-passage from the lungs opens in the floor of the mouth behind the tongue, and in front of the opening of the gullet, so that each particle of food as it is swallowed passes over the opening, but is prevented from falling into it (and thus causing death from choking) by the action of a small cartilaginous shield (the epiglottis), which at the right moment bends back and protects the orifice. Now the kangaroo is born in such an exceedingly imperfect and undeveloped condition, that it is quite unable to suck. The mother therefore places the minute blind and naked young upon the nipple, and then injects milk into it by means of a special muscular envelope of the mammary gland. Did no special provision exist, the young one must infallibly be choked by the intrusion of the milk into the windpipe. But there *is* a special provision. The larynx is so elongated that it rises up into the posterior end of the nasal passage, and is thus enabled to give free entrance to the air for the lungs, while the milk passes harmlessly on each side of this elongated larynx, and so safely attains the gullet behind it.

Adult Cetaceans have a similar contrivance, to exclude water from the windpipe.

Now, on the Darwinian hypothesis, either all mammals descended from marsupial progenitors, or else the marsupials sprung from animals having in most respects the ordinary mammalian structure.

On the first alternative, how did "Natural Selection" remove this (at least perfectly innocent and harmless) structure in almost all other mammals, and, having done so, again reproduce it in precisely those forms which alone require it, namely, the Cetacea? That such a harmless structure *need not* be removed any Darwinian must confess, since a structure exists in both the crocodiles and gavials, which enables the former to breathe themselves while drowning the prey which they hold in their mouths. On Mr. Darwin's hypothesis it could only have been developed where useful, therefore not in the gavials (!) which feed on fish, but which yet retain, as we might expect, this, in them, superfluous but harmless formation.

On the second alternative, how did the elongated larynx itself arise, seeing that if its development had lagged behind that of the maternal structure, the young primeval kangaroo must have been choked: while without the injecting power in the mother, it must have been starved?

The struggle by the sole action of which such a form was developed must indeed have been severe!

The sea-urchins (Echinus) present us also with structures the origin of which it seems impossible to explain by the action of "Natural Selection" only. These lowly animals belong to that group of the star-fish class (Echinodermata), the species of which possess generally spheroidal bodies, built up of multitudinous calcareous plates, and constitute the order Echinoidea. They are also popularly known as sea-eggs. Utterly devoid of limbs, the locomotion of these creatures is effected by means of rows of small tubular suckers (which protrude through pores in the calcareous plates) and by moveable spines scattered over the body.

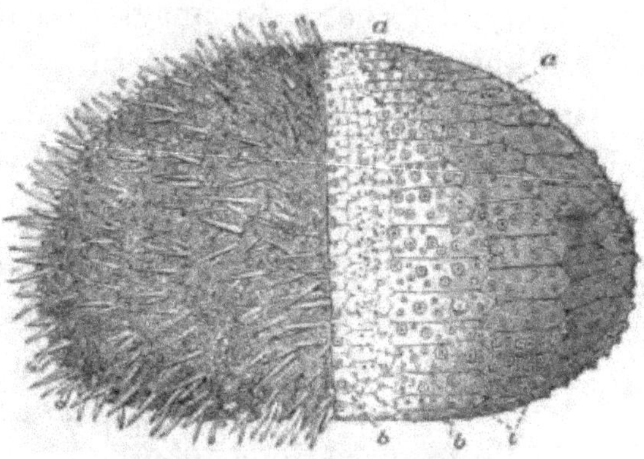

AN ECHINUS, OR SEA-URCHIN.
(The spines removed from one-half.)

Besides these spines and suckers, there are certain very peculiar structures, termed "Pedicellariæ." Each of these consists of a long slender stalk, ending in three short limbs —or rather jaws—the whole supported by a delicate internal skeleton. The three limbs (or jaws), which start from a common point at the of end the stalk, are in the constant habit of opening and closing together again with a snapping action, while the stalk itself sways about. The utility of these appendages is, even now, problematical. It may be that they remove from the surface of the animal's body foreign substances which would be prejudicial to it, and which it cannot otherwise get rid of. But granting this, what would be the utility of the *first rudimentary beginnings* of such structures, and how could such incipient buddings have ever preserved the life of a single Echinus? It is true that on Darwinian principles the ancestral form from which the sea-urchin developed was different, and must not be conceived merely as an Echinus devoid of pedicellariæ; but this makes the difficulty none the less. It is equally hard to imagine that the first rudiments of such structures could have been useful to *any* animal from which the Echinus might have been derived. Moreover, not even the *sudden* development of the snapping action could have been beneficial without the freely moveable stalk, nor could the latter have been efficient without the snapping jaws, yet no minute merely indefinite variations could simultaneously evolve these complex co-ordinations of structure: to deny this seems equivalent to affirming a startling paradox.

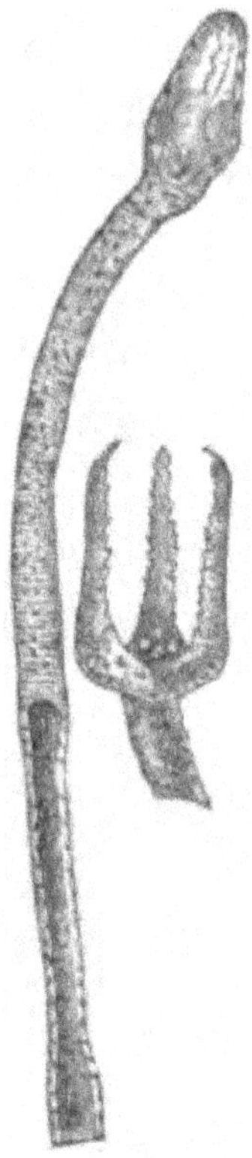

PEDICELLARIÆ.
(Immensely enlarged.)

Mr. Darwin explains the appearance of some structures, the utility of which is not apparent, by the existence of certain "laws of correlation." By these he means that certain parts or organs of the body are so related to other organs or parts, that when the first are modified by the action of "Natural Selection," or what not, the second are simultaneously affected, and increase proportionally, or possibly so decrease. Examples of such are the hair and teeth in the naked Turkish dog, the general deafness of white cats with blue eyes, the relation between the presence of more or less down on young birds when first hatched, and the future colour of their plumage,[1] with many others. But the idea that the modification of any internal or external part of the body of an Echinus carries with it the effect of producing elongated, flexible, triradiate, snapping processes, is, to say the very least, fully as obscure and mysterious as what is here contended for, viz. the efficient presence of an unknown internal natural law or laws conditioning the evolution of new specific forms from preceding ones, modified by the action of surrounding conditions, by "Natural Selection" and by other controlling influences.

The same difficulty seems to present itself in other examples of exceptional structure and action. In the same Echinus, as in many allied forms, and also in some more or less remote ones, a very peculiar mode of development exists. The adult is not formed from the egg directly, but the egg gives rise to a creature which swims freely about, feeds, and is even somewhat complexly organized. Soon a small lump appears on one side of its stomach; this enlarges, and, having established a communication with the exterior, envelopes and appropriates the creature's stomach, with which it swims away and develops into the complete adult form, while the dispossessed individual perishes.

Again, certain flies present a mode of development equally bizarre, though quite different. In these flies, the grub is, as usual, produced from the ovum; but this grub, instead of growing up into the adult in the ordinary way,

[1] "Origin of Species," 5th edit. 1869, p. 179.

undergoes a sort of liquefaction of a great part of its body, while certain patches of formative tissue, which are attached to the ramifying air-tubes, or tracheæ (and which patches bear the name of "imaginal disks"), give rise to the legs, wings, eyes, &c., respectively; and these severally formed parts grow together, and build up the head and body by their mutual approximation. Such a process is unknown outside the class of insects, and inside that class it is only known in a few of the two-winged flies. Now, how "Natural Selection," or any "laws of correlation," can account for the gradual development of such an exceptional process of development—so extremely divergent from that of other insects—seems nothing less than inconceivable. Mr. Darwin himself[1] gives an account of a very peculiar and abnormal mode of development of a certain beetle, the sitaris, as described by M. Fabre. This insect, instead of at first appearing in its grub stage, and then, after a time, putting on the adult form, is at first active, and furnished with six legs, two long antennæ, and four eyes. Hatched in the nests of bees, it at first attaches itself to one of the males, and then crawls, when the opportunity offers, upon a female bee. When the female bee lays her eggs, the young sitaris springs upon them and devours them. Then, losing its eyes, legs, and antennæ, and becoming rudimentary, it sinks into an ordinary grub-like form, and feeds on honey, ultimately undergoing another transformation, re-acquiring its legs, &c., and emerging a perfect beetle! That such a process should have arisen by the accumulation of minute accidental variations in structure and habit, appears to many minds, quite competent to form an opinion on the subject, absolutely incredible.

[1] "Origin of Species," 5th edit., p. 532.

It may be objected, perhaps, that these difficulties are *difficulties of ignorance*—that we cannot explain them because we do not know *enough* of the animals. But it is here contended that this is not the case; it is not that we merely fail to see how Natural Selection acted, but that there is a positive incompatibility between the cause assigned and the results. It will be stated shortly, in illustration of this incompatibility, what wonderful instances of co-ordination and of unexpected utility Mr. Darwin has discovered in orchids. The discoveries are not disputed or undervalued, but the explanation of their *origin* is deemed thoroughly unsatisfactory—utterly insufficient to explain the incipient minute beginnings of structures which are of utility only when they are considerably developed. Let us consider the mammary gland, or breast. Is it conceivable that the young of any animal was ever saved from destruction by accidentally sucking a drop of scarcely nutritious fluid from an accidentally hypertrophied cutaneous gland of its mother? And even if one was so, what chance was there of the perpetuation of such a variation? On the hypothesis of Natural Selection itself, we must assume that up to that time the race had been well adapted to the surrounding conditions; the temporary and accidental trial and change of conditions which caused the so-sucking young one to be the "fittest to survive" under the supposed circumstances, would soon cease to act, and then the progeny of the mother with the accidentally hypertrophied sebaceous glands, would have no tendency to survive the far outnumbering descendants of the normal ancestral form. If, on the other hand, we assume the change of conditions not to have been temporary but permanent, and also assume that this permanent change of conditions was accidentally synchronous with the change of structure, we have a coincidence of very remote probability indeed. But if, again, we accept the presence of some harmonizing law simultaneously determining the two changes, or connecting the second with the first by causation, then, of course, we remove the accidental character of the coincidence.

Again, how explain the external position of the male sexual glands in certain mammals? The utility of the modification, when accomplished, is problematical enough, and no less so the incipient stages of the descent.

As was said in the first chapter, Mr. Darwin explains the brilliant plumage of the peacock or the humming-bird by the action of sexual selection: the more and more brilliant males being selected by the females (attracted by this brilliancy) to become the fathers of the next generation, to which generation they tend to communicate their own bright nuptial vesture.[1] But there are peculiarities of colour and of form which it is not possible to account for

[1] In the opinion of the author of this book, Mr. Darwin has utterly failed to show (in his most recent work) that sexual selection acts efficaciously in modifying species, if indeed it acts at all. Certainly, even in birds, sexual peculiarities occur which cannot be due to sexual selection; as, *e.g.* the colouring of the *inside* of the mouth in the Hornbill (*Buceros bicornis*), and the excess in size, in male pigeons, of the wattle of the "Carrier" and the crop of the "Pouter," an excess not arising "from, but rather in opposition to, the wishes of the breeder." Mr. Darwin himself tells us, "I have received long letters on this subject from Messrs. Hewitt and Tegetmeier, and almost an essay from the late Mr. Brent. It will be admitted by every one that these gentlemen, so well known from their published works, are careful and experienced observers. They do not believe that the females prefer certain males on account of the beauty of their plumage." . . . "Mr. Tegetmeier is convinced that a game-cock, though disfigured by being dubbed with his hackles trimmed, would be accepted as readily as a male retaining all his natural ornaments."—*Descent of Man*, vol. ii. p. 117.

by any such action. Thus, amongst apes, the female is notoriously weaker, and is armed with much less powerful canine tusks, than the male. When we consider what is known of the emotional nature of these animals, and the periodicity of its intensification, it is incredible that a female would often risk life or limb through her admiration of a trifling shade of colour, or a slightly greater though irresistibly fascinating degree of wartiness.

Yet the males of some kinds of ape are adorned with quite exceptionally brilliant local decoration, and the male orang is provided with remarkable, projecting, warty lumps of skin upon the cheeks. As we have said, the weaker female cannot be supposed to have developed these by persevering and long-continued selection,[1] nor can they be thought to tend to the preservation of the individual. On the contrary, the presence of this enlarged appendage must occasion a slight increase in the need of nutriment, and in so far must be a detriment, although its detrimental effect would not be worth speaking of except in relation to "Darwinism;" according to which, "selection" has acted through unimaginable ages, and has ever tended to suppress any useless development by the struggle for life.

In poisonous serpents, also, we have structures which, at all events at first sight, seem positively hurtful to those

[1] Mr. Darwin, in his recently published work on Man, though he abundantly notices these ape sexual characters, does not bring forward a single fact in support of selection on the part of such animals. He assumes that sexual selection has acted in them because he is convinced that it acts in birds. We may, however, turn the argument round and say, since such characters can be formed in apes (as they certainly also are in insects) without the action of sexual selection, the unknown cause which has operated in their case may, most reasonably, be supposed to have also acted in the case of birds.

reptiles. Such are the rattle of the rattlesnake, and the expanding neck (or hood) of the cobra, the former seeming to warn the ear of the intended victim, as the latter warns the eye. It is true we cannot perhaps demonstrate that the victims are alarmed and warned, but, on Darwinian principles, they certainly ought to be so; for the rashest and

RATTLESNAKE.

most incautious of the animals preyed on would always tend to fall victims, and the existing individuals being the long-descended progeny of the timid and cautious, ought to have an inherited tendency to distrust, amongst other objects, both "rattling" and "expanding" snakes. As to any power of fascination exercised by means of these actions, the most distinguished naturalists, certainly the most distinguished erpetologists, entirely deny it, and it is opposed to the careful observations of those known to us.

The mode of formation of both the eye and the ear of the highest animals is such that, if it is (as most Dar-

COBRA.

winians assert processes of development to be) a record of the actual steps by which such structures were first evolved in antecedent forms, it almost amounts to a demonstration that those steps were never produced by "Natural Selection."

The eye is formed by a simultaneous and corresponding ingrowth of one part and outgrowth of another. The skin in front of the future eye becomes depressed; the depression increases and assumes the form of a sac, which changes into the aqueous humour and lens. An outgrowth of brain substance, on the other hand, forms the retina, while a third process is a lateral ingrowth of connective tissue, which afterwards changes into the vitreous humour of the eye.

The internal ear is formed by an involution of the integument, and not by an outgrowth of the brain. But tissue, in connexion with the latter, becomes in part changed, thus forming the auditory nerve, which places the tegumentary sac in direct communication with the brain itself.

Now, these complex and simultaneous co-ordinations could never have been produced by insignificant beginnings, since, until so far developed as to effect the requisite junctions, they are useless. But the eye and ear when fully developed present conditions which are hopelessly difficult to reconcile with the mere action of "Natural Selection." The difficulties with regard to the eye have been well put by Mr. Murphy, especially that of the concordant result of visual development springing from different starting-points and continued on by independent roads.

He says,[1] speaking of the beautiful structure of the perfect eye, "The higher the organization, whether of an entire organism or of a single organ, the greater is the number of the parts that co-operate, and the more perfect is their co-operation; and consequently, the more necessity there is for corresponding variations to take place in all the co-operating parts at once, and the more useless will be any variation whatever unless it is accompanied by corresponding variations in the co-operating parts; while

[1] "Habit and Intelligence," vol. i. p. 319.

it is obvious that the greater the number of variations which are needed in order to effect an improvement, the less will be the probability of their all occurring at once. It is no reply to this to say, what is no doubt abstractedly true, that whatever is possible becomes probable, if only time enough be allowed. There are improbabilities so great that the common sense of mankind treats them as impossibilities. It is not, for instance, in the strictest sense of the word, impossible that a poem and a mathematical proposition should be obtained by the process of shaking letters out of a box; but is improbable to a degree that cannot be distinguished from impossibility; and the improbability of obtaining an improvement in an organ by means of several spontaneous variations, all occurring together, is an improbability of the same kind. If we suppose that any single variation occurs on the average once in m times, the probability of that variation occurring in any individual will be

$$\frac{1}{m};$$

and suppose that x variations must concur in order to make an improvement, then the probability of the necessary variations all occurring together will be

$$\frac{1}{m^x}.$$

Now suppose, what I think a moderate proposition, that the value of m is 1,000, and the value of x is 10, then

$$\frac{1}{m^x} = \frac{1}{1000^{10}} = \frac{1}{10^{30}};$$

a number about ten thousand times as great as the number of waves of light that have fallen on the earth since historical time began. And it is to be further observed, that no improvement will give its possessor a *certainty* of surviving and leaving offspring, but only an *extra chance*, the value of which it is quite impossible to estimate." This difficulty is, as Mr. Murphy points out, greatly intensified by the undoubted fact that the wonderfully complex structure has been arrived at quite independently in beasts on the one hand and in cuttle-fishes on the other; while creatures of the insect and crab division present us with a third and quite separately developed complexity.

As to the ear, it would take up too much space to describe its internal structure;[1] it must suffice to say, that in its interior there is a series of minute rod-like bodies, termed *fibres of Corti*, having the appearance of a key-board, and each fibre being connected with a filament of the auditory nerve: these filaments being like strings to be struck by the keys, *i.e.* by the fibres of Corti. Moreover, this apparatus has been supposed to be a key-board in function as well as in appearance, the vibration of each one fibre giving rise, as some believe, to the sensation of one particular tone, and combinations of such vibrations producing chords. It is by the action of this complex organ, if not by some yet undiscovered auditory structure, that all the wonderful intricacy and charm of Beethoven and Mozart come to be perceived and appreciated.

Now it can hardly be contended that the preservation of any race of men in the struggle for life ever depended on such an extreme delicacy and refinement of the internal ear,—a perfection only exercised in the enjoyment and appreciation of the most exquisite musical performances.

[1] The reader may consult Huxley's "Lessons in Elementary Physiology," p. 204.

How, then, could either the minute incipient stages, or the final perfecting touches of this admirable structure, have been brought about by vague, aimless, and indefinite variations in all conceivable directions of an organ suited to enable the rudest savage to minister to his necessities, but no more?

Mr. Wallace[1] makes an analogous remark with regard to the organ of voice in man—the human larynx. He says of singing: "The habits of savages give no indication of how this faculty could have been developed by Natural Selection, because it is never required or used by them. The singing of savages is a more or less monotonous howling, and the females seldom sing at all. Savages certainly never choose their wives for fine voices, but for rude health, and strength, and physical beauty. Sexual selection could not therefore have developed this wonderful power, which only comes into play among civilized people."

Reverting once more to beauty of form and colour, there is a manifestation of it for which no one will pretend that sexual selection can possibly account. The instance referred to is that presented by bivalve shell-fish.[2] Here we meet with brilliant tints and elegant forms and markings of no direct use to their possessors[3] in the struggle for life, and of no indirect utility as regards sexual selection, for fertilization takes place by the mere action of currents of water, and the least beautiful individual has fully as good

1 "Natural Selection," p. 350.

2 Bivalve shell-fish are creatures belonging to the oyster, scallop, and cockle group, *i.e.* to the class Lamellibranchiata.

3 The attempt has been made to explain these facts as owing to "manner and symmetry of growth, and to colour being incidental on the chemical nature of the constituents of the shell." But surely beauty depends on some such matters in *all* cases!

a chance of becoming a parent as has the one which is the most favoured in beauty of form and colour.

Again, the peculiar outline and coloration of certain orchids—notably of our own bee, fly, and spider orchids—seem hardly explicable by any action of "Natural Selection." Mr. Darwin says very little on this singular resemblance of flowers to insects, and what he does say seems hardly to be what an advocate of "Natural Selection" would require. Surely, for minute accidental indefinite variations to have built up such a striking resemblance to insects, we ought to find that the preservation of the plant, or the perpetuation of its race, depends almost constantly on relations between bees, spiders, and flies respectively and the bee, spider, and fly orchids.[1] This process must have continued for ages constantly and perseveringly, and yet what is the fact? Mr. Darwin tells us, in his work on the Fertilization of Orchids, that neither the spider nor the fly orchids are much visited by insects, while, with regard to the bee orchid, he says, "I have never seen an insect visit these flowers." And he shows how this species is even specially modified to effect self-fertilization.

In the work just referred to, Mr. Darwin gives a series of the most wonderful and minute contrivances by which the visits of insects are utilized for the fertilization of orchids,—structures so wonderful that nothing could well be more so, except the attribution of their origin to minute, fortuitous, and indefinite variations.

The instances are too numerous and too long to quote,

[1] It has been suggested in opposition to what is said above, that there is no real resemblance, but that the likeness is "*fanciful!*" The denial, however, of the fact of a resemblance which has struck so many observers reminds one of the French philosopher's estimate of facts hostile to his theory—"Tant pis pour les faits!"

but in his "Origin of Species"[1] he describes two which must not be passed over. In one (*Coryanthes*) the orchid has its lower lip enlarged into a bucket, above which stand two water-secreting horns. These latter replenish the bucket, from which, when half-filled, the water overflows by a spout on one side. Bees visiting the flower fall into the bucket and crawl out at the spout. By the peculiar arrangement of the parts of the flower, the first bee which does so carries away the pollen-mass glued to his back, and then when he has his next involuntary bath in another flower, as he crawls out the pollen-mass attached to him, comes in contact with the stigma of that second flower and fertilizes it. In the other example (*Catasetum*), when a bee gnaws a certain part of the flower, he inevitably touches a long delicate projection, which Mr. Darwin calls the antenna. "This antenna transmits a vibration to a membrane, which is instantly ruptured; this sets free a spring by which the pollen-mass is shot forth like an arrow in the right direction, and adheres by its viscid extremity to the back of the bee!"

Another difficulty, and one of some importance, is presented by those communities of ants which have not only a population of *sterile* females, or workers, but two distinct and very different castes of such. Mr. Darwin believes that he has got over this difficulty by having found individuals intermediate in form and structure[2] between the two working castes; others may think that we have in this

[1] Fifth Edition, p. 236.

[2] Mr. Smith, of the Entomological department of the British Museum, has kindly informed the author that the individuals intermediate in structure are very few in number—not more than five per cent.—compared with the number of distinctly differentiated individuals. Besides, in the Brazilian kinds these intermediate forms are wanting.

belief of Mr. Darwin an example of the unconscious action of volition upon credence. A vast number of difficulties similar to those which have been mentioned might easily be cited—those given, however, may suffice.

There remains, however, to be noticed a very weighty consideration, which was brought forward in the *North British Review* for June 1867, p. 286, namely, the necessity for the simultaneous modification of *many individuals.* This consideration seems to have escaped Mr. Darwin, for at p. 104 of his last (fifth) edition of "The Origin of Species," he admits, with great candour, that until reading this article he did not "appreciate how rarely single variations, whether slight or strongly marked, could be perpetuated."

The *North British Review* (speaking of the supposition that a species is changed by the survival of a few individuals in a century through a similar and favourable variation) says: "It is very difficult to see how this can be accomplished, even when the variation is eminently favourable indeed; and still more difficult when the advantage gained is very slight, as must generally be the case. The advantage, whatever it may be, is utterly outbalanced by numerical inferiority. A million creatures are born; ten thousand survive to produce offspring. One of the million has twice as good a chance as any other of surviving; but the chances are fifty to one against the gifted individuals being one of the hundred survivors. No doubt the chances are twice as great against any one other individual, but this does not prevent their being enormously in favour of *some* average individual. However slight the advantage may be, if it is shared by half the individuals produced, it will probably be present in at least fifty-one of the survivors, and in a larger proportion of their offspring; but the chances are against the preservation of any one 'sport' (*i.e.* sudden, marked variation) in a numerous tribe. The vague use of an imperfectly understood doctrine of chance has led Darwinian supporters, first, to confuse the two cases above distinguished; and, secondly, to imagine that a very slight balance in favour of some individual sport must lead to its perpetuation. All that can be said is that in the above example the favoured sport would be preserved once in fifty times. Let us consider what will be its influence on the main stock when preserved. It will breed and have a progeny of say 100; now this progeny will, on the whole, be intermediate between the average individual and the sport. The odds in favour of one of this generation of the new breed will be, say one and a half to one, as compared with the average individual; the odds in their favour will, therefore, be less than that of their parents; but owing to their greater number, the chances are that about one and a half of them would survive. Unless these breed together, a most improbable event, their progeny would again approach the average individual; there would be 150 of them, and their superiority would be, say in the ratio of one and a quarter to one; the probability would now be that nearly two of them would survive, and have 200 children, with an eighth superiority. Rather more than two of these would survive; but the superiority would again dwindle, until after a few generations it would no longer be observed, and would count for no more in the struggle for life than any of the hundred trifling advantages which occur in the ordinary organs. An illustration will bring this conception home. Suppose a white man to have been wrecked on an island inhabited by negroes, and to have established himself in friendly relations with a powerful tribe, whose customs he has learnt. Suppose him to possess the physical strength, energy, and ability of a dominant white race, and let the food and climate of the island suit his constitution; grant him every advantage which we can conceive a white to possess over the native; concede that in the struggle for existence his chance of a long life will be much superior to that of the native chiefs; yet from all these admissions, there does not follow the conclusion that, after a limited or unlimited number of generations, the inhabitants of the island will be white. Our shipwrecked hero would probably become king; he would kill a great many blacks in the struggle for existence; he would have a great many wives and children." . . . . "In the first generation there will be some dozens of intelligent young mulattoes, much superior in average intelligence to the negroes. We might expect the throne for some generations to be occupied by a more or less yellow king; but can any one believe that the whole island will gradually acquire a white, or even a yellow, population?" . . . "Darwin says that in the struggle for life a grain may turn the balance in favour of a given structure, which will then be preserved. But one of the weights in the scale of nature is due to the number of a given tribe. Let there be 7000 A's and 7000 B's, representing two varieties of a given animal, and let all the B's, in virtue of a slight difference of structure, have the better chance of life by $\frac{1}{1000}$ part. We must allow that there is a slight probability that the descendants of B will supplant the descendants of A; but let there be only 7001 A's against 7000 B's at first, and the chances are once more equal, while if there be 7002 A's to start, the odds would be laid on the A's. True they stand a greater chance of being killed; but then, they can better afford to be killed. The grain will only turn the scales when these are very nicely balanced, and an advantage in numbers counts for weight, even as an advantage in structure. As the numbers of the favoured variety diminish, so must its relative advantages increase, if the chance of its existence is to surpass the chance of its extinction, until hardly any conceivable advantage would enable the descendants of a single pair to exterminate the descendants of many thousands if they and their descendants are supposed to breed freely with the inferior variety, and so gradually lose their ascendency."

Mr. Darwin himself says of the article quoted: "The justice of these remarks cannot, I think, be disputed. If, for instance, a bird of some kind could procure its food more easily by having its beak curved, and if one were born with its beak strongly curved, and which consequently flourished, nevertheless there would be a very poor chance of this one individual perpetuating its kind to the exclusion of the common form; but there can hardly be a doubt, judging by what we see taking place under domestication, that this result would follow from the preservation during many generations of a large number of individuals with more or less curved beaks, and from the destruction of a still larger number with the straightest beaks." This admission appears to the author to be of compromising significance.[1]

1 Mr. Darwin, in his recent work on Man, makes the further remarkable admission: "I now admit . . . that in the earlier editions of my 'Origin of Species' I probably attributed too much to the action of Natural Selection, or the survival of the fittest. . . . I had not formerly sufficiently considered the existence of many structures which appear to be, as far as

These remarks have been quoted at length, because they so greatly intensify the difficulties brought forward in this chapter. If the most favourable variations have to contend with such difficulties, what must be thought as to the chance of preservation of the slightly displaced eye in a sole, or of the incipient development of baleen in a whale?

SUMMARY AND CONCLUSION.

It has been here contended that certain facts, out of many which might have been brought forward, are inconsistent with the origination of species by "Natural Selection" only or mainly.

Mr. Darwin's theory requires minute, indefinite, fortuitous variations of all parts in all directions, and he insists that the sole operation of "Natural Selection" upon such variations is sufficient to account for the great majority of organic forms, with their most complicated structures, intricate mutual adaptations, and delicate adjustments.

To this conception have been opposed the difficulties presented by such a structure as the form of the giraffe, which ought not to have been the solitary structure it is; also the minute beginnings and the last refinements of protective mimicry equally difficult, or rather impossible to account for by "Natural Selection." Again, the difficulty as to the heads of flat-fishes has been insisted on, as also the origin, and at the same time the constancy, of the limbs of the highest animals. Reference has also been made to the whalebone of whales, and to the impossibility of understanding its origin through "Natural Selection"

we can judge, neither beneficial nor injurious."—See "Descent of Man," vol. i. p. 152.

only; the same as regards the infant kangaroo, with its singular deficiency of power compensated for by maternal structures on the one hand, to which its own breathing organs bear direct relation on the other. Again, the delicate and complex pedicellariæ of Echinoderms, with a certain process of development (through a secondary larva) found in that class, together with certain other exceptional modes of development, have been brought forward. The appearance of colour in certain apes, the hood of the cobra, and the rattle of the rattlesnake, have also been cited. Again, difficulties as to the process of formation of the eye and ear, and as to the fully developed condition of those complex organs, as well as of the voice, have been considered. The beauty of certain shell-fish; the wonderful adaptations of structure, and variety of form and resemblance, found in orchids; together with the complex habits and social conditions of certain ants, have been hastily passed in review. When all these complications are duly weighed and considered, and when it is borne in mind how necessary it is for the permanence of a new variety that many individuals in each case should be simultaneously modified, the cumulative argument against the sole or predominant action of Natural Selection seems irresistible.

The author of this book can say, that, though by no means disposed originally to dissent from the theory of "Natural Selection," if only its difficulties could be solved, he has found each successive year that deeper consideration and more careful examination have more and more brought home to him the inadequacy of Mr. Darwin's theory to account for the preservation and intensification of incipient, specific, and generic characters. That minute, fortuitous, and indefinite variations could have brought about such special forms and modifications as have been enumerated in this chapter, seems to contradict not imagination, but reason.

That either many individuals amongst a species of butterfly should be simultaneously preserved through a similar accidental and minute variation in one definite direction, when variations in many other directions would also preserve; or that one or two so varying should succeed in supplanting the progeny of thousands of other individuals, and that this should by no other cause be carried so far as to produce the appearance (as we have before stated) of spots of fungi, &c.—are alternatives of an improbability so extreme as to be practically equal to impossibility.

In spite of all the resources of a fertile imagination, the Darwinian, pure and simple, is reduced to the assertion of a paradox as great as any he opposes. In the place of a mere assertion of our ignorance as to the way these phenomena have been produced, he brings forward as their explanation a cause which, it is contended in this work, is demonstrably insufficient.

Of course here, as elsewhere throughout nature, we have to do with the operation of fixed and constant natural laws, and the knowledge of these may before long be obtained by human patience or human genius. There seems, however, already enough evidence to show that these as yet unknown natural laws will never be resolved into the action of "Natural Selection," but will constitute or exemplify a mode and condition of organic action of which the Darwinian theory takes no account whatsoever.

CHAPTER III.

THE CO-EXISTENCE OF CLOSELY SIMILAR STRUCTURES OF DIVERSE ORIGIN.

Chances against concordant variations.—Examples of discordant ones.—Concordant variations not unlikely on a non-Darwinian evolutionary hypothesis.—Placental and implacental mammals.—Birds and reptiles.—Independent origins of similar sense organs.—The ear.—The eye.—Other coincidences.—Causes besides "Natural Selection" produce concordant variations, in certain geographical regions.—Causes besides "Natural Selection" produce concordant variations, in certain zoological and botanical groups.—There are homologous parts not genetically related.—Harmony in respect of the organic and inorganic worlds.—Summary and conclusion.

THE theory of "Natural Selection" supposes that the varied forms and structure of animals and plants have been built up merely by indefinite, fortuitous,[1] minute variations in every part and in all directions—those variations only being preserved which are directly or indirectly useful to the individual possessing them, or necessarily correlated with such useful variations.

On this theory the chances are almost infinitely great against the independent accidental occurrence and preservation of two similar series of minute variations resulting

[1] By accidental variations Mr. Darwin does not, of course, mean to imply variations really due to "chance," but to utterly indeterminate antecedents.

in the independent development of two closely similar forms. In all cases, no doubt (on this same theory), *some* adaptation to habit or need would gradually be evolved, but that adaptation would surely be arrived at by different roads.

The organic world supplies us with multitudes of examples of similar functional results being attained by the most diverse means. Thus the body is sustained in the air by birds and by bats. In the first case it is so sustained by a limb in which the bones of the hand are excessively reduced, but which is provided with immense outgrowths

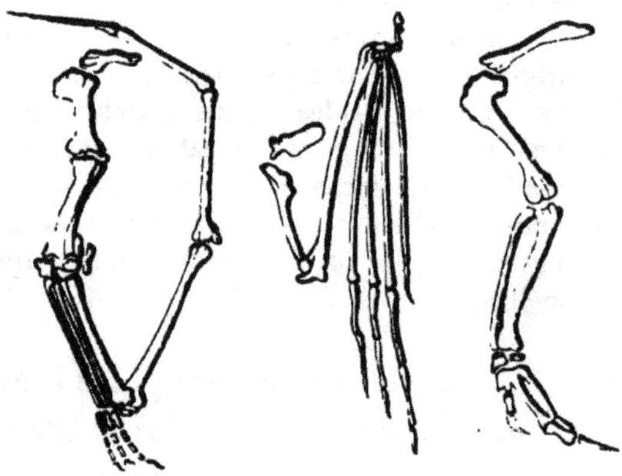

WING-BONES OF PTERODACTYLE, BAT, AND BIRD.

from the skin—namely, the feathers of the wing. In the second case, however, the body is sustained in the air by a limb in which the bones of the hand are enormously ncreased in length, and so sustain a great expanse of naked kin, which is the flying membrane of the bat's wing. Certain fishes and certain reptiles can also flit and take very prolonged jumps in the air. The flying-fish, however takes these by means of a great elongation of the rays of the pectoral fins—parts which cannot be said to be of the same nature as the constituents of the wing of either the bat or the bird. The little lizard, which enjoys the formidable name of "flying-dragon," flits by means of a structure altogether peculiar—namely, by the liberation and great elongation of some of the ribs which support a fold of skin. In the extinct pterodactyles—which were *truly* flying rep-

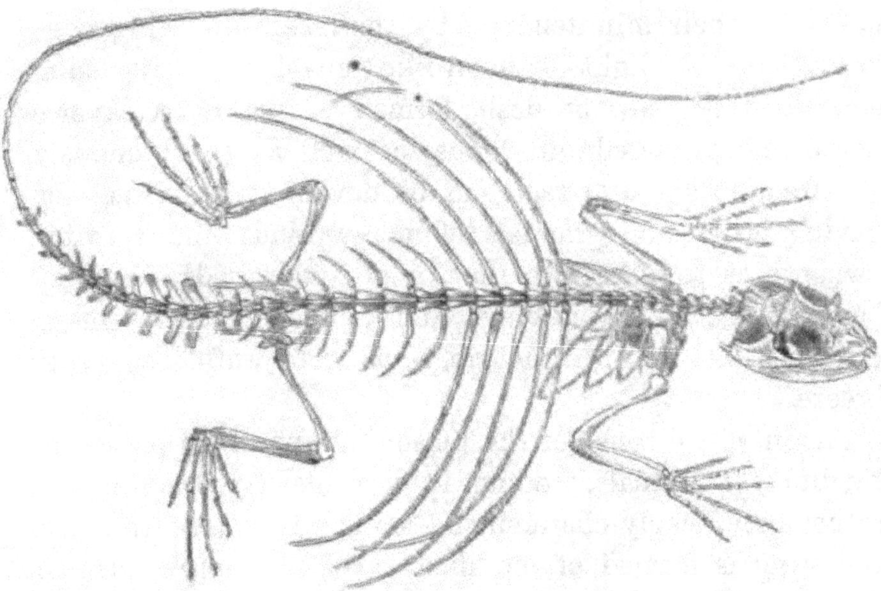

SKELETON OF THE FLYING-DRAGON.
(Showing the elongated ribs which support the flitting organ.)

tiles—we meet with an approximation to the structure of the bat, but in the pterodactyle we have only one finger elongated in each hand: a striking example of how the very same function may be provided for by a modification similar in principle, yet surely manifesting the independence of its origin. When we go to lower animals, we find flight produced by organs, as the wings of insects, which are not modified limbs at all; or we may even find the function subserved by quite artificial means, as in the aërial spiders, which use their own threads to float with in the air. In the vegetable kingdom the atmosphere is often made use of for the scattering of seeds, by their being furnished with special structures of very different kinds. The various modes by which such seeds are dispersed are well expressed by Mr. Darwin. He says:[1] "Seeds are disseminated by their minuteness,—by their capsule being converted into a light balloon-like envelope,—by being embedded in pulp or flesh, formed of the most diverse parts, and rendered nutritious, as well as conspicuously coloured, so as to attract and be devoured by birds,—by having hooks and grapnels of many kinds and serrated awns, so as to adhere to the fur of quadrupeds,—and by being furnished with wings and plumes, as different in shape as elegant in structure, so as to be wafted by every breeze."

Again, if we consider the poisoning apparatus possessed by different animals, we find in serpents a perforated—or rather very deeply channelled—tooth. In wasps and bees the sting is formed of modified parts, accessory in reproduction. In the scorpion, we have the median terminal process of the body specially organized. In the spider, we have a specially constructed antenna; and finally, in the centipede a pair of modified thoracic limbs.

It would be easy to produce a multitude of such instances of similar ends being attained by dissimilar means, and it is here contended that by "the action of Natural Selection" *only* it is so improbable as to be practically impossible for two exactly similar structures to have ever been indepen-

[1] "Origin of Species," 5th edition, p. 235.

dently developed. It is so because the number of possible variations is indefinitely great, and it is therefore an indefinitely great number to one against a similar series of variations occurring and being similarly preserved in any two independent instances.

The difficulty here asserted applies exclusively, however, to pure Darwinism, which makes use *only* of indirect modifications through the survival of the fittest.

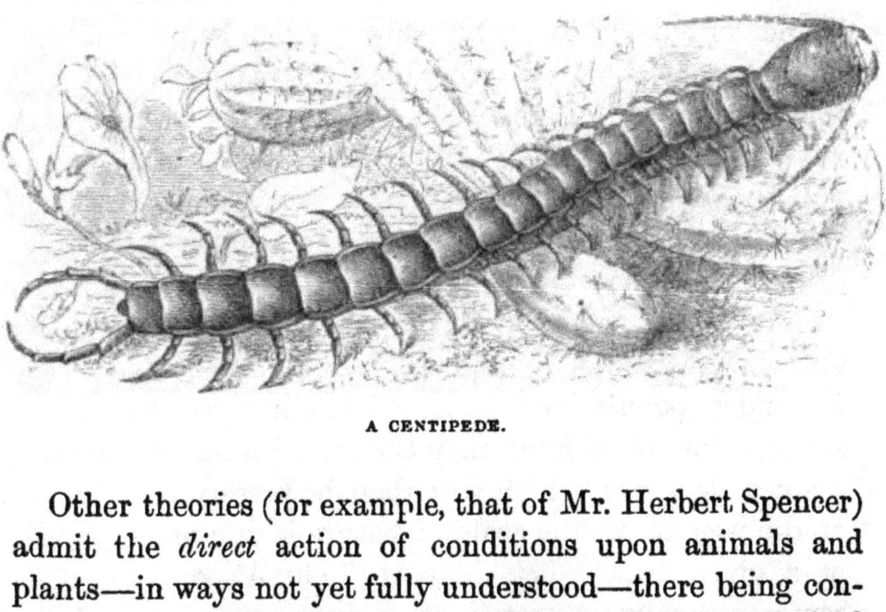

A CENTIPEDE.

Other theories (for example, that of Mr. Herbert Spencer) admit the *direct* action of conditions upon animals and plants—in ways not yet fully understood—there being conceived to be at the same time a certain peculiar but limited power of response and adaptation in each animal and plant so acted on. Such theories have not to contend against the difficulty proposed, and it is here urged that even very complex extremely similar structures have again and again been developed quite independently one of the other, and this because the process has taken place not by merely haphazard, indefinite variations in all directions, but by the

friendly relations with a powerful tribe, whose customs he has learnt. Suppose him to possess the physical strength, energy, and ability of a dominant white race, and let the food and climate of the island suit his constitution; grant him every advantage which we can conceive a white to possess over the native; concede that in the struggle for existence his chance of a long life will be much superior to that of the native chiefs; yet from all these admissions, there does not follow the conclusion that, after a limited or unlimited number of generations, the inhabitants of the island will be white. Our shipwrecked hero would probably become king; he would kill a great many blacks in the struggle for existence; he would have a great many wives and children." . . . . "In the first generation there will be some dozens of intelligent young mulattoes, much superior in average intelligence to the negroes. We might expect the throne for some generations to be occupied by a more or less yellow king; but can any one believe that the whole island will gradually acquire a white, or even a yellow, population?" . . . "Darwin says that in the struggle for life a grain may turn the balance in favour of a given structure, which will then be preserved. But one of the weights in the scale of nature is due to the number of a given tribe. Let there be 7000 A's and 7000 B's, representing two varieties of a given animal, and let all the B's, in virtue of a slight difference of structure, have the better chance of life by $\frac{1}{7000}$ part. We must allow that there is a slight probability that the descendants of B will supplant the descendants of A; but let there be only 7001 A's against 7000 B's at first, and the chances are once more equal, while if there be 7002 A's to start, the odds would be laid on the A's. True they stand a greater chance of being killed; but then, they can better afford to be killed. The grain will only turn the scales when these are very nicely balanced, and an advantage in numbers counts for weight, even as an advantage in structure. As the numbers of the favoured variety diminish, so must its relative advantages increase, if the chance of its existence is to surpass the chance of its extinction, until hardly any conceivable advantage would enable the descendants of a single pair to exterminate the descendants of many thousands if they and their descendants are supposed to breed freely with the inferior variety, and so gradually lose their ascendency."

Mr. Darwin himself says of the article quoted: "The justice of these remarks cannot, I think, be disputed. If, for instance, a bird of some kind could procure its food more easily by having its beak curved, and if one were born with its beak strongly curved, and which consequently flourished, nevertheless there would be a very poor chance of this one individual perpetuating its kind to the exclusion of the common form; but there can hardly be a doubt, judging by what we see taking place under domestication, that this result would follow from the preservation during many generations of a large number of individuals with more or less curved beaks, and from the destruction of a still larger number with the straightest beaks." This admission appears to the author to be of compromising significance.[1]

1 Mr. Darwin, in his recent work on Man, makes the further remarkable admission: "I now admit . . . that in the earlier editions of my 'Origin of Species' I probably attributed too much to the action of Natural Selection, or the survival of the fittest. . . . I had not formerly sufficiently considered the existence of many structures which appear to be, as far as

has elsewhere[1] pointed out, there is a certain similarity of the upper cutting teeth, or incisors.

Now these correspondences are the more striking when we bear in mind that a similar dentition is often put to very different uses. The food of different kinds of apes is very different, yet how uniform is their dental structure! Again, who, looking at the teeth of different kinds of bears, would ever suspect that one kind was frugivorous, and another a devourer exclusively of animal food?

The suggestion made by Professor Huxley was therefore one which had much to recommend it to Darwinians, though it has not met with any notable acceptance, and though he seems himself to have returned to the older notion,—namely, that the pouched-beasts, or marsupials, are a special ancient offshoot from the great mammalian class.

But whichever view may be the correct one, we have in either case a number of forms similarly modified in harmony with surrounding conditions, and eloquently proclaiming some natural plastic power, other than mere fortuitous variation with survival of the fittest. If, however, the reader thinks that teeth are parts peculiarly qualified for rapid variation (in which view the author cannot concur), he is requested to suspend his judgment till he has considered the question of the independent evolution of the *highest organs of sense.* If this seems to establish the existence of some other law than that of "Natural Selection," then the operation of that other law may surely be also traced in the harmonious co-ordinations of dental form.

The other difficulty, kindly suggested to me by the

[1] "Journal of Anatomy and Physiology" (1868), vol. ii. p. 139.

learned Professor, refers to the structure of birds, and of extinct reptiles more or less related to them.

The class of birds is one which is remarkably uniform in its organization. So much is this the case, that the best mode of subdividing the class is a problem of the greatest difficulty. Existing birds, however, present forms which, though closely resembling in the greater part of their structure, yet differ markedly the one from the other in certain respects. One form is exemplified by the ostrich, rhea, emeu, cassowary, apteryx, dinornis, &c.: these are the *struthious* birds. All other existing birds belong to the second division, and are called (from the keel on the breast-bone) *carinate* birds.

Now birds and reptiles have such and so many points in common, that Darwinians must regard the former as modified descendants of ancient reptilian forms. But on Darwinian principles it is impossible that the class of birds so uniform and homogeneous should have had a double reptilian origin. If one set of birds sprang from one set of reptiles, and another set of birds from another set of reptiles, the two sets could never, by "Natural Selection" only, have grown into such a perfect similarity. To admit such a phenomenon would be equivalent to abandoning the theory of "Natural Selection" as the sole origin of species.

Now, until recently it has generally been supposed by evolutionists that those ancient flying reptiles, the pterodactyles, or forms allied to them, were the progenitors of the class of birds; and certain parts of their structure especially support this view. Reference is here made to the bladebone (scapula), and the bone which passes down from the shoulder-joint to the breast-bone (viz. the coracoid). These bones are such remarkable anticipations of the same parts in ordinary (*i.e.* carinate) birds, that it is hardly possible for a Darwinian not to regard the resemblance as due to community of origin. This resemblance was carefully pointed out by Professor Huxley in his "Hunterian Course" for 1867, when attention was called to the existence in *Dimorphodon macronyx* of even that small process which in birds gives attachment to the upper end of the merrythought. Also Mr. Seeley[1] has shown that in pterodactyles, as in birds, the optic lobes of the brain were placed low down on each side—"lateral and depressed," and that several details of cranial structure were remarkably avian. Nevertheless, the view has been put forward and ably maintained by Professor Huxley,[2] as also by Professor Cope in the United States, that the line of descent from reptiles to birds has not been from ordinary reptiles, through pterodactyle-like forms, to ordinary birds, but to the struthious ones from certain extinct reptiles termed Dinosauria; one of the most familiarly known of which is the Iguanodon of the Wealden formation. In these Dinosauria we find skeletal characters unlike those of ordinary (*i.e.* carinate) birds, but closely resembling in certain points the osseous structure of the struthious birds. Thus a difficulty presents itself as to the explanation of the three following relationships:—(1) That of the Pterodactyles with carinate birds; (2) that of the Dinosauria with struthious birds; (3) that of the carinate and struthious birds with each other.

[1] See "Ann. and Mag. of Nat. Hist." for August 1870, p. 140; and for January 1871, p. 20, plates ii. and iii.

[2] See "Proceedings of the Royal Institution," vol. v. part iv. p. 278: Report of a Lecture delivered February 7, 1868. Also "Quarterly Journal of the Geological Society," February 1870: "Contributions to the Anatomy and Taxonomy of the Dinosauria."

Either, birds must have had two distinct origins whence they grew to their present conformity, or the very same skeletal, and probably cerebral, characters must have spontaneously and independently arisen. Here is a dilemma, either horn of which bears a threatening aspect to the exclusive supporter of "Natural Selection," and between which it seems somewhat difficult to choose.

It has been suggested to the author that this difficulty may be evaded by considering pterodactyles and carinate birds as independent branches from one side of an ancient common trunk; while similarly the Dinosauria and struthious birds are taken to be independent branches from the other side of the same common trunk; the two kinds of birds resembling each other so much on account of their later development from that trunk as compared with the development of the reptilian forms. But to this it may be replied, that the ancient common stock could not have had at one and the same time a shoulder structure of *both kinds.* It must have been that of the struthious birds or that of the carinate birds, or something different from both. If it was that of the struthious birds, how did the pterodactyles and carinate birds independently arrive at the very same divergent structure? If it was that of the carinate birds, how did the struthious birds and Dinosauria independently agree to differ? Finally, if it was something different from either, how did the carinate birds and pterodactyles take on independently one special common structure when disagreeing in so many; while the struthious birds, agreeing in many points with the Dinosauria, agree yet more with the carinate birds? Indeed, by no arrangement of branches from a stem can the difficulty be evaded.

Professor Huxley seems inclined[1] to cut the Gordian knot by considering the shoulder structure of the pterodactyle as independently educed, and having relation to physiology only. This conception is one which harmonizes completely with the views here advocated, and with those of Mr. Herbert Spencer, who also calls in direct modification to the aid of "Natural Selection." That merely minute indefinite variations in all directions should unaided have independently built up the shoulder structure of the pterodactyles and carinate birds, and have laterally depressed their optic lobes, at a time so far back as the deposition of the Oolite strata,[2] is a coincidence of the

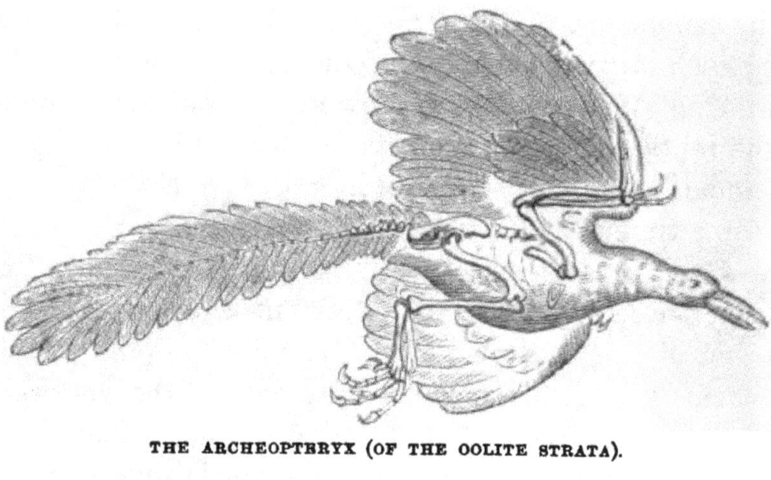

THE ARCHEOPTERYX (OF THE OOLITE STRATA).

highest improbability; but that an innate power and evolutionary law, aided by the corrective action of "Natural Selection," should have furnished like needs with like aids, is not at all improbable. The difficulty does not tell against the theory of evolution, but only

[1] "Proceedings of Geological Society," November 1869, p. 38.

[2] The archeopteryx of the Oolite has the true carinate shoulder structure.

against the specially Darwinian form of it. Now this form has never been expressly adopted by Professor Huxley; so far from it, in his lecture at the Royal Institution before referred to, he observes,[1] "I can testify, from personal experience, it is possible to have a complete faith in the general doctrine of evolution, and yet to hesitate in accepting the Nebular, or the Uniformitarian, or the Darwinian hypotheses in all their integrity and fulness."

It is quite consistent, then, in the Professor to explain the difficulty as he does; but it would not be similarly so with an absolute and pure Darwinian.

Yet stronger arguments of an analogous kind are, however, to be derived from the highest organs of sense. In the most perfectly organized animals—those namely which, like ourselves, possess a spinal column—the internal organs of hearing consist of two more or less complex membranous sacs (containing calcareous particles—otoliths), which are primitively or permanently lodged in two chambers, one on each side of the cartilaginous skull. The primitive cartilaginous cranium supports and protects the base of the brain, and the auditory nerves pass from that brain into the cartilaginous chambers to reach the auditory sacs. These complex arrangements of parts could not have been evolved by "Natural Selection," *i.e.* by minute accidental variations, except by the action of such through a vast period of time; nevertheless, it was fully evolved at the time of deposition of the Upper Silurian rocks.

Cuttle-fishes (*Cephalopoda*) are animals belonging to the molluscous primary division of the animal kingdom, which division contains animals formed upon a type of structure

[1] "Proceedings of the Royal Institution," vol. v. p. 279.

utterly remote from that on which the animals of the higher division provided with a spinal column are constructed. And indeed no transitional form (tending even to bridge over the chasm between those two groups) has ever yet been discovered, either living or in a fossilized condition.[1]

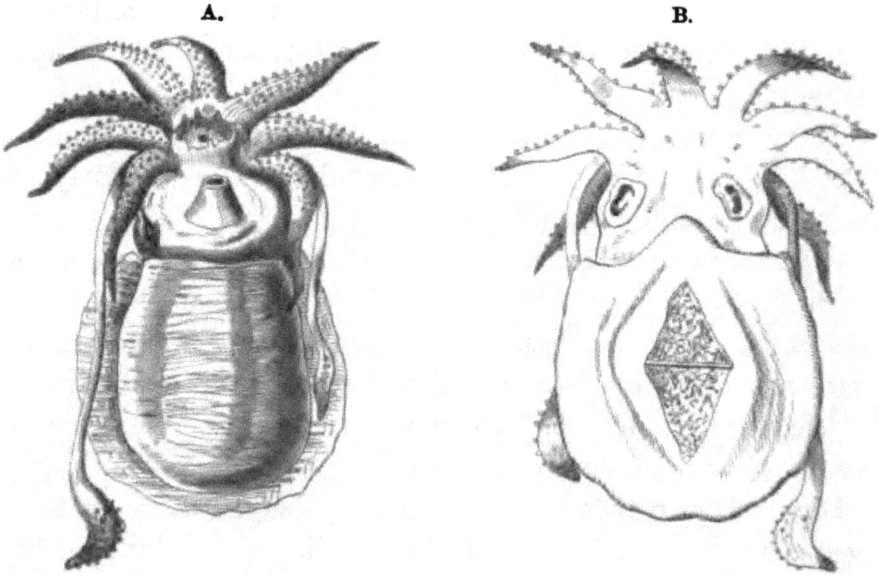

CUTTLE-FISH.

A. Ventral aspect. B. Dorsal aspect.

Nevertheless, in the two-gilled Cephalopods (*Dibranchiata*) we find the brain supported and protected by a cartilaginous cranium. In the base of this cranium are two cartilaginous chambers. In each chamber is a membranous sac containing an otolith, and the auditory nerves pass from the cerebral ganglia into the cartilaginous chambers to reach the auditory sacs. Moreover, it has been

[1] This remark is made without prejudice to possible affinities in the direction of the Ascidians,—an affinity which, if real, would be irrelevant to the question here discussed.

suggested by Professor Owen that sinuosities between processes projecting from the inner wall of each chamber "seem to be the first rudiments of those which, in the higher classes (*i.e.* in animals with a spinal column), are extended in the form of canals and spiral chambers, within the substance of the dense nidus of the labyrinth."[1]

Here, then, we have a wonderful coincidence indeed; two highly complex auditory organs, marvellously similar in structure, but which must nevertheless have been developed in entire and complete independence one of the other! It would be difficult to calculate the odds against the independent occurrence and conservation of two such complex series of merely accidental and minute haphazard variations. And it cannot be maintained that the sense of hearing could not be efficiently subserved otherwise than by such sacs, in cranial cartilaginous capsules so situated in relation to the brain, &c.

Our wonder, moreover, may be increased when we recollect that the two-gilled cephalopods have not yet been found below the lias, where they at once abound; whereas the four-gilled cephalopods are Silurian forms. Moreover, the absence is in this case significant in spite of the imperfection of the geological record; because when we consider how many individuals of various kinds of four-gilled cephalopods have been found, it is fair to infer that at the least a certain small percentage of dibranchs would also have left traces of their presence had they existed. Thus it is probable that some four-gilled form was the progenitor of the dibranch cephalopods. Now the four-gilled kinds (judging from the only existing form, the nautilus) had the

[1] "Lectures on the Comp. Anat. of the Invertebrate Animals," 2nd edit. 1855, p. 619; and Todd's "Cyclopædia of Anatomy," vol. i. p. 554.

auditory organ in a very inferior condition of development to what we find in the dibranch: thus we have not only evidence of the independent high development of the organ in the former, but also evidence pointing towards a certain degree of comparative rapidity in its development.

Such being the case with regard to the organ of hearing, we have another yet stronger argument with regard to the organ of sight, as has been well pointed out by Mr. J. J. Murphy.[1] He calls attention to the fact that the eye must have been perfected in at least "three distinct lines of descent," alluding not only to the molluscous division of the animal kingdom, and the division provided with a spinal column, but also to a third primary division, viz. that which includes all insects, spiders, crabs, &c., which are spoken of as Annulosa, and the type of whose structure is as distinct from that of the molluscous type on the one hand, as it is from that of the vertebrate type on the other.

In the cuttle-fishes we find an eye constructed even more completely on the vertebrate type than is the ear. Sclerotic, retina, choroid, vitreous humour, lens, aqueous humour, all are present. The correspondence is wonderfully complete, and there can hardly be any hesitation in saying that for such an exact, prolonged, and correlated series of similar structures to have been brought about in two independent instances by merely indefinite and minute accidental variations, is an improbability which amounts virtually to impossibility. Moreover, we have here again the same imperfection of the four-gilled cephalopod, as compared with the two-gilled, and therefore (if the latter proceeded from the former) a similar indication of a cer-

[1] See "Habit and Intelligence," vol. i. p. 321.

tain comparative rapidity of development. Finally, and this is perhaps one of the most curious circumstances, the process of formation appears to have been, at least in some respects, the same in the eyes of these molluscous animals as in the eyes of vertebrates. For in these latter the cornea is at first perforated, while different degrees of perforation of the same part are presented by different adult cuttle-fishes—large in the calamaries, smaller in the octopods, and reduced to a minute foramen in the true cuttle-fish sepia.

Some may be disposed to object that the conditions requisite for affecting vision are so rigid that similar results in all cases must be independently arrived at. But to this objection it may well be replied that Nature herself has demonstrated that there is no such necessity as to the details of the process. For in the higher Annulosa, such as the dragon-fly, we meet with an eye of an unquestionably very high degree of efficiency, but formed on a type of structure only remotely comparable with that of the fish or the cephalopod. The last-named animal might have had an eye as efficient as that of a vertebrate, but formed on a distinct type, instead of being another edition, as it were, of the very same structure.

In the beginning of this chapter examples have been given of the very diverse mode in which similar results have in many instances been arrived at; on the other hand, we have in the fish and the cephalopod not only the eye, but at one and the same time the ear also similarly evolved, yet with complete independence.

Thus it is here contended that the similar and complex structures of both the highest organs of sense, as developed in the vertebrates on the one hand, and in the mollusks on the other, present us with residuary phenomena for which "Natural Selection" alone is quite incompetent to account: and that these same phenomena must therefore be considered as conclusive evidence for the action of some other natural law or laws conditioning the simultaneous and independent evolution of these harmonious and concordant adaptations.

Provided with this evidence, it may be now profitable to enumerate other correspondences, which are not perhaps in themselves inexplicable by "Natural Selection," but which are more readily to be explained by the action of the unknown law or laws referred to—which action, as its necessity has been demonstrated in one case, becomes *a priori* probable in the others.

Thus the great oceanic Mammalia—the whales—show striking resemblances to those prodigious, extinct, marine

SKELETON OF AN ICHTHYOSAURUS.

reptiles, the Ichthyosauria, and this not only in structures readily referable to similarity of habit, but in such matters as greatly elongated premaxillary bones, together with the concealment of certain bones of the skull by other cranial bones.

Again, the aërial mammals, the bats, resemble those flying reptiles of the secondary epoch, the pterodactyles; not only to a certain extent in the breast-bone and mode of supporting the flying membrane, but also in the proportions of different parts of the spinal column and the hinder (pelvic) limbs.

Bivalve shell-fish (*i.e.* creatures of the mussel, cockle, and oyster class, which receive their name from the body being protected by a double shell, one valve of which is placed on each side) have their two shells united by one or two powerful muscles, which pass directly across from one shell to the other, and which are termed "adductor muscles," because by their contraction they bring together the valves and so close the shell. Now there are certain animals which belong to the crab and lobster class (Crustacea)—a class

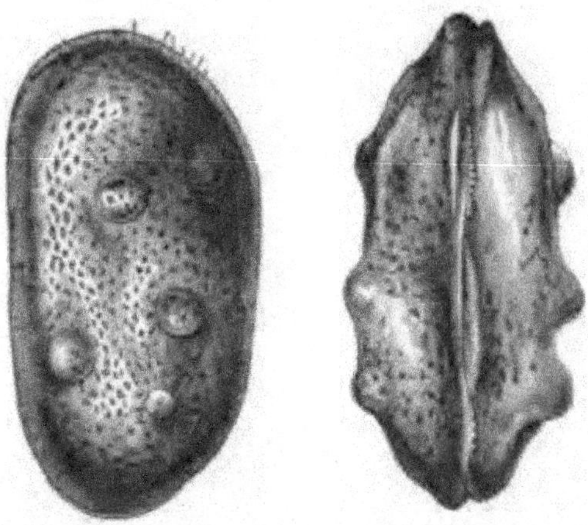

CYTHERIDEA TOROSA.
An ostracod (Crustacean), externally like a bivalve shell-fish (Lamellibranch).

constructed on a different type from that on which the bivalve shell-fish are constructed—which present a very curious approximation to both the form, and, in a certain respect, the structure of true bivalves. Reference is here made to certain small Crustacea—certain phyllopods and ostracods—which have the hard outer coat of their thorax so modified as to look exceedingly like a bivalve shell, although its nature and composition are quite different. But this is by no means all,—not only is there this external resemblance between the thoracic

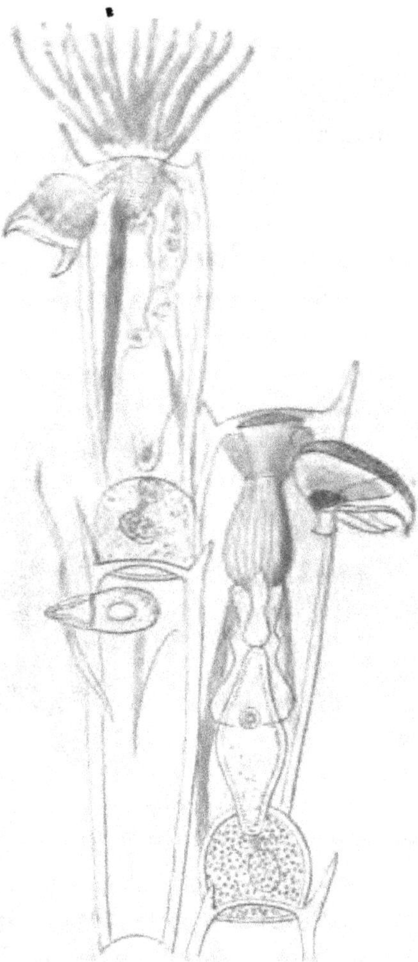

A POLYZOON, WITH BIRD'S-HEAD PROCESSES.

armour of the crustacean and the bivalve shell, but the two sides of the ostracod and phyllopod thorax are connected together also by an adductor muscle!

The pedicellariæ of the echinus have been already spoken of, and the difficulty as to their origin from minute, fortuitous, indefinite variations has been stated. But structures essentially similar (called avicularia, or "bird's-head processes") are developed from the surface of the compound masses of certain of the highest of the polyp-like animals, viz. the Polyzoa or, as they are sometimes called, the Bryozoa.

These compound animals have scattered over the surface of their bodies minute processes, each of which is like the head of a bird, with an upper and lower beak, the whole supported on a slender neck. The beak opens and shuts at intervals, like the jaws of the pedicellariæ of the echinus,

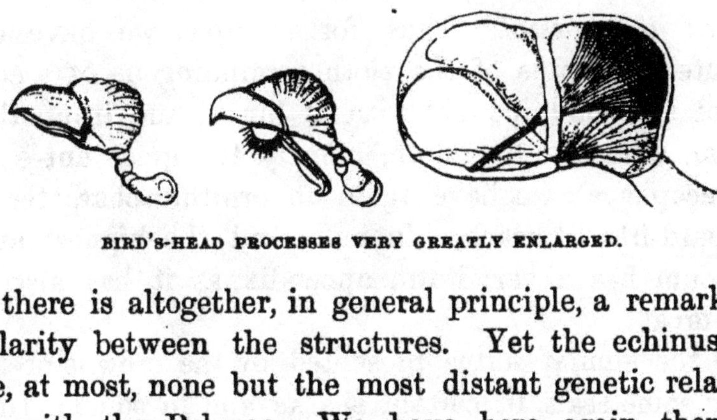

BIRD'S-HEAD PROCESSES VERY GREATLY ENLARGED.

and there is altogether, in general principle, a remarkable similarity between the structures. Yet the echinus can have, at most, none but the most distant genetic relationship with the Polyzoa. We have here again therefore complex and similar organs of diverse and independent origin.

In the highest class of animals (the Mammalia) we have almost always a placental mode of reproduction, *i.e.* the blood of the fœtus is placed in nutritive relation with the blood of the mother by means of vascular prominences. No trace of such a structure exists in any bird or in any reptile, and yet it reappears in certain sharks. There indeed it might be supposed to end; but, strange as it seems, it reappears in very lowly creatures, namely, in certain of the ascidians, sometimes called tunicaries or sea-squirts.

Now, if we were to concede that the ascidians were the common ancestors[1] of both these sharks and of the higher mammals, we should be little, if any nearer to an explanation of the phenomenon by means of "Natural Selection;" for in the sharks in question the vascular prominences are developed from one fœtal structure (the umbilical vesicle), while in the higher mammals they are developed from quite another part, viz. the allantois.

So great, however, is the number of similar, but apparently independent, structures, that we suffer from an *embarras de richesses.* Thus, for example, we have the convoluted windpipe of the sloth, reminding us of a condition of the windpipe met with in birds; and in another mammal, allied to the sloth, namely the great ant-eater (Myrmecophaga), we have again an ornithic character in its gizzard-like stomach. In man and the highest apes the cæcum has a vermiform appendix, as it has also in the wombat!

Also the similar forms presented by the crowns of the teeth in some seals, in certain sharks, and in some extinct Cetacea may be referred to; as also the similarity of the beak in birds, in some reptiles, in the tadpole, and in cuttle-fishes. As to entire external form, may be adduced

[1] A view propounded by Kowalewsky, and since supported by Kupffer, but which has quite recently been strongly controverted by W. Dönitz: see his article entitled "Ueber die sogenannte Chorda der Ascidienlarven und die Vermeintliche Verwandtschaft von Wirbellosen und Wirbelthieren," in Reichert and Reymond's "Archiv für Anatomie und Physiologie," 1870, No. 6, page 761.

the curious similarity between a true mouse (*Mus delicatulus*) and a small marsupial, pointed out by Mr. Andrew Murray in his work on the "Geographical Distribution of Mammals;" but instances enough for the present purpose have been already quoted.

Upper Figure—ANTECHNINUS MINUTISSIMUS (*implacental*).
Lower Figure—MUS DELICATULUS (*placental*).

Additional reasons for believing that similarity of structure is produced by other causes than merely by "Natural Selection" are furnished by certain facts of zoological geography, and by a similarity in the mode of variation being sometimes extended to several species of a genus, or even to widely different groups; while the restriction and the limitation of such similarity are often not less remarkable. Thus Mr. Wallace says,[1] as to local influence: "Larger or smaller districts, or even single islands, give a special character to the majority of their Papilionidæ. For instance:—1. The species of the Indian region (Sumatra, Java, and Borneo) are almost invariably smaller than the allied species inhabiting Celebes and the Moluccas. 2. The species of New Guinea and Australia are also, though in a less degree, smaller than the nearest species or varieties of the Moluccas. 3. In the Moluccas themselves the species of Amboyna are the largest. 4. The species of Celebes equal or even surpass in size those of Amboyna. 5. The species and varieties of Celebes possess a striking character in the form of the anterior wings, different from that of the allied species and varieties of all the surrounding islands. 6. Tailed species in India or the Indian region become tailless as they spread eastward through the Archipelago. 7. In Amboyna and Ceram the females of several species are dull-coloured, while in the adjacent islands they are more brilliant." Again:[2] "In Amboyna and Ceram the female of the large and handsome *Ornithoptera Helena* has the large patch on the hind wings constantly of a pale dull ochre or buff colour; while in the scarcely distinguishable varieties from the adjacent islands of Bouru and New Guinea, it is of a golden yellow, hardly inferior in brilliancy to its colour in the male sex. The female of *Ornithoptera Priamus* (inhabiting Amboyna and Ceram exclusively) is of a pale, dusky brown tint, while in all the allied species the same sex is nearly black, with contracted white markings. As a third example, the female of *Papilio*

[1] "Natural Selection," p. 167.
[2] Ibid. p. 173.

Ulysses has the blue colour obscured by dull and dusky tints; while in the closely allied species from the surrounding islands, the females are of almost as brilliant an azure blue as the males. A parallel case to this is the occurrence, in the small islands of Goram, Matabello, Ké, and Aru, of several distinct species of Euplœa and Diadema, having broad bands or patches of white, which do not exist in any of the allied species from the larger islands. These facts seem to indicate some local influence in modifying colour, as unintelligible and almost as remarkable as that which has resulted in the modifications of form previously described."

After endeavouring to explain some of the facts in a way to be noticed directly, Mr. Wallace adds:[1] "But even the conjectural explanation now given fails us in the other cases of local modification. Why the species of the Western Islands should be smaller than those further east; why those of Amboyna should exceed in size those of Gilolo and New Guinea; why the tailed species of India should begin to lose that appendage in the islands, and retain no trace of it on the borders of the Pacific; and why, in three separate cases, the females of Amboyna species should be less gaily attired than the corresponding females of the surrounding islands, are questions which we cannot at present attempt to answer. That they depend, however, on some general principle is certain, because analogous facts have been observed in other parts of the world. Mr. Bates informs me that, in three distinct groups, Papilios, which, on the Upper Amazon and in most other parts of South America, have spotless upper wings, obtain pale or white spots at Para and on the Lower Amazon; and

[1] "Natural Selection," p. 177.

also that the Æneas group of Papilios never have tails in the equatorial regions and the Amazon valley, but gradually acquire tails in many cases as they range towards the northern or southern tropic. Even in Europe we have somewhat similar facts, for the species and varieties of butterflies peculiar to the Island of Sardinia are generally smaller and more deeply coloured than those of the mainland, and the same has been recently shown to be the case with the common tortoiseshell butterfly in the Isle of Man; while *Papilio Hospiton*, peculiar to the former island, has lost the tail, which is a prominent feature of the closely allied *P. Machaon*."

"Facts of a similar nature to those now brought forward would no doubt be found to occur in other groups of insects, were local faunas carefully studied in relation to those of the surrounding countries; and they seem to indicate that climate and other physical causes have, in some cases, a very powerful effect in modifying specific form and colour, and thus directly aid in producing the endless variety of nature."

With regard to butterflies of Celebes belonging to different families, they present "a peculiarity of outline which distinguishes them at a glance from those of any other part of the world:"[1] it is that the upper wings are generally more elongated and the anterior margin more curved. Moreover, there is, in most instances, near the base an abrupt bend or elbow, which in some species is very conspicuous. Mr. Wallace endeavours to explain this phenomenon by the supposed presence at some time of special persecutors of the modified forms, supporting the opinion by the remark that small, obscure, very

[1] "Malay Archipelago," vol. i. p. 439.

rapidly flying and mimicked kinds have not had the wing modified. Such an enemy occasioning increased powers of

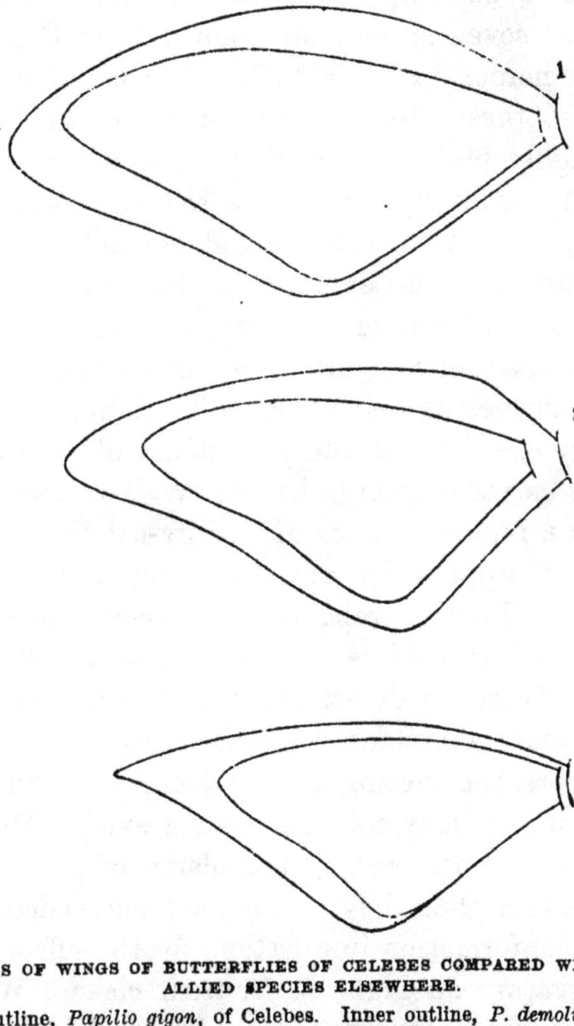

1

2

3

OUTLINES OF WINGS OF BUTTERFLIES OF CELEBES COMPARED WITH THOSE OF ALLIED SPECIES ELSEWHERE.

1. Outer outline, *Papilio gigon*, of Celebes. Inner outline, *P. demolion*, of Singapore and Java.—2. Outer outline, *P. miletus*, of Celebes. Inner outline, *P. sarpedon*, India.—3. Outer outline, *Tachyris zarinda*, Celebes. Inner outline, *T. nero*.

flight, or rapidity in turning, he adds, "one would naturally suppose to be an insectivorous bird; but it is a remarkable fact that most of the genera of fly-catchers of Borneo and Java on the one side, and of the Moluccas on the other, are almost entirely absent from Celebes. Their place seems to be supplied by the caterpillar-catchers, of which six or seven species are known from Celebes, and are very numerous in individuals. We have no positive evidence that these birds pursue butterflies on the wing, but it is highly probable that they do so when other food is scarce. Mr. Bates suggested to me that the larger dragon-flies prey upon butterflies, but I did not notice that they were more abundant in Celebes than elsewhere."[1]

Now, every opinion or conjecture of Mr. Wallace is worthy of respectful and attentive consideration, but the explanation suggested and above referred to hardly seems a satisfactory one. What the past fauna of Celebes may have been is as yet conjectural. Mr. Wallace tells us that now there is a remarkable *scarcity* of fly-catchers, and that their place is supplied by birds of which it can only be said that it is "highly probable" that they chase butterflies "when other food is scarce." The quick eye of Mr. Wallace failed to detect them in the act, as also to note any unusual abundance of other insectivorous forms, which therefore, considering Mr. Wallace's zeal and powers of observation, we may conclude do not exist. Moreover, even if there ever has been an abundance of such, it is by no means certain that they would have succeeded in producing the conformation in question, for the effect of this peculiar curvature on flight is far from clear. We have here, then, a structure hypothetically explained by an uncertain property induced by a cause the presence of which is only conjectural.

Surely it is not unreasonable to class this instance with

[1] "Natural Selection," p. 177.

the others before given, in which a common modification of form or colour coexists with a certain geographical distribution quite independently of the destructive agencies of animals. If physical causes connected with locality can abbreviate or annihilate the tails of certain butterflies, why may not similar causes produce an elbow-like prominence on the wings of other butterflies? There are many such instances of simultaneous modification. Mr. Darwin himself[1] quotes Mr. Gould as believing that birds of the same species are more brightly coloured under a clear atmosphere, than when living on islands or near the coast. Mr. Darwin also informs us that Wollaston is convinced that residence near the sea affects the colour of insects; and finally, that Moquin-Tandon gives a list of plants which, when growing near the sea-shore, have their leaves in some degree fleshy, though not so elsewhere. In his work on "Animals and Plants under Domestication,"[2] Mr. Darwin refers to M. Costa as having (in *Bull. de la Soc. Imp. d'Acclimat.* tome viii. p. 351) stated "that young shells taken from the shores of England and placed in the Mediterranean at once altered their manner of growth, and formed prominent diverging rays *like those on the shells of the proper Mediterranean oyster;*" also to Mr. Meehan, as stating (*Proc. Acad. Nat. Sc. of Philadelphia*, Jan. 28, 1862) "that twenty kinds of American trees all differ from their nearest European allies in a *similar manner*, leaves less toothed, buds and seeds smaller, fewer branchlets," &c. These are indeed striking examples of concordant modification![3]

1 "Origin of Species," 5th edition, p. 166. 2 Vol. ii. p. 280.

3 "Again, what, at first sight, can more accord with 'natural selection' than the fact that so many animals turn white in winter in Arctic regions?

 [Those

But cases of simultaneous and similar modifications

THE GREAT SHIELDED GRASSHOPPER.

abound on all sides. Even as regards the human species, there is a very generally admitted opinion that a new

Those that did not so turn would much more easily become the prey of others (if they were vegetarians), or (if they were carnivorous animals) their prey would more readily perceive and avoid them. Here, then, it seems at first that we have the obvious action of natural selection. Yet, in fact, this faculty now appears to be rather the result of some obscure internal tendency, intensified, no doubt, by natural selection, but by no means due to the action of the latter on mere accidental minute variations. For in Siberia it is not only timid or predacious animals that tend to become light-coloured in winter, since Pallas tells us that such a phenomenon is observable in domestic cattle and in horses. In such animals, of course, this character cannot be due to natural selection, and therefore, as we *must* admit it in this case to be due to some spontaneous internal tendency, it immediately becomes probable that a similar tendency also exists in the other cases, and the *onus probandi* lies with him who denies that such is the case."—*Novæ Species Quadrupedum e Glirium ordine*, 1778, p. 7, quoted by Mr. Darwin in "Descent of Man:" see vol. i. p. 282.

type has been developed in the United States, and this in about a couple of centuries only, and in a vast multitude of individuals of diverse ancestry. The instances here given, however, must suffice, though more could easily be adduced.

It may be well now to turn to groups presenting similar variations, not through, but independently of, geographical distribution, and, as far as we know, independently of conditions other than some peculiar nature and tendency (as

THE SIX-SHAFTED BIRD OF PARADISE.

yet unexplained) common to members of such groups, which nature and tendency seem to induce them to vary in certain definite lines or directions which are different in different groups. Thus with regard to the group of insects of which the walking leaf is a member, Mr. Wallace observes:[1] "The *whole family*[2] of the Phasmidæ,

[1] See "Natural Selection," p. 64.

[2] The italics are not Mr. Wallace's.

or spectres, to which this insect belongs, is more or less imitative, and a great number of the species are called 'walking-stick insects,' from their singular resemblance to twigs and branches."

Again, Mr. Wallace[1] tells us of as many as four kinds of orioles, which birds mimic, more or less, four species of

THE LONG-TAILED BIRD OF PARADISE.

a genus of honey-suckers, the weak orioles finding their profit in being mistaken by certain birds of prey for the strong, active, and gregarious honey-suckers. Now many other birds would be benefited by similar mimicry, which is none the less confined, in this part of the world, to the oriole genus. It is true that the absence of mimicry in

[1] "Malay Archipelago," vol. ii. p. 150; and "Natural Selection," p. 104.

THE RED BIRD OF PARADISE.

other forms may be explained by their possessing some other (as yet unobserved) means of preservation; but it is nevertheless remarkable, not so much that one species should mimic, as that no less than four should do so in different ways and degrees, all these four belonging to *one and the same genus.*

In other cases, however, there is not even the help of

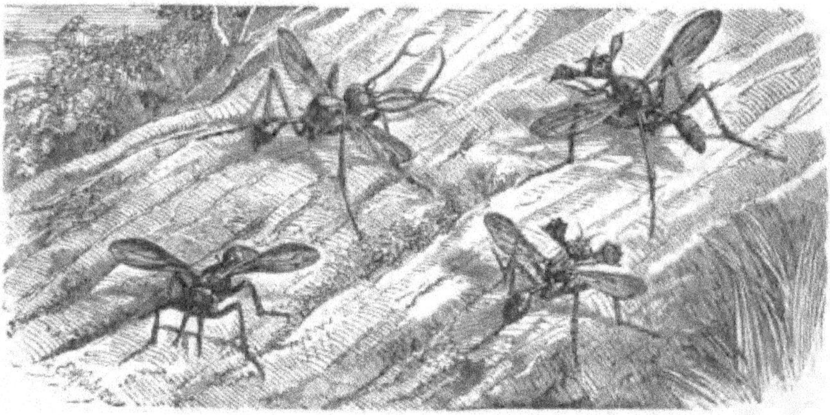

HORNED FLIES.

protective action to account for the phenomenon. Thus we have the wonderful birds of Paradise,[1] which agree in

THE MAGNIFICENT BIRD OF PARADISE.

developing plumage unequalled in beauty, but a beauty

[1] See "Malay Archipelago," vol. ii. chap. xxxviii.

which as to details is of different kinds, and produced in different ways in different species. To develop "beauty and singularity of plumage" is a character of the group, but not of any one definite kind, to be explained merely by inheritance.

Again, we have the very curious horned flies,[1] which agree indeed in a common peculiarity, but in one singularly different in detail in different species, and not known to have any protecting effect.

Amongst plants also we meet with similar resemblances. The great group of Orchids includes species which exhibit strange and bizarre approximations to different animal forms, and which have often the appearance of cases of mimicry, as it were in an incipient stage.

The number of similar instances which could be brought forward from amongst animals and plants is very great, but the examples given are, it is hoped, amply sufficient to point towards the conclusion which other facts will establish, viz. that there are causes operating (in the evocation of these harmonious diverging resemblances) other than "Natural Selection," or heredity, and other even than merely geographical, climatal, or any simply external conditions.

Many cases have been adduced of striking likenesses between different animals, not due to inheritance; but this should be the less surprising, in that the very same individual presents us with likenesses between different parts of its body (*e.g.* between the several joints of the backbone), which are certainly not explicable by inheritance. This, however, leads to a rather large subject, which will be treated of in the eighth chapter of the present work.

[1] Loc. cit. p. 314.

Here it will be enough to affirm (leaving the proof of the assertion till later) that parts are often homologous which have no direct genetic relationship—a fact which harmonizes well with the other facts here given, but which "Natural Selection," pure and simple, seems unable to explain.

But surely the independent appearance of similar organic forms is what we might expect, *a priori*, from the independent appearance of similar inorganic ones. As Mr. G. H. Lewes well observes:[1] "We do not suppose the carbonates and phosphates found in various parts of the globe—we do not suppose that the families of alkaloids and salts have any nearer kinship than that which consists in the similarity of their elements, and the conditions of their combination. Hence, in organisms, as in salts, morphological identity may be due to a community of causal connexion, rather than community of descent."

"Mr. Darwin justly holds it to be incredible that individuals identically the same should have been produced through Natural Selection from parents *specifically distinct;* but he will not deny that identical forms may issue from parents *genetically distinct*, when these parent forms and the conditions of production are identical. To deny this would be to deny the law of causation."

Professor Huxley has, however, suggested[2] that such mineral identity may be explained by applying also to minerals a law of descent; that is, by considering such similar forms as the descendants of atoms which inhabited one special part of the primitive nebular cosmos, each considerable space of which may be supposed to have been under the influence of somewhat different conditions.

[1] *Fortnightly Review*, New Series, vol. iii. (April 1868), p. 372.
[2] "Lay Sermons," p. 339.

Surely, however, there can be no real parity between the relationship of existing minerals to nebular atoms, and the relationship of existing animals and plants to the earliest organisms. In the first place, the latter have produced others by generative multiplication, which mineral atoms never did. In the second, existing animals and plants spring from the living tissues of preceding animals and plants, while existing minerals spring from the chemical affinity of separate elements. Carbonate of soda is not formed, by a process of reproduction, from other carbonate of soda, but directly by the suitable juxtaposition of carbon, oxygen, and sodium.

Instead of approximating animals and minerals in the mode suggested, it may be that they are to be approximated in quite a contrary fashion; namely, by attributing to mineral species an internal innate power. For, as we must attribute to each elementary atom an innate power and tendency to form (under the requisite external conditions) certain unions with other atoms, so we may attribute to certain mineral species—as crystals—an innate power and tendency to exhibit (the proper conditions being supplied) a definite and symmetrical external form. The distinction between animals and vegetables on the one hand, and minerals on the other, is that, while in the organic world close similarity is the result sometimes of inheritance, sometimes perhaps of direct production independently of parental action, in the inorganic world the latter is the constant and only mode in which such similarity is produced.

When we come to consider the relations of species to space—in other words, the geographical distribution of organisms—it will be necessary to return somewhat to the subject of the independent origin of closely similar forms, in regard to which some additional remarks will be found towards the end of the seventh chapter.

In this third chapter an effort has been made to show that while on the Darwinian theory concordant variations are extremely improbable, yet Nature presents us with abundant examples of such; the most striking of which are, perhaps, the higher organs of sense. Also that an important influence is exercised by conditions connected with geographical distribution, but that a deeper-seated influence is at work, which is hinted at by those special tendencies in definite directions, which are the properties of certain groups. Finally, that these facts, when taken together, afford strong evidence that "Natural Selection" has not been the exclusive or predominant cause of the various organic structural peculiarities. This conclusion has also been re-enforced by the consideration of phenomena presented to us by the inorganic world.

CHAPTER IV.

MINUTE AND GRADUAL MODIFICATIONS.

There are difficulties as to minute modifications, even if not fortuitous.—Examples of sudden and considerable modifications of different kinds.—Professor Owen's view.—Mr. Wallace.—Professor Huxley.—Objections to sudden changes.—Labyrinthodont.—Potto.—Cetacea.—As to origin of bird's wing.—Tendrils of climbing plants.—Animals once supposed to be connecting links.—Early specialization of structure.—Macrauchenia.—Glyptodon.—Sabre-toothed tiger.—Conclusion.

NOT only are there good reasons against the acceptance of the exclusive operation of "Natural Selection" as the one means of specific origination, but there are difficulties in the way of accounting for such origination by the sole action of modifications which are insignificant and minute whether fortuitous or not.

Arguments may yet be advanced in favour of the view that new species have from time to time manifested themselves with suddenness, and by modifications appearing at once (as great in degree as are those which separate *Hipparion* from *Equus*), the species remaining stable in the intervals of such modifications: by stable being meant that their variations only extend for a certain degree in various directions, like oscillations in a stable equilibrium. This is the conception of Mr. Galton,[1] who compares the

[1] "Hereditary Genius, an Inquiry into its Laws," &c. By Francis Galton, F.R.S. (London : Macmillan.)

development of species with a many facetted spheroid tumbling over from one facet, or stable equilibrium, to another. The existence of internal conditions in animals corresponding with such facets is denied by pure Darwinians, but it is contended in this work, though not in this chapter, that something may also be said for their existence.

The considerations brought forward in the last two chapters, namely, the difficulties with regard to incipient and closely similar structures respectively, together with palæontological considerations to be noticed later, appear to point strongly in the direction of sudden and considerable changes. This is notably the case as regards the young oysters already mentioned, which were taken from the shores of England and placed in the Mediterranean, and which at once altered their mode of growth and formed prominent diverging rays, *like those of the proper Mediterranean oyster*; as also the twenty-nine kinds of American trees, all differing from their nearest European allies *similarly*—"leaves less toothed, buds and seeds smaller, fewer branchlets," &c. To these may be added other facts given by Mr. Darwin. Thus he says "that climate, to a certain extent, directly modifies the form of dogs."[1]

The Rev. R. Everett found that setters at Delhi, though most carefully paired, yet had young with "nostrils more contracted, noses more pointed, size inferior, and limbs more slender." Again, cats at Mombas, on the coast of Africa, have short stiff hairs instead of fur; and a cat at Algoa Bay, when left only eight weeks at Mombas, "underwent a complete metamorphosis, having parted with its

[1] "Animals and Plants under Domestication," vol. i. p. 37.

sandy-coloured fur."[1] The conditions of life seem to produce a considerable effect on horses, and instances are given by Mr. Darwin of pony breeds[2] having independently arisen in different parts of the world, possessing a certain similarity in their physical conditions. Also changes due to climate may be brought about at once in a second generation, though no appreciable modification is shown by the first. Thus "Sir Charles Lyell mentions that some Englishmen, engaged in conducting the operations of the Real del Monte Company in Mexico, carried out with them some greyhounds of the best breed to hunt the hares which abound in that country. It was found that the greyhounds could not support the fatigues of a long chase in this attenuated atmosphere, and before they could come up with their prey they lay down gasping for breath; but these same animals have produced whelps, which have grown up, and are not in the least degree incommoded by the want of density in the air, but run down the hares with as much ease as do the fleetest of their race in this country."[3]

[1] "Animals and Plants under Domestication," vol. i. p. 47.

[2] Ibid. p. 52.

[3] Carpenter's "Comparative Physiology," p. 987, quoted by Mr. J. J. Murphy, "Habit and Intelligence," vol. i. p. 171. Mr. Darwin, in his "Descent of Man," vol. i. p. 119, mentions that certain South American Indians (Aymaras), inhabiting a lofty region, have remarkably long bodies and short legs—especially the femora. He adds: "These men are so thoroughly acclimatized to their cold and lofty abode, that when carried down by the Spaniards to the low eastern plains, and when now tempted down by high wages to the gold-washings, they suffer a frightful rate of mortality. Nevertheless, Mr. Forbes found a few pure families which had survived during two generations; and he observed that they still inherited their characteristic peculiarities. But it was manifest, even without measurement, that these peculiarities had all decreased; and, on measurement, their bodies were found not to be so much elongated as

We have here no action of "Natural Selection;" it was not that certain puppies happened accidentally to be capable of enduring more rarefied air, and so survived, but the offspring were directly modified by the action of surrounding conditions. Neither was the change elaborated by minute modifications in many successive generations, but appeared at once in the second.

Further, with regard to sudden alterations of form, Nathusius is said to state positively as to pigs,[1] that the result of common experience and of his experiments was that rich and abundant food, given during youth, tends by some direct action to make the head broader and shorter. Curious jaw appendages often characterize Normandy pigs, according to M. Eudes Deslongchamps. Richardson figures these appendages on the old "Irish greyhound pig," and they are said by Nathusius to appear occasionally in all the long-eared races. Mr. Darwin observes,[2] "As no wild pigs are known to have analogous appendages, we have at present no reason to suppose that their appearance is due to reversion; and if this be so, we are forced to admit that somewhat complex, though apparently useless structures may be suddenly developed without the aid of selection." Again, "Climate directly affects the thickness

those of the men on the high plateau; whilst their femora had become somewhat lengthened, as had their tibiæ, but in a less degree." Here the rapidity of the change—only two generations—points rather to a direct action of conditions than to that of "Natural Selection." In favour of direct modification, another passage from Mr. Darwin may be quoted. He says, "In young persons whose heads from disease have become fixed either sideways or backways, one of the eyes has changed its position, and the bones of the skull have been modified."—*Descent of Man*, vol. i. p. 147.

[1] "Animals and Plants under Domestication," vol. i. p. 72.

[2] Ibid. p. 76.

of the skin and hair" of cattle.[1] In the English climate an individual Porto Santo rabbit[2] recovered the proper colour of its fur in rather less than four years. The effect of the climate of India on the turkey is considerable. Mr. Blyth[3] describes that bird as being much degenerated in size, "utterly incapable of rising on the wing," of a black colour, and "with long pendulous appendages over the beak enormously developed." Mr. Darwin again tells us that there has suddenly appeared in a bed of common broccoli a peculiar variety, faithfully transmitting its newly acquired and remarkable characters;[4] also that there has been a rapid transformation of American varieties of maize;[5] that certainly "the Ancon and Manchamp breeds of sheep," and that (all but certainly) Niata cattle, turnspit and pug dogs, jumper and frizzled fowls, short-faced tumbler pigeons, hook-billed ducks, &c., and a multitude of vegetable varieties, have suddenly appeared in nearly the same state as we now see them.[6] Lastly, Mr. Darwin tells us, that there has been an occasional development (in five distinct cases) in England of the "japanned" or "black-shouldered peacock" (*Pavo nigripennis*); a distinct species, according to Dr. Sclater,[7] yet arising in Sir J. Trevelyan's flock composed entirely of the common kind, and increasing, "*to the extinction of the previously existing breed.*"[8] Mr. Darwin's only explanation of the phenomenon (on the supposition of the species being distinct) is by reversion, owing to a supposed

1 "Animals and Plants under Domestication," vol. i. p. 71.

2 Ibid. p. 114.

3 Quoted, Ibid. p. 274.

4 Ibid. p. 324.

5 Ibid. p. 322.

6 Ibid. vol. ii. p. 414.

7 Proc. Zool. Soc. of London, April 24, 1860.

8 "Animals and Plants under Domestication," vol. i. p. 291.

ancestral cross. But he candidly admits, "I have heard of no other such case in the animal or vegetable kingdom." On the hypothesis of its being only a variety, he observes, "The case is the most remarkable ever recorded of the abrupt appearance of a new form, which so closely resembles a true species that it has deceived one of the most experienced of living ornithologists."

As to plants, M. C. Naudin[1] has given the following instances of the sudden origination of apparently permanent forms: "The first case mentioned is that of a poppy, which took on a remarkable variation in its fruit—a crown of secondary capsules being added to the normal central capsule. A field of such poppies was grown, and M. Göppert, with seed from this field, obtained still this monstrous form in great quantity. Deformities of ferns are sometimes sought after by fern-growers. They are now always obtained by taking spores from the abnormal parts of the monstrous fern; from which spores ferns presenting the same peculiarities invariably grow. . . . . The most remarkable case is that observed by Dr. Godron, of Nancy. In 1861 that botanist observed, amongst a sowing of *Datura tatula*, the fruits of which are very spinous, a single individual of which the capsule was perfectly smooth. The seeds taken from this plant all furnished plants having the character of this individual. The fifth and sixth generations are now growing without exhibiting the least tendency to revert to the spinous form. More remarkable still, when crossed with the normal *Datura tatula*, hybrids were produced, which, in the

[1] Extracted by J. J. Murphy, vol. i. p. 197, from the *Quarterly Journal of Science*, of October 1867, p. 527.

second generation, reverted to the original types, as true hybrids do."[1]

There are, then, abundant instances to prove that considerable modifications may suddenly develop themselves, either due to external conditions or to obscure internal causes in the organisms which exhibit them. Moreover, these modifications, from whatever cause arising, are capable of reproduction—the modified individuals "breeding true."

The question is whether new species have been developed by non-fortuitous variations which are insignificant and minute, or whether such variations have been comparatively sudden and of appreciable size and importance? Either hypothesis will suit the views here maintained equally well (those views being opposed only to fortuitous indefinite variations), but the latter is the more remote from the Darwinian conception, and yet has much to be said in its favour.

Professor Owen considers, with regard to specific origination, that natural history "teaches that the change would be sudden and considerable: it opposes the idea that species are transmitted by minute and slow degrees."[2] "An innate tendency to deviate from parental type, operating through periods of adequate duration," being

1 In confirmation of the suddenness of occasional changes, a remark recently made by Mr. Darwin should be quoted. He says: "It is also well to reflect on such facts as the wonderful growth of galls on plants caused by the poison of an insect, and on the remarkable changes of colour in the plumage of parrots when fed on certain fishes, or inoculated with the poison of toads; for we can thus see that the fluids of the system, if altered for some special purpose, might induce other strange changes."—*Descent of Man*, vol. i. p. 152.

2 "Anatomy of Vertebrates," vol. iii. p. 795.

"the most probable nature, or way of operation of the secondary law, whereby species have been derived one from the other."[1]

Now, considering the number of instances adduced of sudden modifications in domestic animals, it is somewhat startling to meet with Mr. Darwin's positive assertion that it is "a *false belief*" that natural species have often originated in the same abrupt manner. The belief *may* be false, but it is difficult to see how its falsehood can be positively asserted.

It is demonstrated by Mr. Darwin's careful weighings and measurements, that, though little used parts in domestic animals get reduced in weight and somewhat in size, yet that they show no inclination to become truly "rudimentary structures." Accordingly, he asserts,[2] that such rudimentary parts are formed "suddenly, by arrest of development" in domesticated animals, but in wild animals slowly. The latter assertion however is a *mere assertion;* necessary perhaps for the theory of "Natural Selection," but as yet unproved by facts.

But why should not these changes take place suddenly in a state of nature? As Mr. Murphy says:[3] "It may be true that we have no evidence of the origin of wild species in this way. But this is not a case in which negative evidence proves anything. We have never witnessed the origin of a wild species by any process whatever; and if a species were to come suddenly into being in the wild state, as the Ancon Sheep did under domestication, how could you ascertain the fact? If the first of a newly-

1 "Anatomy of Vertebrates," vol. iii. p. 807.

2 "Animals and Plants under Domestication," vol. ii. p. 318.

3 "Habit and Intelligence," vol. i. p. 344.

begotten species were found, the fact of its discovery would tell nothing about its origin. Naturalists would register it as a very rare species, having been only once met with, but they would have no means of knowing whether it were the first or the last of its race."

To this Mr. Wallace has replied (in his review, in *Nature*,[1] of Mr. Murphy's work), by objecting that sudden changes could very rarely be useful, because each kind of animal is a nicely balanced and adjusted whole, any one sudden modification of which would in most cases be hurtful unless accompanied by other simultaneous and harmonious modifications. If, however, it is not unlikely that there is an innate tendency to deviate at certain times, and under certain conditions, it is not more unlikely that that innate tendency should be an harmonious one, calculated to simultaneously adjust the various parts of the organism to their new relations. The objection as to the sudden abortion of rudimentary organs may be similarly met.

Professor Huxley seems now disposed to accept the, at least occasional, intervention of sudden and considerable variations. In his review of Professor Kölliker's criticisms,[2] he himself says,[3] "We greatly suspect that she" (*i.e.* Nature) "does make considerable jumps in the way of variation now and then, and that these saltations give rise to some of the gaps which appear to exist in the series of known forms."

In addition to the instances brought forward in the second chapter against the minute action of "Natural Selection," may be mentioned such structures as the

[1] See Dec. 2, 1869, vol. i. p. 132.

[2] "Über die Darwin'sche Schöpfungstheorie:" ein Vortrag, von Kölliker; Leipzig, 1864.

[3] See "Lay Sermons," p. 342.

wonderfully folded teeth of the labyrinthodonts. The marvellously complex structure of these organs is not merely unaccountable as due to "Natural Selection," but its production by insignificant increments of complexity is hardly less difficult to comprehend.

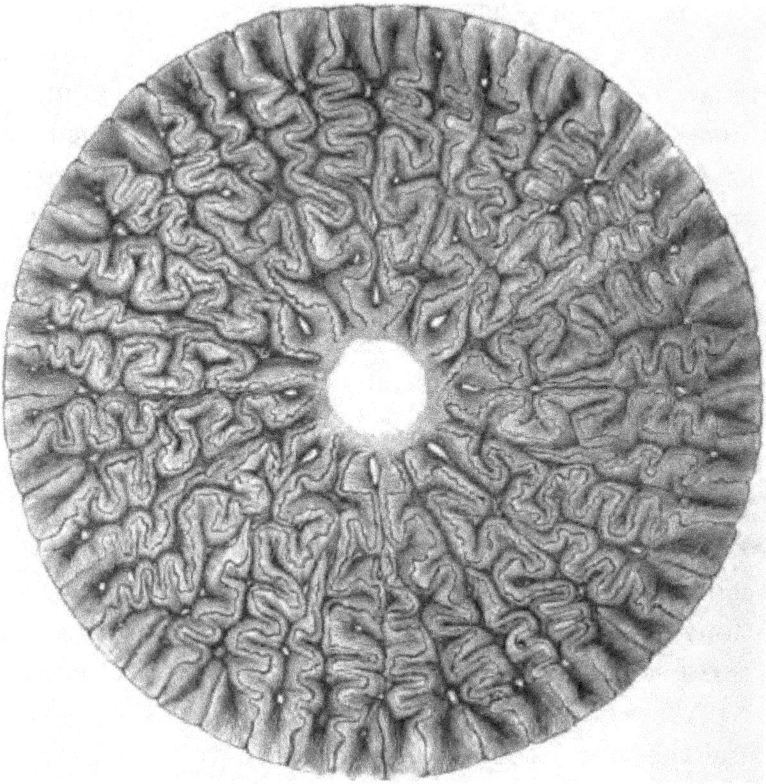

MUCH ENLARGED HORIZONTAL SECTION OF THE TOOTH OF A LABYRINTHODON.

Similarly the aborted index of the Potto (*Perodicticus*) is a structure not likely to have been induced by minute changes; while, as to "Natural Selection," the reduction of the forefinger to a mere rudiment is inexplicable indeed! "How this mutilation can have aided in the struggle for life, we must confess, baffles our conjectures on the subject; for that any very appreciable gain to the individual can have resulted from the slightly lessened degree of required nourishment thence resulting (*i.e.* from the suppression), seems to us to be an almost absurd proposition."[1]

HAND OF THE POTTO (PERODICTICUS), FROM LIFE.

Again to anticipate somewhat, the great group of whales (Cetacea) was fully developed at the deposition of the Eocene strata. On the other hand, we may pretty safely conclude that these animals were absent as late as the latest secondary rocks, so that their development could not have been so very slow, unless geological time is (although we shall presently see there are grounds to believe it is not) practically infinite. It is true that it is generally very unsafe to infer the absence of any animal forms during a certain geological period because no remains of them have as yet been found in the strata then deposited: but in the case of the Cetacea it is safe to do so; for, as Sir Charles Lyell remarks,[2] they are animals the remains of which are singularly likely to have been preserved had they existed, in the same way

1 "Anatomy of the Lemuroidea." By James Murie, M.D., and St. George Mivart. Trans. Zool. Soc., March 1866, p. 91.

2 "Principles of Geology," last edition, vol. i. p. 163.

that the remains were preserved of the Ichthyosauri and Plesiosauri, which appear to have represented the Cetacea during the secondary geological period.

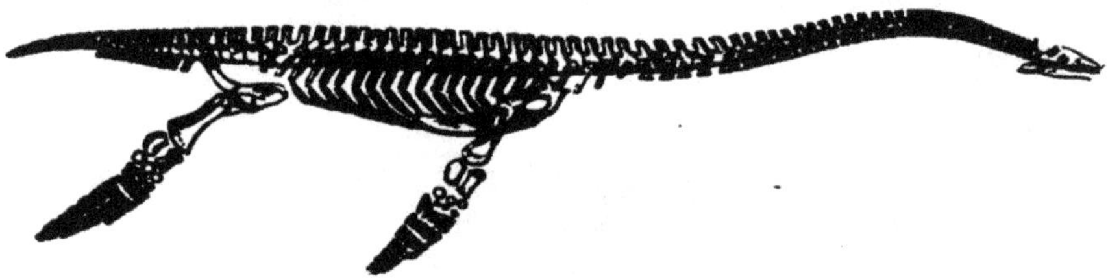

SKELETON OF A PLESIOSAURUS.

As another example let us consider the origin of wings, as they exist in birds. Here we find in fact an arm, the bones of the hand of which are atrophied and reduced in number, as compared with those of most other Vertebrates. Now, if the wing took its origin from a terrestrial or subaërial organ, this abortion of the bones could hardly have been serviceable—hardly have preserved individuals in the struggle for life. If it arose from an aquatic organ, like

SKELETON OF AN ICHTHYOSAURUS.

the wing of the penguin, we have then a singular divergence from the ordinary vertebrate fin-limb. In the ichthyosaurus, in the plesiosaurus, in the whales, in the porpoises, in the seals, and in others, we have shortening of the bones, but no reduction in the number either of the fingers or of their joints, which are, on the contrary, multiplied in Cetacea and the ichthyosaurus. And even in the turtles we have eight carpal bones and five digits, while no finger has less than two phalanges. It is difficult, then, to believe that the Avian limb was developed in any other way than by a comparatively sudden modification of a marked and important kind.

How, once more, can we conceive the peculiar actions of the tendrils of some climbing plants to have been produced by minute modifications? These, according to Mr. Darwin,[1] oscillate till they touch an object, and then embrace it. It is stated by that observer, "that a thread weighing no more than the thirty-second of a grain, if placed on the tendril of the *Passiflora gracilis*, will cause it to bend; and merely to touch the tendril with a twig causes it to bend; but if the twig is at once removed, the tendril soon straightens itself. But the contact of other tendrils of the plant, or of the falling of drops of rain, do not produce these effects."[2]

Some of the zoological and anatomical discoveries of late years tend rather to diminish than to augment the evidence in favour of minute and gradual modification. Thus all naturalists now admit that certain animals, which were at one time supposed to be connecting links between groups, belong altogether to one group, and not at all to the other. For example, the aye-aye[3] (*Chiromys Madagas-*

[1] *Quarterly Journal of Science*, April 1866, pp. 257–8.

[2] "Habit and Intelligence," vol. i. p. 178.

[3] This animal belongs to the order Primates, which includes man, the apes, and the lemurs. The lemurs are the lowest kinds of the order, and differ much from the apes. They have their head-quarters in the Island of Madagascar. The aye-aye is a lemur, but it differs singularly from all its congeners, and still more from all apes. In its dentition it strongly approximates to the rodent (rat, squirrel, and guinea-pig) order, as it has two cutting teeth above, and two below, growing from permanent pulps, and in the adult condition has no canines.

cariensis) was till lately considered to be allied to the squirrels, and was often classed with them in the rodent order, principally on account of its dentition; at the same time that its affinities to the lemurs and apes were admitted. The thorough investigation into its anatomy which has now been made demonstrates that it has no more essential affinity to rodents than any other lemurine creature has.

THE AYE-AYE.

Bats were, by the earliest observers, naturally supposed to have a close relationship to birds, and cetaceans to fishes. It is almost superfluous to observe that all now agree that these mammals make not even an approach to either one or other of the two inferior classes.

In the same way it has been till recently supposed that those extinct flying saurians, the pterodactyles, had an affinity with birds more marked than any other known animals. Now, however, as has been already said, it is contended that not only had they no such close affinity, but that other extinct reptiles had a far closer one.

The *amphibia* (*i.e.* frogs, toads, and efts) were long considered (and are so still by some) to be reptiles, showing an affinity to fishes. It now appears that they form with the latter one great group—the ichthyopsida of Professor Huxley—which differs widely from reptiles; while its two component classes (fishes and amphibians) are difficult to separate from each other in a thoroughly satisfactory manner.

If we admit the hypothesis of gradual and minute modification, the succession of organisms on this planet must have been a progress from the more general to the more special, and no doubt this has been the case in the majority of instances. Yet it cannot be denied that some of the most recently formed fossils show a structure singularly more generalized than any exhibited by older allied forms; while others are more specialized than are any similar creatures of the existing creation.

A notable example of the former circumstance is offered by macrauchenia, a hoofed animal, which was at first supposed to be a kind of great llama (whence its name)—the llama being a ruminant, which, like all the rest, has two toes to each foot. Now hoofed animals are divisible into two very distinct series, according as the number of functional toes on each hind foot is odd or even. And many other characters are found to go with this obvious one. Even the very earliest Ungulata show this distinction, which is completely developed and marked even in the Eocene palæotherium and anoplotherium found in Paris by Cuvier. The former of these has the toes odd (perissodactyle), the other has them even (artiodactyle).

Now, the macrauchenia, from the first relics of it which were found, was thought to belong, as has been said, to the even-toed division. Subsequent discoveries, however, seemed to give it an equal claim to rank amongst the perissodactyle forms. Others again inclined the balance of probability towards the artiodactyle. Finally, it appears that this very recently extinct beast presents a highly generalized type of structure, uniting in one organic form both artiodactyle and perissodactyle characters, and that in a manner not similarly found in any other known creature living, or fossil. At the same time the differentiation of artiodactyle and perissodactyle forms existed as long ago as in the period of the Eocene ungulata, and even in a marked degree, as has been before observed.

Again, no armadillo *now living* presents nearly so remarkable a speciality of structure as was possessed by the *extinct* glyptodon. In that singular animal the spinal column had most of its joints fused together, forming a rigid cylindrical rod, a modification, as far as yet known, absolutely peculiar to it.

In a similar way the *extinct* machairodus, or sabre-toothed tiger, is characterized by a more highly differentiated and specially carnivorous dentition than is shown by any predacious beast of the *present day*. The specialization is of this kind. The grinding teeth (or molars) of beasts are divided into premolars and true molars. The premolars are molars which have deciduous vertical predecessors (or milk teeth), and any which are in front of such, *i.e.* between such and the canine tooth. The true molars are those placed behind the molars having deciduous vertical predecessors. Now, as a dentition becomes more distinctly carnivorous, so the hindermost molars and the foremost premolars disappear. In the existing cats this process is carried so far that in the upper jaw only one true molar is left on each side. In the machairodus there is no upper true molar at all, while the premolars are reduced to two, there being only these two teeth above, on each side, behind the canine.

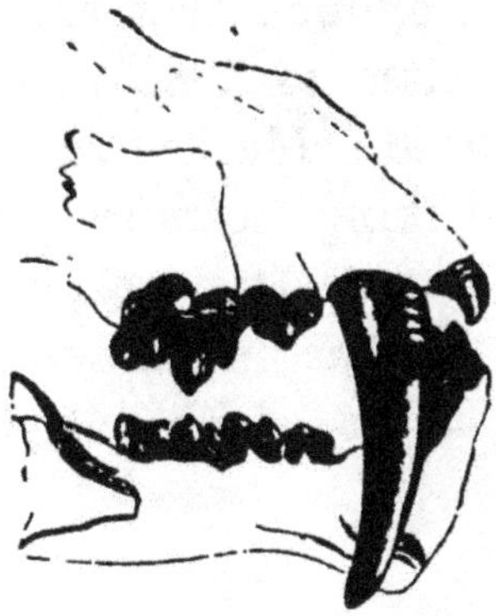

DENTITION OF THE SABRE-TOOTHED TIGER (MACHAIRODUS).

With regard to these instances of early specialization, as also with regard to the changed estimate of the degrees of affinity between forms, it is not pretended for a moment that such facts are irreconcilable with "Natural Selection." Nevertheless, they point in an opposite direction. Of course not only is it conceivable that certain antique types arrived at a high degree of specialization and then disappeared; but it is manifest they did do so. Still the fact of this early degree of excessive specialization tells to a certain, however small, extent against a progress through excessively minute steps, whether fortuitous or not; as also does the distinctness of kinds formerly supposed to constitute connecting links. For, it must not be forgotten, that if species have manifested themselves generally by gradual and minute modifications, then the absence, not in one but in *all cases*, of such connecting links, is a phenomenon which remains to be accounted for.

It appears then that, apart from fortuitous changes, there are certain difficulties in the way of accepting extremely minute modifications of any kind, although these difficulties may not be insuperable. Something, at all events, is to be said in favour of the opinion that sudden and appreciable changes have from time to time occurred, however they may have been induced. Marked *races* have undoubtedly so arisen (some striking instances having been here recorded), and it is at least conceivable that such may be the mode of *specific* manifestation generally, the possible conditions as to which will be considered in a later chapter.

CHAPTER V.

AS TO SPECIFIC STABILITY.

What is meant by the phrase "specific stability;" such stability to be expected *a priori*, or else considerable changes at once.—Increasing difficulty of intensifying race characters; alleged causes of this phenomenon; probably an internal cause co-operates.—A certain definiteness in variations.—Mr. Darwin admits the principle of specific stability in certain cases of unequal variability.—The goose.—The peacock.—The guinea-fowl.—Exceptional causes of variation under domestication.—Alleged tendency to reversion.—Instances.—Sterility of hybrids.—Prepotency of pollen of same species, but of different race.—Mortality in young gallinaceous hybrids.—A bar to intermixture exists somewhere.—Guinea-pigs.—Summary and conclusion.

As was observed in the preceding chapters, arguments may yet be advanced in favour of the opinion that species are stable (at least in the intervals of their comparatively sudden successive manifestations); that the organic world may be symbolized according to Mr. Galton's before-mentioned conception, by many facetted spheroids, each of which can repose upon any one facet, but, when too much disturbed, rolls over till it finds repose in stable equilibrium upon another and distinct facet. It is here contended then that something may be urged in favour of the existence of such facets—of such intermitting conditions of stable equilibrium.

A view as to the stability of species, in the intervals of change, has been well expressed in an able article, before quoted from, as follows:[1]—"A given animal or plant appears to be contained, as it were, within a sphere of variation: one individual lies near one portion of the surface; another individual, of the same species, near another part of the surface; the average animal at the centre. Any individual may produce descendants varying in any direction, but is more likely to produce descendants varying towards the centre of the sphere, and the variations in that direction will be greater in amount than the variations towards the surface." This might be taken as the representation of the normal condition of species (*i.e.* during the periods of repose of the spheroids upon their several facets) assuming as true that specific stability which has been before defended.

Judging the organic world from the inorganic, we might expect *a priori* that each species of the former, like crystallized species, would have an approximate limit of form and even of size, and at the same time that the organic, like the inorganic forms, would present modifications in correspondence with surrounding conditions; yet that these modifications would be, not minute and insignificant, but definite and appreciable, equivalent to the shifting of the spheroid on to another facet for support.

Mr. Murphy says,[2] "Crystalline formation is also dependent in a very remarkable way on the medium in which it takes place." "Beudant has found that common salt crystallizing from pure water forms cubes, but if the water contains a little boracic acid, the angles of the cubes are truncated. And the Rev. E. Craig has found that carbonate of copper, crystallizing from a solution containing sulphuric

[1] *North British Review*, New Series, vol. vii., March 1867, p. 282.

[2] "Habit and Intelligence," vol. i. p. 75.

acid, forms hexagonal tabular prisms; but if a little ammonia is added, the form changes to that of a long rectangular prism, with secondary planes in the angles. If a little more ammonia is added, several varieties of rhombic octahedra appear; if a little nitric acid is added, the rectangular prism appears again. The changes take place not by the addition of new crystals, but by changing the growth of the original ones." These, however, may be said to be the same species, after all; but recent researches by Dr. H. Charlton-Bastian seem to show that modifications in the conditions may result in the evolution of forms so diverse as to constitute different organic species.

Mr. Murphy observes:[1] "It is scarcely possible to doubt that the various forms of fungi which are characteristic of particular situations are not really distinct species, but that the same germ will develop into different forms, according to the soil on which it falls." It is possible, however, to interpret the facts differently, and it may be that these are the manifestations of really different and distinct species, developed according to the different and distinct circumstances in which each is placed. Mr. Murphy quotes Dr. Carpenter[2] to the effect that "No *Puccinia* but the *Puccinia rosæ* is found upon rose bushes, and this is seen nowhere else; *Omygena exigua* is said to be never seen but on the hoof of a dead horse; and *Isaria felina* has only been observed upon the dung of cats, deposited in humid and obscure situations." He adds, "We can scarcely believe that the air is full of the germs of distinct species of fungi, of which one never vegetates until it falls on the hoof of a dead horse, and another until it falls on cat's dung in a

[1] "Habit and Intelligence," vol. i. p. 202.
[2] "Comparative Physiology," p. 214, note.

damp and dark place." This indeed is scarcely credible, but it does not quite follow that the forms developed are necessarily the same species, if, as Dr. Bastian seems to show, thoroughly different and distinct organic forms[1] can be evolved one from another by modifying the conditions. The last-named observer has brought forward arguments and facts from which it would appear that such definite, sudden, and considerable transformations may take place in the lowest organisms. If such is really the case, we might expect, *a priori*, to find in the highest organisms a tendency (much more impeded and rare in its manifestations) to similarly appreciable and sudden changes, under certain stimuli; but a tendency to continued stability, under normal and ordinary conditions. The proposition that species have, normally, a definite limit to their variability, is largely supported by facts brought forward by the zealous industry of Mr. Darwin himself. It is unquestionable that the degrees of variation which have been arrived at in domestic animals have been obtained more or less readily in a moderate amount of time; but that further development in certain desired directions is in some a matter of extreme difficulty, and in others appears to be all but, if not quite, an impossibility. It is also unquestionable that the degree of divergence which has been attained in one domestic species is no criterion of the amount of divergence which has been attained in another. It is contended on the other side, that we have no evidence of any limits to variation other than those imposed by physical conditions, such, *e.g.*, as those which determine the greatest degree of speed possible to

[1] See *Nature*, June and July 1870, Nos. 35, 36, and 37, pp. 170, 193, and 219.

any animal (of a given size) moving over the earth's surface ; also it is said that the differences in degree of change shown by different domestic animals depend in a great measure upon the abundance or scarcity of individuals subjected to man's selection, together with the varying direction and amount of his attention in different cases ; finally, it is urged that the changes found in nature are within the limits to which the variation of domestic animals extends,—it being the case that when changes of a certain amount have occurred to a species under nature, it becomes *another species*, or sometimes *two or more other species* by divergent variations, each of these species being able again to vary and diverge in any useful direction.

But the fact of the increasing difficulty found in producing, by ever such careful selection, any further extreme in some change already carried very far (such as the tail of the "fantailed pigeon" or the crop of the "pouter"), is certainly, so far as it goes, on the side of the existence of definite limits to variability. It is asserted in reply, that physiological conditions of health and life may bar any such further development. Thus, Mr. Wallace says[1] of these developments: "Variation seems to have reached its limits in these birds. But so it has in nature. The fantail has not only more tail-feathers than any of the three hundred and forty existing species of pigeons, but more than any of the eight thousand known species of birds. There is, of course, some limit to the number of feathers of which a tail useful for flight can consist, and in the fantail we have probably reached that limit. Many birds have the œsophagus or the skin of the neck more or less dilatable, but in no known bird is it so dilatable as in the pouter pigeon.

1 "Natural Selection," p. 293.

Here again the possible limit, compatible with a healthy existence, has probably been reached. In like manner, the differences in the size and form of the beak in the various breeds of the domestic pigeon is greater than that between the extreme forms of beak in the various genera and sub-families of the whole pigeon tribe. From these facts, and many others of the same nature, we may fairly infer, that if rigid selection were applied to any organ, we could in a comparatively short time produce a much greater amount of change than that which occurs between species and species in a state of nature, since the differences which we do produce are often comparable with those which exist between distinct genera or distinct families."

But in a domestic bird like the fantail where Natural Selection does not come into play, the tail-feathers could hardly be limited by "utility for flight," yet two more tail-feathers could certainly exist in a fancy breed if "utility for flight" were the only obstacle. It seems probable that the real barrier is an *internal* one in the nature of the organism, and the existence of such is just what is contended for in this chapter. As to the differences between domestic races being greater than those between species or even genera of wild animals, that is not enough for the argument. For upon the theory of "Natural Selection" all birds have a common origin, from which they diverged by insignificant modifications, so that we ought to meet with changes sufficient to warrant the belief that a hornbill could be produced from a creature as different from it as a humming-bird, proportionate time being allowed.

But not only does it appear that there are barriers which oppose change in certain directions, but that there are positive tendencies to development along certain special lines.

In a bird which has been kept and studied like the pigeon, it is difficult to believe that any remarkable spontaneous variations would pass unnoticed by breeders, or that they would fail to be attended to and developed by some one fancier or other. On the hypothesis of *indefinite* variability, it is then hard to say why pigeons with bills like toucans, or with certain feathers lengthened like those of trogans, or those of birds of paradise, have never been produced. This, however, is a question which may be settled by experiment. Let a pigeon be bred with a bill like a toucan's, and with the two middle tail-feathers lengthened like those of the king bird of paradise, or even let individuals be produced which exhibit any marked tendency of the kind, and the claim to indefinite variability shall be at once conceded.

As yet all the changes which have taken place in pigeons are of a few definite kinds only, such as may be well conceived to be compatible with a species possessed of a certain inherent capacity for considerable yet definite variation, a capacity for the ready production of certain degrees of abnormality which once attained cannot be further increased.

Mr. Darwin himself has already acquiesced in the proposition here maintained, inasmuch as he distinctly affirms the existence of a marked internal barrier to change in certain cases. And if this is admitted in one case, the *principle*[1] is conceded, and it immediately becomes pro-

[1] Mr. Darwin, in his "Descent of Man," just published, distinctly admits the existence of such internal powers. Thus, in vol. i. p. 154, he says, of the exciting causes of modification, "they relate much more closely to the constitution of the varying organism, than to the nature of the conditions to which it has been subjected." In a note on page 223 he speaks of "incidental results of certain unknown differences in the con-

bable that such internal barriers exist in all, although enclosing a much larger field for variation in some cases than in others. Mr. Darwin abundantly demonstrates the variability of dogs, horses, fowls, and pigeons, but he none the less shows clearly the *very small* extent to which the goose, the peacock, and the guinea-fowl have varied.[1] Mr. Darwin attempts to explain this fact as regards the goose by the animal being valued only for food and feathers, and from no pleasure having been felt in it on other accounts. He adds, however, at the end the striking remark,[2] which concedes the whole position, "but the goose seems to have *a singularly inflexible organization.*" This is not the only place in which such expressions are used. He elsewhere makes use of phrases which quite harmonize with the conception of a normal specific constancy, but varying greatly and suddenly at intervals. Thus he speaks[3] of a *whole organization seeming to have become plastic, and tending to depart from the parental type.* That different organisms should have different degrees of variability, is only what might have been expected *a priori* from the existence of parallel differences in inorganic species, some of these having but a single form, and others being polymorphic.

To return to the goose, however, it may be remarked that it is at least as probable that its fixity of character is

stitution of the reproductive system of the species crossed;" and in vol. ii. at p. 388 may be read the following passage:—"In the greater number of cases we can only say that the cause of each slight variation and of each monstrosity lies much more in the nature or constitution of the organism than in the nature of the surrounding conditions; though new and changed conditions certainly play an important part in exciting organic changes of all kinds."

[1] "Animals and Plants under Domestication," vol. i. pp. 289—295.

[2] "Origin of Species," 5th edition, 1869, p. 45.

[3] Ibid. p. 13.

the cause of the neglect, as the reverse. It is by no means unfair to assume that *had* the goose shown a tendency to vary similar in degree to the tendency to variation of the fowl or pigeon, it would have received attention at once on that account.

As to the peacock, it is excused on the pleas (1), that the individuals maintained are so few in number, and (2), that its beauty is so great it can hardly be improved. But the individuals maintained *have not been too few* for the independent origin of the black-shouldered form, or for the supplanting of the commoner one by it. As to any neglect in selection, it can hardly be imagined that with regard to this bird (kept as it is all but exclusively for its beauty), any spontaneous beautiful variation in colour or form would have been neglected. On the contrary, it would have been seized upon with avidity and preserved with anxious care. Yet apart from the black-shouldered and white varieties, no tendency to change has been known to show itself. As to its being too beautiful for improvement, that is a proposition which can hardly be maintained. Many consider the Javan bird much handsomer than the common peacock, and it would be easy to suggest a score of improvements as regards either species.

The guinea-fowl is excused, as being "no general favourite, and scarcely more common than the peacock;" but Mr. Darwin himself shows and admits that it is a noteworthy instance of constancy under very varied conditions.

These instances alone (and there are yet others) seem sufficient to establish the assertion that degree of change is different in different domestic animals. It is, then, somewhat unwarrantable in any Darwinian to assume that *all* wild animals have a capacity for change similar to that existing in *some* of the domestic ones. It seems more reasonable to maintain the opposite, namely, that if, as Mr. Darwin says, the capacity for change is different in different domestic animals, it must surely be limited in those domestic animals which have it least, and *a fortiori* limited in wild animals.

Indeed, it cannot be reasonably maintained that wild species certainly vary as much as do domestic races; it is possible that they may do so, but at least this has not been yet shown. Indeed, the much greater degree of variation amongst domestic animals than amongst wild ones is asserted over and over again by Mr. Darwin, and his assertions are supported by an overwhelming mass of facts and instances.

Of course, it may be maintained that a tendency to indefinite change exists in all cases, and that it is only the circumstances and conditions of life which modify the effects of this tendency to change so as to produce such different results in different cases. But assertion is not proof, and this assertion has not been proved. Indeed, it may be equally asserted (and the statement is more consonant with some of the facts given), that domestication in certain animals induces and occasions a capacity for change which is wanting in wild animals—the introduction of new causes occasioning new effects. For, though a certain degree of variability (normally, in all probability, only oscillation) exists in all organisms, yet domestic ones are exposed to new and different causes of variability, resulting in such striking divergencies as have been observed. Not even in this latter case, however, is it necessary to believe that the variability is indefinite, but only that the small oscillations become in certain instances intensified into large and conspicuous ones. Moreover, it is possible that some of our domestic animals have been in part chosen and domesticated through possessing variability in an eminent degree.

That each species exhibits certain oscillations of structure is admitted on all hands. Mr. Darwin asserts that this is the exhibition of a tendency to vary which is absolutely indefinite. If this indefinite variability *does* exist, of course no more need be said. But we have seen that there are arguments *a priori* and *a posteriori* against it, while the occurrence of variations in certain domestic animals greater in degree than the differences between many wild species, is no argument in favour of its existence, until it can be shown that the causes of variability in the one case are the same as in the other. An argument against indefinite variability, however, may be drawn from the fact, that certain animals, though placed under the influence of those exceptional causes of variation to which domestic animals are subject, have yet never been known to vary, even in a degree equal to that in which certain wild kinds have been ascertained to vary.

In addition to this immutability of character in some animals, it is undeniable that domestic varieties have little stability, and much tendency to reversion, whatever be the true explanation of such phenomena.

In controverting the generally received opinion as to "reversion," Mr. Darwin has shown that it is not all breeds which in a few years revert to the original form; but he has shown no more. Thus, the feral rabbits of Porto Santo, Jamaica, and the Falkland Islands, have not yet so reverted in those several parts of the world.[1] Nevertheless, a Porto

[1] "Animals and Plants under Domestication," vol. i. p. 115.

Santo rabbit brought to England reverted in a manner the most striking, recovering the proper colour of its fur "in rather less than four years."[1] Again, the white silk fowl, in our climate, "reverts to the ordinary colour of the common fowl in its skin and bones, due care having been taken to prevent any cross."[2] This reversion taking place in spite of careful selection is very remarkable.

Numerous other instances of reversion are given by Mr. Darwin, both as regards plants and animals; amongst others, the singular fact of bud reversion.[3] The curiously recurring development of black sheep, in spite of the most careful breeding, may also be mentioned, though, perhaps, reversion has no part in the phenomenon.

These facts seem certainly to tell in favour of limited variability, while the cases of non-reversion do not contradict it, as it is not contended that all species have the same tendency to revert, but rather that their capacities in this respect, as well as for change, are different in different kinds, so that often reversion may only show itself at the end of very long periods indeed.

Some of the instances given as probable or possible causes of reversion by Mr. Darwin, can hardly be such. He cites, for example, the occasional presence of supernumerary digits in man.[4] For this notion, however, he is not responsible, as he rests his remark on the authority of a passage published by Professor Owen. Again, he refers[5]

[1] "Animals and Plants under Domestication," vol. i. p. 114.

[2] Ibid. vol. i. p. 243.

[3] Ibid. vol. ii. p. 361.

[4] Ibid. vol. ii. p. 16. Since the publication of the first edition of the "Genesis of Species," Mr. Darwin has admitted his mistake in this matter, as also in the attribution by him of supernumerary mammæ to reversion.—See "Descent of Man," vol. i. p. 125.

[5] "Animals and Plants under Domestication," vol. ii. p. 57.

to "the greater frequency of a monster proboscis in the pig than in any other animal." But with the exception of the peculiar muzzle of the Saiga (or European Antelope), the only known proboscidian Ungulates are the elephants and tapirs, and to neither of these has the pig any close affinity. It is rather in the horse than in the pig that we might look for the appearance of a reversionary proboscis, as both the elephants and the tapirs have the toes of the hind foot of an odd number. It is true that the elephants are generally considered to form a group apart from both the odd and the even-toed Ungulata. But of the two, their affinities with the odd-toed division are more marked.[1]

Another argument in favour of the, at least intermitting, constancy of specific forms and of sudden modification, may be drawn from the absence of minute transitional forms, but this will be considered in the next chapter.

It remains now to notice in favour of specific stability, that the objection based upon the physiological difference between "species" and "races" still exists unrefuted.

Mr. Darwin freely admits difficulties regarding the sterility of different species when crossed, and shows satisfactorily that it could never have arisen from the action of "Natural Selection." He remarks[2] also: "With some few exceptions in the case of plants, domesticated varieties, such as those of the dog, fowl, pigeon, several fruit trees, and culinary vegetables, which differ from each other in external characters more than many species, are perfectly fertile when crossed, or even fertile in excess, whilst

[1] This has been shown by my late friend, Mr. H. N. Turner, jun., in an excellent paper by him in the "Proceedings of the Zoological Society for 1849," p. 147. The untimely death, through a dissecting wound, of this promising young naturalist, was a great loss to zoological science.

[2] "Animals and Plants under Domestication," vol. ii. p. 189.

closely allied species are almost invariably in some degree sterile."

Again, after speaking of "the general law of good being derived from the intercrossing of distinct individuals of the same species," and of the evidence that the pollen of a distinct *variety* or race is prepotent over a flower's own pollen, Mr. Darwin adds the very significant remark:[1] "When distinct *species* are crossed, the case is directly the reverse, for a plant's own pollen is almost always prepotent over foreign pollen."

Again he says:[2] "I believe from observations communicated to me by Mr. Hewitt, who has had great experience in hybridizing pheasants and fowls, that the early death of the embryo is a very frequent cause of sterility in first crosses. Mr. Salter has recently given the results of an examination of about 500 eggs produced from various crosses between three species of Gallus and their hybrids. The majority of these eggs had been fertilized, and in the majority of the fertilized eggs the embryos either had been partially developed and had then aborted, or had become nearly mature, but the young chickens had been unable to break through the shell. Of the chickens which were born, more than four-fifths died within the first few days, or at latest weeks, 'without any obvious cause, apparently from mere inability to live,' so that from 500 eggs only twelve chickens were reared. The early death of hybrid embryos probably occurs in like manner with plants; at least it is known that hybrids raised from very distinct species are sometimes weak and dwarfed, and perish at an early age, of which fact Max Wichura has recently given some striking cases with hybrid willows."

[1] "Origin of Species," 5th edition, 1869, p. 115.

[2] Ibid. p. 323.

Mr. Darwin objects to the notion that there is any peculiar sterility imposed to check specific intermixture and change, saying,[1] "To grant to species the special power of producing hybrids, and then to stop their further propagation by different degrees of sterility, not strictly related to the facility of the first union between their parents, seems a strange arrangement."

But this only amounts to saying that the author himself would not have so acted had he been the Creator. A "strange arrangement" must be admitted anyhow, and all who acknowledge teleology at all, must admit that the strange arrangement was designed. Mr. Darwin says, as to the sterility of species, that the cause lies exclusively in their sexual constitution; but all that need be affirmed is that sterility is brought about somehow, and it is undeniable that "crossing" *is* checked. All that is contended for is that there *is* a bar to the intermixture of *species*, but not of *breeds;* and if the conditions of the generative products are that bar, it is enough for the argument, no special kind of barring action being contended for.

He, however, attempts to account for the modification of the sexual products of species as compared with those of varieties, by the exposure of the former to more uniform conditions during longer periods of time than those to which varieties are exposed; and that as wild animals, when captured, are often rendered sterile by captivity, so the influence of union with another species may produce a similar effect. It seems to the author an unwarrantable assumption that a cross with what, on the Darwinian theory, can only be a slightly diverging descendant from a

[1] "Origin of Species," 5th edition, 1869, p. 314.

common parent, should produce an effect equal to that of captivity, and consequent change of habit, as well as considerable modification of food.

No clear case has been given by Mr. Darwin in which mongrel animals, descended from the same undoubted species, have been persistently infertile *inter se;* nor any clear case in which hybrids between animals generally admitted to be of distinct species, have been continuously fertile *inter se.*

It is true that facts are brought forward tending to establish the probability of the doctrine of Pallas, that species may sometimes be rendered fertile by domestication. But even if this were true, it would be no approximation towards proving the converse, *i.e.* that races and varieties may become sterile when wild. And whatever may be the preference occasionally shown by certain breeds to mate with their own variety, no sterility is recorded as resulting from unions with other varieties. Indeed, Mr. Darwin remarks:[1] "With respect to sterility from the crossing of domestic races, I know of no well-ascertained case with animals. This fact (seeing the great difference in structure between some breeds of pigeons, fowls, pigs, dogs, &c.) is extraordinary when contrasted with the sterility of many closely-allied natural species when crossed."

It has been alleged that the domestic and wild guinea-pig do not breed together, but the specific identity of these forms is very problematical. Mr. A. D. Bartlett, superintendent of the Zoological Gardens, whose experience is so great, and observation so quick, believes them to be of decidedly distinct species.

[1] "Animals and Plants under Domestication," vol. ii. p. 104.

Thus, then, it seems that a certain normal specific stability in species, accompanied by occasional sudden and considerable modifications, might be expected *a priori* from what we know of crystalline inorganic forms and from what we may suspect with regard to the lowest organic ones. This presumption is strengthened by the knowledge of the increasing difficulties which beset any attempt to indefinitely intensify any race characteristics. The obstacles to this indefinite intensification, as well as to certain lines of variation in certain cases, appear to be not only external, but to depend on internal causes or an internal cause. We have seen that Mr. Darwin himself implicitly admits the principle of specific stability in asserting the singular inflexibility of the organization of the goose. We have also seen that it is not fair to conclude that all wild races can vary as much as the most variable domestic ones. It has been shown besides that there are grounds for believing in a tendency to reversion generally, as it is distinctly present in certain instances; further, that the doctrine of specific stability is confirmed by the fact that physiological obstacles oppose themselves to any considerable or continued intermixture of species, while no such barriers oppose themselves to the blending of varieties. All these considerations taken together may fairly be looked upon as strengthening the belief that specific manifestations are relatively stable. At the same time the view advocated in this book does not depend upon, and is not identified with, any such stability. All that the author contends for is that specific manifestation takes place along certain lines, and according to law; and not in an exceedingly minute, indefinite, and fortuitous manner. Finally, he cannot but feel justified, from all that has been brought forward, in reiterating the opening assertion of this chapter, that something is still to be said for the view which maintains that species are stable, at least in the intervals of their comparatively rapid successive manifestations.

CHAPTER VI.

SPECIES AND TIME.

Two relations of species to time.—No evidence of past existence of minutely graduated intermediate forms when such might be expected *a priori.*—Bats, Pterodactyles, Dinosauria, and Birds.—Ichthyosauria, Chelonia, and Anoura.—Horse ancestry.—Labyrinthodonts and Trilobites.—Two subdivisions of the second relation of species to time.—Sir Wm. Thomson's views.—Probable period required for ultimate specific evolution from primitive ancestral forms.—Geometrical increase of time required for rapidly multiplying increase of structural differences.—Proboscis monkey.—Time required for deposition of strata necessary for Darwinian evolution.—High organization of Silurian forms of life.—Absence of fossils in oldest rocks.—Summary and conclusion.

Two considerations present themselves with regard to the necessary relation of species to time, if the theory of "Natural Selection" is valid and sufficient.

The first is with regard to the evidences of the past existence of intermediate forms, their duration and succession.

The second is with regard to the total amount of time required for the evolution of all organic forms from a few original ones, and the bearing of other sciences on this question of time.

As to the first consideration, evidence is as yet against the modification of species by "Natural Selection" alone, because not only are minutely transitional forms generally absent, but they are absent in cases where we might certainly *a priori* have expected them to be present.

Now it has been said:[1] "If Mr. Darwin's theory be true, the number of varieties differing one from another a very little must have been indefinitely great, so great indeed as probably far to exceed the number of individuals which have existed of any one variety. If this be true, it would be more probable that no two specimens preserved as fossils should be of one variety than that we should find a great many specimens collected from a very few varieties, provided, of course, the chances of preservation are equal for all individuals." "It is really strange that vast numbers of perfectly similar specimens should be found, the chances against their perpetuation as fossils are so great; but it is also very strange that the specimens should be so exactly alike as they are, if, in fact, they came and vanished by a gradual change."

Mr. Darwin attempts[2] to show cause why we should believe *a priori* that intermediate varieties would exist in lesser numbers than the more extreme forms; but though they would doubtless do so sometimes, it seems too much to assert that they would do so generally, still less universally. Now little less than universal and very marked inferiority in numbers would account for the absence of certain series of minutely intermediate fossil specimens. The mass of palæontological evidence is indeed overwhelmingly against minute and gradual modification. It is true that when once an animal has obtained powers of flight its means of diffusion are indefinitely increased, and we might expect to find many relics of an aërial form and

[1] *North British Review*, New Series, vol. vii., March 1867, p. 317.
[2] "Origin of Species," 5th edition, 1869, p. 212.

few of its antecedent state—with nascent wings just commencing their suspensory power. Yet had such a slow mode of origin, as Darwinians contend for, operated exclusively in all cases, it is absolutely incredible that birds, bats, and pterodactyles should have left the remains they have, and yet not a single relic be preserved in any one instance of any of these different forms of wing in their incipient and relatively imperfect functional condition!

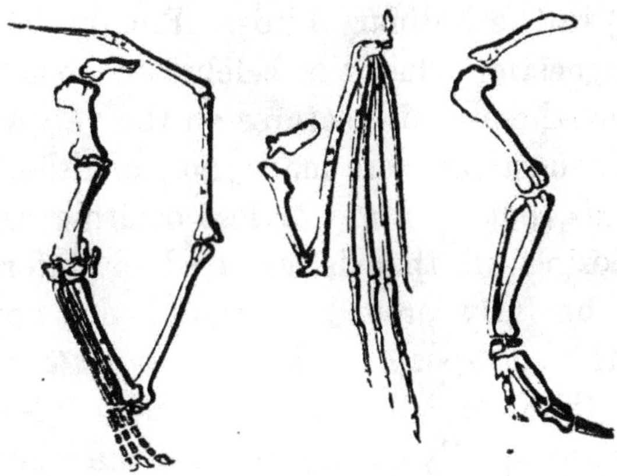

WING-BONES OF PTERODACTYLE, BAT, AND BIRD.

Whenever the remains of bats have been found they have presented the exact type of existing forms, and there is as yet no indication of the conditions of an incipient elevation from the ground.

The pterodactyles, again, though a numerous group, are all true and perfect pterodactyles, though surely *some* of the many incipient forms, which on the Darwinian theory have existed, must have had a good chance of preservation.

As to birds, the only notable instance in which discoveries recently made appear to fill up an important hiatus, is that concerning the remains of some Dinosaurian reptiles, the interpretation of which, as given by Professor

Huxley,[1] has been noticed in the third chapter of this work. The learned Professor has (as also has Professor Cope in America) shown that in very important and significant points the skeletons of the Iguanodon and of its allies approach very closely to that existing in the ostrich, emeu, rhea, &c. He has given weighty reasons for thinking that the line of affinity between birds and reptiles passes to the birds last named from the Dinosauria, rather than from the Pterodactyles (through Archeopteryx-like forms) to the ordinary birds. Finally, he has thrown out the suggestion that the celebrated footsteps left by some extinct three-toed creatures on the very ancient sandstone of Connecticut were made, not, as hitherto supposed, by true birds, but by more or less ornithic reptiles. But even supposing all that is asserted or inferred on this subject to be fully proved, it would not approach to a demonstration of specific origin by *minute* modification; for though the facts harmonize well with "Natural Selection," they are equally consistent with the rapid and sudden development of new specific forms of life. Indeed, Professor Huxley, with a laudable caution and moderation too little observed by some Teutonic Darwinians, guarded himself carefully from any imputation of asserting dogmatically the theory of "Natural Selection," while upholding fully the doctrine of evolution.

But, after all, it is by no means certain, though very probable, that the Connecticut footsteps were made by very ornithic reptiles, or extremely sauroid birds. And it must not be forgotten that a completely carinate bird (the Archeopteryx) existed at a time when, as yet, we have no evidence of some of the Dinosauria having come into being.

[1] See also the *Popular Science Review* for July 1868.

Moreover, if the remarkable and minute similarity of the coracoid of a pterodactyle to that of a bird be merely the result of function and no sign of genetic affinity, it is not inconceivable that the pelvic and leg resemblances of

THE ARCHEOPTERYX (OF THE OOLITE STRATA).

Dinosauria to birds may be functional likewise, though such an explanation is, of course, by no means necessary to support the view maintained in this book.

But the number of forms represented by many individuals, yet by *no transitional ones*, is so great that only

SKELETON OF AN ICHTHYOSAURUS.

two or three can be selected as examples. Thus those remarkable fossil reptiles, the Ichthyosauria and Plesiosauria, extended, through the secondary period, probably over the greater part of the globe. Yet no single transitional form has yet been met with in spite of the multitudinous individuals preserved. Again, with regard to their modern representatives the Cetacea, one or two aberrant forms alone have been found, but no series of transitional ones indicating minutely the line of descent. This group, the whales, is a very marked one; and it is curious, on Darwinian principles, that so few instances tending to indicate its mode of origin should have presented themselves. Here, as in the bats, we might surely expect that some relics of unquestionably incipient stages of its development would have been left.

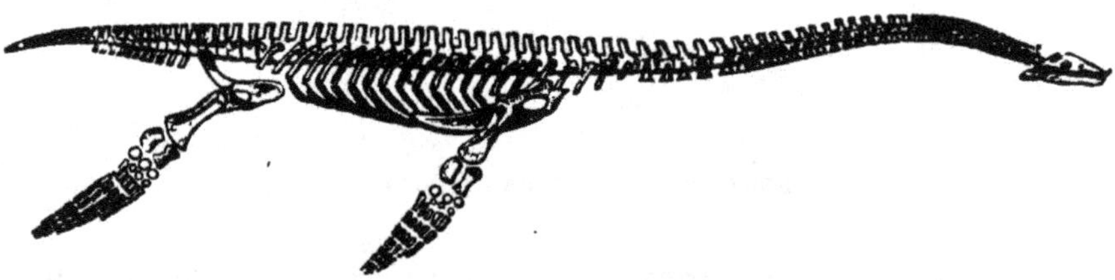

SKELETON OF A PLESIOSAURUS.

The singular order Chelonia, including the tortoises, turtles, and terrapins (or fresh-water tortoises), is another instance of an extreme form without any, as yet known, transitional stages. Another group may be finally mentioned, viz. the frogs and toads (anourous Batrachians), of which we have at present no relic of any kind linking them on to the Eft group on the one hand, or to Reptiles on the other.

The only instance in which an approach towards a series of nearly related forms has been obtained is that of the existing horse, its predecessor Hipparion and other extinct allies. But even here we have no proof whatever of modification by minute and infinitesimal steps; *a fortiori* no approach to a proof of modification by "Natural Selection" acting upon indefinite fortuitous variations. On the contrary, the series is an admirable example of successive modification in one special direction along one beneficial line, and the teleologist must here be allowed to consider that one motive of this modification (among probably an indefinite number of motives inconceivable to us) was the relationship in which the horse was to stand to the human inhabitants of this planet. These extinct forms, as Professor Owen remarks,[1] "differ from each other in a greater degree than do the horse, zebra, and ass," which are not only good *zoological* species as to form, but are species *physiologically*—*i.e.* they cannot produce a race of hybrids fertile *inter se*.

As to the mere action of surrounding conditions, the same Professor remarks:[2] "Any modification affecting the density of the soil might so far relate to the changes of limb-structure, as that a foot with a pair of small hoofs dangling by the sides of the large one, like those behind the cloven hoof of the ox, would cause the foot of Hipparion, *e.g.*, and *a fortiori* the broader based three-hoofed foot of the Palæothere, to sink less deeply into swampy soil, and be more easily withdrawn than the more concentratively simplified and specialized foot of the horse. Rhinoceroses and zebras, however, tread together the arid plains of Africa in the present day; and the horse has multiplied in that half of America where two or more kinds of tapir still exist. That the continents of the Eocene or Miocene periods were less diversified in respect of swamp and sward, pampas or desert, than those of the

1 "Anatomy of Vertebrates," vol. iii. p. 792.

2 Ibid. p. 793.

Pliocene period, has no support from observation or analogy."

Not only, however, do we fail to find any traces of the incipient stages of numerous very peculiar groups of animals, but it is undeniable that there have been instances which appeared at first to indicate a *gradual transition*, and yet these instances have been shown by further investigation and discovery not truly to indicate anything of the kind. Thus at one time the remains of Labyrinthodonts which up till then had been discovered, seemed to justify the opinion that, as time went on, forms had successively appeared with more and more complete segmentation and

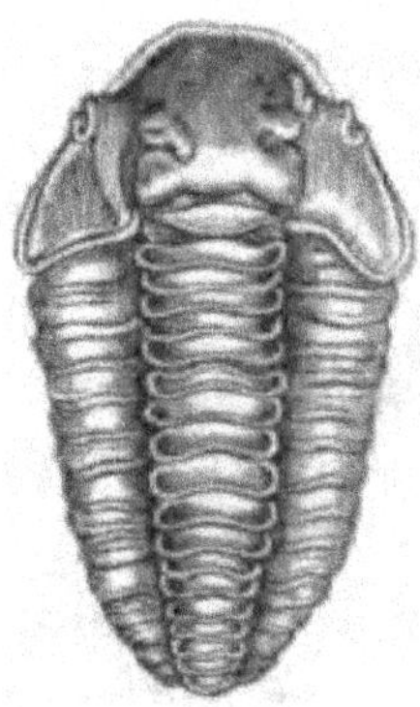

TRILOBITE.

ossification of the backbone, which in the earliest forms was (as it is in the lowest fishes now) a soft continuous rod or notochord. Now, however, it is considered probable that the soft back-boned Labyrinthodont (Archegosaurus) was an immature or larval form,[1] while Labyrinthodonts with completely developed vertebræ have been found to exist amongst the very earliest forms yet discovered. The same may be said regarding the eyes of the trilobites, some of

[1] As a tadpole is the *larval form* of a frog.

the oldest forms having been found as well furnished with organs of sight as the very last of the group which has left its remains accessible to observation.

Such instances, however, as well as the abrupt way in which marked and special forms (as the Pterodactyles, &c., before referred to) appear and disappear from the geological record, are of course explicable on the Darwinian theory, provided a sufficiently enormous amount of past time be allowed. The alleged extreme, and probably great, imperfection of that record may indeed be pleaded in excuse for the absence of transitional forms. But it *is* an excuse.[1] Nor is it possible to deny the *a priori* probability of the preservation of at least a few *minutely transitional* forms in some instances, if *every* species without exception has arisen exclusively by such minute and gradual transitions.

It remains now to turn to the other considerations with regard to the relation of species to time: namely (1) the total amount of time which other sciences show to be allowable for organic evolution; and (2) the proportion existing, on Darwinian principles, between the time anterior to the earlier fossils, and the time since; as evidenced by the proportion between the amount of evolutionary change during the latter epoch and that which must have occurred anteriorly.

Sir William Thomson has lately [2] advanced arguments from three distinct lines of inquiry, agreeing in one approximate result. The three lines of inquiry are—1, The action of the tides upon the earth's rotation; 2, The probable length of time during which the sun has illuminated this

[1] As Professor Huxley, with his characteristic candour, fully admitted in his lecture on the Dinosauria before referred to.

[2] "Transactions of the Geological Society of Glasgow," vol. iii.

planet; and 3, The temperature of the interior of the earth. The result arrived at by these investigations is a conclusion that the existing state of things on the earth, life on the earth, all geological history showing continuity of life, must be limited within some such period of past time as one hundred million years. The first question which suggests itself, supposing Sir W. Thomson's views to be correct, is: Has this period been anything like enough for the evolution of all organic forms by "Natural Selection"? The second is: Has this period been anything like enough for the deposition of the strata which must have been deposited if all organic forms have been evolved by *minute* steps, according to the Darwinian theory?

As to Sir William Thomson's views the author of this book cannot presume to advance any opinion; but the fact that they have not been refuted pleads strongly in their favour, when we consider how much they tell against the theory of Mr. Darwin. The last-named author only remarks that "many of the elements in the calculation are more or less doubtful,"[1] and Professor Huxley[2] does not attempt to *refute* Sir William Thomson's arguments, but only to show cause for suspense of judgment, inasmuch as the facts *may be* capable of other explanations.

Mr. Wallace, on the other hand,[3] seems more disposed to accept them, and, after considering Sir William's objections and those of Mr. Croll, puts the probable date of the beginning of the Cambrian deposits[4] at only

1 "Origin of Species," 5th edition, p. 354.
2 See his address to the Geological Society, on February 19, 1869.
3 See *Nature*, vol. i. p. 399, February 17, 1870.
4 Ibid. vol. i. p. 454.

twenty-four million years ago. On the other hand, he seems to consider that specific change has been more rapid than generally supposed, and exceptionally stable during the last score or so of thousand years.

Now, first, with regard to the time required for the evolution of all organic forms by merely accidental, minute, and fortuitous variations, the useful ones of which have been preserved:

Mr. Murphy[1] is of opinion that there has not been time enough. He says, "I am inclined to think that geological time is too short for the evolution of the higher forms of life out of the lower by that accumulation of imperceptibly slow variations to which alone Darwin ascribes the whole process."

"Darwin justly mentions the greyhound as being equal to any natural species in the perfect co-ordination of its parts, 'all adapted for extreme fleetness and for running down weak prey.'" "Yet it is an artificial species (and not *physiologically* a species *at all*), formed by long-continued selection under domestication; and there is no reason to suppose that any of the variations which have been selected to form it have been other than gradual and almost imperceptible. Suppose that it has taken five hundred years to form the greyhound out of his wolf-like ancestor. This is a mere guess, but it gives the order of the magnitude." Now, if so, "how long would it take to obtain an elephant from a protozoon, or even from a tadpole-like fish? Ought it not to take much more than a million times as long?"[2]

Mr. Darwin[3] would compare with the natural origin of

[1] "Habit and Intelligence," vol. i. p. 344. [2] Ibid. vol. i. p. 345.
[3] "Origin of Species," 5th edition, p. 353.

a species "unconscious selection, that is, the preservation of the most useful or beautiful animals, with no intention of modifying the breed." He adds: "But by this process of unconscious selection, various breeds have been sensibly changed in the course of two or three centuries."

"Sensibly changed!" but not formed into "new species." Mr. Darwin, of course, could not mean that species *generally* change so rapidly, which would be strangely at variance with the abundant evidence we have of the stability of animal forms as represented on Egyptian monuments and as shown by recent deposits. Indeed, he goes on to say,—"Species, however, probably change much more slowly, and within the same country only a few change at the same time. This slowness follows from all the inhabitants of the same country being already so well adapted to each other, that places in the polity of nature do not occur until after long intervals, when changes of some kind in the physical conditions, or through immigration, have occurred, and individual differences and variations of the right nature, by which some of the inhabitants might be better fitted to their new places under altered circumstances, might not at once occur." This is true, and not only will these changes occur at distant intervals, but it must be borne in mind that, in tracing back an animal to a remote ancestry, we pass through modifications of such rapidly increasing number and importance that a geometrical progression can alone indicate the increase of periods which such profound alterations would require for their evolution through "Natural Selection" only.

Thus let us take for an example the proboscis monkey of Borneo (*Semnopithecus nasalis*). In Mr. Darwin's own opinion, this form might have been "sensibly changed" in the course of two or three centuries. According to this, for evolving it as a true and perfect species one thousand years would be a very moderate period. Let ten thousand years be taken to represent approximately the period of substantially constant conditions during which no considerable change would be brought about. Now, if one thousand years may represent the period required for the evolution of the species *S. nasalis*, and of the other species of the genus Semnopithecus; ten times that period should, I think, be allowed for the differentiation of that genus, the African Cercopithecus and the other genera of the family Simiidæ—the differences between the genera being certainly more than tenfold greater than those between the species of the same genus. Again we may perhaps interpose a period of ten thousand years' comparative repose.

For the differentiation of the families Simiidæ and Cebidæ—so very much more distinct and different than any two genera of either family—a period ten times greater should, I believe, be allowed than that required for the evolution of the subordinate groups. A similarly increasing ratio should be granted for the successive developments of the differences between the Lemuroid and the higher forms of primates; for those between the original primate and other root-forms of placental mammals; for those between primary placental and implacental mammals, and perhaps also for the divergence of the most ancient stock of these and of the monotremes; since in all these cases modifications of structure appear to increase in complexity in at least that ratio. Finally, a vast period must be granted for the development of the lowest mammalian type from the primitive stock of the whole vertebrate sub-kingdom. Supposing this primitive stock to have arisen directly from a very lowly organized animal indeed (such as a nematoid worm, or an ascidian, or a jelly-fish), yet it is not easy to believe that less than two thousand million years would be required for the totality of animal development by no other means than minute, fortuitous, occasional, and intermitting variations in all conceivable directions. If this be even an approximation to the truth, then there seem to be strong reasons for believing that geological time is not sufficient for such a process.

The second question is, whether there has been time enough for the deposition of the strata which must have been deposited, if all organic forms have been evolved according to the Darwinian theory?

Now this may at first seem a question for geologists only, but, in fact, geology in this matter must rather take its time from zoology than the reverse; for if Mr. Darwin's theory be true, past time down to the deposition of the Upper Silurian strata can have been but a very small fraction of the whole time during which strata have been deposited. For when those Upper Silurian strata were formed, organic evolution had already run a great part of its course, perhaps the longest, slowest, and most difficult part of that course.

At that ancient epoch not only were the vertebrate, molluscous, and arthropod types distinctly and clearly differentiated, but highly developed forms had been produced in each of these sub-kingdoms. Thus in the Vertebrata there were fishes not belonging to the lowest but to the very highest groups which are known to have ever been developed, namely, the Elasmobranchs (the highly organized sharks and rays) and the Ganoids, a group now poorly represented, but for which the sturgeon may stand as a type, and which in many important respects more nearly resemble higher Vertebrata than do the ordinary or osseous fishes. Fishes in which the ventral fins are placed in front of the pectoral ones (*i.e.* jugular fishes) have been generally considered to be comparatively modern forms. But Professor Huxley has obligingly informed the author that he has discovered a jugular fish in the Permian deposits.

Amongst the molluscous animals we have members of the very highest known class, namely, the Cephalopods, or cuttle-fish class; and amongst articulated animals we find Trilobites and Eurypterida, which do not belong to any incipient worm-like group, but are distinctly differentiated Crustacea of no low form.[1]

We have in all these animal types nervous systems differentiated on distinctly different patterns; fully formed organs of circulation, digestion, excretion, and generation; complexly constructed eyes and other sense organs. In fact we have all the most elaborate and complete animal structures built up, and not only once; for in the fishes and mollusca we have (as described in the third chapter of this work) the coincidence of the independently developed organs of sense attaining a nearly similar complexity in two quite distinct forms. If, then, so small an advance in organization has been made in fishes, molluscs,

[1] Dr. Scudder "has lately found a fossil insect in the Devonian formation of New Brunswick, which is furnished with the well-known tympanum or stridulating apparatus of the male Locustidæ." (Trans. Ent. Soc., Third Series, vol. ii., quoted in Darwin's "Descent of Man," vol. i. p. 360.)

and arthropods since the Upper Silurian deposits, it will probably be within the mark to consider that the period before those deposits (during which all these organs would, on the Darwinian theory, have slowly built up their different perfections and complexities) occupied time at least a hundredfold greater.

A. B.

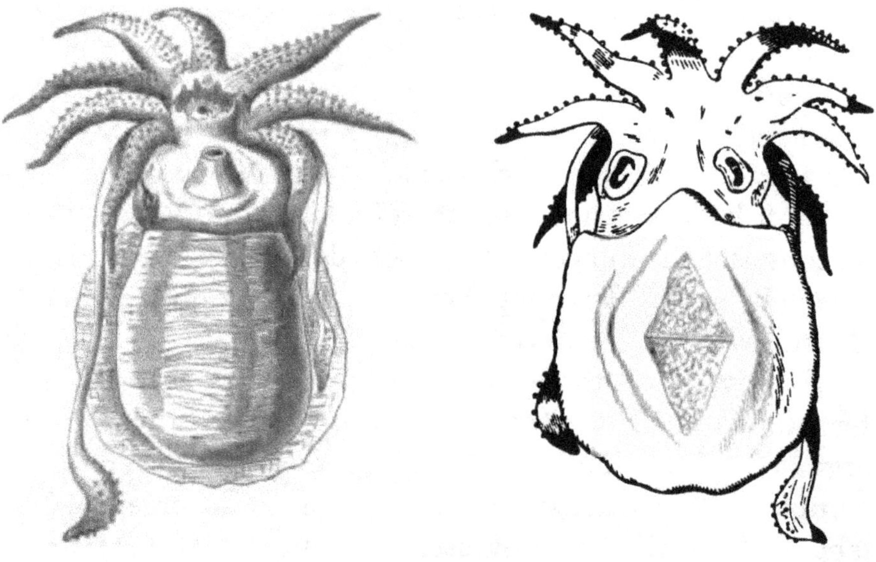

CUTTLE-FISH.
A. Ventral aspect. B. Dorsal aspect.

Now it will be a moderate computation to allow 25,000,000 years for the deposit of the strata down to and including the Upper Silurian. If, then, the evolutionary work done during this deposition only represents a hundredth part of the sum total, we shall require 2,500,000,000 (two thousand five hundred million) years for the complete development of the whole animal kingdom to its present state. Even one quarter of this, however, would far exceed the time which physics and astronomy seem able to allow for the completion of the process.

Finally, a difficulty exists as to the reason of the absence of rich fossiliferous deposits in the oldest strata—if life was then as abundant and varied as, on the Darwinian theory, it must have been. Mr. Darwin himself admits[1] "the case at present must remain inexplicable; and may be truly urged as a valid argument against the views" entertained in his book.

Thus, then, we find a remarkable (and on Darwinian principles an inexplicable) absence of minutely graduated transitional forms. All the most marked groups—bats, pterodactyles, chelonians, ichthyosauria, anoura, &c.—appear at once upon the scene. Even the horse, the animal whose pedigree has been probably best preserved, affords no conclusive evidence of specific origin by insignificant fortuitous variations; while some forms, as the labyrinthodonts and trilobites, which seemed to exhibit gradual change, are shown by further investigation to do nothing of the sort. As regards the time required for evolution (whether estimated by the probably minimum period required for organic change, or for the deposition of strata which accompanied that change), reasons have been suggested why it is likely that the past history of the earth does not supply us with enough. First, because of the prodigious increase in the importance and number of differences and modifications which we meet with as we traverse successively greater and more primary zoological groups; and, secondly, because of the vast series of strata necessarily deposited if the period since the Lower Silurian marks but a small fraction of the whole

[1] "Origin of Species," 5th edition, p. 381.

period of organic evolution. Finally, the absence or rarity of fossils in the oldest rocks is a point at present inexplicable, and not to be forgotten or neglected.

Now all these difficulties are avoided if we admit that new forms of animal life of all degrees of complexity appear from time to time with comparative suddenness, being evolved according to laws in part depending on surrounding conditions, in part internal—similar to the way in which crystals (and, perhaps from recent researches, the lowest forms of life) build themselves up according to the internal laws of their component substance, and in harmony and correspondence with all environing influences and conditions.

CHAPTER VII.

SPECIES AND SPACE.

The geographical distribution of animals presents difficulties.—These not insurmountable in themselves; harmonize with other difficulties.—Fresh-water fishes.—Forms common to Africa and India; to Africa and South America; to China and Australia; to North America and China; to New Zealand and South America; to South America and Tasmania; to South America and Australia.—Pleurodont lizards.—Insectivorous mammals.—Similarity of European and South American frogs.—Analogy between European salmon and fishes of New Zealand, &c.—An ancient Antarctic continent probable.—Other modes of accounting for facts of distribution.—Independent origin of closely similar forms.—Conclusion.

THE study of the distribution of animals over the earth's surface presents us with many facts having certain not unimportant bearings on the question of specific origin. Amongst these are instances which, at least at first sight, appear to conflict with the Darwinian theory of "Natural Selection." It is not, however, here contended that such facts do by any means constitute of themselves obstacles which cannot be got over. Indeed, it would be difficult to imagine any obstacles of the kind which could not be surmounted by an indefinite number of terrestrial modifications of surface—submergences and emergences—junctions and separations of continents in all directions, and combinations of any desired degree of frequency.

All this being supplemented by the intercalation of armies of enemies, multitudes of ancestors of all kinds, and myriads of connecting forms, whose *raison d'être* may be simply their utility or necessity for the support of the theory of "Natural Selection."

Nevertheless, when brought in merely to supplement and accentuate considerations and arguments derived from other sources, in that case difficulties connected with the geographical distribution of animals are not without significance, and are worthy of mention even though by themselves they constitute but simple problems, the solution or non-solution of which could not alone vitally affect any theory of specific origination.

Many facts as to the present distribution of animal life over the world are very readily explicable by the hypothesis of slight elevations and depressions of larger and smaller parts of its surface, but there are others which it is much more difficult so to explain.

The distribution either of animals possessing the power of flight, or of inhabitants of the ocean, is of course easily to be accounted for; the difficulty, if there is really any, must mainly be with strictly terrestrial animals of moderate or small powers of locomotion and with inhabitants of fresh water. Mr. Darwin himself observes,[1] "In regard to fish, I believe that the same species never occur in the fresh waters of distant continents." Now, the author is enabled, by the labours and through the kindness of Dr. Günther, to show that this belief cannot be maintained; that naturalist having called his attention to the following facts with regard to fish-distribution. These facts show that though only one species which is absolutely

[1] "Origin of Species," 5th edition, 1869, p. 463.

and exclusively an inhabitant of fresh water is as yet known to be found in distant continents, yet that in several other instances fishes identical in species (though not exclusively fresh-water) *are* found in the fresh waters of distant continents, and that very often the same *genus* is so distributed.

The genus *Mastacembelus* belongs to a family of fresh-water Indian fishes. Eight species of this genus are described by Dr. Günther in his catalogue.[1] These forms extend from Java and Borneo on the one hand, to Aleppo on the other. Nevertheless, a new species (*M. cryptacanthus*) has been described by the same author,[2] which is an inhabitant of the Camaroon country of *Western* Africa. He observes: "The occurrence of Indian forms on the West Coast of Africa, such as *Periophthalmus, Psettus, Mastacembelus,* is of the highest interest, and an almost new fact in our knowledge of the geographical distribution of fishes."

Ophiocephalus, again, is a truly Indian genus, there being no less than twenty-five species,[3] all from the fresh waters of the East Indies. Yet Dr. Günther informs me that there is a species in the Upper Nile and in West Africa.

The Acanthopterygian family (*Labyrinthici*) contains nine fresh-water genera, and these are distributed between the East Indies and South and Central Africa.

The Carp fishes (Cyprinoids) are found in India, Africa, and Madagascar, but there are none in South America.

Thus existing fresh-water fishes point to an immediate

[1] See his Catalogue of Acanthopterygian Fishes in the British Museum, vol. iii. p. 540.

[2] Proc. Zool. Soc. 1867, p. 102, and Ann. Mag. of Nat. Hist. vol. xx. p. 110.

[3] See Catalogue, vol. iii. p. 469.

connexion between Africa and India, harmonizing with what we learn from Miocene mammalian remains.

On the other hand, the Characinidæ (a family of the physostomous fishes) are found in Africa and South America, and not in India; and even the component groups of the family are so distributed,—namely, the *Tetragonopterina*[1] and the *Hydrocyonina.*[2]

Again, we have similar phenomena in that almost exclusively fresh-water group the Siluroids.

Thus the genera *Clarias*[3] and *Heterobranchus*[4] are found both in Africa and the East Indies. *Plotosus* is found in Africa, India, and Australia, and the species *P. anguillaris*[5] has been brought from both China and Moreton Bay. Here, therefore, we have the same species in two distinct geographical regions. It is however a coast fish, which, though entering rivers, yet lives in the sea.

Eutropius[6] is an African genus, but *E. obtusirostris* comes from India. On the other hand, *Amiurus* is a North American form; but one species, *A. cantonensis,*[7] comes from China.

The genus *Galaxias*[8] has at least one species common to New Zealand and South America, and one common to South America and Tasmania. In this genus we thus have an absolutely and completely fresh-water form *of the very same species* distributed between different and distinct geographical regions.

Of the lower fishes, a lamprey, *Mordacia mordax,*[9] is common to South Australia and Chile; while another form

[1] See Catalogue, vol. v. p. 311. [2] Ibid. p. 345.
[3] Ibid. p. 13. [4] Ibid. p. 21. [5] Ibid. p. 24.
[6] Ibid. p. 52. [7] Ibid. p. 100. [8] Ibid. vol. vi. p. 208.
[9] Ibid. vol. viii. p. 507.

of the same family, namely, *Geotria chilensis*,[1] is found not only in South America and Australia, but in New Zealand also. These fishes, however, probably pass part of their lives in the sea.

We thus certainly have several species which *are* common to the fresh waters of distant continents, although it cannot be certainly affirmed that they are exclusively and entirely fresh-water fishes throughout all their lives, except in the case of *Galaxias*.

Existing forms point to a close union between South America and Africa on the one hand, and between South America, Australia, Tasmania, and New Zealand on the other; but these unions were not synchronous any more than the unions indicated between India and Australia, China and Australia, China and North America, and India and Africa.

Pleurodont lizards are such as have the teeth attached by their sides to the inner surface of the jaw, in contra-

INNER SIDE OF LOWER JAW OF PLEURODONT LIZARD.
(Showing the teeth attached to the inner surface of its side.)

distinction to acrodont lizards, which have the bases of their teeth anchylosed to the summit of the margin of the jaw. Now pleurodont iguanian lizards abound in the South American region, but nowhere else, and are not as yet known to inhabit any part of the present continent of Africa. Yet pleurodont lizards, strange to say, are found in

[1] See Catalogue, vol. viii. p. 509.

Madagascar. This is the more remarkable, as we have no evidence yet of the existence in Madagascar of fresh-water fishes common to Africa and South America.

Again, that interesting island Madagascar is the home of very singular and special insectivorous beasts of the genera Centetes, Ericulus, and Echinops; while the only other member of the group to which they belong is Solenodon, which is a resident in the West India Islands,

SOLENODON.

Cuba and Hayti. The connexion, however, between the West Indies and Madagascar must surely have been at a time when the great lemurine group was absent; for it is difficult to understand the spread of such a form as Solenodon, and at the same time the non-extension of the active lemurs, or their utter extirpation, in such a congenial situation as the West Indian Archipelago.

The close connexion of South America and Australia is demonstrated (on the Darwinian theory), not only from the marsupial fauna of both, but also from the frogs and toads which respectively inhabit those regions. A truly remarkable similarity and parallelism exist, however, between certain of the same animals inhabiting South-Western America and Europe. Thus Dr. Günther has described[1] a frog from Chile by the name of cacotus, which singularly resembles the European bombinator.

Again of the salmons, two genera from South America, New Zealand, and Australia, are analogous to European salmons.

In addition to this may be mentioned a quotation from Professor Dana, given by Mr. Darwin,[2] to the effect that "it is certainly a wonderful fact that New Zealand should have a closer resemblance in its crustacea to Great Britain, its antipode, than to any other part of the world:" and Mr. Darwin adds, "Sir J. Richardson also speaks of the reappearance on the shores of New Zealand, Tasmania, &c., of northern forms of fish. Dr. Hooker informs me that twenty-five species of algæ are common to New Zealand and to Europe, but have not been found in the intermediate tropical seas."

Many more examples of the kind could easily be brought forward, but these may suffice. As to the last-mentioned cases, Mr. Darwin explains them by the influence of the glacial epoch, which influence he would extend actually across the equator,[3] and thus account for, amongst other

[1] Proc. Zool. Soc. 1868, p. 482.

[2] "Origin of Species," 5th edition, 1869, p. 454.

[3] Mr. J. J. Murphy, in a very interesting paper read before the Geological Society, June 9th, 1869, advances weighty reasons for believing that "the equatorial regions were never glaciated at all" (p. 355).

matters, the appearance in Chile of frogs having close genetic relations with European forms. But it is difficult to understand the persistence and preservation of such exceptional forms with the extirpation of all the others which probably accompanied them, if so great a migration of northern kinds had been occasioned by the cold of the glacial epoch.

Mr. Darwin candidly says,[1] "I am far from supposing that all difficulties in regard to the distribution and affinities of the identical and allied species, which now live so widely separated in the north and south, and sometimes on the intermediate mountain-ranges, are removed." . . . "We cannot say why certain species and not others have migrated; why certain species have been modified and have given rise to new forms, whilst others have remained unaltered." Again he adds, "Various difficulties also remain to be solved; for instance, the occurrence, as shown by Dr. Hooker, of the same plants at points so enormously remote as Kerguelen Land, New Zealand, and Fuegia; but icebergs, as suggested by Lyell, may have been concerned in their dispersal. The existence, at these and other distant points of the southern hemisphere, of species which, though distinct, belong to a genera exclusively confined to the south, is a more remarkable case. Some of these species are so distinct that we cannot suppose that there has been time since the commencement of the last glacial period for their migration and subsequent modification to the necessary degree." Mr. Darwin goes on to account for these facts by the probable existence of a rich antarctic flora in a warm period anterior to the last glacial epoch. There are indeed many reasons

[1] "Origin of Species," 5th edition, p. 459.

for thinking that a southern continent, rich in living forms, once existed. Among these reasons is the distribution of struthious birds around the antarctic region: as the ostrich in Africa, the rhea in South America, the emeu in Australia, the apteryx, dinornis, &c. in New Zealand, the epiornis in Madagascar. Still the existence of such a land would not alone explain the various geographical cross relations which have been given above. It would not, for example, account for the resemblance between the crustacea or fishes of New Zealand and of England. It would, however, go far to explain the identity (specific or generic) between fresh-water and other forms now simultaneously existing in Australia and South America, or in either or both of these, and New Zealand.

Again, mutations of elevation small and gradual (but frequent and intermitting), through enormous periods of time—waves, as it were, of land rolling many times in many directions—might be made to explain numerous difficulties as to geographical distribution, and any cases that remained would probably be capable of explanation, as being isolated but allied animal forms, now separated indeed, but being merely remnants of extensive groups which, at an earlier period, were spread over the surface of the earth. Thus none of the facts here given are any serious difficulty to the doctrine of "evolution;" but it is contended in this book that if other considerations render it improbable that the manifestation of the successive forms of life has been brought about by minute, indefinite, and fortuitous variations, then these facts as to geographical distribution intensify that improbability, and are so far worthy of attention.

All geographical difficulties of the kind would be evaded

if we could concede the probability of the independent origin, in different situations, of the same organic forms in animals high in the scale of nature. Similar causes must produce similar results, and new reasons have been lately adduced for believing, as regards the *lowest organisms*, that the same forms can arise and manifest themselves independently. The difficulty as to higher animals is, however, much greater, as (on the theory of evolution) one acting force must always be the ancestral influences in each case, and this force must always tend to go on acting in the same groove and direction in the future as it has done in the past. So that it is difficult to conceive that individuals the ancestral history of which is very different, can be acted upon by all influences, external and internal, in such diverse ways and proportions that the results (unequals being added to unequals) shall be equal and similar. Still, though highly improbable, this cannot be said to be impossible; and if there *is* an innate law of any kind helping to determine specific evolution, this may more or less, or entirely, neutralize or even reverse the effect of ancestral habit. Thus, it is quite conceivable that a pleurodont lizard might have arisen in Madagascar in perfect independence of the similarly-formed American lacertilia: just as certain teeth of carnivorous and insectivorous marsupial animals have been seen most closely to resemble those of carnivorous and insectivorous placental beasts; just as, again, the paddles of the Cetacea resemble, in the fact of a multiplication in the number of the phalanges, the many-jointed feet of extinct marine reptiles, and as the beak of the cuttle-fish or of the tadpole resembles that of birds. We have already seen (in Chapter III.) that it is impossible, upon any hypothesis, to escape admitting the independent origins of closely similar forms. It may be that they are both more frequent and more important than is generally thought.

That closely similar structures may arise without a genetic relationship has been lately well urged by Mr. Ray Lankester.[1] He has brought this notion forward even as regards the bones of the skull in osseous fishes and in mammals. He has done this on the ground that the probable common ancestor of mammals and of osseous fishes was a vertebrate animal of so low a type that it could not be supposed to have possessed a skull differentiated into distinct bony elements—even if it was bony at all. If the ancestral cranium was thus undifferentiated, then the cranial bones must have had an independent origin in each class, and in this case we have the most strikingly harmonious and parallel results from independent actions. For the bones of the skull in an osseous fish are so closely conformed to those of a mammal, that "both types of skull exhibit many bones in common," though "in each type some of these bones acquire special arrangements and very different magnitudes."[2] And no investigator of homologies doubts that a considerable number of the bones which form the skull of any osseous fish are certainly homologous with the cranial bones of man. The occipital, the parietal, and frontal, the bones which surround the internal ear, the vomer, the premaxilla, and the quadrate bones, may be given as examples. Now, if such close relations of homology can be brought about independently of any but the most remote

[1] See Ann. and Mag. of Nat. Hist., July 1870, p. 37.

[2] Professor Huxley's Lectures on the Elements of Comp. Anat. p. 184.

genetic affinity, it would be rash to affirm dogmatically that there is any impossibility in the independent origin of such forms as centetes and solenodon, or of genetically distinct batrachians, as similar to each other as are some of the frogs of South America and of Europe. At the same time, such phenomena must at present be considered as very improbable, from the action of ancestral habit, as before stated.

We have seen, then, that the geographical distribution of animals presents difficulties, though not insuperable ones, for the Darwinian hypothesis. If, however, other reasons against it seem to have any weight—if, especially, there is reason to believe that geological time has not been sufficient for it, then it will be well to bear in mind the facts here enumerated. These facts, however, are not opposed to the doctrine of evolution; and if it could be established that closely similar forms had really arisen in complete independence one of the other, they would rather tend to strengthen and to support that theory.

CHAPTER VIII.

HOMOLOGIES.

Animals made-up of parts mutually related in various ways.—What homology is.—Its various kinds.—Serial homology.—Lateral homology.—Vertical homology.—Mr. Herbert Spencer's explanations.—An internal power necessary, as shown by facts of comparative anatomy.—Of teratology.—M. St. Hilaire.—Professor Burt Wilder.—Foot-wings.—Facts of pathology.—Mr. James Paget.—Dr. William Budd.—The existence of such an internal power of individual development diminishes the improbability of an analogous law of specific origination.

THAT concrete whole which is spoken of as "an individual" (such, *e.g.*, as a bird or a lobster) is formed of a more or less complex aggregation of parts which are actually (from whatever cause or causes) grouped together in a harmonious interdependency, and which have a multitude of complex relations amongst themselves.

The mind detects a certain number of these relations as it contemplates the various component parts of an individual in one or other direction—as it follows up different lines of thought. These perceived relations, though subjective, *as relations*, have nevertheless an objective foundation as real parts, or conditions of parts, of real wholes; they are, therefore, true relations, such, *e.g.*, as those between the right and left hand, between the hand and the foot, &c.

The component parts of each concrete whole have also a relation of resemblance to the parts of other concrete wholes, whether of the same or of different kinds, as the resemblance between the hands of two men, or that between the hand of a man and the fore-paw of a cat.

Now, it is here contended that the relationships borne one to another by various component parts, imply the existence of some innate, internal condition, conveniently spoken of as a power or tendèncy, which is quite as mysterious as is any innate condition, power, or tendency resulting in the orderly evolution of successive specific manifestations. These relationships, as also this developmental power, will doubtless, in a certain sense, be somewhat further explained as science advances. But the result will be merely a shifting of the inexplicability a point backwards, by the intercalation of another step between the action of the internal condition or power and its external result. In the meantime, even if by "Natural Selection" we could eliminate the puzzles of the "origin of species," yet other phenomena, not less remarkable (namely, those noticed in this chapter), would still remain unexplained and inexplicable. It is not improbable that, could we arrive at the causes conditioning all the complex inter-relations between the several parts of one animal, we should at the same time obtain the key to unlock the secrets of specific origination.

It is desirable, then, to see what facts there are in animal organization which point to innate conditions (powers and tendencies) as yet unexplained, and upon which the theory of "Natural Selection" is unable to throw any explanatory light.

The facts to be considered are the phenomena of "homology," and especially of serial, bilateral, and vertical homology.

The word "homology" indicates such a relation between two parts that they may be said in some sense to be "the same," or at least "of similar nature." This similarity, however, does not relate to the *use* to which parts are put, but only to their relative position with regard to other parts, or to their mode of origin. There are many kinds of homology,[1] but it is only necessary to consider the three kinds above enumerated.

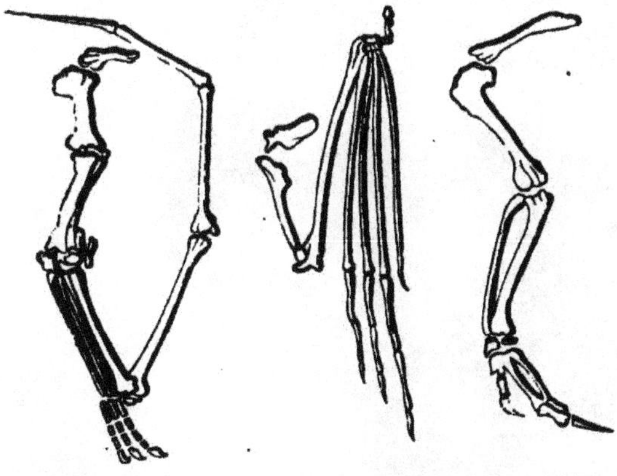

WING-BONES OF PTERODACTYLE, BAT, AND BIRD.

The term "homologous" may be applied to parts in two individual animals of different kinds, or to different parts of the same individual. Thus "the right and left hands," or "joints of the backbone," or "the teeth of the two jaws," are homologous parts of the same individual. But the arm of man, the foreleg of the horse, the paddle of the whale, and the wing of the bat and of the bird, are all

1 For an enumeration of the more obvious homological relationships see Ann. and Mag. of Nat. Hist. for August 1870, p. 118.

likewise homologous parts, yet of another kind; that is they are the same parts existing in animals of different species.

In contrast to this, the wing of the humming-bird and the wing of the humming-bird moth are not homologous at all, or in any sense; for the resemblance between them consists solely in the use to which they are put, and is

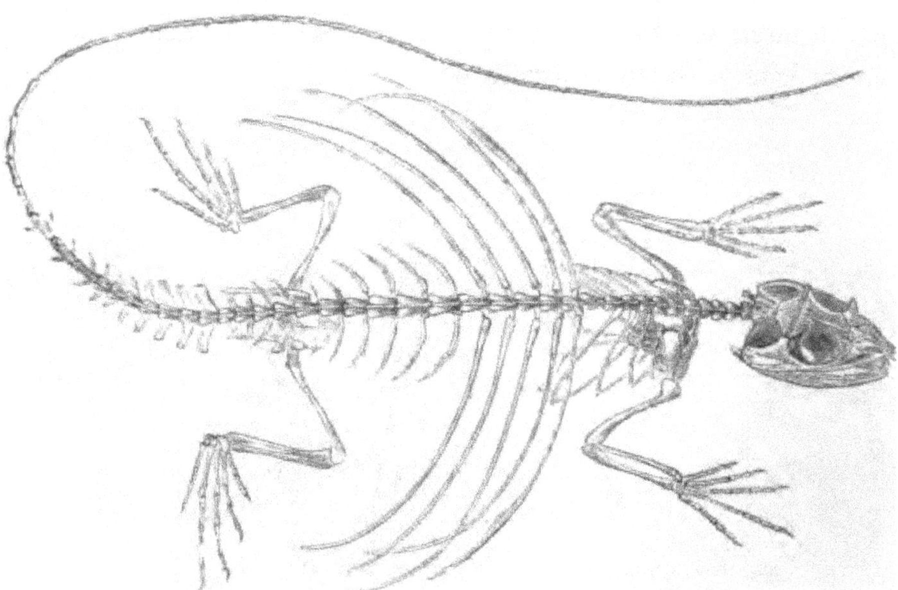

SKELETON OF THE FLYING DRAGON.
(Showing the elongated ribs which support the flitting organ.)

therefore only a relation of *analogy.* There is no relation of *homology* between them, because they have no common resemblance as to their relations to surrounding parts, or as to their mode of origin. Similarly, there is no homology between the wing of the bat and that of the flying-dragon, for the latter is formed of certain ribs, and not of limb bones.

Homology may be further distinguished into (1) a relationship which, on evolutionary principles, would be due to descent from a common ancestor, as the homological

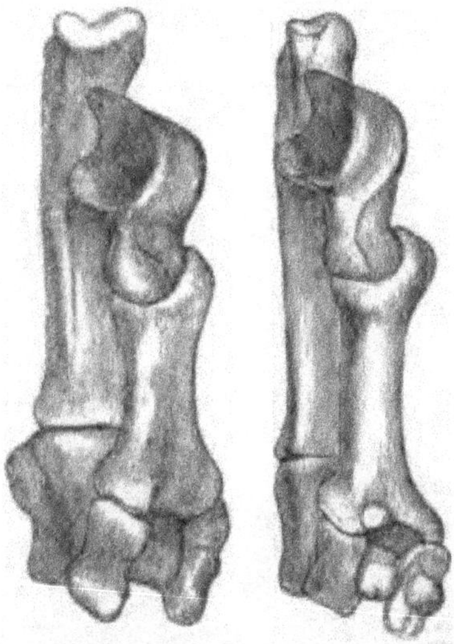

TARSAL BONES OF DIFFERENT LEMUROIDS.
ig ht-hand figure, Tarsus of Galago ; *left-hand figure*, Tarsus of Cheirogaleus.)

relation between the arm-bone of the horse and that of the ox, or between the singular ankle-bones of the two lemurine genera, cheirogaleus and galago, and which relation has

A CENTIPEDE.

N 2

been termed by Mr. Ray Lankester "homogeny;"[1] and (2) a relationship induced, not derived—such as exists between parts closely similar in relative position, but with

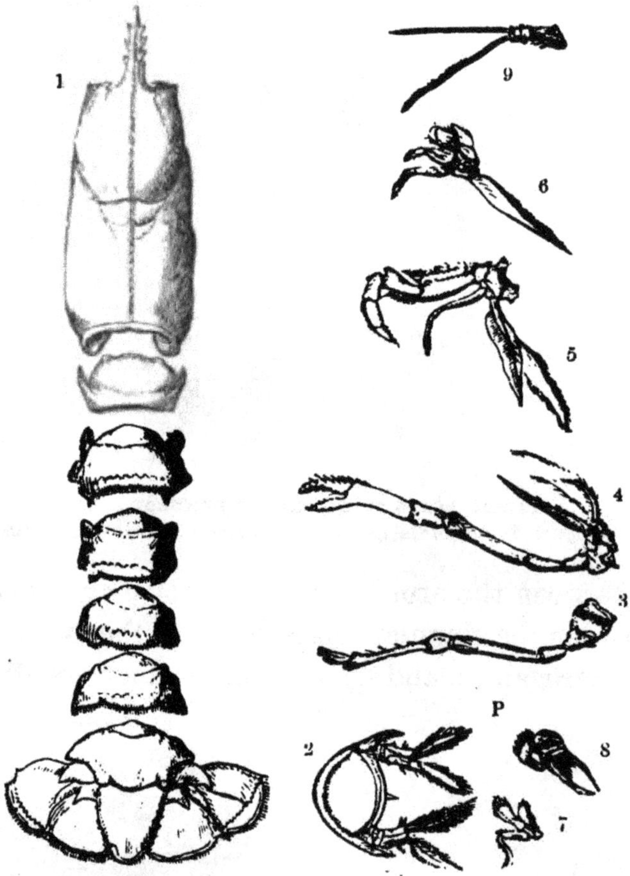

PART OF THE SKELETON OF THE LOBSTER.

no genetic affinity, or only a remote one, as the homological relation between the chambers of the heart of a bat and those of a bird, or the similar teeth of the thylacine

[1] See Ann. and Mag. of Nat. Hist., July 1870.

and the dog before spoken of.[1] For this relationship Mr. Ray Lankester has proposed the term "homoplasy."

"Serial homology" is a relation of resemblance existing between two or more parts placed in series one behind the other in the same individual. Examples of such homologues are the ribs, or joints of the backbone of a horse, or the limbs of a centipede. The latter animal is a striking example of serial homology. The body (except at its two ends) consists of a longitudinal series of similar segments. Each segment supports a pair of limbs, and the appendages of all the segments (except as before) are completely alike.

A less complete case of serial homology is presented by Crustacea (animals of the crab class), notably by the squilla and by the common lobster. In the latter animal we have a six-jointed abdomen (the so-called tail), in front of which is a large solid mass (the cephalo-thorax), terminated anteriorly by a median process (the rostrum). On the under-surface of the body we find a quantity of moveable appendages. Such are, *e.g.*, feelers (Fig. 9), jaws (Figs. 6, 7, and 8), foot-jaws (Fig. 5), claws and legs (Figs. 3 and 4), beneath the cephalo-thorax; and flat processes (Fig. 2), called "swimmerets," beneath the so-called tail or abdomen.

Now, these various appendages are distinct and different enough as we see them in the adult, but they all appear in the embryo as buds of similar form and size, and the thoracic limbs at first consist each of two members, as the swimmerets always do.

This shows what great differences may exist in size, in form, and in function, between parts which are develop-

[1] See *antè*, p. 76.

[illegible] are modifica- [illegible] structure, which becomes [illegible] In other words, [illegible]

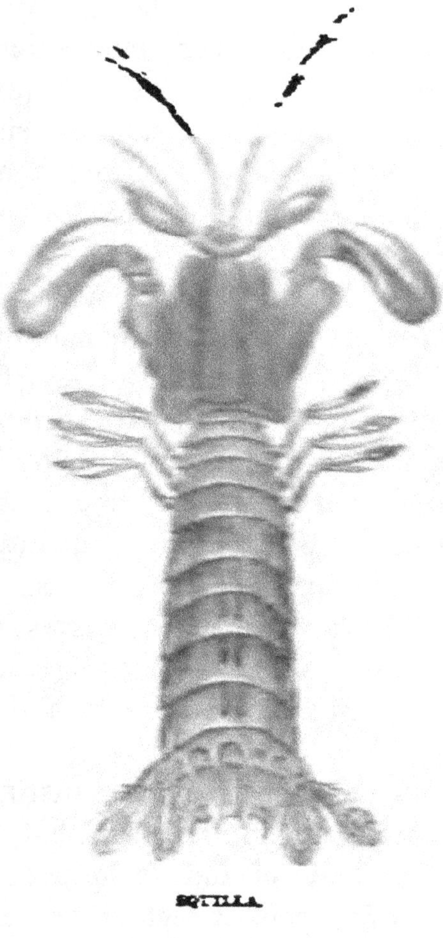

SQUILLA.

The segments of the body, as they follow one behind the other, are also serially alike, as is plainly seen in the abdomen or tail. In the cephalo-thorax of the lobster, however, this is disguised. It is therefore very interesting to find that in the other crustacean before mentioned, the Squilla, the segmentation of the body is more completely preserved, and even the first three segments, which go to compose the head, remain permanently distinct.

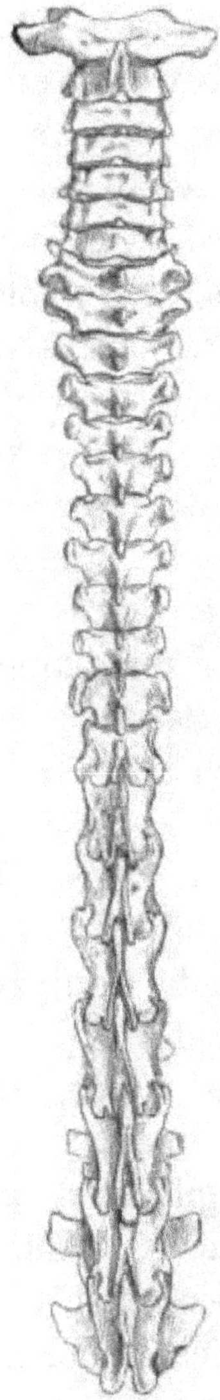

SPINE OF GALAGO ALLENII.

Such an obvious and unmistakeable serial repetition of parts does not obtain in the highest, or backboned animals, the Vertebrata. Thus in man, and other mammals, nothing of the kind is *externally* visible, and we have to penetrate to his skeleton to find such a series of homologous parts.

There, indeed, we discover a number of pairs of bones, each pair so obviously resembling the others that they all receive a common name—the ribs. There also (*i.e.* in the skeleton) we find a still more remarkable series of similar parts, the joints of the spine or backbone (vertebræ), which are admitted by all to possess a certain community of structure.

It is in their limbs, however, that the Vertebrata present their most conspicuous example of serial homology—almost the only serial homology noticeable externally.

The facts of serial homology seem hardly to have excited the amount of interest they certainly merit.

Very many writers, indeed, have occupied themselves with investigations and speculations as to what portions of the leg and foot answer to what parts of the arm and hand, a question which has only recently received a more or less satisfactory solution through the successive concordant efforts of Professor Humphry,[1] Professor Huxley,[2] the author of this work,[3] and Professor Flower.[4] Very few writers, however, have devoted much time or thought to the question of serial homology in general. Mr. Herbert Spencer, indeed, in his very interesting "First Principles of Biology," has given forth ideas on this subject, which are well worthy of careful perusal and consideration, and some of which apply also to the other kinds of homology mentioned above. He would explain the serial homologies of such creatures as the lobster and centipede thus: Animals of a very low grade propagate themselves by spontaneous fission. If certain creatures found benefit from this process of division remaining incomplete, they would (on the theory of "Natural Selection") transmit their selected tendency to such incomplete division to their posterity. In this way, it is conceivable that animals might arise in the form of long chains of similar segments, each of which chains would consist of a number of imperfectly separated individuals, and be equivalent to a series of separate individuals belonging to kinds in which the fission was complete. In other words, Mr. Spencer would explain it as the coalescence of organisms of a lower degree of aggregation in one ongitudinal series, through survival of the fittest aggregations. This may be so. It is certainly an ingenious speculation, but facts have not yet been brought forward which demonstrate it; otherwise, this kind of serial homology might be termed "homogenetic."

[1] Treatise on the Human Skeleton, 1858.
[2] Hunterian Lectures for 1864.
[3] Linnæan Transactions, vol. xxv. p. 395, 1866.
[4] Hunterian Lectures for 1870, and Journal of Anat. for May 1870.

The other kind of serial repetitions, namely, those of the vertebral column, are explained by Mr. Spencer as the results of alternate strains and compressions acting on a primitively homogeneous cylinder. The serial homology of the fore and hind limbs is explained by the same writer as the result of a similarity in the influences and conditions to which they are exposed. Serial homologues so formed might be called, as Mr. Ray Lankester has proposed, "homoplastic." But there are, it is here contended, abundant reasons for thinking that the predominant agent in the production of the homologies of the limbs is an *internal* force or tendency. And if such a power can be shown to be necessary in this instance, it may also be legitimately used to explain such serial homologies as those of the centipede's segments and of the joints of the backbone. At the same time it is not, of course, pretended that external conditions do not contribute their own effects in addition. The presence of this internal power will be rendered more probable if valid arguments can be brought forward against the explanations which Mr. Herbert Spencer has offered.

Lateral homology (or bilateral symmetry) is the resemblance between the right and left sides of an animal, or of part of an animal; as, *e.g.*, between our right hand and our left. It exists more or less at one or other time of life in all animals, except some very lowly organized creatures. In the highest animals this symmetry is laid down at the very dawn of life, the first trace of the future creature being a longitudinal streak—the embryonic "primitive groove." This kind of homology is explained by Mr. Spencer as the result of the similar way in which conditions affect the right and left sides respectively.

Vertical homology (or vertical symmetry) is the resemblance existing between parts which are placed one above, the other beneath. It is much less general and marked than serial, or lateral homology. Nevertheless, it is plainly to be seen in the tail region of most fishes, and in the far-extending dorsal and ventral fins of such kinds as the sole and the flounder.

It is also strikingly shown in the bones of the tail of certain efts, as in *Chioglossa*, where the complexity of the upper (neural) arch is closely repeated by the inferior one. Again, in *Spelerpes rubra*, where almost vertically ascending articular processes above are repeated by almost vertically descending articular processes below. Also in the axolotl, where there are double pits, placed side by side, not only superiorly, but at the same time inferiorly.[1]

VERTEBRÆ OF AXOLOTL.

This kind of homology is also explained by Mr. Spencer as the result of the similarity of conditions affecting the two parts. He explains the very general absence of symmetry between the dorsal and ventral surfaces of animals by the different conditions to which these two surfaces are respectively exposed, and in the same way he explains the asymmetry of the flat-fishes (*Pleuronectidæ*), of snails, &c.

Now, first, as regards Mr. Spencer's explanation of animal forms by means of the influence of external conditions, the following observations may be made. Abundant instances are brought forward by him of admirable adaptation of structure to circumstances, but in the immense majority of these instances it is very difficult, if not impos-

[1] See a Paper on the "Axial Skeleton of the Urodela," in Proc. Zool. Soc. 1870, p. 266.

sible, to see *how* external conditions can have produced, or even have tended to produce them. For example, we may take the migration of an eye of the sole from one side of the head to the other. What is there here either in the darkness, or the friction, or in any other conceivable external cause, to have produced the first beginning of such an unprecedented displacement of the eye? Mr. Spencer has beautifully illustrated that correlation which all must admit to exist between the forms of organisms and their surrounding external conditions, but by no means proved that the latter are *the cause* of the former.

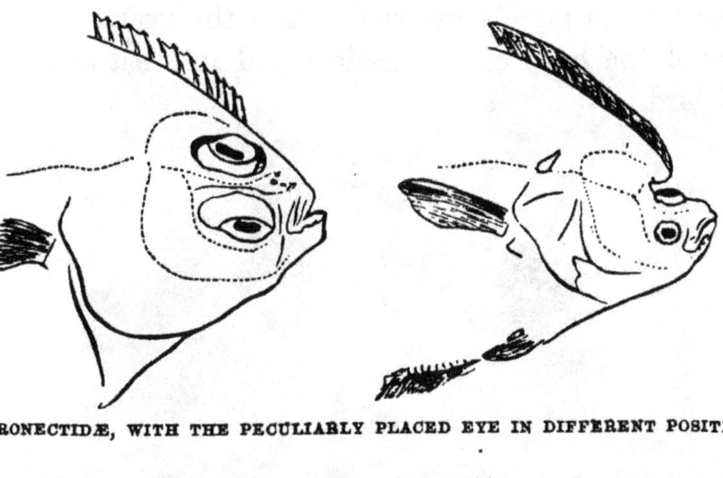

PLEURONECTIDÆ, WITH THE PECULIARLY PLACED EYE IN DIFFERENT POSITIONS.

Some internal conditions (or in ordinary language some internal power and force) must be conceded to living organisms, otherwise incident forces must act upon them and upon non-living aggregations of matter in the same way and with similar effects.

If the mere presence of these incident forces produces so ready a response in animals and plants, it must be that there are, in their case, conditions disposing and enabling them so to respond, according to the old maxim, *Quicquid recipitur, recipitur ad modum recipientis,* as the same rays of light which bleach a piece of silk, blacken nitrate of silver. If, therefore, we attribute the forms of organisms to the action of external conditions, *i.e.* of incident forces on their modifiable structure, we give but a partial account of the matter, removing a step back, as it were, the action of the internal condition, power, or force which must be conceived as occasioning such ready modifiability. But indeed it is not at all easy to see how the influence of the surface of the ground, or any conceivable condition or force, can produce the difference which exists between the ventral and dorsal shields of the carapace of a tortoise, or by what differences of merely external causes the ovaries of the two sides of the body can be made equal in a bat and unequal in a bird.

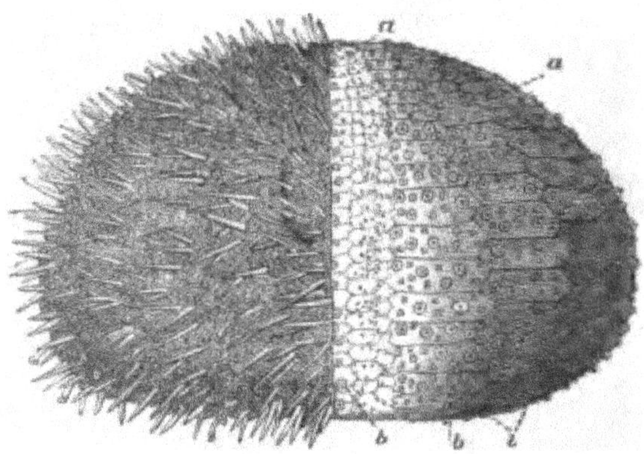

AN ECHINUS, OR SEA-URCHIN.
(The spines removed from one-half.)

There is, on the other hand, an *a priori* reason why we should expect to find that the symmetrical forms of all animals are due to internal causes. This reason is the fact that the symmetrical forms of minerals are undoubtedly due to such causes. It is unnecessary here to do more than refer to the beautiful and complex forms presented by inorganic structures. With regard to organisms, however, the wonderful Acanthometræ and the Polycystina may be mentioned as presenting complexities of form which cannot be explained except by the action of *internal* causes. The same may be said of the great group of Echinoderms, with their amazing variety of component parts. If then internal forces can so build up the most varied structures, they are surely capable of producing the serial, lateral, and vertical symmetries which higher animal forms exhibit. Mr. Spencer is the more bound to admit this, inasmuch as in his doctrine of "physiological units" he maintains that these organic atoms of his have an innate power of building up and evolving the whole and perfect animal from which they were in each case derived. To build up and evolve the various symmetries here spoken of is not one whit more mysterious. Directly to refute Mr. Spencer's hypothesis as to the effects of surrounding conditions would require, however, the bringing forward of examples of organisms which are ill-adapted to their positions, and out of harmony with their surroundings—a difficult task indeed.[1]

[1] Just as Buffon's superfluous lament over the unfortunate organization of the sloth has been shown, by the increase of our knowledge, to have been uncalled for and absurd, so other supposed instances of non-adaptation will, no doubt, similarly disappear. Mr. Darwin, in his "Origin of Species," 5th edition, p. 220, speaks of a woodpecker (*Colaptes campestris*) as having an organization quite at variance with its habits, and as never climbing a tree, though possessed of the special arboreal structure of other woodpeckers. It now appears, however, from the observations of Mr. W. H. Hudson, C.M.Z.S., that its habits are in harmony with its structure. See Mr. Hudson's third letter to the Zoological Society, published in the Proceedings of that Society for March 24, 1870, p. 159; also Mr. Darwin's reply in the Proceedings for November 1st, 1870.

Secondly, as regards the last-mentioned author's explanation of such serial homology as exists in the centipede and its allies, the very groundwork is open to objection. Multiplication by spontaneous fission seems from some recent researches to be much less frequent than has been

AN ANNELID DIVIDING SPONTANEOUSLY.
(A new head having been formed towards the hinder end of the body of the parent.)

supposed, and more evidence is required as to the fact of the habitual propagation of *any* planariæ in such fashion.[1]

[1] Dr. Cobbold has informed the author that he has never observed a *planaria* divide spontaneously, and he is sceptical as to that process taking place at all. Dr. H. Charlton Bastian has also stated that, in spite of much observation, he has never seen the process in *vorticella*.

But even if this were as asserted, it nevertheless fails to explain the peculiar condition presented by *Syllis* and some other annelids, where a new head is formed at intervals in certain segments of the body. Here we have evidently an innate tendency to the development at intervals of a complex whole. It is not the budding out from, or spontaneous fission of, certain segments; but the transformation in a definite and very peculiar manner of parts which already exist into other and more complex parts. Again, the processes of development presented by some of these creatures do not by any means point to an origin through the linear coalescence of primitively distinct animals by means of imperfect segmentation. Here reference may be made to those flies before spoken of (see *antè*, p. 51), in the development of which the legs, wings, eyes, &c., are derived from masses of formative tissue (termed imaginal disks), which, by their mutual approximation, together build up parts of the head and body,[1] recalling to mind the development of Echinoderms.

Again, Nicholas Wagner found in certain other Diptera, the Hessian flies, that the larva gives rise to secondary larvæ within it, which develop, and burst the body of the primary larva. The secondary larvæ give rise, similarly, to another set within them, and these again to another set.[2]

Again, the fact that in *Tænia echinococcus* one egg produces numerous individuals, tends to invalidate the argument that the increase of segments during development is a relic of specific genesis.

Mr. H. Spencer seems to deny serial homology to the

1 Professor Huxley's Hunterian Lecture, March 16, 1868.

2 Ibid., March 18.

mollusca, but it is difficult to see why the shell segments of chiton are not such homologues because the segmentation is superficial. The external processes of eolis, doris, &c., are good examples of serial homology, as also are plainly the successive chambers of the orthoceratidæ. Nor are parts of a series less serial because arranged spirally, as in most gasteropods. Mr. Spencer observes of the molluscous as of the vertebrate animal, "You cannot cut it into transverse slices, each of which contains a digestive organ, a respiratory organ, a reproductive organ, &c."[1] But the same may be said of every single arthropod and annelid, if it be meant that all these organs are not contained in every possible slice. While if it be meant that parts of all such organs are contained in certain slices, then some of the mollusca may also be included.

Another objection to Mr. Spencer's speculation is derived from considerations which have already been stated, as to past time. For if the annulose animals have been formed by aggregation, we ought to find this process much less perfect in the oldest form. But a complete development, such as already obtains in the lobster, &c., was reached by the Eurypterida and Trilobites of the palæozoic strata; and annelids, in all probability formed mainly like those of the present day, abounded during the deposition of the oldest fossiliferous rocks.

Thirdly, and lastly, as regards such serial homology as is exemplified by the backbone of man, there are also several objections to Mr. Spencer's mechanical explanation.

On the theory of evolution most in favour, the first Vertebrata were aquatic. Now, as natation is generally

[1] "Principles of Biology," vol. ii. p. 105.

effected by repeated and vigorous lateral flexions of the body, we ought to find the segmentation much more complete laterally than on the dorsal and ventral aspects of the spinal column. And yet, in those species which, taken together, constitute a series of more and more distinctly segmented forms, the segmentation gradually increases *all round* the central part of the spinal column.

Mr. Spencer[1] thinks it probable that the sturgeon has retained the notochordal (that is, the primitive, unsegmented) structure because it is sluggish. But Dr. Günther

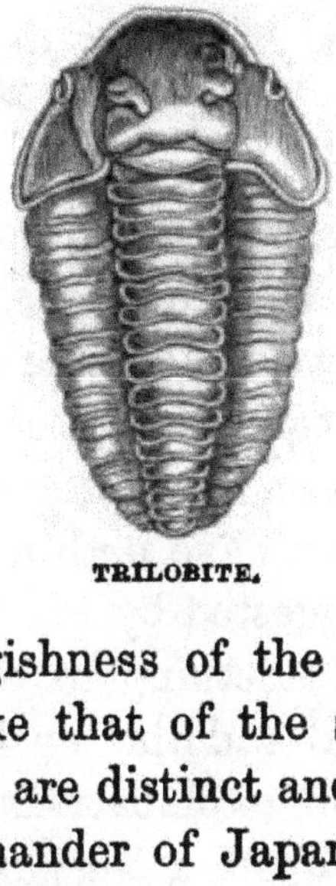

TRILOBITE.

states that the sluggishness of the common tope (*Galeus vulgaris*) is much like that of the sturgeon, and yet the bodies of its vertebræ are distinct and well ossified. Moreover, the great salamander of Japan is much more inert and sluggish than either, and yet it has a well-developed bony spine.

The author can learn nothing of the habits of the sharks *Hexanchus*, *Heptanchus*, and *Echinorhinus*, but Müller describes them as possessing a persistent *chorda dorsalis*.[2] It

1 "Principles of Biology," vol. ii. p. 203.

2 Quoted by H. Stannius in his "Handbuch der Anatomie der Wirbelthiere," Zweite Auflage, Erstes Buch, § 7, p. 17.

may be they have the habits of the tope, but other sharks are amongst the very swiftest and most active of fishes.

In the bony pike (*lepidosteus*), the rigidity of the bony scales by which it is completely enclosed must prevent any excessive flexion of the body, and yet its vertebral column presents a degree of ossification and vertebral completeness greater than that found in any other fish whatever.

Mr. Spencer supports his mechanical hypothesis by the non-segmentation of the anterior end of the skeletal axis, *i.e.* by the non-segmentation of the skull. But in fact the skull *is* segmented, and, according to the quasi-vertebral theory of the skull put forward by Professor Huxley,[1] is probably formed of a number of coalesced segments, of some of which the trabeculæ cranii and the mandibular and hyoidean arches are indications. What is perhaps most remarkable, however, is that the segmentation of the skull—its separation into the three occipital, parietal, and frontal elements—is most complete and distinct in the highest class, and this can have nothing, however remotely, to do with the cause suggested by Mr. Spencer.

Thus, then, there is something to be said in opposition to both the aggregational and the mechanical explanations of serial homology. The explanations suggested are very ingenious, yet repose upon a very small basis of fact. Not but that the process of vertebral segmentation may have been sometimes assisted by the mechanical action suggested.

It remains now to consider what are the evidences in support of the existence of an internal power, by the action of which these homological manifestations are evolved. It

[1] In his last Hunterian Course of Lectures, 1869.

is here contended that there *is* good evidence of the existence of some such special internal power, and that not only from facts of comparative anatomy, but also from those of teratology[1] and pathology. Such facts appear to show, not only that there are homological internal relations, but that they are so strong and energetic as to reassert and re-exhibit themselves in creatures which, on the Darwinian theory, are the descendants of others in which they were much less marked. They are, in fact, sometimes even more plain and distinct in animals of the highest types than in inferior forms, and, moreover, this deep-seated tendency acts even in diseased and abnormal conditions.

Mr. Darwin recognizes[2] these homological relations, and does "not doubt that they may be mastered more or less completely by Natural Selection." He does not, however, give any explanation of these phenomena other than the imposition on them of the name "laws of correlation;" and indeed he says: "The nature of the bond of correlation is frequently quite obscure." Now, it is surely more desirable to make use, if possible, of one conception than to imagine a number of, to all appearance, separate and independent "laws of correlation" between different parts of each animal.

But even some of his reasons for accepting these alleged laws hardly appear well founded. Thus Mr. Darwin, in support of the existence of such a law of concomitant variation as regards hair and teeth, brings forward the cases of Julia Pastrana[3] and a man of the Burmese Court,

1 The science of abnormal forms.

2 "Animals and Plants under Domestication," vol. ii. p. 322; and "Origin of Species," 5th edition, 1869, p. 178.

3 A remarkable woman exhibited in London a few years ago.

and adds :[1] "These cases and those of the hairless dogs forcibly call to mind the fact that the two orders of mammals, namely, the Edentata and Cetacea, which are the most abnormal in their dermal covering, are likewise the most abnormal either by deficiency or redundancy of teeth." The assertion with regard to these orders is certainly true, but it should be borne in mind at the same time that the armadillos, which are much more abnormal than are the American ant-eaters as regards their dermal covering, in their dentition are less so. On the other hand, the Cape ant-eater, or Aard-vark (Orycteropus), has teeth

THE AARD-VARK (ORYCTEROPUS).

formed on a type quite different from any existing in other mammals ; yet its hairy coat does not exhibit any such strange peculiarity. Again, those remarkable scaly ant-eaters of the Old World—the pangolins (Manis)—stand alone amongst mammals as regards their dermal covering ;

[1] "Animals and Plants under Domestication," vol. ii. p. 328.

having been classed with lizards by early naturalists on account of their clothing of scales, yet their mouth is like that of the hairy ant-eaters of the New World. The duck-billed platypus of Australia (Ornithorhynchus) is the only

THE PANGOLIN (MANIS).

mammal which has teeth formed of horn, yet its furry coat is normal and ordinary. Again, the Dugong and Manatee are dermally alike, yet extremely different as regards the structure and number of their teeth. The Porcupine also, in spite of its enormous armature of quills, is furnished

DUGONG.

with as good a supply of teeth as are the hairy members of the same family, but not with a better one; and in spite of the deficiency of teeth in the hairless dogs, no converse redundancy of teeth has, it is believed, been remarked in Angora cats and rabbits. To say the least, then, this law of correlation presents numerous and remarkable exceptions.

To return, however, to the subject of homological relations: it is surely inconceivable that indefinite variation with survival of the fittest can ever have built up these serial, bilateral, and vertical homologies, without the action of some special innate power or tendency so to build up, possessed by the organism itself in each case. By "special tendency" is meant one the laws and conditions of which are as yet unknown, but which is analogous to the innate power and tendency possessed by crystals similarly to build up certain peculiar and very definite forms.

First, with regard to comparative anatomy. The correspondence between the thoracic and pelvic limbs is notorious. Professor Gegenbaur has lately endeavoured[1] to explain this resemblance by the derivation of each limb from a primitive form of fin. This fin is supposed to have had a marginal external (radial) series of cartilages, each of which supported a series of secondary cartilages, starting from the inner (ulnar) side of the distal part of the supporting marginal piece. The root marginal piece would become the humerus or femur, as the case might be; the second marginal piece, with the piece attached to the inner side of the distal end of the root marginal piece, would together form either the radius and ulna or the tibia and fibula, and so on.

Now there may be little doubt (from *a priori* considerations) as to the special differentiation of the limb-bones of the higher Vertebrates having been evolved from anterior conditions existing in some fish-like form or other. But

[1] "Ueber das Gliedmaassenskelet der Enaliosaurier," Jenaischen Zeitschrift, Bd. v. Heft 3, Taf. xiii.

the particular view advocated by the learned Professor is open to criticism. Thus, it may be objected against his view, first, that it takes no account of the radial ossicle which becomes so enormous in the mole; secondly, that it does not explain the extra series of ossicles which are formed on the *outer* (radial or marginal) side of the paddle in the Ichthyosaurus; and thirdly, and most importantly, that even if this had been the way in which the limbs had been differentiated, it would not be at all inconsistent with the possession of an innate power of producing, and an

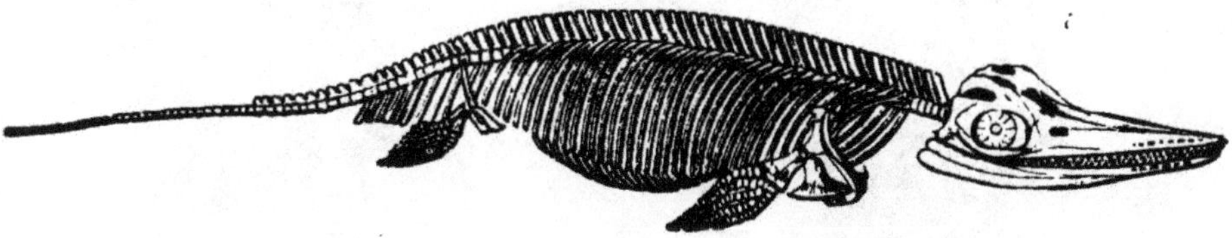

SKELETON OF AN ICHTHYOSAURUS.

innate tendency to produce, similar and symmetrical homological resemblances. It would not be so because resemblances of the kind are found to exist, which, on the Darwinian theory, must be subsequent and secondary, not primitive and ancestral. Thus we find in animals of the eft kind (certain amphibians), in which the tarsus is cartilaginous, that the carpus is cartilaginous likewise. And we shall see in cases of disease and of malformation what a tendency there is to a similar affection of homologous parts. In efts, as Professor Gegenbaur himself has pointed out,[1] there is a striking correspondence between the bones or cartilages supporting the arm, wrist, and fingers,

[1] In his work on the Carpus and Tarsus.

and those sustaining the leg, ankle, and toes, with the exception that the toes exceed the fingers in number by one.

Yet these animals are far from being the root-forms from which all the Vertebrata have diverged, as is evidenced from the degree of specialization which their structure presents. If they have descended from such primitive forms as Professor Gegenbaur imagines, then

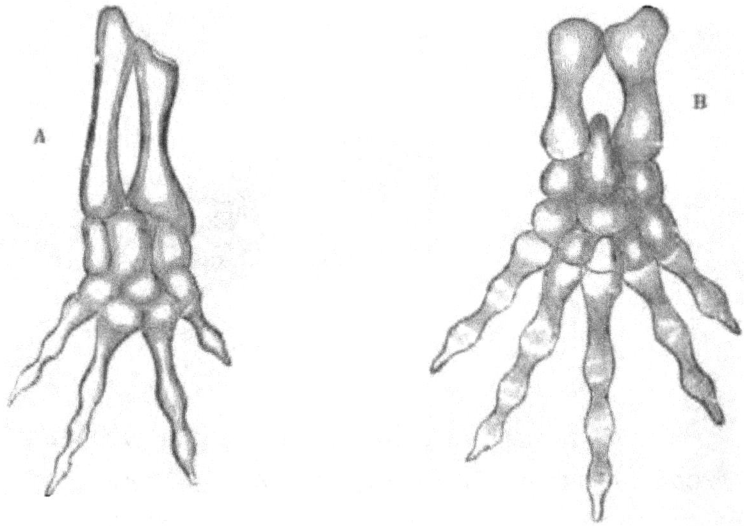

A. SKELETON OF ANTERIOR EXTREMITY OF AN EFT.
B. SKELETON OF POSTERIOR EXTREMITY OF THE SAME.

they have built up a secondary serial homology—a repetition of similar modifications—fully as remarkable as if it were primary. The Plesiosauria—those extinct marine reptiles of the Secondary period, with long necks, small heads, and paddle-like limbs—are of yet higher organization than are the efts and other Amphibia: nevertheless they present us with a similarity of structure between the fore and hind limb, which is so great as almost to be identity. But the Amphibia and Plesiosauria, though not themselves primitive vertebrate types, may be thought by some to have derived their limb-structure by direct descent from such. Tortoises, however, must be admitted to be not only highly differentiated organisms, but to be far indeed removed from primeval vertebrate structure.

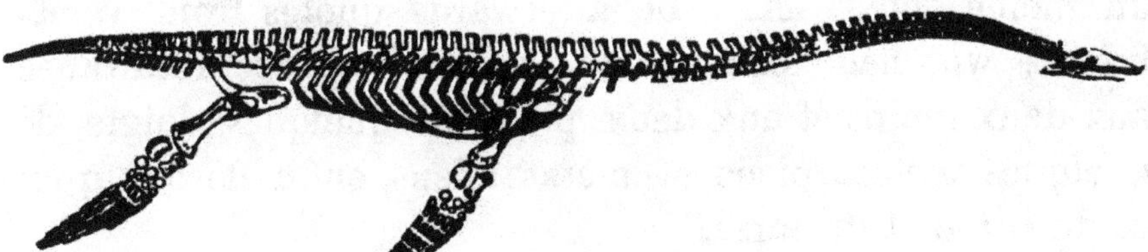

SKELETON OF A PLESIOSAURUS.

Yet certain tortoises[1] (notably *Chelydra Temminckii*) exhibit such a remarkable uniformity in fore and hind limb-structure (extending even up to the proximal ends of the humerus and femur) that it is impossible to doubt its independent development in these forms.

Again in the Potto (Perodicticus) there is an extra bone in the foot, situate in the transverse ligament enclosing the flexor tendons. It is noteworthy that in the *hand* of the same animal a serially homologous structure should also be developed.[2] In the allied form called the Slow Lemur (Nycticebus) we have certain arrangements of the muscles and tendons of the hand which reproduce in great measure those of the foot and *vice versâ*.[3] And in the Hyrax another myological resemblance appears.[4] It is,

[1] An excellent specimen displaying this resemblance is preserved in the Museum of the Royal College of Surgeons.

[2] Phil. Trans. 1867, p. 353.

[3] Proc. Zool. Soc. 1865, p. 255.

[4] Ibid. p. 351.

however, needless to multiply instances, which can easily be produced in large numbers if required.

Secondly, with regard to teratology, it is notorious that similar abnormalities are often found to co-exist in both the pelvic and thoracic limbs.

M. Isidore Geoffroy St. Hilaire remarks,[1] "L'anomalie se répète d'un membre thoracique au membre abdominal du même côté." And he afterwards quotes from Weitbrecht,[2] who had "observé dans un cas l'absence simultanée aux deux mains et aux deux pieds, de quelques doigts, de quelques metacarpiens et metatarsiens, enfin de quelques os du carpe et du tarse."

Professor Burt G. Wilder, in his paper on extra digits,[3] has recorded no less than twenty-four cases where such excess co-existed with regard to both little fingers; also one case in which the right little finger and little toe were so affected; six in which it was both the little fingers and both the little toes; and twenty-two other cases more or less the same, but in which the details were not accurately to be obtained.

Mr. Darwin cites [4] a remarkable instance of what he is inclined to regard as the development in the foot of birds of a sort of representation of the wing-feathers of the hand. He says: "In several distinct breeds of the pigeon and fowl the legs and the two outer toes are heavily feathered, so that, in the trumpeter pigeon, they appear like little wings. In the feather-legged bantam,

1 "Hist. Générale des Anomalies," t. i. p. 228. Bruxelles, 1837.

2 Nov. Comment. Petrop. t. ix. p. 269.

3 Read on June 2, 1868, before the Massachusetts Medical Society. See vol. ii. No. 3.

4 "Animals and Plants under Domestication," vol. ii. p. 322.

the 'boots,' or feathers which grow from the outside of the leg, and generally from the two outer toes, have, according to the excellent authority of Mr. Hewitt, been seen to exceed the wing-feathers in length, and in one

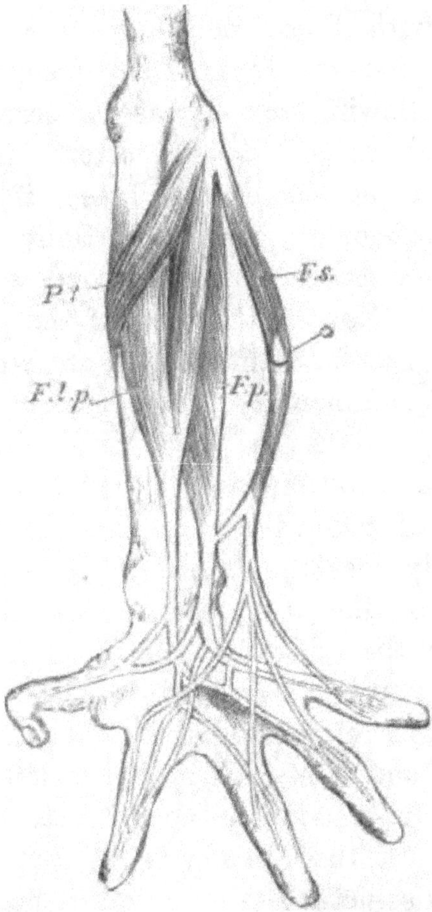

LONG FLEXOR MUSCLES AND TENDONS OF THE HAND OF NYCTICEBUS.
P.t. Pronator teres. *F.s.* Flexor sublimis digitorum. *F.p.* Flexor profundus digitorum. *F.l.p.* Flexor longus pollicis.

case were actually nine and a half inches in length! As Mr. Blyth has remarked to me, these leg-feathers resemble the primary wing-feathers, and are totally unlike the fine down which naturally grows on the legs of some birds, such as grouse and owls. Hence it may be suspected that excess of food has first given redundancy to the plumage, and then that the law of homologous variation has led to the development of feathers on the legs, in a position corresponding with those on the wing, namely, on the outside of the tarsi and toes. I am strengthened in this belief by the following curious case of correlation, which for a long time seemed to me utterly inexplicable,—namely, that in pigeons of any breed, if the legs are feathered, the two outer toes are partially connected by skin. These two outer toes correspond with our third and fourth toes. Now, in the wing of the pigeon, or any other bird, the first and fifth digits are wholly aborted; the second is rudimentary, and carries the so-called 'bastard wing;' whilst the third and fourth digits are completely united and enclosed by skin, together forming the extremity of the wing. So that in feather-footed pigeons not only does the exterior surface support a row of long feathers like wing-feathers, but the very same digits which in the wing are completely united by skin become partially united by skin in the feet; and thus, by the law of the correlated variation of homologous parts, we can understand the curious connexion of feathered legs and membrane between the outer toes."

Irregularities in the circulating system are far from uncommon, and sometimes illustrate this homological tendency. My friend and colleague Mr. George G. Gascoyen, surgeon at St. Mary's Hospital, has supplied me with two instances of symmetrical affections which have come under his observation.

In the first of these the brachial artery bifurcated almost

at its origin, the two halves re-uniting at the elbow-joint, and then dividing into the radial and ulnar arteries in the usual manner. In the second case an aberrant artery was given off from the radial side of the brachial artery, again almost at its origin. This aberrant artery anastomosed below the elbow-joint with the radial side of the radial artery. In each of these cases the right and left sides varied in precisely the same manner.

Thirdly, as to pathology. Mr. James Paget,[1] speaking of symmetrical diseases, says: "A certain morbid change of structure on one side of the body is repeated in the exactly corresponding part of the other side." He then quotes and figures a diseased lion's pelvis from the College of Surgeons Museum, and says of it: "Multiform as the pattern is in which the new bone, the product of some disease comparable with a human rheumatism, is deposited—a pattern more complex and irregular than the spots upon a map—there is not one spot or line on one side which is not represented, as exactly as it would be in a mirror, on the other. The likeness has more than daguerreotype exactness." He goes on to observe: "I need not describe many examples of such diseases. Any out-patients' room will furnish abundant instances of exact symmetry in the eruptions of eczema, lepra, and psoriasis; in the deformities of chronic rheumatism, the paralyses from lead; in the eruptions excited by iodide of potassium or copaiba. And any large museum will contain examples of equal symmetry in syphilitic ulcerations of the skull; in rheumatic and syphilitic deposits on the tibiæ and other bones; in all the effects of chronic rheumatic arthritis, whether in the bones, the ligaments, or the cartilages;

[1] "Lectures on Surgical Pathology," 1853, vol. i. p. 18.

in the fatty and earthy deposits in the coats of arteries."[1]

He also considers it to be proved that, "Next to the parts which are symmetrically placed, none are so nearly identical in composition as those which are homologous. For example, the backs of the hands and of the feet, or the palms and soles, are often not only symmetrically, but similarly, affected with psoriasis. So are the elbows and the knees; and similar portions of the thighs and the arms may be found affected with ichthyosis. Sometimes also specimens of fatty and earthy deposits in the arteries occur, in which exact similarity is shown in the plan, though not in the degree, with which the disease affects severally the humeral and femoral, the radial and peroneal, the ulnar and posterior tibial arteries."

Dr. William Budd[2] gives numerous instances of symmetry in disease, both lateral and serial. Thus, amongst others, we have one case (William Godfrey) in which the hands and feet were distorted. "The distortion of the right hand is greater than that of the left, of the right foot greater than that of the left foot." In another (Elizabeth Alford) lepra affected the extensor surfaces of the thoracic and pelvic limbs. Again, in the case of skin disease illustrated in Plate III., "The analogy between the elbows and knees is clearly expressed in the fact that these were the only parts affected with the disease."[3]

Professor Burt Wilder,[4] in his paper on "Pathological

1 "Lectures on Surgical Pathology," 1853, vol. i. p. 22.

2 See "Medico-Chirurgical Transactions," vol. xxv. (or vii. of 2nd series), 1842, p. 100, Pl. III.

3 Ibid., p. 122.

4 See *Boston Medical and Surgical Journal* for April 5, 1866, vol. lxxiv. p. 189.

Polarities," strongly supports the philosophical importance of these peculiar relations, adding arguments in favour of antero-posterior homologies, which it is here unnecessary to discuss, enough having been said, it is believed, to thoroughly demonstrate the existence of those deep internal relations which are named lateral and serial homologies.

What explanation can be offered of these phenomena? To say that they exhibit a "nutritional relation" brought about by a "balancing of forces" is no explanation of the fact. The changes are, *of course,* brought about by a "nutritional" process, and the symmetry is undoubtedly the result of a "balance of forces," but to say so is a truism. The question is, what is the cause of this "nutritional balancing"? It is here contended that this "balancing" must be due to an internal cause which at present science is utterly incompetent to explain. It is an internal property possessed by each living organic whole as well as by each non-living crystalline mass, and that there is such internal power or tendency, which may be termed a "polarity," seems to be demonstrated by the instances above given, which can easily be multiplied indefinitely. Mr. H Spencer[1] (speaking of the reproduction, by budding, of a Begònia-leaf) recognizes a power of the kind. He says: "We have therefore no alternative but to say, that the living particles composing one of these fragments, have an innate tendency to arrange themselves into the shape of the organism to which they belong. We must infer that a plant or animal of any species, is made up of special units, in all of which there dwells the intrinsic aptitude to aggregate into the form of that species: just as in the

[1] "Principles of Biology," vol. i p. 180.

atoms of a salt, there dwells the intrinsic aptitude to crystallize in a particular way. It seems difficult to conceive that this can be so; but we see it *is* so." . . . . "For this property there is no fit term. If we accept the word polarity, as a name for the force by which inorganic units are aggregated into a form peculiar to them; we may apply this word to the analogous force displayed by organic units."[1]

Dr. Jeffries Wyman,[2] in his paper on the "Symmetry and Homology of Limbs," has a distinct chapter on the "Analogy between Symmetry and Polarity," illustrating it by the effects of magnets on "particles in a polar condition."

Mr. J. J. Murphy, after noticing[3] the power which crystals have to repair injuries inflicted on them and the modifications they undergo through the influence of the medium in which they may be formed, goes on to say:[4] "It needs no proof that in the case of spheres and crystals the forms and the structures are the effect, and not the cause, of the formative principles. Attraction, whether gravitative or

[1] Mr. Spencer, in an appendix to the first volume of the "Principles of Biology," has explained more fully what he means by the word "innate." He attributes "innate tendencies" entirely to the inherited structures of the "physiological units" produced in them by the total forces of the organisms through which they have been transmitted during the serial evolution of such organisms. This, however, is a mere moving of the difficulty a step backwards; and he by no means gets rid of (what never can be got rid of) the conception of innate power—of force proceeding from the organism as distinguished from force proceeding towards the organism. At the very least, Mr. Spencer must attribute to his ultimate units an innate power of inheriting effects of ancestral modifications, and this is, in principle, a power fully as mysterious as any for which the author of this book here contends.

[2] See the "Proceedings of the Boston Society of Natural History," vol. xi. June 5, 1867.

[3] "Habit and Intelligence," vol. i. p. 75.

[4] Ibid. p. 112.

capillary, produces the spherical form; the spherical form does not produce attraction. And crystalline polarities produce crystalline structure and form; crystalline structure and form do not produce crystalline polarities. The same is not quite so evident of organic forms, but it is equally true of them also." . . . . . "It is not conceivable that the microscope should reveal peculiarities of structure corresponding to peculiarities of habitual tendency in the embryo, which at its first formation has no structure whatever;"[1] and he adds that "there is something quite inscrutable and mysterious" in the formation of a new individual from the germinal matter of the embryo. In another place[2] he says: "We know that in crystals, notwithstanding the variability of form within the limits of the same species, there are definite and very peculiar formative laws, which cannot possibly depend on anything like organic functions, because crystals have no such functions; and it ought not to surprise us if there are similar formative or morphological laws among organisms, which, like the formative laws of crystallization, cannot be referred to any relation of form or structure to function. Especially, I think, is this true of the lowest organisms, many of which show great beauty of form, of a kind that appears to be altogether due to symmetry of growth; as the beautiful star-like rayed forms of the *acanthometræ*, which are low animal organisms not very different from the Foraminifera." Their "definiteness of form does not appear to be accompanied by any corresponding differentiation of function between different parts; and, so far as I can see, the beautiful regularity and symmetry of their radiated forms are altogether due to unknown laws

1 "Habit and Intelligence," vol. i. p. 170. 2 Ibid. p. 229.

of symmetry of growth, just like the equally beautiful and somewhat similar forms of the compound six-rayed, star-shaped crystals of snow."

Altogether, then, it appears that each organism has an innate tendency to develop in a symmetrical manner, and that this tendency is controlled and subordinated by the action of external conditions, and not that this symmetry is superinduced only *ab externo.* In fact, that each organism has its own internal and special laws of growth and development.

If, then, it is still necessary to conceive an internal law or "substantial form," moulding each organic being and directing its development as a crystal is built up, only in an indefinitely more complex manner, it is congruous to imagine the existence of some internal law accounting at the same time for specific divergence as well as for specific identity.

A principle regulating the successive evolution of different organic forms is not one whit more mysterious than is the mysterious power by which a particle of structureless sarcode develops successively into an egg, a grub, a chrysalis, a butterfly, all the conditions, cosmical, physical, chemical, and vital, being supplied which are the requisite accompaniments to determine such evolution.

CHAPTER IX.

EVOLUTION AND ETHICS.

The origin of morals an inquiry not foreign to the subject of this book.—Modern utilitarian view as to that origin.—Mr. Darwin's speculation as to the origin of the abhorrence of incest.—Cause assigned by him insufficient.—Care of the aged and infirm opposed by "Natural Selection;" also self-abnegation and asceticism.—Distinctness of the ideas "right" and "useful."—Mr. John Stuart Mill.—Insufficiency of "Natural Selection" to account for the origin of the distinction between duty and profit.—Distinction of moral acts into "material" and "formal."—No ground for believing that formal morality exists in brutes.—Evidence that it does exist in savages.—Facility with which savages may be misunderstood.—Objections as to diversity of customs.—Mr. Hutton's review of Mr. Herbert Spencer.—Anticipatory character of morals.—Sir John Lubbock's explanation.—Summary and conclusion.

ANY inquiry into the origin of the notion of "morality"—the conception of "right"—may, perhaps, be considered as somewhat remote from the question of the Genesis of Species; the more so since Mr. Darwin at one time disclaimed any pretension to explain the origin of the higher psychical phenomena of man. His disciples, however, were never equally reticent, and indeed he himself is now not only about to produce a work[1] on man (in which this

[1] The work referred to is the "Descent of Man," which has appeared since the publication of the first edition of this book. Mr. Darwin has therein justified the author's anticipations, and has asserted in the strongest terms the identity in kind of the mental faculties of men and brutes, and has thoroughly confounded our moral judgments with the gregarious instincts of beasts.

question must be considered), but he has distinctly announced the extension of the application of his theory to the very phenomena in question. He says:[1] "In the distant future I see open fields for far more important researches. Psychology will be based on a new foundation, that of the necessary acquirement of each mental power and capacity by gradation. Light will be thrown on the origin of man and his history." It may not be amiss then to glance at the question, so much disputed, concerning the origin of ethical conceptions and its bearing on the theory of "Natural Selection."[2]

The followers of Mr. John Stuart Mill, of Mr. Herbert Spencer, and apparently, also, of Mr. Darwin, assert that in spite of the great *present* difference between the ideas "useful" and "right," they are, nevertheless, one as to their *origin*, and that that origin consisted ultimately of pleasurable and painful sensations.

They say that "Natural Selection" has evolved moral conceptions from perceptions of what was useful, *i.e.* pleasurable, by having through long ages preserved a

[1] "Origin of Species," 5th edition, 1869, p. 577.

[2] Since the first edition of this work appeared, Mr. Darwin has fully explained his views as to morality, and has identified the "moral sense" with "stronger and more persistent instincts." No argument, however, has been employed, and no facts adduced, which even tend to answer the objections here urged. Mr. Darwin seems not adequately to recognize the points which require to be met, and while he brings forward instances bearing on the acquisition of *materially* moral habits (which are utterly trivial and beside the point), he literally does not say one word in explanation of the genesis of *formal* morality (with which we are alone concerned), nor even pretend to show how the gregarious instinct of a herd becomes metamorphosed into a common moral judgment. While therefore the author has the satisfaction of feeling that he has not misrepresented Mr. Darwin, he also feels that he has nothing whatever substantial to retract, or even to modify, in his former assertions and arguments.

predominating number of those individuals who have had a natural and spontaneous liking for practices and habits of mind useful to the race, and that the same power has destroyed a predominating number of those individuals who possessed a marked tendency to contrary practices. The descendants of individuals so preserved have, they say, come to inherit such a liking and such useful habits of mind, and at last (finding this inherited tendency thus existing in themselves, distinct from their tendency to conscious self-gratification) have become apt to regard it as fundamentally distinct, *innate*, and independent of all experience. In fact, according to this school, the idea of "right" is only the result of the gradual accretion of useful predilections which, from time to time, arose in a series of ancestors naturally selected. In this way, "morality" is, as it were, the congealed past experience of the race, and "virtue" becomes no more than a sort of "retrieving," which the thus improved human animal practises by a perfected and inherited habit, regardless of self-gratification, just as the brute animal has acquired the habit of seeking prey and bringing it to his master, instead of devouring it himself.

Though Mr. Darwin has not as yet expressly advocated this view, yet some remarks made by him appear to show his disposition to sympathise with it. Thus, in his work on "Animals and Plants under Domestication,"[1] he asserts that "the savages of Australia and South America hold the crime of incest in abhorrence;" but he considers that this abhorrence has probably arisen through "Natural Selection," the ill effects of close interbreeding having caused the less numerous and less healthy offspring of

[1] Vol. ii. p. 122.

incestuous unions to disappear by degrees, in favour of the descendants (greater both in number and strength) of individuals who naturally, from some cause or other, as he suggests, preferred to mate with strangers rather than with close blood-relations; this preference being transmitted and becoming thus instinctive, or habitual, in remote descendants.

But on Mr. Darwin's own ground, it may be objected that this notion fails to account for "abhorrence," and "moral reprobation;" for, as no stream can rise higher than its source, the original "slight feeling" which was *useful* would have been perpetuated, but would never have been augmented beyond the degree requisite to ensure this beneficial preference, and therefore would not certainly have become magnified into "abhorrence." It will not do to assume that the union of males and females, each possessing the required "slight feeling," must give rise to offspring with an intensified feeling of the same kind; for, apart from reversion, Mr. Darwin has called attention to the unexpected modifications which sometimes result from the union of *similarly* constituted parents. Thus, for example, he tells us:[1] "If two top-knotted canaries are matched, the young, instead of having very fine top-knots, are generally bald." From examples of this kind, it is fair, on Darwinian principles, to infer that the union of parents who possessed a similar inherited aversion might result in phenomena quite other than the augmentation of such aversion, even if the two aversions should be altogether of the same kind; while, very probably, they might be so different in their nature as to tend to neutralize each other. Besides, the union of parents so similarly emotional

[1] "Animals and Plants under Domestication," vol. i. p. 295.

would be rare indeed amongst savages, where marriages would be owing to almost anything rather than to congeniality of mind between the spouses. Mr. Wallace tells us,[1] that they choose their wives for "rude health and physical beauty," and this is just what might be naturally supposed. Again, we must bear in mind the necessity there is that *many individuals* should be similarly and simultaneously affected with this aversion from consanguineous unions; as we have seen, in the second chapter, how infallibly variations presented by only a few individuals tend to be eliminated by mere force of numbers. Mr. Darwin indeed would throw back this aversion, if possible, to a pre-human period; since he speculates as to whether the gorillas or orang-utans, in effecting their matrimonial relations, show any tendency to respect the prohibited degrees of affinity.[2] No tittle of evidence, however, has yet been adduced pointing in this direction; though, surely, if it were of such importance and efficiency as to result (through the aid of "Natural Selection" alone) in that "abhorrence" before spoken of, we might expect to be able to detect unmistakeable evidence of its incipient stages. On the contrary, as regards the ordinary apes (for with regard to the highest there is no evidence of the kind) as we see them in confinement, it would be difficult to name any animals less restricted, by even a generic bar, in the gratification of the sexual instinct. And although the conditions under which they have been observed are abnormal, yet these are hardly the animals to present us, in a state of nature, with an extraordinary and exceptional sensitiveness in such matters.

1 "Natural Selection," p. 350.

2 "Animals and Plants under Domestication," vol. ii.

To take an altogether different case. Care of, and tenderness towards, the aged and infirm are actions on all hands admitted to be "right;" but it is difficult to see how such actions could ever have been so useful to a community as to have been seized on and developed by the exclusive action of the law of the "survival of the fittest." On the contrary, it seems probable that on strict utilitarian principles the rigid political economy of Tierra del Fuego would have been eminently favoured and diffused by the impartial action of "Natural Selection" alone. By the rigid political economy referred to, is meant that destruction and utilization of "useless mouths" which Mr. Darwin himself describes in his highly interesting "Journal of Researches."[1] He says: "It is certainly true, that when pressed in winter by hunger, they kill and devour their old women before they kill their dogs. The boy being asked why they did this, answered, 'Doggies catch otters, old women no.' They often run away into the mountains, but they are pursued by the men and brought back to the slaughter-house at their own firesides." Mr. Edward Bartlett, who has recently returned from the Amazons, reports that at one Indian village, where the cholera made its appearance, the whole population immediately dispersed into the woods, leaving the sick to perish uncared for and alone. Now, had the Indians remained, undoubtedly far more would have died; as doubtless, in Tierra del Fuego, the destruction of the comparatively useless old women has often been the means of preserving the healthy and reproductive young. Such acts surely must be greatly favoured by the stern and unrelenting action of exclusive "Natural Selection."

[1] See 2nd edition, vol. i. p. 214.

In the same way, that admiration which all feel for acts of self-denial done for the good of others, and tending even towards the destruction of the actor, could hardly be accounted for on Darwinian principles alone; for self-immolators must but rarely leave direct descendants, while the community they benefit must by their destruction tend, so far, to morally deteriorate. But devotion to others of the same community is by no means *all* that has to be accounted for. Devotion to the whole human race, and devotion to God—in the form of asceticism—have been and are very generally recognized as "good;" and the author contends that it is simply impossible to conceive that such ideas and sanctions should have been developed by "Natural Selection" alone, from only that degree of unselfishness necessary for the preservation of brutally barbarous communities in the struggle for life. That degree of unselfishness once attained, further improvement would be checked by the mutual opposition of diverging moral tendencies and spontaneous variations in all directions. Added to which, we have the principle of reversion and atavism, tending powerfully to restore and reproduce that more degraded anterior condition whence the later and better state painfully emerged.

Very few, however, dispute the complete distinctness, here and now, of the ideas of "duty" and "interest," whatever may have been the origin of those ideas. No one pretends that ingratitude may, in any past abyss of time, have been a virtue, or that it may be such now in Arcturus or the Pleiades. Indeed, a certain eminent writer of the utilitarian school of ethics has amusingly and instructively shown how radically distinct even in his own mind are the two ideas which he nevertheless endeavours to identify.

Mr. John Stuart Mill, in his examination of "Sir William Hamilton's Philosophy," says:[1] "If I am informed that the world is ruled by a being whose attributes are infinite, but what they are we cannot learn, nor what the principles of his government, except that 'the highest human morality which we are capable of conceiving' does not sanction them; convince me of it, and I will bear my fate as I may. But when I am told that I must believe this, and at the same time call this being by the names which express and affirm the highest human morality, I say in plain terms that I will not. Whatever power such a being may have over me, there is one thing which he shall not do: he shall not compel me to worship him. I will call no being good, who is not what I mean when I apply that epithet to my fellow-creatures; and if such a being can sentence me to hell for not so calling him, to hell I will go."

This is unquestionably an admirable sentiment on the part of Mr. Mill (with which every absolute moralist will agree), but it contains a complete refutation of his own position, and is a capital instance[2] of the vigorous life of moral intuition in one who professes to have eliminated any fundamental distinction between the "right" and the "expedient." For if an action is morally good, and to be done merely in proportion to the amount of pleasure it secures, and morally bad and to be avoided as tending to misery, and if it could be *proved* that by calling God

[1] Page 103.

[2] I have not the merit of detecting this inconsistency; it was pointed out to me by my friend the Rev. W. W. Roberts. It is a good example of the refutations which Mr. Mill, every now and then, gives himself—much the kind of thing which Professor Masson calls "a trap-door opened by Mr. Mill himself in the floor of his own philosophy."—*Recent British Philosophy*, p. 339.

good—whether He is so or not, in our sense of the term,—we could secure a maximum of pleasure, and by refusing to do so we should incur endless torment, clearly, on utilitarian principles, the flattery would be good.

Mr. Mill, of course, must also mean that, in the matter in question, all men would do well to act with him. Therefore, he must mean that it would be well for all to accept (on the hypothesis above given) infinite and final misery for all as the result of the pursuit of happiness as the only end.

It must be recollected that in consenting to worship this unholy God, Mr. Mill is not asked to do harm to his neighbour, so that his refusal reposes simply on his perception of the immorality of the requisition.

It is also noteworthy that an omnipotent Deity is supposed incapable of altering Mr. Mill's mind and moral perceptions!

Mr. Mill's decision is right, but it is difficult indeed to see how, without the recognition of an "absolute morality," he can justify so utter and final an abandonment of all utility in favour of a clear moral perception.

These two ideas, the "right" and the "useful," being so distinct here and now, a greater difficulty meets us with regard to their origin from some common source, than met us when considering the difficulties as to the incipient stages of certain bodily structures. For the distinction between the "right" and the "useful" is so fundamental and essential, that not only does the idea of benefit not enter into the idea of duty, but we see that the very fact of an act *not* being beneficial to us makes it the more praiseworthy, while gain tends to diminish the merit of an action. Yet this idea, "right," thus excluding, as it does, all reference to utility or pleasure, has nevertheless to be constructed and evolved from utility and pleasure, and ultimately from pleasurable sensations, if we are to accept pure Darwinianism: if we are to accept, that is, the evolution of man's psychical nature and highest powers, by the exclusive action of "Natural Selection," from such faculties as are possessed by brutes; in other words, if we are to believe that the conceptions of the highest human morality arose through minute and fortuitous variations of brutal desires and appetites in all conceivable directions.

It is here contended, on the other hand, that no conservation of any such variations could ever have given rise to the faintest beginning of any such moral perceptions; that by "Natural Selection" alone the maxim *fiat justitia, ruat cœlum*, could not have been excogitated, still less have found a widespread acceptance; that it is impotent to suggest even an approach towards an explanation of the *first beginning* of the idea of "right." It need hardly be remarked that acts may be distinguished not only as pleasurable, useful, or beautiful, but also as good, in two different senses: (1) *materially* moral acts, and (2) acts which are *formally* moral. The first are acts good in themselves, *as acts*, apart from any intention of the agent which may or may not have been directed towards "right." The second are acts which are good not only in themselves, as acts, but also in the deliberate *intention* of the agent who recognizes his actions as being "right." Thus acts may be *materially* moral or immoral, in a very high degree, without being in the least *formally* so. For example, a person may tend and minister to a sick man with scrupulous care and exactness, having in view all the time nothing but the future reception of a good legacy. Another may, in the dark, shoot his own father, taking him to be an assassin, and so commit what is *materially* an act of parricide, though *formally* it is only an act of self-defence of more or less culpable rashness. A woman may innocently, because ignorantly, marry a married man, and so commit a *material* act of adultery. She may discover the facts, and persist, and so make her act *formal* also.

Actions of brutes, such as those of the bee, the ant, or the beaver, however materially good as regards their relation to the community to which such animals belong, are absolutely destitute of the most incipient degree of real, *i.e.* formal "goodness," because unaccompanied by mental acts of conscious will directed towards the fulfilment of duty. Apology is due for thus stating so elementary a distinction,[1] but the statement is not superfluous, for confusion of thought, resulting from confounding together these very distinct things, is unfortunately far from uncommon.

Thus, some Darwinians assert that the germs of morality exist in brutes, and we have seen that Mr. Darwin himself speculates on the subject as regards the highest apes. It may safely be affirmed, however, that there is no trace in brutes of any actions simulating morality which are not explicable by the fear of punishment, by the hope of pleasure, or by personal affection. No sign of moral reprobation is given by any brute, and yet had such existed in germ through Darwinian abysses of past time, some evidence of its existence must surely have been rendered perceptible through "survival of the fittest" in other forms

[1] Since the publication of Mr. Darwin's "Descent of Man," it has become evident that this apology was an unnecessary one.

besides man, if that "survival" has alone and exclusively produced it in him.

Abundant examples may indeed be brought forward of useful acts which simulate morality, such as parental care of the young, &c. But did the most undeviating habits guide all brutes in such matters, were even aged and infirm members of a community of insects or birds carefully tended by young which benefited by their experience, such acts would not indicate even the faintest rudiment of real, *i.e.* formal, morality. "Natural Selection" would, of course, often lead to the prevalence of acts beneficial to a community, and to acts *materially* good; but unless they can be shown to be *formally* so, they are not in the least to the point, they do not offer any explanation of the origin of an altogether new and fundamentally different motive and conception.

It is interesting, on the other hand, to note Mr. Darwin's statement as to the existence of a distinct moral feeling even in perhaps the very lowest and most degraded of all the human races known to us. Thus, in the same "Journal of Researches"[1] before quoted, bearing witness to the existence of moral reprobation on the part of the Fuegians, he says: "The nearest approach to religious feeling which I heard of was shown by York Minster (a Fuegian so named), who, when Mr. Bynoe shot some very young ducklings as specimens, declared in the most solemn manner, 'Oh, Mr. Bynoe, much rain, snow, blow much.' This was evidently a retributive punishment for wasting human food."

Mr. Wallace gives valuable testimony, in his "Malay Archipelago," to the existence of a very distinct, and even

[1] Vol. i. p. 215.

highly developed moral sense in the natives with whom he became acquainted. In one case,[1] a Papuan who had been paid in advance for bird-skins, and who had not been able to fulfil his contract before Mr. Wallace was on the point of starting, "came running down after us holding up a bird, and saying with great satisfaction, 'Now I owe you nothing!'" And this though he could have withheld payment with complete impunity.

Mr. Wallace's observations and opinions on this head seem hardly to meet with due appreciation in Sir John Lubbock's recent work on Primitive Man.[2] But considering the acute powers of observation and the industry of Mr. Wallace, and especially considering the years he passed in familar and uninterrupted intercourse with natives, his opinion and testimony should surely carry with it great weight. He has informed the author that he found a strongly marked and widely diffused modesty, in sexual matters, amongst all the tribes with which he came in contact. In the same way Mr. Bonwick, in his work on the Tasmanians, testifies to the modesty exhibited by the naked females of that race, who by the decorum of their postures gave evidence of the possession in germ of what under circumstances would become the highest chastity and refinement.

Hasty and incomplete observations and inductions are prejudicial enough to physical science, but when their effect is to degrade untruthfully our common humanity, there is an additional motive to regret them. A hurried visit to a tribe, whose language, traditions, and customs are unknown,

1 "Malay Archipelago," vol. ii. p. 365.

2 "The Origin of Civilization and the Primitive Condition of Man," p. 261. Longmans, 1870.

is sometimes deemed sufficient for "smart" remarks as to "ape characters," &c., which are as untrue as irrelevant. It should not be forgotten how extremely difficult it is to enter into the ideas and feelings of an alien race. If in the nineteenth century a French theatrical audience can witness with acquiescent approval, as a type of English manners and ideas, the representation of a marquis who sells his wife at Smithfield, &c. &c., it is surely no wonder if the ideas of a tribe of newly visited savages should be more or less misunderstood. To enter into such ideas requires long and familiar intimacy, like that experienced by the explorer of the Malay Archipelago. From him and others, we have abundant evidence that moral ideas exist, at least in germ, in savage races of men, while they sometimes attain even a highly developed state. No amount of evidence as to acts of moral depravity is to the point, as the object here aimed at is to establish that moral intuitions *exist* in savages, not that their actions are good.[1]

Objections, however, are sometimes drawn from the different notions, as to the moral value of certain acts, entertained by men of various countries or of different epochs; also from the difficulty of knowing what particular actions

[1] As to the fundamental and essential similarity between men of the most diverse races, Mr. Darwin's recent work on the "Descent of Man," vol. i. pp. 34 and 232, may be quoted with advantage. He there tells us: "The Fuegians rank amongst the lowest barbarians; but I was continually struck with surprise how closely the three natives on board H.M.S. 'Beagle,' who had lived some years in England and could talk a little English, resembled us in disposition and in most of our mental faculties." Again: "The American aborigines, Negroes and Europeans differ as much from each other in mind as any three races that can be named; yet I was incessantly struck, whilst living with the Fuegians on board the 'Beagle,' with the many little traits of character showing how similar their minds were to ours; and so it was with a full-blooded negro with whom I happened once to be intimate."

in certain cases are the right ones, and from the effects which prejudice, interest, passion, habit, or even, indirectly, physical conditions, may have upon our moral perceptions. Thus Sir John Lubbock speaks[1] of certain Feejeeans, who, according to the testimony of Mr. Hunt,[2] have the custom of piously choking their parents under certain circumstances, in order to insure their happiness in a future life. Should any one take such facts as telling *against* the belief in an absolute morality, he would show a complete misapprehension of the point in dispute; for such facts tell in *favour* of it.

Were it asserted that man possesses a distinct innate power and faculty of infallibly applying the moral rule in each particular case, the illustration would be to the point. But all that need be contended for is that the intellect can perceive not only truth, but also a quality of "higher" which ought to be followed, and of "lower" which ought to be avoided when two lines of conduct are presented to the will for choice, the intellect so acting being the conscience.

This has been well put by Mr. James Martineau in his excellent essay on Whewell's Morality. He says:[3] "If moral good were a quality resident in each action, as whiteness in snow, or sweetness in fruits; and if the moral faculty was our appointed instrument for detecting its presence; many consequences would ensue which are at variance with fact. The wide range of differences observable in the ethical judgments of men would not exist; and even if they did, could no more be reduced and modified by discussion than constitutional differences of

1 "Primitive Man," p. 248.

2 "Fiji and the Fijians," vol. i. p. 183.

3 "Essays," Second Series, vol. ii. p. 13.

hearing or of vision. And, as the quality of moral good either must or must not exist in every important operation of the will, we should discern its presence or absence separately in each; and even though we never had the conception of more than one insulated action we should be able to pronounce upon its character. This, however, we have plainly no power to do. Every moral judgment is relative, and involves a comparison of two terms. When we praise what *has been* done, it is with the coexistent conception of something *else* that *might have been* done; and when we resolve on a course as right, it is to the exclusion of some other that is wrong. This fact, that every ethical decision is in truth a *preference*, an election of one act as higher than another, appears of fundamental importance in the analysis of the moral sentiments."

From this point of view it is plain how trifling are arguments drawn from the acts of a savage, since an action highly immoral in us might be one exceedingly virtuous in him—being the highest presented to his choice in his degraded intellectual condition and peculiar circumstances.

It need only be contended, then, that there *is* a perception of "right" incapable of further analysis; not that there is any infallible internal guide as to all the complex actions which present themselves for choice. The *principle* is given in our nature, the *application* of the principle is the result of a thousand educational influences.

It is no marvel then that in complex "cases of conscience" it is sometimes a matter of exceeding difficulty to determine which of two courses of action is the less objectionable. This no more invalidates the truth of moral principles than does the difficulty of a mathematical problem cast doubt on mathematical principles.

Habit, education, and intellectual gifts facilitate the correct application of both.

Again, if our moral insight is intensified or blunted by our habitual wishes or, indirectly, by our physical condition, the same may be said of our perception of the true relations of physical facts one to another. An eager wish for marriage has led many a man to exaggerate the powers of a limited income, and a fit of dyspepsia has given an unreasonably gloomy aspect to more than one balance-sheet.

Considering that moral intuitions have to do with *insensible* matters, they cannot be expected to be more clear than the perception of physical facts. And if the latter perceptions may be influenced by volition, desire, or health, our moral views may also be expected to be so influenced, and this in a higher degree because they so often run counter to our desires. A bottle or two of wine may make a sensible object appear double; what wonder, then, if our moral perceptions are sometimes warped and distorted by such powerful agencies as an evil education or an habitual absence of self-restraint? In neither case does occasional distortion invalidate the accuracy of normal and habitual perception.

The distinctness here and now of the ideas of "right" and "useful" is however, as before said, fully conceded by Mr. Herbert Spencer, although he contends that these conceptions are one in root and origin.

His utilitarian Genesis of Morals, however, has been recently combated by Mr. Richard Holt Hutton in a paper which appeared in *Macmillan's Magazine.*[1]

This writer objects an *argumentum ad hominem*, applying

[1] See No. 117, July 1869, p. 272.

to morals the same argument that has been applied in this work to our sense of musical harmony, and by Mr. Wallace to the vocal organs of man.

Mr. Herbert Spencer's notions on the subject are thus expressed by himself: "To make my position fully understood, it seems needful to add that, corresponding to the fundamental propositions of a developed moral science, there have been, and still are developing in the race certain fundamental moral intuitions; and that, though these moral intuitions are the result of accumulated experiences of utility gradually organized and inherited, they have come to be quite independent of conscious experience. Just in the same way that I believe the intuition of space possessed by any living individual to have arisen from organized and consolidated experiences of all antecedent individuals, who bequeathed to him their slowly-developed nervous organizations; just as I believe that this intuition, requiring only to be made definite and complete by personal experiences, has practically become a form of thought quite independent of experience;—so do I believe that the experiences of utility, organized and consolidated through all past generations of the human race, have been producing corresponding nervous modifications which, by continued transmissions of accumulation, have become in us certain faculties of moral intuition, active emotions responding to right and wrong conduct, which have no apparent basis in the individual experiences of utility. I also hold that, just as the space intuition responds to the exact demonstrations of geometry, and has its rough conclusions interpreted and verified by them, so will moral intuitions respond to the demonstrations of moral science, and will have their rough conclusions interpreted and verified by them."[1]

Against this view of Mr. Herbert Spencer, Mr. Hutton objects—"1. That even as regards Mr. Spencer's illustration from geometrical intuitions, his process would be totally inadequate, since you could not deduce the necessary space intuition of which he speaks from any possible accumulations of familiarity with space relations. . . . We cannot *inherit* more than our fathers *had*: no amount of

[1] Mr. H. Spencer has published in the *Fortnightly Review* for April 1871, a paper on "Morals and Moral Sentiments," in reply to Mr. Hutton, wherein he complains that the last-named writer has misrepresented him, and says: "Mr. Hutton has so used the word 'utility,' and so interpreted it on my behalf, as to make me appear to mean that moral sentiment is formed out of *conscious generalizations* respecting what is beneficial and what detrimental." Mr. Spencer then goes on to say: "The experiences of utility I refer to are those which become registered, not as distinctly recognized connexions between certain kinds of acts and certain kinds of remote results, but those which become registered in the shape of associations between groups of feelings that have often recurred together, though the relation between them has not been consciously generalized." Mr. Spencer then gives some examples of emotions unconsciously resulting from previous associated sensations. The author of this book can say that he did not understand Mr. Hutton to have laid the stress, which Mr. Spencer imagines he has, upon the fact that the experiences in question were *reasoned-out, consciously* accumulated, and generalized. If Mr. Spencer will say his meaning is that the universe being governed by Infinite Goodness, utility and virtue ultimately coincide, and that experiences of utility and sympathetic feelings are consequently the occasions of the full development in us of moral perceptions—then it must be owned he has been strangely misunderstood and misrepresented. But if the moral perceptions are, in their ultimate analysis, mere inherited utilitarian experiences—the consciousness or unconsciousness of the generalizations is a matter of comparatively no importance whatever. It may be here added that Mr. Spencer's illustrations seem to tell *against* his cause. As in the cases mentioned, the intensity of emotion felt will be increased by recalling to consciousness the sense associations on which it is based, while with moral perceptions it is directly the reverse, if these are based, as Mr. Spencer asserts them to be, on unconscious utilitarian generalizations.

experience of facts, however universal, can give rise to that particular characteristic of intuitions and *a priori* ideas, which compels us to deny the possibility that in any other world, however otherwise different, our experience (as to space relations) could be otherwise."

"2. That the case of moral intuitions is very much stronger."

"3. That if Mr. Spencer's theory accounts for anything, it accounts not for the deepening of a sense of utility and inutility into right and wrong, but for the drying up of the sense of utility and inutility into mere inherent tendencies, which would exercise over us not *more* authority but *less*, than a rational sense of utilitarian issues."

"4. That Mr. Spencer's theory could not account for the intuitional sacredness now attached to *individual* moral rules and principles, without accounting *a fortiori* for the general claim of the greatest happiness principle over us as the final moral intuition—which is conspicuously contrary to the fact, as not even the utilitarians themselves plead any instinctive or intuitive sanction for their great principle."

"5. That there is no trace of positive evidence of any single instance of the transformation of a utilitarian rule of right into an intuition, since we find no utilitarian principle of the most ancient times which is now an accepted moral intuition, nor any moral intuition, however sacred, which has not been promulgated thousands of years ago, and which has not constantly had to stop the tide of utilitarian *objections* to its authority—and this age after age, in our own day quite as much as in days gone by. . . . . Surely, if anything is remarkable in the history of morality, it is the *anticipatory* character, if I may use the expression, of moral principles—the intensity and absoluteness with which they are laid down ages before the world has approximated to the ideal thus asserted."

Sir John Lubbock, in his work on Primitive Man before referred to, abandons Mr. Spencer's explanation of the genesis of morals while referring to Mr. Hutton's criticisms on the subject. Sir John proposes to substitute "deference to authority" instead of "sense of interest" as the origin of our conception of "duty," saying that what has been found to be beneficial has been traditionally inculcated on the young, and thus has become to be dissociated from "interest" in the mind, though the inculcation itself originally sprung from that source. This, however, when analysed, turns out to be a distinction without a difference. It is nothing but utilitarianism, pure and simple, after all. For it can never be intended that authority is obeyed because of an intuition that it *should be deferred to,* since that would be to admit the very principle of absolute morality which Sir John combats. It must be meant, then, that authority is obeyed through fear of the consequences of disobedience, or through pleasure felt in obeying the authority which commands. In the latter case we have "pleasure" as the end, and no rudiment of the conception "duty." In the former we have fear of punishment, which appeals directly to the sense of "utility to the individual," and no amount of such a sense will produce the least germ of "ought," which is a conception different *in kind,* and in which the notion of "punishment" has no place. Thus, Sir John Lubbock's explanation only concerns a *mode* in which the sense of "duty" may be stimulated or appealed to, and makes no approximation to an explanation of its origin.

Could the views of Mr. Herbert Spencer, of Mr. Mill, or of Mr. Darwin on this subject be maintained, or should they come to be generally accepted, the consequences would be disastrous indeed! Were it really the case that virtue was a *mere kind of "retrieving,"* then certainly we should have to view with apprehension the spread of intellectual cultivation, which would lead the human "retrievers" to regard from a new point of view their fetching and carrying. We should be logically compelled to acquiesce in the vociferations of some continental utilitarians, who would banish altogether the senseless words "duty" and "merit;" and then, one important influence which has aided human progress being withdrawn, we should be reduced to hope that in this case the maxim *cessante causa cessat ipse effectus* might through some incalculable accident fail to apply.

It is true that Mr. Spencer tries to erect a safeguard against such moral disruption, by asserting that for every immoral act, word, or thought, each man during this life receives minute and exact retribution, and that thus a regard for individual self-interest will effectually prevent any moral catastrophe. But by what means will he enforce the acceptance of a dogma which is not only incapable of proof, but is opposed to the commonly received opinion of mankind in all ages? Ancient literature, sacred and profane, teems with protests against the successful evil-doer, and certainly, as Mr. Hutton observes:[1] "Honesty must have been associated by our ancestors with many unhappy as well as many happy consequences, and

[1] *Macmillan's Magazine*, No. 117, July 1869.

we know that in ancient Greece dishonesty was openly and actually associated with happy consequences . . . . when the concentrated experience of previous generations was held, *not* indeed to justify, but to excuse by utilitarian considerations, craft, dissimulation, sensuality, selfishness."

This dogma is opposed to the moral consciousness of many as to the events of their own lives; and the author, for one, believes that it is absolutely contrary to fact.

History affords multitudes of instances: an example may be selected from one of the most critical periods of modern times. Let it be granted that Lewis the Sixteenth of France and his queen had all the defects attributed to them by the most hostile of serious historians; let all the excuses possible be made for his predecessor, Lewis the Fifteenth, and also for Madame de Pompadour: can it be pretended that there are grounds for affirming that the vices of the two former so far exceeded those of the latter, that their respective fates were plainly and evidently just? that while the two former died in their beds, after a life of the most extreme luxury, the others merited to stand forth through coming time as examples of the most appalling and calamitous tragedy?[1]

[1] The same period supplies us with a yet more striking example. H. Von Sybel, in his "French Revolution" (translated by W. C. Perry), vol. iv. p. 321, says of the unfortunate young Lewis the Seventeenth: "No one can read the reports of the martyrdom of this unhappy child without the deepest emotion. Simon the Cobbler, a neighbour and admirer of Marat, had been appointed, on his recommendation, by Robespierre, as the jailer of the young Capet." . . . . "The ill-treatment of the feeble child became his daily refreshment from the ennui of the prison, his pastime and his patriotic office. He clothed the Prince in a *sansculotte* dress, compelled him to wear a Jacobin cap, made him drunk with ardent spirits, and forced him to sing indecent songs. This treatment was varied by abuse, blows, and cruelties of every kind whenever the child made mention of his parents, whenever he showed the slightest

This theme, however, is too foreign to the immediate matter in hand to be further pursued, tempting as it is. But a passing protest against a superstitious and deluding dogma may stand,—a dogma which, like any other dogma, may be vehemently asserted and maintained, but which is remarkable for being destitute, at one and the same time, of both authoritative sanction and the support of reason and observation.

To return to the bearing of moral conceptions on "Natural Selection," it seems that, from the reasons given in this chapter, we may safely affirm—1. That "Natural Selection" could not have produced, from the sensations of pleasure and pain experienced by brutes, a higher degree of morality than was useful; therefore it could have produced any amount of "beneficial habits," but not abhorrence of certain acts as impure and sinful.

symptom of resistance to the humiliations inflicted on him, whenever news arrived of a victory of the Vendeans or the Austrians." . . . . "The brutal monster one day beat and kicked the boy because he would not repeat the words, 'My mother is a harlot.' Another time Simon was awakened in the night, and heard the child praying as he knelt by his bedside. 'I'll teach you,' he cried, 'to whine your paternosters,' and, pouring a pail of cold water over his body and his bed, he compelled him by blows from an iron-heeled shoe to pass the rest of the winter night in the wet, cold bed." After the death of Simon he was imprisoned in a little cell for six months, at the end of which time when his new jailer, Laurent, entered, "He was astonished when they led him by the dim light of a lantern to the entrance of a pestiferous den, from which a feeble voice answered him after repeated calls; but what was his horror, when, on the following day, he caused the door to be broken open, and penetrated the scene of misery itself! In this poisonous atmosphere a pale and emaciated child, with matted hair, lay upon a filthy lair, clothed with half-rotten rags, his head covered with an eruption, his neck with festering sores, and his whole body with swarms of vermin." Mr. Herbert Spencer may be safely challenged to explain by what crimes this child had merited so frightful and long-continued a chastisement.

2. That it could not have developed that high esteem for acts of care and tenderness to the aged and infirm which actually exists, but would rather have perpetuated certain low social conditions which obtain amongst certain savage tribes.

3. That it could not have evolved from ape sensations the noble virtue of a Marcus Aurelius, or the loving but manly devotion of a St. Lewis.

4. That, alone, it could not have given rise to the maxim *fiat justitia, ruat cœlum.*

5. That the interval between material and formal morality is one altogether beyond its power to traverse.

Also, that the anticipatory character of moral principles is a fatal bar to that explanation of their origin which is offered to us by Mr. Herbert Spencer. And, finally, that the solution of that origin proposed recently by Sir John Lubbock is a mere version of simple utilitarianism, appealing to the pleasure or safety of the individual, and therefore utterly incapable of solving the riddle it endeavours to explain.

Such appearing to be the case as to the power of "Natural Selection," we nevertheless find moral conceptions—*formally* moral ideas—not only spread over the civilized world, but manifesting themselves unmistakably (in however rudimentary a condition, and however misapplied) amongst the lowest and most degraded of savages. If from amongst these, individuals can be brought forward who seem to be destitute of any moral conception, similar cases also may easily be found in highly civilized communities. Such cases tell no more against moral intuitions than do cases of colour-blindness or idiotism tell against sight and reason. We have then, in distinct moral perception, a highly important and conspicuous fact, the existence of which is fatal to the theory of "Natural Selection," as put forward of late by Mr. Darwin and his most ardent followers. It must be remarked, however, that whatever force this fact may have against a belief in the origination of man from brutes by minute, fortuitous variations, it has no force whatever against the conception of the orderly evolution and successive manifestation of specific forms by ordinary natural law—even if we include amongst such the upright frame, the ready hand and massive brain of man himself.

CHAPTER X.

PANGENESIS.

A "provisional hypothesis" supplementing "Natural Selection."—Statement of the hypothesis.—Difficulty as to multitude of gemmules—as to certain modes of reproduction—as to formations without the requisite gemmules.—Mr. Lewes and Professor Delpino.—Difficulty as to developmental force of gemmules—as to their spontaneous fission.—Pangenesis and Vitalism.—Paradoxical reality.—Pangenesis scarcely superior to anterior hypotheses.—Buffon.—Owen.—Herbert Spencer.—"Gemmules" as mysterious as "physiological units."—Conclusion.

In addition to the theory of "Natural Selection," by which it has been attempted to account for the origin of species, Mr. Darwin has also put forward what he modestly terms "a provisional hypothesis" (that of *Pangenesis*), by which to account for the origin of each and every individual form.

Now, though the hypothesis of Pangenesis is no necessary part of "Natural Selection," still any treatise on specific origination would be incomplete if it did not take into consideration this last speculation of Mr. Darwin's. The hypothesis in question may be stated as follows: That each living organism is ultimately made up of an almost infinite number of minute particles, or organic atoms, termed "gemmules," each of which has the power of reproducing its kind. Moreover, these particles are supposed to circulate freely about the organism (which is made up of them), and to be derived from all the parts of all the organs of the less remote ancestors of each such organism during all the states and stages of such several ancestors' existence; and therefore of the several states of each of such ancestors' organs. It is further supposed that such a complete collection of gemmules is aggregated in each ovum and spermatozoon in most animals, and in each part capable of reproducing by gemmation (budding) in the lowest animals and in plants.

In many of such lower organisms, therefore, such a congeries of ancestral gemmules must exist in every part of their bodies, since in them every part is capable of reproducing by gemmation. Mr. Darwin must evidently admit this, since he says: "It has often been said by naturalists that each cell of a plant has the actual or potential capacity of reproducing the whole plant; but it has this power only in virtue of containing gemmules *derived from every part*."[1]

Moreover, these gemmules are supposed to tend to aggregate themselves, and to reproduce in certain definite relations to other gemmules. Thus, when the foot of an eft is cut off, its reproduction is explained by Mr. Darwin as resulting from the aggregation of those floating gemmules which come next in order to those of the cut surface, and the successive aggregations of the other kinds of gemmules which come after in regular order. Also, the most ordinary processes of repair are similarly accounted for, and the successive development of similar parts and organs in creatures in which such complex evolutions occur is explained in the same way, by the independent action of separate gemmules.

[1] "Animals and Plants under Domestication," vol. ii. p. 403.

In order that every living creature may be thus furnished, the number of such gemmules in each must be inconceivably great. Mr. Darwin says:[1] "In a highly organized and complex animal the gemmules thrown off from each different cell or unit throughout the body must be inconceivably numerous and minute. Each unit of each part, as it changes during development—and we know that some insects undergo at least twenty metamorphoses—must throw off its gemmules. All organic beings, moreover, include many dormant gemmules derived from their grandparents and more remote progenitors, but not from all their progenitors. These *almost infinitely numerous* and minute gemmules must be included in each bud, ovule, spermatozoon, and pollen grain." We have seen also that in certain cases a similar multitude of gemmules must be included in every considerable part of the whole body of each organism; but where are we to stop? There must be gemmules not only from every organ, but from every component part of such organ, from every subdivision of such component part, and from every cell, thread or fibre entering into the composition of such subdivision. Moreover, not only from all these, but from each and every single stage of the evolution and development of such successively more and more elementary parts. At the first glance this new atomic theory has charms from its apparent simplicity, but the attempt thus to follow it out into its ultimate limits and extreme consequences seems to indicate that it is at once insufficient and cumbrous.

Mr. Darwin himself is, of course, fully aware that there must be *some* limit to this aggregation of gemmules. He

[1] "Animals and Plants under Domestication," vol. ii. p. 366.

says :[1] "Excessively minute and numerous as they are believed to be, an infinite number derived, during a long course of modification and descent, from each cell of each progenitor, could not be supported and nourished by the organism."

But apart from these matters, which will be more fully considered further on, the hypothesis not only does not appear to account for certain phenomena which, in order to be a valid theory, it ought to account for; but it seems absolutely to conflict with patent and notorious facts.

How, for example, does it explain the peculiar reproduction which is found to take place in certain marine worms —certain annelids?

In such creatures we see that, from time to time, one of the segments of the body gradually becomes modified till it assumes the condition of a head, and this remarkable phenomenon is repeated again and again, the body of the worm thus multiplying serially into new individuals which successively detach themselves from the older portion. The development of such a mode of reproduction by "Natural Selection" seems not less inexplicable than does its continued performance through the aid of "pangenesis." For how can gemmules attach themselves to others to which they do not normally or generally succeed? Scarcely less difficult to understand is the process of the stomach-carrying-off mode of metamorphosis before spoken of as existing in the Echinoderms. Next, as to certain patent and notorious facts: On the hypothesis of pangenesis, no creature can develop an organ unless it possesses the component gemmules which serve for its formation. No creature can possess such gemmules unless

[1] "Animals and Plants under Domestication," vol. ii. p. 402.

it inherits them from its parents, grandparents, or its less remote ancestors. Now, the Jews are remarkably scrupulous as to marriage, and rarely contract such a union with individuals not of their own race. This practice has gone on for thousands of years; and similarly also for

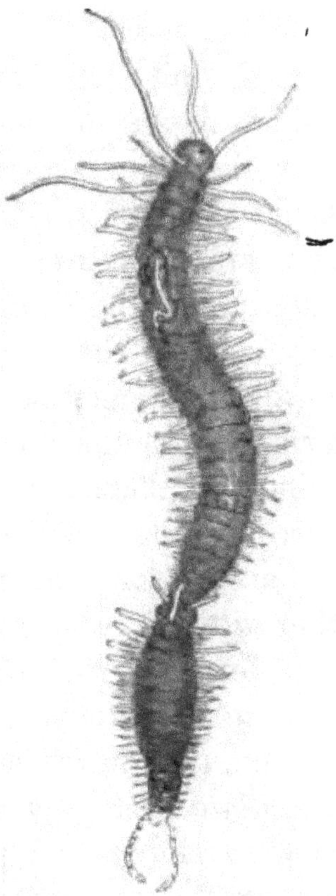

AN ANNELID DIVIDING SPONTANEOUSLY
(A new head having been formed towards the hinder end of the body of the parent).

thousands of years the rite of circumcision has been unfailingly and carefully performed. If then the hypothesis of pangenesis is well founded, that rite ought to be now absolutely or nearly superfluous from the necessarily continuous absence of certain gemmules through so many centuries and so many generations. Yet it is not at all so, and this fact seems to amount almost to an experimental demonstration that the hypothesis of pangenesis is an insufficient explanation of individual evolution.

Two exceedingly good criticisms of Mr. Darwin's hypothesis have appeared. One of these is by Mr. G. H. Lewes,[1] the other by Professor Delpino of Florence.[2] The latter gentleman gives a report of an observation made by him upon a certain plant, which observation adds force to what has just been said about the Jewish race. He says:[3] "If we examine and compare the numerous species of the genus *Salvia,* commencing with *Salvia officinalis,* which may pass as the main state of the genus, and concluding with *Salvia verticillata,* which may be taken as the most highly developed form, and as the most distant from the type, we observe a singular phenomenon. The lower cell of each of the two fertile anthers, which is much reduced and different from the superior even in *Salvia officinalis,* is transmuted in other *salviæ* into an organ (nectarotheca) having a very different form and function, and finally disappears entirely in *Salvia verticillata.*"

"Now, on one occasion, in a flower belonging to an individual of *Salvia verticillata,* and only on the left stamen, I observed a perfectly developed and pollinigerous lower cell, perfectly homologous with that which is normally developed in *Salvia officinalis.* This case of atavism is

[1] See *Fortnightly Review,* New Series, vol. iii. April 1868, p. 352.

[2] This appeared in the *Rivista Contemporanea Nazionale Italiana,* and was translated and given to the English public in *Scientific Opinion* of September 29, October 6, and October 13, 1869, pp. 365, 391, and 407.

[3] See *Scientific Opinion* of October 13, 1869, p. 407.

truly singular. According to the theory of Pangenesis, it is necessary to assume that all the gemmules of this anomalous formation, and therefore the mother-gemmule of the cell, and the daughter-gemmules of the special epidermic tissue, and of the very singular subjacent tissue of the endothecium, have been perpetuated, and transmitted from parent to offspring in a dormant state, and through a number of generations, such as startles the imagination, and leads it to refuse its consent to the theory of Pangenesis, however seductive it may be." This seems a further confirmation of what has been advanced as to the Jews.

The main objection raised against Mr. Darwin's hypothesis is that it (Pangenesis) requires so many subordinate hypotheses for its support, and that some of these are not tenable.

Professor Delpino considers[1] that as many as eight of these subordinate hypotheses are required, namely, that—

"1. The emission of the gemmules takes place, or may take place, in all states of the cell."

"2. The quantity of gemmules emitted from every cell is very great."

"3. The minuteness of the gemmules is extreme."

"4. The gemmules possess two sorts of affinity, one of which might be called *propagative*, and the other *germinative* affinity.

"5. By means of the propagative affinity all the gemmules emitted by all the cells of the individual flow together and become condensed in the cells which compose the sexual organs, whether male or female (embryonal vesicle, cells of the embryo, pollen grains, fovilla, antherozoids, spermatozoids), and likewise flow together and be-

[1] See *Scientific Opinion* of September 29, 1869, p. 366.

come condensed in the cells which constitute the organs of a sexual or agamic reproduction (buds, spores, bulbilli, portions of the body separated by scission, &c.)."

"6. By means of the germinative affinity, every gemmule (except in cases of anomalies or monstrosities) can be developed only in cells homologous with the mother-cells of the cell from which they originated. In other words, the gemmules from any cell can only be developed in unison with the cell preceding it in due order of succession, and whilst in a nascent state."

"7. Of each kind of gemmule a great number perishes; a great number remains in a dormant state through many generations in the bodies of descendants; the remainder germinate and reproduce the mother-cell."

"8. Every gemmule may multiply itself by a process of scission into any number of equivalent gemmules."

Mr. Darwin has published a short notice in reply to Professor Delpino, in *Scientific Opinion* of October 20, 1869, p. 426. In this reply he admits the justice of Professor Delpino's attack, but objects to the alleged necessity of the first subordinate hypothesis, namely, "that the emission of gemmules takes place in all states of the cell." But if this is not the case, then a great part of the utility and distinction of Pangenesis is destroyed, or, as Mr. Lewes justly says:[1] "If gemmules produce whole cells, we have the very power which was pronounced mysterious in larger organisms."

Mr. Darwin also does not see the force of the objection to the power of self-division which must be asserted of the gemmules themselves if Pangenesis be true. The objection, however, appears to many to be a serious one.

[1] *Fortnightly Review*, New Series, vol. iii. April 1868, p. 508.

To admit the power of spontaneous division and multiplication in such rudimentary structures seems a complete contradiction. The gemmules, by the hypothesis of Pangenesis, are the ultimate organized components of the body, the absolute organic atoms of which each body is composed; how then *can* they be divisible? Any part of a gemmule would be an impossible (because a *less* than possible) quantity. If it is divisible into still smaller organic wholes, as a germ-cell is, it must be made up as the germ-cell is, of subordinate component atoms, which are then the *true* gemmules. This process may be repeated *ad infinitum*, unless we get to true organic atoms, the true gemmules, whatever they may be, and they necessarily will be incapable of any process of spontaneous fission. It is remarkable that Mr. Darwin brings forward in support of gemmule fission the observation that "Thuret has seen the zoospore of an alga divide itself, and both halves germinate." Yet on the hypothesis of Pangenesis, the zoospore of an alga must contain gemmules from all the cells of the parent algæ, and from all the parts of all their less remote ancestors in all their stages of existence. What wonder, then, that such an excessively complex body should divide and multiply; and what parity is there between such a body and a gemmule? A steam-engine and a steel-filing might equally well be compared together.

Professor Delpino makes a further objection, which, however, will only be of weight in the eyes of Vitalists. He says,[1] Pangenesis is not to be received because "it leads directly to the negation of a specific vital principle, co-ordinating and regulating all the movements, acts, and functions of the individuals in which it is incarnated. For

[1] *Scientific Opinion* of October 13, 1869, p. 408.

Pangenesis of the individual is a term without meaning. If, in contemplating an animal of high organization, we regard it purely as an aggregation of developed gemmules, although these gemmules have been evolved successively one after the other, and one within the other, notwithstanding they elude the conception of the *real and true individual,* these problematical and invisible gemmules must be regarded as so many individuals. Now, that real, true, living individuals exist in nature, is a truth which is persistently attested to us by our consciousness. But how, then, can we explain that a great quantity of dissimilar elements, like the atoms of matter, can unite to form those perfect unities which we call individuals, if we do not suppose the existence of a specific principle, proper to the individual but foreign to the component atoms, which aggregates these said atoms, groups them into molecules, and then moulds the molecules into cells, the cells into tissues, the tissues into organs, and the organs into apparatus?"

"But, it may be urged in opposition by the Pangenesists, your vital principle is an unknown and irresolute *x*. This is true; but, on the other hand, let us see whether Pangenesis produces a clearer formula, and one free from unknown elements. The existence of the gemmules is a first unknown element; the propagative affinity of the gemmules is a second; their germinative affinity is a third; their multiplication by fission is a fourth—and what an unknown element!"

"Thus, in Pangenesis, everything proceeds by force of unknown elements, and we may ask whether it is more logical to prefer a system which assumes a multitude of unknown elements to a system which assumes only a single one?"

Mr. Darwin appears, by "Natural Selection," to destroy the reality of species, and by Pangenesis that of the individual. Mr. Lewes observes[1] of the individual that "This whole is only a subjective conception which summarizes the parts, and that in point of fact it is the parts which are reproduced." But the parts are also, from the same point of view, merely subjective until we come to the absolute organic atoms. These atoms, on the other hand, are utterly invisible, intangible; indeed, in the words of Mr. Darwin, inconceivable. Thus, then, it results from the theories in question, that the organic world is reduced to utter unreality as regards all that can be perceived by the senses or distinctly imagined by the mind; while the only reality consists of the invisible, the insensible, the inconceivable; in other words, nothing is known that really is, and only the non-existent can be known. A somewhat paradoxical outcome of the speculations of those who profess to rely exclusively on the testimony of sense. "*Les extrêmes se touchent,*" and extreme sensationalism shakes hands with the "das Seyn ist das nichts" of Hegel.

Altogether, the hypothesis of Pangenesis seems to be little, if at all, superior to earlier hypotheses of a more or less similar nature.

Apart from the atoms of Democritus, and apart also from the speculations of mediæval writers, the molecules of Bonnet and of Buffon almost anticipated the hypothesis of Pangenesis. According to the last-named author,[2] organic particles from every part of the body assemble in

[1] *Fortnightly Review*, New Series, vol. iii. April 1868, p. 509.

[2] "Histoire Naturelle, générale et particulière," tome ii. 1749, p. 327. "Ces liqueurs séminales sont toutes deux un extrait de toutes les parties du corps," &c.

the sexual secretions, and by their union build up the embryo, each particle taking its due place, and occupying in the offspring a similar position to that which it occupied in the parent. In 1849 Professor Owen, in his treatise on "Parthenogenesis," put forward another idea. According to this, the cells resulting from the subdivision of the germ-cell preserve their developmental force, unless employed in building up definite organic structures. In certain creatures, and in certain parts of other creatures, germ-cells unused are stored up, and by their agency lost limbs and other mutilations are repaired. Similar unused products of the germ-cell are also supposed to become situate in the generative products.

According to Mr. Herbert Spencer, in his "Principles of Biology," each living organism consists of certain so-called "physiological units." Each of these units has an innate power and capacity, by which it tends to build up and reproduce the entire organism of which it forms a part, unless in the meantime its force is exhausted by its contributing to the production of some distinct and definite tissue—a condition somewhat similar to that conceived by Professor Owen.[1]

Now, at first sight, Mr. Darwin's atomic theory appears to be more simple than any of the others. It has been objected, that while Mr. Spencer's theory requires the assumption of an innate power and tendency in each physiological unit, Mr. Darwin's, on the other hand, re-

[1] Mr. Spencer, however, holds that so long as the process of growth and multiplication by gemmation goes on actively, so that the aggregates and their units, in a continual state of change, are not held in such constant relation as to bring about an equilibrium between the form of the one and the polarities of the other, the process of growth and multiplication may go on without limit.

quires nothing of the kind, but explains the evolution of each individual by purely mechanical conceptions. In fact, however, it is not so. Each gemmule, according to Mr. Darwin, is really the seat of powers, elective affinities, and special tendencies as marked and mysterious as those possessed by the physiological unit of Mr. Spencer, with the single exception that the former has no tendency to build up the whole living, complex organism of which it forms a part. Some may think this an important distinction, but such can hardly be the case, for Mr. Darwin considers that his gemmule has the innate power and tendency to increase and transform itself into the whole living, complex cell of which it forms a part; and the one tendency is, in principle, fully as difficult to understand, fully as mysterious, as the other. The difference is but one of degree, not of kind. Moreover, the one conception in the case of the "physiological unit" explains all, while with regard to the gemmule, as we have seen, its power of growth has to be supplemented by other powers and tendencies, each distinct, and each in itself inexplicable and profoundly mysterious.

That there should be physiological units possessed of the power attributed to them, harmonizes with what has recently been put forward by Dr. H. Charlton Bastian;[1] who maintains that under fit conditions the simplest organisms develop themselves into relatively large and complex ones. This is not supposed by him to be due to any inheritance of ancestral gemmules, but to direct

[1] As this sheet of the second edition is passing through the press, a work has appeared written by Dr. H. Charlton Bastian, and entitl "The Modes of Origin of Lowest Organisms." London and New York: Macmillan and Co.

growth and transformation of the most minute and the simplest organisms, which themselves, by all reason and analogy, owe their existence to immediate transformation from the inorganic world.

On the whole, then, we seem justified in asserting that there are grave difficulties in the way of the reception of the hypothesis of Pangenesis, which moreover, if established, would leave the evolution of individual organisms, when thoroughly analysed, little if at all less mysterious or really explicable than it is at present.

As was said at the beginning of this chapter, "Pangenesis" and "Natural Selection" are quite separable and distinct hypotheses. The fall of one of these by no means necessarily includes that of the other. Nevertheless, Mr. Darwin has associated them closely together, and, therefore, the refutation of Pangenesis may render it advisable for those who have hitherto accepted "Natural Selection" to reconsider their acceptance of that theory.

CHAPTER XI.

SPECIFIC GENESIS.

Review of the statements and arguments of the preceding chapters.—Cumulative argument against predominant action of "Natural Selection."—Whether anything positive as well as negative can be enunciated.—Constancy of laws of nature does not necessarily imply constancy of specific evolution.—Possible exceptional stability of existing epoch.—Probability that an internal cause of change exists.—Innate powers must be conceived as existing somewhere or other.—Symbolism of molecular action under vibrating impulses.—Professor Owen's statement.—Statement of the author's view.—It avoids the difficulties which oppose "Natural Selection."—It harmonizes apparently conflicting conceptions.—Summary and conclusion.

HAVING now severally reviewed the principal biological facts which bear upon specific manifestation, it remains to sum up the results, and to endeavour to ascertain what, if anything, can be said *positively*, as well as negatively, on this deeply interesting question.

In the preceding chapters it has been contended, in the first place, that no mere survival of the fittest accidental and minute variations can account for the incipient stages of useful structures, such as, *e.g.*, the heads of flat-fishes, the baleen of whales, limbs of vertebrates, the laryngeal structures of the new-born kangaroo, the pedicellariæ of Echinoderms, or for many of the facts of mimicry, and especially those last touches of mimetic perfection, where an insect not only mimics a leaf, but one worm-eaten and attacked by fungi.

Also, that structures like the hood of the cobra and the rattle of the rattlesnake seem to require another explanation.

Again, it has been contended that instances of colour, as in some apes; of beauty, as in some shell-fish; and of utility, as in many orchids, are examples of conditions which are quite beyond the power of Natural Selection to originate and develop.

Next, the peculiar mode of origin of the eye (by the simultaneous and concurrent modification of distinct parts), with the wonderful refinement of the human ear and voice, have been insisted on; as also, that the importance of all these facts is intensified through the necessity (admitted by Mr. Darwin) that many individuals should be similarly and simultaneously modified in order that slightly favourable variations may hold their own in the struggle for life, against the overwhelming force and influence of mere number.

Again, we have considered, in Chapter III., the great improbability that from minute variations in all directions, alone and unaided, (save by the survival of the fittest), closely similar structures should independently arise; though, on a non-Darwinian evolutionary hypothesis, their development might be expected *a priori*. We have seen, however, that there are many instances of wonderfully close similarity which are not due to genetic affinity; the most notable instance, perhaps, being that brought forward by Mr. Murphy, namely, the appearance of the same eye-structure in the vertebrate and molluscous sub-kingdoms. A curious resemblance, though less in degree, has also been seen to exist between the auditory organs of fishes and of Cephalopods. Remarkable similarities between certain placental and implacental mammals, between the bird's-head processes of Polyzoa and the pedicellariæ of Echinoderms, between Ichthyosauria and Cetacea, with very many other similar coincidences, have also been indicated as instances in point.

Evidence has also been brought forward to show that similarity is sometimes directly induced by very obscure conditions, at present quite inexplicable, *e.g.* by causes immediately connected with geographical distribution; as in the loss of the tail in certain forms of Lepidoptera and in simultaneous modifications of colour in others, and in the direct modification of young English oysters when transported to the shore of the Mediterranean.

Again, it has been asserted that certain groups of organic forms seem to have an innate tendency to remarkable developments of some particular kind, as beauty and singularity of plumage in the group of birds of paradise.

It has also been contended that there is something to be said in favour of sudden, as opposed to exceedingly minute and gradual, modifications, even if the latter are not fortuitous. Cases were brought forward, in Chapter IV., such as the bivalve just mentioned; twenty-seven kinds of American trees simultaneously and similarly modified; also the independent production of pony breeds; and the case of the English greyhounds in Mexico, the offspring of which produced directly acclimated progeny. Besides these, the cases of the Normandy pigs, of *Datura tatula*, and also of the black-shouldered peacock, have been spoken of. The teeth of the labyrinthodon, the hand of the potto, the whalebone of whales, the wings of birds, the climbing tendrils of some plants, &c. have also been adduced as instances of structures, the origin and production of which are probably due rather to considerable modifications than to minute increments.

It has also been shown that certain forms which were once supposed to be especially transitional and intermediate (as, *e.g.*, the aye-aye) are really not so; while the ordinary rule, that the progress of forms has been "from the more general to the more special," has been shown to have remarkable exceptions, as, *e.g.* Macrauchenia, the Glyptodon, and the sabre-toothed tiger (Machairodus).

Next, as to specific stability, it has been seen that there may be a certain limit to normal variability, and that if changes take place they may be expected *a priori* to be marked and considerable ones, from the facts presented by the inorganic world, and perhaps also by the lowest forms of the organic world. It has also been seen that with regard to minute spontaneous variations in races, there is a rapidly increasing difficulty in intensifying them, in any one direction, by ever such careful breeding. Moreover, it has appeared that different species show a tendency to variability in definite directions, and probably in different degrees, and that at any rate Mr. Darwin himself concedes the existence of an internal barrier to change when he credits the goose with "a singularly inflexible organization;" also, that he admits the presence of an *internal* proclivity to change when he speaks of "a whole organization seeming to have become plastic, and tending to depart from the parental type."

We have seen also that a marked proclivity to reversion

does exist, inasmuch as it sometimes takes place in a striking manner, as exemplified in the white silk fowl in England, *in spite of* careful selection in breeding.

Again, we have found that a tendency exists in nature to eliminate hybrid races, by whatever means that elimination is effected, while no similar tendency bars the way to an indefinite blending of varieties. This has also been enforced by statements as to the prepotency of certain pollen of identical species, but of distinct races.

To all the preceding considerations have been added others derived from the relations of species to past time. It has been contended that we have as yet no evidence of minutely intermediate forms connecting uninterruptedly together undoubtedly distinct species. It has also been maintained that while even "horse ancestry" fails to supply such a desideratum, in very strongly marked and exceptional kinds (such as the Ichthyosauria, Chelonia, and Anoura), the absence of links is both important and significant. For if every species, without exception, has arisen by minute modifications, it seems incredible that a small percentage of such transitional forms should not have been preserved. This, of course, is especially the case as regards the marine Ichthyosauria and Plesiosauria, of which so very many remains have been discovered.

Sir William Thomson's great authority has been seen to oppose itself to "Natural Selection," by limiting, on astronomical and physical grounds, the duration of life on this planet to about one hundred million years. This period, it has been contended, is not nearly enough, on the one hand, for the evolution of all organic forms by the exclusive action of mere minute, fortuitous variations; on the other hand, for the deposition of all the strata which must have been deposited, if minute fortuitous variation was the manner of successive specific manifestation.

Again, the geographical distribution of existing animals has been seen to present difficulties which, though not themselves of any great weight, yet have a certain value when taken in conjunction with all the other objections.

The facts of homology, serial, bilateral and vertical, have also been passed in review. Such phenomena, it has been contended, are not explicable without admitting the action of what may most conveniently be spoken of as an *internal* power, the existence of which is supported by facts not only of comparative anatomy, but of teratology and pathology also. Besides this, "Natural Selection" has been shown to be impotent to explain these phenomena, while the existence of such an internal power of homologous evolution diminishes the *a priori* improbability of an analogous law of specific origination.

All these various considerations have been supplemented by an endeavour to show the utter inadequacy of Mr. Darwin's theory with regard to the higher psychical phenomena of man (especially the evolution of moral perceptions), and with regard to the evolution of individual organisms by the action of Pangenesis. And it has been implied that if Mr. Darwin's latter hypothesis could be shown to be untenable, an antecedent doubt would be thrown upon his other conception, namely, the theory of "Natural Selection."

A cumulative argument thus arises against the prevalent action of "Natural Selection," which, to the mind of the author, is conclusive. As before observed, he was not originally disposed to reject Mr. Darwin's fascinating theory. Reiterated endeavours to solve its difficulties have, however, had the effect of convincing him that that theory, as the one or as the leading explanation of the successive evolution and manifestation of specific forms, is untenable. At the same time he admits fully that "Natural Selection" acts, and must act, and that it plays in the organic world a certain though a secondary and subordinate part.

The one *modus operandi* yet suggested having been found insufficient, the question arises: Can another be substituted in its place? If not, can anything that is positive, and if anything, what, be said as to the question of specific origination?

Now in the first place, it is of course axiomatic that the laws which conditioned the evolution of extinct and of existing species are of as much efficacy at this moment as at any preceding period, that they *tend* to the manifestation of new forms as much now as ever before. It by no means necessarily follows, however, that this tendency is actually being carried into effect, and that new species of the higher animals and plants are now being produced. They may be so or they may not, according as existing circumstances favour, or conflict with, the action of those laws. It is possible that lowly organized creatures may be continually evolved at the present day, the requisite conditions being more or less easily supplied. There is, however, no such evidence at present as to higher forms; while, as we have seen in Chapter VII., there are *a priori* considerations which militate against their being similarly evolved.

The presence of wild varieties, and the difficulty which often exists in the determination of species, are sometimes adduced as arguments that high forms are now in process of evolution. These facts, however, do not necessarily prove more than that some species possess a greater variability than others, and (what is indeed unquestionable) that species have often been unduly multiplied by geologists and botanists. It may be, for example, that Wagner was right, and that all the American monkeys of the genus cebus may be reduced to a single species, or to two.

With regard to the lower organisms, and supposing views recently advanced to become fully established, there is no reason to think that the forms said to be evolved were new species, but rather reappearances of definite kinds which had appeared before and will appear again under the same conditions. So with higher forms, similar conditions must educe similar results; but here practically similar conditions can rarely obtain, because of the large part which "descent" and "inheritance" always play in such highly organized forms.

Still it is conceivable that different combinations at different times may have occasionally the same outcome, just as the multiplications of different numbers may have severally the same result.

There are reasons, however, for thinking it possible that the human race is a witness of an exceptionally unchanging and stable condition of things, if the calculations of Mr. Croll are valid as to how far variations in the eccentricity in the earth's orbit, together with the precession of the equinoxes, have produced changes in climate. Mr. Wallace has pointed out[1] that, as during the last 60,000 years

[1] See *Nature*, March 3, 1870, p. 454. Mr. Wallace says (referring to Mr. Croll's paper in the *Phil. Mag.*), "As we are now, and have been for 60,000 years, in a period of low eccentricity, *the rate of change of species during that time may be no measure of the rate that has generally obtained in past geological epochs.*"

these conditions have been exceptionally unchanging, specific evolution may have been exceptionally rare. It becomes then possible to suppose that for a similar period stimuli to change in the manifestation of animal forms may have been unusually few and feeble,—that is, if the conditions of the earth's orbit have been as exceptional as stated. However, even if new species are now being evolved as actively as ever, or if they have been so quite recently, no conflict thence necessarily arises with the view here advocated. For it by no means follows that if some examples of new species have recently been suddenly produced from individuals of antecedent species, we ought to be able to put our fingers on such cases; as Mr. Murphy well observes[1] in a passage before quoted, "If a species were to come suddenly into being in a wild state, as the Ancon sheep did under domestication, how could we ascertain the fact? If the first of a newly-born species were found, the fact of its discovery would tell nothing about its origin. Naturalists would register it as a very rare species, having been only once met with, but they would have no means of knowing whether it were the first or the last of its race."

But are there any grounds for thinking that in the genesis of species an *internal* force or tendency intervenes, co-operating with and controlling the action of external conditions?

It is here contended that there are such grounds, and that though inheritance, reversion, atavism, Natural Selection, &c., play a part not unimportant, yet that such an internal power is a great, perhaps the main, determining agent.

[1] "Habit and Intelligence," vol. i. p. 344.

the sexual secretions, and by their union build up the embryo, each particle taking its due place, and occupying in the offspring a similar position to that which it occupied in the parent. In 1849 Professor Owen, in his treatise on "Parthenogenesis," put forward another idea. According to this, the cells resulting from the subdivision of the germ-cell preserve their developmental force, unless employed in building up definite organic structures. In certain creatures, and in certain parts of other creatures, germ-cells unused are stored up, and by their agency lost limbs and other mutilations are repaired. Similar unused products of the germ-cell are also supposed to become situate in the generative products.

According to Mr. Herbert Spencer, in his "Principles of Biology," each living organism consists of certain so-called "physiological units." Each of these units has an innate power and capacity, by which it tends to build up and reproduce the entire organism of which it forms a part, unless in the meantime its force is exhausted by its contributing to the production of some distinct and definite tissue—a condition somewhat similar to that conceived by Professor Owen.[1]

Now, at first sight, Mr. Darwin's atomic theory appears to be more simple than any of the others. It has been objected, that while Mr. Spencer's theory requires the assumption of an innate power and tendency in each physiological unit, Mr. Darwin's, on the other hand, re-

[1] Mr. Spencer, however, holds that so long as the process of growth and multiplication by gemmation goes on actively, so that the aggregates and their units, in a continual state of change, are not held in such constant relation as to bring about an equilibrium between the form of the one and the polarities of the other, the process of growth and multiplication may go on without limit.

quires nothing of the kind, but explains the evolution of each individual by purely mechanical conceptions. In fact, however, it is not so. Each gemmule, according to Mr. Darwin, is really the seat of powers, elective affinities, and special tendencies as marked and mysterious as those possessed by the physiological unit of Mr. Spencer, with the single exception that the former has no tendency to build up the whole living, complex organism of which it forms a part. Some may think this an important distinction, but such can hardly be the case, for Mr. Darwin considers that his gemmule has the innate power and tendency to increase and transform itself into the whole living, complex cell of which it forms a part; and the one tendency is, in principle, fully as difficult to understand, fully as mysterious, as the other. The difference is but one of degree, not of kind. Moreover, the one conception in the case of the "physiological unit" explains all, while with regard to the gemmule, as we have seen, its power of growth has to be supplemented by other powers and tendencies, each distinct, and each in itself inexplicable and profoundly mysterious.

That there should be physiological units possessed of the power attributed to them, harmonizes with what has recently been put forward by Dr. H. Charlton Bastian;[1] who maintains that under fit conditions the simplest organisms develop themselves into relatively large and complex ones. This is not supposed by him to be due to any inheritance of ancestral gemmules, but to direct

[1] As this sheet of the second edition is passing through the press, a work has appeared written by Dr. H. Charlton Bastian, and entitl "The Modes of Origin of Lowest Organisms." London and New York: Macmillan and Co.

growth and transformation of the most minute and the simplest organisms, which themselves, by all reason and analogy, owe their existence to immediate transformation from the inorganic world.

On the whole, then, we seem justified in asserting that there are grave difficulties in the way of the reception of the hypothesis of Pangenesis, which moreover, if established, would leave the evolution of individual organisms, when thoroughly analysed, little if at all less mysterious or really explicable than it is at present.

As was said at the beginning of this chapter, "Pangenesis" and "Natural Selection" are quite separable and distinct hypotheses. The fall of one of these by no means necessarily includes that of the other. Nevertheless, Mr. Darwin has associated them closely together, and, therefore, the refutation of Pangenesis may render it advisable for those who have hitherto accepted "Natural Selection" to reconsider their acceptance of that theory.

CHAPTER XI.

SPECIFIC GENESIS.

Review of the statements and arguments of the preceding chapters.—Cumulative argument against predominant action of "Natural Selection."—Whether anything positive as well as negative can be enunciated.—Constancy of laws of nature does not necessarily imply constancy of specific evolution.—Possible exceptional stability of existing epoch.—Probability that an internal cause of change exists.—Innate powers must be conceived as existing somewhere or other.—Symbolism of molecular action under vibrating impulses.—Professor Owen's statement.—Statement of the author's view.—It avoids the difficulties which oppose "Natural Selection."—It harmonizes apparently conflicting conceptions.—Summary and conclusion.

HAVING now severally reviewed the principal biological facts which bear upon specific manifestation, it remains to sum up the results, and to endeavour to ascertain what, if anything, can be said *positively*, as well as negatively, on this deeply interesting question.

In the preceding chapters it has been contended, in the first place, that no mere survival of the fittest accidental and minute variations can account for the incipient stages of useful structures, such as, *e.g.*, the heads of flat-fishes, the baleen of whales, limbs of vertebrates, the laryngeal structures of the new-born kangaroo, the pedicellariæ of Echinoderms, or for many of the facts of mimicry, and especially

instead of being supported by his relatives and friends. In the same way, there is fully as real a distinction between the production of new specific manifestations entirely *ab externo*, and the production of the same through an innate force and tendency, the determination of which into action is occasioned by external circumstances.

To say that organisms possess this innate power, and that by it new species are from time to time produced, is by no means a mere assertion that they *are* produced, and in an unknown mode. It is the negation of that view which deems external forces alone sufficient, and is at the same time the assertion of something positive, to be arrived at by the process of elimination.

All physical explanations result ultimately in such conceptions of innate power, or else in that of will force. The far-famed explanation of the celestial motions ends in the conception that every particle of matter has the innate power of attracting every other particle directly as the mass, and inversely as the square of the distance.

We are logically driven to this positive conception, if we do not accept the view that there is no force but volition, and that all phenomena whatever are the immediate results of the action of intelligent and self-conscious will.

We have seen that the notion of sudden changes—saltatory actions in nature—has received countenance from Professor Huxley.[1] We must conceive that these jumps are orderly, and according to law, inasmuch as the whole cosmos is such. Such orderly evolution harmonizes with a teleology derived, not indeed from external nature directly, but from the mind of man. On this point, however, more will be said in the next chapter.

[1] "Lay Sermons," p. 342.

Again, if new species have not been manifested by the action of external conditions upon minute indefinite individual differences, in what precise way may we conceive that manifestation to have taken place?

Are new species now evolving, as they have been from time to time evolved? If so, in what way and by what conceivable means?

In the first place, they must be produced by natural action in pre-existing material, or by supernatural action.

For reasons to be given in the next chapter, the second hypothesis need not be considered.

If, then, new species are and have been evolved from pre-existing material, must that material have been organic or inorganic?

As before said, additional arguments have lately been brought forward to show that individual organisms *do* arise from a basis of *in*-organic material only. As, however, this at the most appears to be the case exclusively, if at all, with the lowest and most minute organisms, the process cannot be observed, though it may perhaps be fairly inferred.

We may therefore, if for no other reason, dismiss the notion that highly organized animals and plants can be suddenly or gradually built up by any combination of physical forces and natural powers acting externally and internally upon and in merely inorganic material as a base.

But the question is, how have the highest kinds of animals and plants arisen? It seems impossible that they can have appeared otherwise than by the agency of antecedent organisms not greatly different from them.

A multitude of facts, ever increasing in number and

importance, all point to such a mode of specific manifestation.

One very good illustration has been adduced by Professor Flower in the introductory lecture of his first Hunterian Course.[1] It is the reduction in size, to a greater or less degree, of the second and third digits of the foot in Australian marsupials, and this, notwithstanding the very different form and function of the foot in different groups of those animals.

A similarly significant evidence of relationship is afforded by processes of the zygomatic region of the skull in certain edentates existing and extinct.

Again, the relation between existing and recent faunas of the different regions of the world, and the fact that the progress in organization has been for the most part from the more general to the more special, tend to support the doctrine of evolution.

Almost all the facts brought forward by the patient industry of Mr. Darwin in support of his theory of "Natural Selection" are of course available as evidence in favour of the agency of pre-existing and similar animals in specific evolution.

Now the new forms must be produced by changes taking place in organisms at, after, or before their birth, either in their embryonic or towards or in their adult condition.

Examples of strange births are sufficiently numerous, and they may arise either from direct embryonic modifications or apparently from some obscure change in the parental action. To the former category belong the hosts of instances of malformation through arrest of develop-

[1] Introductory Lecture of February 14, 1870, pp. 24—30, Figs. 1—4. (Churchill and Sons.)

ment, and perhaps generally monstrosities of some sort are the result of such affections of the embryo. To the second category belong cases of hybridism, of cross breed, and in all probability the new varieties and forms, such as the memorable one of the black-shouldered peacock. In these cases we do not have abortions or monstrosities, but more or less harmonious forms often of great functional activity, endowed with marked viability and generative prepotency,[1] except in the case of hybrids, when we often find even a more marked generative impotency.

It seems probable therefore that new species may arise from some constitutional affection of parental forms—an affection mainly, if not exclusively, of their generative system. Mr. Darwin has carefully collected [2] numerous instances to show how excessively sensitive to various influences this system is. He says:[3] "Sterility is independent of general health, and is often accompanied by excess of size, or great luxuriance," and "No one can tell, till he tries, whether any particular animal will breed under confinement, or any exotic plant seed freely under culture." Again, "When a new character arises, whatever its nature may be, it generally tends to be inherited, at least in a temporary and sometimes in a most persistent manner."[4] Yet the obscure action of conditions will alter

[1] In the "Descent of Man," vol. i. p. 223, the following passage occurs: "When any character has suddenly appeared in a race or species as the result of a single act of variation" . . . . "and this race is crossed with another not thus characterised, the characters in question do not commonly appear in a blended condition in the young, but are transmitted to them either perfectly developed or not at all."

[2] See especially "Animals and Plants under Domestication," vol. ii. chap. xviii.

[3] "Origin of Species," 5th edition, pp. 323, 324.

[4] "Animals and Plants under Domestication," vol. ii. p. 2.

characters long inherited, as the grandchildren of Aylesbury ducks, removed to a distant part of England, completely lost their early habit of incubation, and hatched their eggs at the same time with the common ducks of the same place."[1]

Mr. Darwin quotes Mr. Bartlett as saying: "It is remarkable that lions breed more freely in travelling collections than in the zoological gardens; probably the constant excitement and irritation produced by moving from place to place, or change of air, may have considerable influence in the matter."[2]

Mr. Darwin also says: "There is reason to believe that insects are affected by confinement like the higher animals," and he gives examples.[3]

Again, he gives examples of change of plumage in the linnet, bunting, oriole, and other birds, and of the temporary modification of the horns of a male deer during a voyage.[4]

Finally, he adds that these changes cannot be attributed to loss of health or vigour, "when we reflect how healthy, long-lived, and vigorous many animals are under captivity, such as parrots, and hawks when used for hawking, chetahs when used for hunting, and elephants. The reproductive organs themselves are not diseased; and the diseases from which animals in menageries usually perish are not those which in any way affect their fertility. No domestic animal is more subject to disease than the sheep, yet it is remarkably prolific. . . . It would appear that any change in the habits of life, whatever these habits may be, if great enough, tends to affect in an inexplicable manner the powers of reproduction."

[1] "Animals and Plants under Domestication," vol. ii. p. 25.
[2] Ibid. p. 151. [3] Ibid. p. 157. [4] Ibid. p. 158.

Such, then, is the singular sensitiveness of the generative system.

As to the means by which that system is affected, we see that a variety of conditions affect it; bût as to the modes in which they act upon it, we have as yet little if any clue.

We have also seen the singular effects (in tailed Lepidoptera, &c.) of causes connected with geographical distribution, the mode of action of which is as yet quite inexplicable; and we have also seen that there appears to be an innate tendency in certain groups (birds of paradise, &c.) to develop characters of a peculiar kind.

It is, to say the least, probable that other influences exist, terrestrial and cosmical, as yet unnoted. The gradually accumulating or diversely combining actions of all these on highly sensitive structures, which are themselves possessed of internal responsive powers and tendencies, may well result in occasional repeated productions of forms harmonious and vigorous, and differing from the parental forms in proportion to the result of the combining or conflicting action of all external and internal influences. If, in the past history of this planet, more causes ever intervened, or intervened more energetically than at present, we might *a priori* expect a richer evolution of forms more radically differing one from another than any which could be produced under conditions of more perfect equilibrium. At the same time, if it be true that the last few thousand years have been a period of remarkable and exceptional uniformity as regards this planet's astronomical relations, there are then some grounds for thinking that organic evolution may have been exceptionally depressed during the same epoch.

Now, as to the fact that sudden changes and sudden developments have occurred, and as to the probability that such changes are likely to occur, evidence was given in Chapter IV.

In Chapter V. we also saw that minerals become modified suddenly and considerably by the action of incident forces—as, *e.g.*, in the production of hexagonal tabular crystals of carbonate of copper by sulphuric acid, and of long rectangular prisms by ammonia, &c.

We have thus an antecedent probability that if changes are produced in specific manifestation through incident forces, these changes will be sensible and considerable, not minute and infinitesimal.

Consequently, it is probable that new species have appeared from time to time with comparative suddenness, and that they still continue so to arise if all the conditions necessary for specific evolution now obtain.[1]

This probability will be increased if the observations of

[1] Professor Humphry has remarked: "We are familiarized with the fact that in the inorganic world combinations take place only in certain definite proportions; for instance, that oxygen unites with nitrogen in one proportion to make nitrous oxide, in a second proportion, a multiple of the first, to make nitric oxide, and so on to the fifth proportion or multiple, which gives nitric acid, and that between these five several fixed proportions no combinations take place: so that the resultants of these and other similar combinations—the inorganic species, as we may call them—are remarkably constant and fixed in their characters. Each has its one form, as in the case of a crystal of chloride of sodium, or sulphate of magnesia, which may be broken down or dissolved but which cannot be modified or made to approach, still less to pass into, any other form." "May there not be something analogous—some corresponding law of combining proportion—presiding over living matter, educing the various forms, fixing their characters, giving them constancy, in fact, evolving and fixing the species?"—*Journal of Anatomy and Physiology*, vol. i. p. 11.

Dr. Bastian are confirmed by future investigation. According to his report, when the requisite conditions were supplied, the transformations which appeared to take place (from very low to higher organisms) were sudden, definite, and complete.

If this is so, there most probably exists in higher forms a similar tendency to such change. That tendency may indeed be long suppressed, and ultimately modified by the action of heredity—an action which would increase in force with the increase in the perfection and complexity of the organism affected. Still we might expect that such changes as do take place would be also sudden, definite, and complete.

Moreover, as the same causes produce the same effects, several individual parent forms must often have been similarly and simultaneously affected. That they should be so affected—at least that several similarly modified individuals should simultaneously arise—has been seen to be a generally necessary circumstance for the permanent continuance of such new modifications.

It is also conceivable that such new forms may be endowed with excessive constitutional strength and viability, and with generative prepotency, as was the case with the black-shouldered peacock in Sir J. Trevelyan's flock. This flock was entirely composed of the common kind, and yet the new form rapidly developed itself "*to the extinction of the previously existing breed.*"[1]

Indeed, the notion accepted by both Mr. Darwin and Mr. Herbert Spencer, and which is plainly the fact (namely, that changes of conditions and incident forces, within limits, augment the viability and fertility of indi-

[1] "Animals and Plants under Domestication," vol. i. p. 291.

viduals), harmonizes well with the suggested possibility as to an augmented viability and prepotency in new organic forms evolved by peculiar consentaneous actions of conditions and forces, both external and internal.

The remarkable series of changes noted by Dr. Bastian were certainly not produced by external incident forces *only*, but by these acting on a peculiar *materia*, having special properties and powers. Therefore, the changes were induced by the consentaneous action of internal and external forces.[1] In the same way, then, we may expect changes in higher forms to be evolved by similar united action of internal and external forces.

One other point may here be adverted to. When the remarkable way in which structure and function simultaneously change, is borne in mind; when those numerous instances in which nature has supplied similar wants by similar means, as detailed in Chapter III., are remembered; when also all the wonderful contrivances of orchids, of mimicry, and the strange complexity of certain instinctive actions are considered: then the conviction forces itself on many minds that the organic world is the expression of an intelligence of some kind. This view has been well advocated by Mr. Joseph John Murphy, in his recent work so often here referred to.

This intelligence, however, is evidently not altogether such as ours, or else has other purposes than those most obvious to us. For the end is often attained in singularly roundabout ways, or with a prodigality of means which seems out of all proportion with the result: not with the

[1] Though hardly necessary, it may be well to remark that the views here advocated in no way depend upon the truth of the doctrine of Spontaneous Generation.

simple action directed to one end which generally marks human activity.

Organic nature then speaks clearly to many minds of the action of an intelligence resulting, on the whole and in the main, in order, harmony, and beauty, yet of an intelligence the ways of which are not as our ways.

This view of evolution harmonizes well with Theistic conceptions; not, of course, that this harmony is brought forward as an argument in its favour generally, but it will have weight with those who are convinced that Theism reposes upon solid grounds of reason as *the* rational view of the universe. To such it may be observed that, thus conceived, the Divine action has that slight amount of resemblance to, and that wide amount of divergence from what human action would be, which might be expected *a priori*—might be expected, that is, from a Being whose nature and aims are utterly beyond our power to imagine, however faintly, but whose truth and goodness are the fountain and source of our own perceptions of such qualities.

The view of evolution maintained in this work, though arrived at in complete independence,[1] yet seems to agree in many respects with the views advocated by Professor Owen in the last volume of his "Anatomy of Vertebrates," under the term "derivation." He says:[2] "Derivation holds that every species changes in time, by virtue of inherent tendencies thereto. 'Natural Selection' holds that no such

[1] Since the publication of the first edition of this book, its author has become aware that similar views were enunciated more than ten years ago by Professor Theophilus Parsons, of Harvard University, Cambridge, Massachusetts They were published in the July Number of the *American Journal of Science and Arts* for 1860.

[2] Vol. iii. p. 808.

change can take place without the influence of altered external circumstances.[1] 'Derivation' sees, among the effects of the innate tendency to change irrespective of altered circumstances, a manifestation of creative power in the variety and beauty of the results; and, in the ultimate forthcoming of a being susceptible of appreciating such beauty, evidence of the pre-ordaining of such relation of power to the appreciation. 'Natural Selection' acknowledges that if ornament or beauty, in itself, should be a purpose in creation, it would be absolutely fatal to it as a hypothesis."

"'Natural Selection' sees grandeur in the view of life, with its several powers, having been originally breathed by the Creator into a few forms or into one. 'Derivation' sees therein a narrow invocation of a special miracle and an unworthy limitation of creative power, the grandeur of which is manifested daily, hourly, in calling into life many forms, by conversion of physical and chemical into vital modes of force, under as many diversified conditions of the requisite elements to be so combined."

The theory propounded in this work allows, however, a greater and more important share to external influences, it being believed by the author that these external influences equally with the internal ones are the results of one harmonious action underlying the whole of nature, organic and inorganic, cosmical, physical, chemical, terrestrial, vital, and social.

According to this view, an internal law controls the action of every part of every individual, and of every

[1] This is hardly an exact representation of Mr. Darwin's view. On his theory, if a favourable variation happens to arise (the external circumstances remaining the same), it will yet be preserved.

organism as a unit, and of the entire organic world as a whole.

It is believed: That this conception of an internal innate force will ever remain necessary, however much its subordinate processes and actions may become explicable. That by such a force, from time to time, new species are manifested by ordinary generation, just as *Pavo nigripennis* appeared suddenly, these new forms not being monstrosities but harmonious self-consistent wholes. That thus, as specific distinctness is manifested by obscure sexual conditions, so in obscure sexual modifications specific distinctions arise.

That these "jumps" are considerable in comparison with the minute variations of "Natural Selection"—are in fact sensible steps, such as discriminate species from species.

That the latent tendency which exists to these sudden evolutions is determined to action by the stimulus of external conditions.

That "Natural Selection" rigorously destroys monstrosities, and abortive and feeble attempts at the performance of the evolutionary process.

That "Natural Selection" removes the antecedent species rapidly when the new one evolved is more in harmony with surrounding conditions.

That "Natural Selection" favours and develops useful variations, though it is impotent to originate them or to erect the physiological barrier which seems to exist between species.

By some such conception as this, the difficulties here enumerated, which beset the theory of "Natural Selection" pure and simple, are to be got over.

Thus, for example, the difficulties discussed in the first chapter—namely, those as to the origins and first beginnings of certain structures—are completely evaded.

Again, as to the independent origin of closely similar structures, such as the eyes of the Vertebrata and cuttle-fishes, the difficulty is removed if we may adopt the conception of an innate force similarly directed in each case, and assisted by favourable external conditions.

Specific stability, limitation to variability, and the facts of reversion, all harmonize with the view here put forward. The same may be said with regard to the significant facts of homology, and of organic symmetry; and our consideration of the hypothesis of Pangenesis in Chapter X. has seemed to result in a conception as to innate powers which also accords well with the view just mentioned.

The evolutionary hypothesis here advocated also serves to explain all those remarkable facts which were stated in the first chapter to be explicable by the theory of Natural Selection, namely, the relation of existing to recent faunas and floras; the phenomena of homology and of rudimentary structures; also the processes gone through in development, and lastly the wonderful facts of mimicry.

Finally, the view adopted is the synthesis of many distinct and, at first sight, conflicting conceptions, each of which contains elements of truth, and all of which it appears to be able more or less to harmonize.

Thus it has been seen that "Natural Selection" is accepted. It acts and must act, though alone it does not appear capable of fulfilling the task assigned to it by Mr. Darwin.

Pangenesis has probably also much truth in it, and has

certainly afforded valuable and pregnant suggestions, but unaided and alone it seems inadequate to explain the evolution of the individual organism.

Those three conceptions of the organic world which may be spoken of as the teleological, the typical, and the transmutationist, have often been regarded as mutually antagonistic and conflicting.

The genesis of species as here conceived, however, accepts, distributes, and harmonizes all the three.

Teleology concerns the ends for which organisms were designed. The recognition, therefore, that their formation took place by an evolution not fortuitous, in no way invalidates the acknowledgment of their final causes if on other grounds there are reasons for believing that such final causes exist.

Conformity to type, or the creation of species according to certain "divine ideas," is in no way interfered with by such a process of evolution as is here advocated. Such "divine ideas" must be accepted or declined upon quite other grounds than the mode of their realization, and of their manifestation in the world of sensible phenomena.

Transmutationism (an old name for the evolutionary hypothesis), which was considered at one time to be the very antithesis of the two preceding conceptions, harmonizes well with them if the evolution be understood to be orderly and designed. It will in the next chapter be shown to be completely in harmony with conceptions, upon the acceptance of which "final causes" and "divine ideal archetypes" alike depend.

Thus then, if the cumulative argument put forward in this book is valid, we must admit the insufficiency of Natural Selection both on account of the residuary phenomena it fails to explain, and on account of certain other phenomena which seem actually to conflict with that theory. We have seen that though the laws of nature are constant, yet some of the conditions which determine specific change may be exceptionally absent at the present epoch of the world's history; also that it is not only possible, but highly probable, that an internal power or tendency is an important if not the main agent in producing the manifestation of new species on the scene of realized existence, and that in any case, from the facts of homology, innate internal powers to the full as mysterious must be accepted, whether they act in specific origination or not. Besides all this, we have seen that it is probable that the action of this innate power is stimulated, evoked, and determined by external conditions, and also that the same external conditions, in the shape of "Natural Selection," play an important part in the evolutionary process: and finally, it has been affirmed that the view here advocated, while it is supported by the facts on which Darwinism rests, is not open to the objections and difficulties which oppose themselves to the reception of "Natural Selection" as the exclusive or even as the main agent in the successive and orderly evolution of organic forms in the *genesis of species*.

CHAPTER XII.

THEOLOGY AND EVOLUTION.

Prejudices on the subject.—"Creation" sometimes denied from prejudice.—The Unknowable.—Mr. Herbert Spencer's objections to theism; to creation.—Meanings of term "creation."—Confusion from not distinguishing between "primary" and "derivative" creation.—Mr. Darwin's objections.—Bearing of Christianity on the theory of evolution.—Supposed opposition, the result of a mi conception.—Theological authority not opposed to evolution—St. Augustin.—St. Thomas Aquinas.—Certain consequences of want of flexibility of mind.—Reason and imagination.—The first cause and demonstration.—Parallel between Christianity and natural theology.—What evolution of species is.—Professor Agassiz.—Innate powers must be recognized.—Bearing of evolution on religious belief.—Professor Huxley.—Professor Owen.—Mr. Wallace.—Mr. Darwin.—*A priori* conception of Divine action.—Origin of Man.—Absolute creation and dogma.—Mr. Wallace's view.—A supernatural origin for man's body not necessary.—Two orders of being in man.—Two modes of origin.—Harmony of the physical, hyperphysical, and supernatural.—Reconciliation of science and religion as regards evolution.—Conclusion.

THE special "Darwinian Theory" and that of an evolutionary process neither excessively minute nor fortuitous having now been considered, it is time to turn to the important question, whether both or either of these conceptions may have any bearing, and if any, what, upon Christian belief?

Some readers will consider such an inquiry to be a work of supererogation. Seeing clearly themselves the absurdity of prevalent popular views, and the shallowness of popular objections, they may be impatient of any discussion on the subject. But it is submitted that there are many minds worthy of the highest esteem and of every consideration, which have regarded the subject hitherto almost exclusively from one point of view; that there are some persons who are opposed to the progress (in their own minds or in that of their children or dependants) of physical scientific truth —the natural revelation—through a mistaken estimate of its religious bearings, while there are others who are zealous in its promotion from a precisely similar error. For the sake of both these the author may be pardoned for entering upon some elementary matters relating to the question whether evolution or Darwinism have any, and if any, what, bearing on theology?

There are at least two classes of men who will doubtless assert that they have a very important and highly significant bearing upon it.

One of these classes consists of persons zealous for religion indeed, but who identify orthodoxy with their own private interpretation of Scripture or with narrow opinions in which they have been brought up—opinions doubtless widely spread, but at the same time destitute of any distinct and authoritative sanction on the part of the Christian Church.

The other class is made up of men hostile to religion, and who are glad to make use of any and every argument which they think may possibly be available against it.

Some individuals within this latter class may not believe in the existence of God, but may yet abstain from publicly avowing their absence of belief, contenting themselves with denials of "creation" and "design," though these denials are really consequences of their negative attitude of mind respecting the most important and fundamental of all beliefs.

Without a distinct belief in a personal God it is impossible to have any religion worthy of the name, and no one can at the same time accept the Christian religion and deny the dogma of creation.

"I believe in God," "the Creator of Heaven and Earth," the first clauses of the Apostles' Creed, formally commit those who accept them to the assertion of this belief. If, therefore, any theory of physical science really conflicts with such an authoritative statement, its importance to Christians is unquestionable.

As, however, "creation" forms a part of "revelation," and as "revelation" appeals for its acceptance to "reason," which has to prepare a basis for it by an intelligent acceptance of theism on *purely rational grounds*, it is necessary to start with a few words as to the reasonableness of belief in God, which indeed are less superfluous than some readers may imagine; "a few words," because this is not the place where the argument can be drawn out, but only certain suggestions offered in reply to some modern objections.

No better example perhaps can be taken, as a type of this negative position, than a passage in Mr. Herbert Spencer's "First Principles."[1] That author constantly speaks of the "ultimate cause of things" as "the Unknowable," a term singularly unfortunate, and, as Mr. James Martineau has pointed out,[2] even self-contradictory; for that entity, the

[1] See 2nd edition, p. 113.

[2] "Essays, Philosophical and Theological," Trübner and Co., First Series, 1866, p. 190. "Every relative disability may be read two ways. A disqualification in the nature of thought for knowing x is, from the other side, a

knowledge of the existence of which presses itself ever more and more upon the cultivated intellect, cannot be the unknown, still less *the unknowable*, because we certainly know it, in that we know for certain that it exists. Nay more, to predicate incognoscibility of it, is even an actual knowledge of the mode of its existence. Mr. Herbert Spencer says: [1] "The consciousness of an Inscrutable Power manifested to us through all phenomena has been growing ever clearer; and must eventually be freed from its imperfections. The certainty that on the one hand such a Power exists, while on the other hand its nature transcends intuition, and is beyond imagination, is the certainty towards which intelligence has from the first been progressing." One would think that the familiar and accepted word "the Inscrutable" (which is in this passage actually employed, and to which no theologian would object) would have been a far better term than "the Unknowable." The above extract has, however, such a

disqualification in the nature of x from being known. To say then that the First Cause is wholly removed from our apprehension is not simply a disclaimer of faculty on our part: it is a charge of inability against the First Cause too. The dictum about it is this: 'It is a Being that may exist out of knowledge, but that is precluded from entering within the sphere of knowledge.' We are told in one breath that this Being must be in every sense 'perfect, complete, total—including in itself all power, and transcending all law' (p. 38); and in another that this perfect and omnipotent One is totally incapable of revealing any one of an infinite store of attributes. Need we point out the contradictions which this position involves? If you abide by it, you deny the Absolute and Infinite in the very act of affirming it, for, in debarring the First Cause from self-revelation, you impose a limit on its nature. And in the very act of declaring the First Cause incognizable, you do not permit it to remain unknown. For that only is unknown of which you can neither affirm nor deny any predicate: here you deny the power of self-disclosure to the 'Absolute,' of which therefore something is known;—viz., that nothing can be known!"

[1] Loc. cit. p. 108.

theistic aspect that some readers may think the opposition here offered superfluous; it may be well, therefore, to quote two more sentences. In another place he observes,[1] "Passing over the consideration of credibility, and confining ourselves to that of conceivability, we see that atheism, pantheism, and theism, when rigorously analysed, severally prove to be absolutely unthinkable;" and speaking of "every form of religion," he adds,[2] "The analysis of every possible hypothesis proves, not simply that no hypothesis is sufficient, but that no hypothesis is even thinkable." The unknowable is admitted to be a power which cannot be regarded as having sympathy with us, but as one to which no emotion whatever can be ascribed, and we are expressly forbidden "by *duty*," to affirm personality of God as much as to deny it of Him. How such a being can be presented as an object on which to exercise religious emotion it is difficult indeed to understand.[3] Aspiration, love, devotion to be poured forth upon what we can never know, upon what we can never affirm to know, or care for, us, our thoughts or actions, or to possess the attributes of wisdom and goodness! The worship offered in such a religion must be, as Professor Huxley says,[4] "for the most part of the silent sort"—silent not only as to the spoken

[1] Loc. cit. p. 43. [2] Loc. cit. p. 46.

[3] Mr. J. Martineau, in his "Essays," vol. i. p. 211, observes: "Mr. Spencer's conditions of pious worship are hard to satisfy; there must be between the Divine and human no communion of thought, relations of conscience, or approach of affection." . . . . "But you cannot constitute a religion out of mystery alone, any more than out of knowledge alone; nor can you measure the relation of doctrines to humility and piety by the mere amount of conscious darkness which they leave. All worship, being directed to what is *above* us and transcends our comprehension, stands in presence of a mystery. But not all that stands before a mystery is worship."

[4] "Lay Sermons," p. 20.

word, but silent as to the mental conception also. It will be difficult to distinguish the follower of this religion from the follower of none, and the man who declines either to assert or to deny the existence of God is practically in the position of an atheist. For theism enjoins the cultivation of sentiments of love and devotion to God, and the practice of their external expression. Atheism forbids both, while the simply non-theist abstains in conformity with the prohibition of the atheist and thus practically sides with him. Moreover, since man cannot imagine that of which he has no experience in any way whatever, and since he has experience only of *human* perfections and of the powers and properties of *inferior* existences; if he be required to deny human perfections and to abstain from making use of such conceptions, he is thereby necessarily reduced to others of an inferior order. Mr. H. Spencer says,[1] "Those who espouse this alternative position, make the erroneous assumption that the choice is between personality and something lower than personality; whereas the choice is rather between personality and something higher. Is it not just possible that there is a mode of being as much transcending intelligence and will, as these transcend mechanical motion?"

"It is true we are totally unable to conceive any such higher mode of being. But this is not a reason for questioning its existence; it is rather the reverse." "May we not therefore rightly refrain from assigning to the 'ultimate cause' any attributes whatever, on the ground that such attributes, derived as they must be from our own natures, are not elevations but degradations?" The way however to arrive at the object aimed at (*i.e.* to acquire the best

[1] Loc. cit. p. 109.

attainable conception of the First Cause) is not to refrain from *the only conceptions possible to us*, but to seek the very highest of these, and then declare their utter inadequacy; and this is precisely the course which has been pursued by theologians. It is to be regretted that before writing on this matter Mr. Spencer did not more thoroughly acquaint himself with the ordinary doctrine on the subject. It is always taught in the Church schools of divinity, that nothing, not even *existence*, is to be predicated *univocally*[1] of "God" and "creatures;" that after exhausting ingenuity to arrive at the loftiest possible conceptions, we must declare them to be *utterly inadequate;* that, after all, they are but accommodations to human infirmity; that they are in a sense objectively false (because of their inadequacy), though subjectively and very practically true. But the difference between this mode of treatment and that adopted by Mr. Spencer is wide indeed; for the practical result of the mode inculcated by the Church is that each one may freely affirm and act upon the highest human conceptions he can attain of the power, wisdom, and good-

1 "Deus in hac vita non potest a nobis videri per suam essentiam, sed cognoscitur a nobis ex creaturis secundum habitudinem principii, et per modum excellentiæ et remotionis: *Sic igitur potest nominari a nobis ex creaturis: non tamen ita, quod nomen significans ipsum exprimat divinam essentiam, secundum quod est.* Sicut ut hoc nomen exprimit sua significatione essentiam hominis secundum quod est."—ST. THOMAS, *Summa.* Pars i. qu. xiii. art. i.

"Cum hoc nomen sapiens de homine dicitur, quodammodo describit, et comprehendit rem significatam, non autem, cum dicitur de Deo: relinquit rem significatam, ut incomprehensam, et excedentem nominis significationem, unde patet, quod non secundum eandem rationem hoc nomen sapiens de Deo, et de homine dicitur. Et eadem ratio est de aliis. Unde *nullum nomen univoce de Deo, et creaturis prædicatur.* . . . Dicendum est igitur, quod hujusmodi nomina dicuntur de Deo, et creaturis secundum analogiam, id est, proportionem."—ST. THOMAS, loc. cit. art. v.

ness of God, His watchful care, His loving providence for every man, at every moment and in every need; for the Christian knows that the falseness of his conceptions lies only in their *inadequacy;* he may therefore strengthen and refresh himself, may rejoice and revel in conceptions of the goodness of God, drawn from the tenderest human images of fatherly care and love, or he may chasten and abase himself by consideration of the awful holiness and unapproachable majesty of the Divinity derived from analogous sources, knowing that no thought of man can ever be *true enough*, can ever attain the incomprehensible reality, which nevertheless really *is* all that can be conceived, *plus* an inconceivable infinity beyond.

A good illustration of what is here meant, and of the difference between the theistic position and Mr. Spencer's, may be supplied by an example he has himself proposed. Thus,[1] he imagines an intelligent watch speculating as to its maker, and conceiving of him in terms of watch-being, and figuring him as furnished with springs, escapements, cogged wheels, &c., his motions facilitated by oil—in a word, like himself. It is assumed by Mr. Spencer that this necessary watch conception would be completely false, and the illustration is made use of to show "the presumption of theologians"—the absurdity and unreasonableness of those men who figure the incomprehensible cause of all phenomena as a Being in some way comparable with man. Now, putting aside for the moment all other considerations, and accepting the illustration, surely the example demonstrates rather the unreasonableness of the *objector himself!* It is true, indeed, that a man is an organism indefinitely more complex and perfect than any watch; but if the

[1] Loc. cit. p. 111.

watch could only conceive of its maker in watch terms, or else in terms altogether inferior, the watch would plainly be right in speaking of its maker as a, to it, inconceivably perfect kind of watch, acknowledging at the same time that this, its conception of him, was *utterly inadequate*, although the best its inferior nature allowed it to form. For if, instead of so conceiving of its maker, it refused to make use of these relative perfections as a makeshift, and so necessarily thought of him as amorphous metal, or mere oil, or by the help of any other inferior conception which a watch might be imagined capable of entertaining, that watch would be wrong indeed. For man can much more properly be compared with, and has much more affinity to, a perfect watch in full activity than to a mere piece of metal or drop of oil. But the watch is even more in the right still, for its maker, man, virtually *has* the cogged wheels, springs, escapements, oil, &c., which the watch's conception has been supposed to attribute to him; inasmuch as all these parts must have existed as distinct ideas in the human watchmaker's mind before he could actually construct the clock formed by him. Nor is even this all, for, by the hypothesis, the watch *thinks*. It must, therefore, think of its maker as "a thinking being," and in this it is *absolutely and completely right*.[1] Either, therefore, the hypothesis is *absurd* or it actually *demonstrates the very position it was chosen to refute*. Unquestionably, then, on the mere ground taken by Mr. Herbert Spencer himself, if we are compelled to think of the First Cause either in human terms (but with human imperfections abstracted and human perfections carried to the highest conceivable

[1] In this criticism on Mr. Herbert Spencer, the author finds he has been anticipated by Mr. James Martineau. (See "Essays," vol. i. p. 208.)

degree), or, on the other hand, in terms decidedly inferior, such as those are driven to who think of Him, yet decline to accept as a help the term "personality;" there can be no question but that the first conception is immeasurably nearer the truth than the second. Yet the latter is the one put forward and advocated by that author in spite of its unreasonableness, and in spite also of its conflicting with the whole moral nature of man and all his noblest aspirations.[1]

Again, Mr. Herbert Spencer objects to the conception of God as "first cause," on the ground that "when our symbolic conceptions are such that no cumulative or indirect processes of thought can enable us to ascertain that there are corresponding actualities, nor any predictions be made whose fulfilment can prove this, then they are altogether vicious and illusive, and in no way distinguishable from pure fictions."[2]

[1] In an excellent article on "Variety as an Aim in Nature," in the Number of the *Contemporary Review* for May 1871, the Duke of Argyll remarks: "If there be any work in Nature which reflects any image of the Creator, the human mind is that work. Nor is there any difficulty in conceiving how such an image may be true and yet be faint—how it may be real and yet be distant. For nothing in the human mind is more wonderful than this, that it is conscious of its own limitations. The bars which we feel so much, and against which we so often beat in vain, are bars which would not be felt at all unless there were something in us against which they press. It is as if these bars were a limit of Opportunity rather than a boundary of Power. It is as if we might understand immensely more than we can discover—if only some one would explain it to us! There is hardly one of the higher powers or faculties of our mind in respect of which we do not feel daily that we are tied and bound by the weight of our infirmities. Therefore we can have no difficulty in conceiving all our own powers exalted to an indefinite degree. And thus it is that although all goodness, and power, and knowledge, must be conceived of as we know them in ourselves, it does not follow that they must be conceived of according to the measure which we ourselves supply."

[2] Loc. cit. p. 29.

Now, it is quite true that "symbolic conceptions," which are not to be justified either (1) by presentations of sense, or (2) by intuitions, are invalid as representations of real truth. Yet the conception of God referred to *is* justified by our primary intuitions, and we can assure ourselves that it *does* stand for an actuality by comparing it with (1) our intuitions of free-will and causation, and (2) our intuitions of morality and responsibility. That we *have* these intuitions is a point on which the author joins issue with Mr. Spencer, and confidently affirms that they cannot logically be denied without at the same time complete and absolute scepticism resulting from such denial—scepticism wherein vanishes any certainty as to the existence both of Mr. Spencer and his critic, and by which it is equally impossible to have a thought free from doubt, or to go so far as to affirm the existence of that very doubt or of the doubter who doubts it.

It may not be amiss here to protest against the intolerable assumption of men of a certain school, who are continually talking in lofty terms of "science," but who actually speak of primary religious conceptions as "unscientific," and habitually employ the word "science" when they should limit it by the prefix "physical." This is the more amazing as not a few of this school adopt the idealist philosophy, and affirm that "matter and force" are but names for certain "modes of consciousness." It might be expected of them at least to admit that opinions which repose on primary and fundamental intuitions are especially and *par excellence* scientific.

The foregoing are some of the objections to the Christian conception of God. We may now turn to those which are directed against God as the Creator, *i.e.* as the absolute originator of the universe, without the employment of any pre-existing means or material. This is again considered by Mr. Spencer as a thoroughly illegitimate symbolic conception, as much so as the atheistic one—the difficulty as to a *self-existent Creator* being in his opinion equal to that of a *self-existent universe.* To this it may be replied that both are of course equally *unimaginable,* but that it is not a question of facility of conception—not which is easiest to conceive, but which best accounts for, and accords with, psychological facts ; namely, with the above-mentioned intuitions. It is contended that *we have* these primary intuitions, and that with these the conception of a self-existent Creator is perfectly harmonious. On the other hand, the notion of a self-existent universe — that there is no real distinction between the finite and the infinite—that the universe and ourselves are one and the same things with the infinite and the self-existent; these assertions, in *addition to* being unimaginable, *contradict* our primary intuitions.

Mr. Darwin's objections to "Creation" are of quite a different kind, and, before entering upon them, it will be well to endeavour clearly to understand what we mean by "Creation," in the various senses in which the term may be used.

In the strictest and highest sense "Creation" is the absolute origination of anything by God without pre-existing means or material, and is a *supernatural* act.[1]

In the secondary and lower sense, "Creation" is the formation of anything by God *derivatively;* that is, that the pre-existing matter has been created with the potentiality to

[1] The author means by this, that it is *directly* and *immediately* the act of God, the word "supernatural" being used in a sense convenient for the purposes of this work, and not in its ordinary theological sense.

evolve from it, under suitable conditions, all the various forms it subsequently assumes. And this power having been conferred by God in the first instance, and those laws and powers having been instituted by Him, through the action of which the suitable conditions are supplied, He is said in this lower sense to create such various subsequent forms. This is the *natural* action of God in the physical world, as distinguished from His direct, or, as it may be here called, supernatural action.

In yet a third sense, the word "Creation" may be more or less improperly applied to the construction of any complex formation or state by a voluntary self-conscious being who makes use of the powers and laws which God has imposed, as when a man is spoken of as the creator of a museum, or of "his own fortune," &c. Such action of a created conscious intelligence is purely natural, but more than physical, and may be conveniently spoken of as hyperphysical.

We have thus (1) direct or supernatural action; (2) physical action; and (3) hyperphysical action—the last two belonging both to the order of nature.[1] Neither the physical nor the hyperphysical actions, however, exclude the idea of the Divine concurrence, and with every consistent theist that idea is necessarily included. Dr. Asa Gray has given expression to this.[2] He says, "Agreeing that plants and animals were produced by Omnipotent fiat, does not exclude the idea of natural order and what we call secondary causes. The record of the fiat—'Let the earth

[1] The phrase "order of nature" is not here used in its theological sense as distinguished from the "order of grace," but as a term, here convenient, to denote actions not due to direct and immediate Divine intervention.

[2] "A Free Examination of Darwin's Treatise," p. 29, reprinted from the *Atlantic Monthly* for July, August, and October, 1860.

bring forth grass, the herb yielding seed,' &c., 'let the earth bring forth the living creature after his kind'—seems even to imply them," and leads to the conclusion that the various kinds were produced through natural agencies.

Now, much confusion has arisen from not keeping clearly in view this distinction between *absolute* creation and *derivative* creation. With the first, physical science has plainly nothing whatever to do, and is impotent to prove or to refute it. The second is also safe from any attack on the part of physical science, for it is primarily derived from psychical not physical phenomena. The greater part of the apparent force possessed by objectors to creation, like Mr. Darwin, lies in their treating the assertion of derivative creation as if it was an assertion of absolute creation, or at least of supernatural action. Thus, he asks whether some of the opponents believe "that, at innumerable periods in the earth's history, certain elemental atoms have been commanded suddenly to flash into living tissues."[1] Certain of Mr. Darwin's objections, however, are not physical, but *metaphysical*, and really attack the dogma of secondary or derivative creation, though to some perhaps they may appear to be directed against absolute creation only.

Thus he uses, as an illustration, the conception of a man who builds an edifice from fragments of rock at the base of a precipice, by selecting for the construction of the various parts of the building the pieces which are the most suitable owing to the shape they happen to have broken into. Afterwards, adverting to this illustration, he says,[2] "The shape of the fragments of stone at the base of our precipice may be called accidental, but this is not

[1] "Origin of Species," 5th edit. p. 571.

[2] "Animals and Plants under Domestication," vol. ii. p. 431.

strictly correct, for the shape of each depends on a long sequence of events, all obeying natural laws, on the nature of the rock, on the lines of stratification or cleavage, on the form of the mountain which depends on its upheaval and subsequent denudation, and lastly, on the storm and earthquake which threw down the fragments. But in regard to the use to which the fragments may be put, their shape may strictly be said to be accidental. And here we are led to face a great difficulty, in alluding to which I am aware that I am travelling beyond my proper province."

"An omniscient Creator must have foreseen every consequence which results from the laws imposed by Him; but can it be reasonably maintained that the Creator intentionally ordered, if we use the words in any ordinary sense, that certain fragments of rock should assume certain shapes, so that the builder might erect his edifice? If the various laws which have determined the shape of each fragment were not predetermined for the builder's sake, can it with any greater probability be maintained that He specially ordained, for the sake of the breeder, each of the innumerable variations in our domestic animals and plants—many of these variations being of no service to man, and not beneficial, far more often injurious, to the creatures themselves? Did He ordain that the crop and tail-feathers of the pigeon should vary, in order that the fancier might make his grotesque pouter and fantail breeds? Did He cause the frame and mental qualities of the dog to vary, in order that a breed might be formed of indomitable ferocity, with jaws fitted to pin down the bull for man's brutal sport? But, if we give up the principle in one case—if we do not admit that the variations of the primeval dog were intentionally guided, in order that the greyhound, for instance, that perfect image of symmetry and vigour, might be formed,—no shadow of reason can be assigned for the belief that the variations, alike in nature, and the result of the same general laws, which have been the groundwork through Natural Selection of the formation of the most perfectly adapted animals in the world, man included, were intentionally and specially guided. However much we may wish it, we can hardly follow Professor Asa Gray in his belief that 'variation has been led along certain beneficial lines,' like a stream 'along definite and useful lines of irrigation.'"

"If we assume that each particular variation was from the beginning of all time pre-ordained, the plasticity of the organization, which leads to many injurious deviations of structure, as well as that redundant power of reproduction which inevitably leads to a struggle for existence, and, as a consequence, to the Natural Selection and survival of the fittest, must appear to us superfluous laws of nature. On the other hand, an omnipotent and omniscient Creator ordains everything and foresees everything. Thus we are brought face to face with a difficulty as insoluble as is that of free-will and predestination."

Before proceeding to reply to this remarkable passage, it may be well to remind some readers that belief in the existence of God, in His primary creation of the universe, and in His derivative creation of all kinds of being, inorganic and organic, do not repose upon physical phenomena, but, as has been said, on primary intuitions. To deny or ridicule any of these beliefs on physical grounds is to commit the fallacy of *ignoratio elenchi.* It is to commit an absurdity analogous to that of saying a blind child could not recognize his father because he could not *see* him, forgetting that he could *hear* and *feel* him. Yet there are some persons who appear to find it unreasonable and absurd that men should regard phenomena in a light not furnished by or to be obtained from the very phenomena themselves, although the men so regarding them avow that the light in which they do view them comes from quite another source. It is as if a man, A, coming into B's room and finding there a butterfly, should insist that B had no right to believe that the butterfly had not flown in at the open window, inasmuch as there was nothing about the room or insect to lead to any other belief; while B can well sustain his right so to believe, he having met C, who told him he brought in the chrysalis and, having seen the insect emerge, took away the skin.

Owing to a similarly narrow and incomplete view men sometimes ridicule the assertion that human conceptions, such as "the vertebrate idea," &c., are ideas in the mind of God; as if the assertors either on the one hand pretended to some prodigious intellectual power—a far-reaching genius not possessed by most naturalists—or, on the other hand, as if they detected in the very phenomena furnishing such special conception evidences of Divine imaginings. But let the idea of God according to the highest conceptions of Christianity be once accepted, and then it becomes simply a truism to say that the mind of the Deity contains all that is *good* and *positive* in the mind of man, *plus*, of course, an absolutely inconceivable infinity beyond. Thus such human conceptions may, nay must, be asserted to be at the same time ideas in the Divine mind also, as every real and separate individual that has been, is, or shall be, is present to the same mind; nay, more, such human conceptions are but faint and obscure adumbrations of corresponding ideas which exist in the mind of God in perfection and fulness.[1]

The theist, having arrived at his theistic convictions from quite other sources than a consideration of zoological or botanical phenomena, comes to the consideration of such phenomena and views them in a theistic light without of course asserting or implying that such light has been derived *from them*, or that there is an obligation of reason so to view them on the part of others who refuse to enter upon or to accept those other sources whence have been derived the theistic convictions of the theist.

But Mr. Darwin is not so inconsequent as to argue against metaphysical ideas on physical data only, for he employs very distinctly metaphysical ones; namely, his

[1] The Rev. Baden Powell says: "All sciences approach perfection as they approach to a unity of first principles,—in all cases occurring to or tending towards certain high elementary conceptions which are the representatives of the unity of the great archetypal ideas according to which the whole system is arranged. Inductive conceptions, very partially and imperfectly realized and apprehended by human intellect, are the exponents in our minds of these great principles in nature."

"All science is but the partial reflexion in the *reason of man*, of the great all-pervading *reason of the universe*. And thus the *unity* of science is the reflexion of the *unity* of nature, and of the *unity* of that supreme reason and intelligence which pervades and rules over nature, and from whence all reason and all science is derived." (Unity of Worlds, Essay i., § ii.; Unity of Sciences, pp. 79 and 81.) Also he quotes from Oersted's "Soul in Nature" (pp. 12, 16, 18, 87, 92, and 377): "If the laws of reason did not exist in nature, we should vainly attempt to force them upon her: if the laws of nature did not exist in our reason, we should not be able to comprehend them." . . . . "We find an agreement between our reason and works which our reason did not produce." . . . . "All existence is a dominion of reason." "The laws of nature are laws of reason, and altogether form an endless unity of reason; . . . . one and the same throughout the universe."

conceptions of the nature and attributes of the First Cause. But what conceptions does he offer us! Nothing but that low anthropomorphism which, unfortunately, he so often seems to treat as the necessary result of Theism. Here we have again the dummy, helpless and deformed, set up merely for the purpose of being knocked down.

It must once more be insisted on, that though man is indeed compelled to conceive of God in human terms, and to speak of Him by epithets objectively false, from their hopeless inadequacy, yet nevertheless the Christian thinker declares that inadequacy in the strongest manner, and vehemently rejects from his idea of God all terms distinctly implying infirmity or limitation.

Now, Mr. Darwin speaks as if all who believe in the Almighty were compelled to accept as really applicable to the Deity conceptions which affirm limits and imperfections. Thus he says: "Can it be reasonably maintained that the Creator intentionally ordered" "that certain fragments of rock should assume certain shapes, so that the builder might erect his edifice?"

Why, surely every theist must maintain that in the first foundation of the universe—the primary and absolute creation—God saw and knew every purpose which every atom and particle of matter should ever subserve in all suns and systems, and throughout all coming æons of time. It is almost incredible, but nevertheless it seems necessary to think that the difficulty thus proposed rests on a sort of notion that amidst the boundless profusion of nature there is too much for God to superintend; that the number of objects is too great for an infinite and *omnipresent* Being to attend singly to each and all in their due proportions and needs! In the same way Mr. Darwin asks whether God can have ordered the race-variations referred to in the passage last quoted, for the considerations therein mentioned. To this it may be at once replied that even man often has *several* distinct intentions and motives for a *single* action, and the theist has no difficulty in supposing that, out of an infinite number of motives, the motive mentioned in each case may have been an exceedingly subordinate one. The theist, though properly attributing to God what, for want of better terms, he calls "purpose" and "design," yet affirms that the limitations of human purposes and motives are by no means applicable to the Divine "purposes." Out of many, say a thousand million, reasons for the institution of the laws of the physical universe, some few are to a certain extent conceivable by us; and amongst these the benefits material and moral accruing from them to men and to each individual man in every circumstance of his life, play a certain, perhaps a very subordinate part.[1] As Baden Powell observes: "How

[1] In the same spirit Mr. Lewes, in criticising the Duke of Argyll's "Reign of Law" (*Fortnightly Review*, July 1867, p. 100), asks whether we should consider that man wise who spilt a gallon of wine in order to fill a wine-glass? But, because we should not do so, it by no means follows that we can argue from such an action to the action of God in the visible universe. For the man's object, in the case supposed, is simply to fill the wine-glass, and the wine spilt is so much loss. With God it may be entirely different in both respects. All these objections are fully met by the principle thus laid down by St. Thomas Aquinas: "Quod si aliqua causa particularis deficiat a suo effectu, hoc est propter aliquam causam particularem impedientem quæ continetur sub ordine causæ universalis. Unde effectus ordinem causæ universalis nullo modo potest exire." . . . . "Sicut indigestio contingit præter ordinem virtutis nutritivæ ex aliquo impedimento, puta ex grossitie cibi, quam necesse est reducere in aliam causam, et sic usque ad causam primam universalem. Cum igitur Deus sit prima causa universalis non unius generi tantum, sed universaliter totius entis, impossibile est quod aliquid contingat præter ordinem divinæ gubernationis; sed ex hoc ipso

can we undertake to affirm, amid all the possibilities of things of which we confessedly know so little, that a thousand ends and purposes may not be answered, because we can trace none, or even imagine none, which seem to our short-sighted faculties to be answered in these particular arrangements?"[1]

The objection to the bull-dog's ferocity in connexion with "man's brutal sport" opens up the familiar but vast question of the existence of evil, a problem the discussion of which would be out of place here. Considering, however, the very great stress which is laid in the present day on the subject of animal suffering by so many amiable and excellent persons, one or two remarks on that matter may not be superfluous. To those who accept the belief in God, the soul and moral responsibility, and recognize the full results of that acceptance—to such, physical suffering and moral evil are simply incommensurable. To them the placing of non-moral beings in the same scale with moral agents will be utterly unendurable. But even considering physical pain only, all must admit that this depends greatly on the mental condition of the sufferer. Only during consciousness does it exist, and only in the most highly-organized men does it reach its acme. The author has been assured that lower races of men appear less keenly sensitive to physical pain than do more cultivated and refined human beings. Thus only in man can there really be any intense degree of suffering, because only in him is

quod aliquid ex unâ parte videtur exire ab ordine divinæ providentiæ, quo consideratur secundam aliquam particularem causam, necesse est quod in eundem ordinem relabatur secundum aliam causam."—*Sum. Theol.* p. i. q. 19, a. 6, and q. 103, a. 7.

[1] "Unity of Worlds," Essay ii., § ii. p. 260.

there that intellectual recollection of past moments and that anticipation of future ones which constitute in great part the bitterness of suffering.[1] The momentary pang, the present pain, which beasts endure, though real enough, is yet, doubtless, not to be compared as to its intensity with the suffering which is produced in man through his high prerogative of self-consciousness.[2]

As to the "beneficial lines" (of Dr. Asa Gray, before referred to), some of the facts noticed in the preceding chapters seem to point very decidedly in that direction, but all must admit that the actual existing outcome is far more "beneficial" than the reverse. The natural universe has resulted in the development of an unmistakable harmony and beauty, and in a decided preponderance of good and of happiness over their opposites.

Even if "laws of nature" did appear, on the theistic hypothesis, to be "superfluous" (which it is by no means intended here to admit), it would surely be puerile to prefer rejecting the hypothesis to conceiving that the appearance of superfluity was due to human ignorance; and this especially might be expected from naturalists to whom the interdependence of nature and the harmony and utility of obscure phenomena are becoming continually more apparent, as, *e.g.*, the structure of orchids to their illustrious expositor.

Having now somewhat cleared the ground, we may turn to the question as to the bearing of Christian dogma upon

[1] See the exceedingly good passage on this subject by the Rev. Dr. Newman, in his "Discourses for Mixed Congregations," 1850, p. 345.

[2] See Mr. G. H. Lewes's "Sea-Side Studies," for some excellent remarks, beginning at p. 329, as to the small susceptibility of certain animals to pain.

evolution, and whether Christians, as such, need take up any definite attitude concerning it.

As has been said, it is plain that physical science and "evolution" *can* have nothing whatever to do with absolute or primary creation. The Rev. Baden Powell well expresses this: "Science demonstrates incessant past changes, and dimly points to yet earlier links in a more vast series of development of material existence; but the idea of a *beginning*, or of *creation*, in the sense of the original operation of the Divine volition to constitute nature and matter, is beyond the province of physical philosophy."[1]

With secondary or derivative creation, physical science is also incapable of conflict; for the objections drawn by some writers seemingly from physical science, are, as has been already argued, really metaphysical, not physical.

Derivative creation is not a supernatural act, but is simply the Divine action by and through natural laws. To recognize such action in such laws is a religious mode of regarding phenomena, which a consistent theist must necessarily accept, and which an atheistic believer must similarly reject. But this conception, if deemed superfluous by certain naturalists, can never be shown to be *false* by any investigations concerning natural laws, the constant action of which it presupposes.

The conflict has arisen through a misunderstanding. Some have supposed that by "creation" was necessarily meant either primary, that is, absolute creation, or, at least, some supernatural action; they have therefore opposed the dogma of "creation" in the imagined interest of physical science.

[1] "Philosophy of Creation," Essay iii., § iv., p. 480.

Others have supposed that by "evolution" was necessarily meant a denial of Divine action, a negation of the providence of God. They have therefore combated the theory of "evolution" in the imagined interest of religion.

It appears then that Christian thinkers are perfectly free to accept the general evolution theory. But are there any theological authorities to justify this view of the matter?

Now, considering how extremely recent are these biological speculations, it might hardly be expected *a priori* that writers of earlier ages should have given expression to doctrines harmonizing in any degree with such very modern views,[1] nevertheless this is certainly the case, and

[1] It seems almost strange that modern English thought should so long hold aloof from familiar communion with Christian writers of other ages and countries. It is rarely indeed that acquaintance is shown with such authors, though a bright example to the contrary was set by Sir William Hamilton. Sir Charles Lyell (in his "Principles of Geology," 7th edition, p. 35) speaks with approval of the early Italian geologists. Of Vallisneri he says, "I return with pleasure to the geologists of Italy who preceded, as has been already shown, the naturalists of other countries in their investigations into the ancient history of the earth, and who still maintained a decided pre-eminence. They refuted and ridiculed the physico-theological systems of Burnet, Whiston, and Woodward; while Vallisneri, in his comments on the Woodwardian theory, remarked how much the interests of religion, as well as of those of sound philosophy, had suffered by perpetually mixing up the sacred writings with questions of physical science." Again, he quotes the Carmelite friar Generelli, who, illustrating Moro before the Academy of Cremona in 1749, strongly opposed those who would introduce the supernatural into the domain of nature. "I hold in utter abomination, most learned Academicians, those systems which are built with their foundations in the air, and cannot be propped up without a miracle, and I undertake, with the assistance of Moro, to explain to you how these marine monsters were transported into the mountains by natural causes."

Sir Charles Lyell notices with exemplary impartiality the spirit of intolerance on both sides: how in France, Buffon, on the one hand, was

it would be easy to give numerous examples. It will be better, however, only to cite one or two authorities of weight. Perhaps no writer of the earlier Christian ages could be quoted whose authority is more generally recognized than that of St. Augustin. The same may be said, of the mediæval period, for St. Thomas Aquinas; and, since the movement of Luther, Suarez may be taken as a writer widely venerated as an authority and one whose orthodoxy has never been questioned.

It must be borne in mind that for a considerable time after even the last of these writers no one had disputed the generally received belief as to the small age of the world or at least of the kinds of animals and plants inhabiting it. It becomes therefore much more striking if views formed under such a condition of opinion are found to harmonize with modern ideas regarding "Creation" and organic life.

Now St. Augustin insists in a very remarkable manner on the merely derivative sense in which God's creation of

influenced by the theological faculty of the Sorbonne to recant his theory of the earth, and how Voltaire, on the other, allowed his prejudices to get the better, if not of his judgment, certainly of his expression of it. Thinking that fossil remains of shells, &c., were evidence in favour of orthodox views, Voltaire, Sir Charles Lyell (Principles, p. 56) tells us, "endeavoured to inculcate scepticism as to the real nature of such shells, and to recall from contempt the exploded dogma of the sixteenth century, that they were sports of nature. He also pretended that vegetable impressions were not those of real plants." . . . . "He would sometimes, in defiance of all consistency, shift his ground when addressing the vulgar; and, admitting the true nature of the shells collected in the Alps and other places, pretend that they were Eastern species, which had fallen from the hats of pilgrims coming from Syria. The numerous essays written by him on geological subjects were all calculated to strengthen prejudices, partly because he was ignorant of the real state of the science, and partly from his bad faith." As to the harmony between many early Church writers of great authority and modern views regarding certain matters of geology, see "Geology and Revelation," by the Rev. Gerald Molloy, D.D., London, 1870.

organic forms is to be understood; that is, that God created them by conferring on the material world the power to evolve them under suitable conditions. He says in his book on Genesis:[1] "Terrestria animalia, tanquam ex ultimo elemento mundi ultima; nihilominus *potentialiter,* quorum numeros tempus postea visibiliter explicaret."

Again he says:—

"Sicut autem in ipso grano invisibiliter erant omnia simul, quæ per tempora in arborem surgerent; ita ipse mundus cogitandus est, cum Deus *simul omnia creavit,* habuisse simul omnia quæ in illo et cum illo facta sunt quando factus est dies; non solum cœlum cum sole et lunâ et sideribus . . . .; sed etiam illa quæ aqua et terra produxit potentialiter atque causaliter, priusquam per temporum moras ita exorirentur, quomodo nobis jam nota sunt in eis operibus, quæ Deus usque nunc operatur."[2]

"Omnium quippe rerum quæ corporaliter visibiliterque nascuntur, occulta quædam semina in istis corporeis mundi hujus elementis latent."[3]

And again: "Ista quippe originaliter ac primordialiter in quadam textura elementorum cuncta jam creata sunt; sed acceptis opportunitatibus prodeunt."[4]

St. Thomas Aquinas, as was said in the first chapter, quotes with approval the saying of St. Augustin that in the first institution of nature we do not look for *Miracles,* but for the *laws of Nature:* "In prima institutione naturæ non quæritur miraculum, sed quid natura rerum habeat, ut Augustinus dicit."[5]

[1] "De Genesi ad Litt." lib. v. cap. v., No. 14 in Ben. Edit., vol. iii. p. 186.
[2] Lib. cit., cap. xxii., No. 44.
[3] Lib. cit., "De Trinitate," lib. iii. cap. viii.. No. 13.
[4] Lib. cit., cap. ix., No. 16.
[5] St. Thomas, Summa, i. quest. 67, art. 4, ad 3.

Again, he quotes with approval St. Augustin's assertion that the kinds were created only derivatively, "*potentialiter tantum.*"[1]

Also he says, "In prima autem rerum institutione fuit principium activum verbum Dei, quod de materia elementari produxit animalia, vel in actu vel *virtute*, secundum Aug. lib. 5 de Gen. ad lit. c. 5."[2]

Speaking of "kinds" (in scholastic phraseology "substantial forms") latent in matter, he says: "Quas quidam posuerunt non incipere per actionem naturæ sed prius in materia exstitisse, ponentes latitationem formarum. Et hoc accidit eis ex ignorantia materiæ, quia nesciebant distinguere inter potentiam et actum. Quia enim formæ præexistunt eas simpliciter præexistere."[3]

Also Cornelius à Lapide[4] contends that at least certain animals were not absolutely, but only derivatively created, saying of them, "Non fuerunt creata formaliter, sed potentialiter."

As to Suarez, it will be enough to refer to Disp. xv. § 2, n. 9, p. 508, t. i., edition *Vives*, Paris; also Nos. 13—15. Many other references to the same effect could easily be given, but these may suffice.

It is then evident that ancient and most venerable theological authorities distinctly assert *derivative* creation, and thus their teachings harmonize with all that modern science can possibly require.

It may indeed truly be said with Roger Bacon: "The saints never condemned many an opinion which the moderns think ought to be condemned."[5]

[1] Primæ Partis, vol. ii., quest. 74, art. 2. [2] Lib. cit., quest. 71, art. 1.
[3] Lib. cit., quest. 45, art. 8. [4] *Vide* In Genesim Comment. cap. i.
[5] Roger Bacon, Opus tertium, c. ix. p. 27, quoted in the *Rambler* for 1859, vol. xii. p. 375.

The various extracts given show clearly how far "evolution" is from any necessary opposition to the most orthodox theology. The same may be said of spontaneous generation. The most recent doctrine, lately advocated by Dr. H. Charlton Bastian,[1] teaches that matter exists in two different states, the crystalline (or statical) and the colloidal (or dynamical) conditions. It also teaches that colloidal matter, when exposed to certain conditions, presents the phenomena of life, and that it can be formed from crystalline matter, and thus that the *prima materia* of which these are diverse forms contains potentially all the multitudinous kinds of animal and vegetable existence. This theory moreover quite harmonizes with the views here advocated, for just as crystalline matter builds itself, under suitable conditions, along *certain definite lines*, so analogously colloidal matter has *its definite lines and directions* of development. Such matter is not collected in haphazard, accidental aggregations, but evolves according to its proper laws and special properties.

The perfect orthodoxy of these views is unquestionable. Nothing is plainer from the venerable writers quoted, as well as from a mass of other authorities, than that "the supernatural" is not to be looked for or expected in the sphere of mere nature. For this statement there is a general *consensus* of theological authority.

The teaching which the author has received is, that God is inscrutable and incomprehensible to us from the infinity

[1] See *Nature*, June and July, 1870. Those who, like Professors Huxley and Tyndall, do not accept his conclusions, none the less agree with him in principle, though they limit the evolution of the organic world from the inorganic to a very remote period of the world's history. (See Professor Huxley's address to the British Association at Liverpool, 1870, p. 17.)

of His attributes, so that our minds can, as it were, only apprehend, in a most fragmentary and imperfect manner (as through a glass darkly), dim perceptions of infinitesimal portions of His inconceivable perfection. In this way the partial glimpses obtained by us in various modes differ from each other; not that God is anything but the most perfect unity, but that apparently conflicting views arise from our inability to apprehend Him, except in this imperfect manner, *i.e.* by successive slight approximations along different lines of approach. Sir William Hamilton has said:[1] "Nature conceals God, and man reveals Him." It is not, according to the teaching above mentioned, exactly thus; but rather that physical nature reveals to us one side, one aspect of the Deity, while the moral and religious worlds bring us in contact with another, and at first, to our apprehension, a very different one. The difference and discrepancy, however, which are at first perceived, is soon found to proceed not from the reason but from a want of flexibility in the imagination. This want is far from surprising. Not only may a man be expected, as a matter of course, to be an adept in his own art, but at the same time to show an incapacity for a very different mode of activity.[2] We rarely find an artist who takes much

1 "Lectures on Metaphysics and Logic," vol. i. Lecture ii., p. 40.

2 In the same way that an undue cultivation of any one kind of knowledge is prejudicial to philosophy. Mr. James Martineau well observes: "Nothing is more common than to see maxims, which are unexceptionable as the assumptions of particular sciences, coerced into the service of a universal philosophy, and so turned into instruments of mischief and distortion. That 'we can know nothing but phenomena,'—that 'causation is simply constant priority,'—that 'men are governed invariably by their interests,' are examples of rules allowable as dominant hypotheses in physics or political economy, but exercising a desolating tyranny when thrust on to the throne of universal empire. He who seizes upon these and similar

interest in jurisprudence, or a prizefighter who is an acute metaphysician. Nay, more than this, a positive tendency may be developed, which, in the intellectual order, may result in a spontaneous and unreasoning disbelief in whatever appears at first sight to be in opposition to the more familiar concept. It has been aptly said "that past ages were pre-eminently credulous as compared with our own, yet the difference is not so much in the amount of the credulity as in the direction which it takes."[1]

Dr. Newman observes: "Any one study, of whatever kind, exclusively pursued, deadens in the mind the interest, nay the perception of any other. Thus, Cicero says that Plato and Demosthenes, Aristotle and Isocrates, might have respectively excelled in each other's province, but that each was absorbed in his own. Specimens of this peculiarity occur every day. You can hardly persuade some men to talk about anything but their own pursuit; they refer the whole world to their own centre, and measure all matters by their own rule, like the fisherman in the drama, whose eulogy on his deceased lord was, that 'he was so fond of fish.'"[2]

The same author urther says:[3] "When anything which comes before us is very unlike what we commonly experience, we consider it on that account untrue; not because it really shocks our reason as improbable, but because it startles our imagination as strange. Now, revelation

maxims, and carries them in triumph on his banner, may boast of his escape from the uncertainties of metaphysics, but is himself all the while the unconscious victim of their very vulgarest deception." ("Essays," Second Series, *A Plea for Philosophical Studies*, p. 421.)

1 Lecky's "History of Rationalism," vol. i. p. 73.

2 "Lectures on University Subjects," by J. H. Newman, D.D., p. 322.

3 Loc. cit. p. 324.

presents to us a perfectly different aspect of the universe from that presented by the sciences. The two informations are like the distinct subjects represented by the lines of the same drawing, which, accordingly as they are read on their concave or convex side, exhibit to us now a group of trees with branches and leaves, and now human faces." . . . "While then reason and revelation are consistent in fact, they often are inconsistent in appearance; and this seeming discordance acts most keenly on the imagination, and may suddenly expose a man to the temptation, and even hurry him on to the commission of definite acts of unbelief, in which reason itself really does not come into exercise at all."[1]

Thus we find just that distinctness between the ideas derived from physical science on the one hand and from religion on the other, which we might *a priori* expect if there exists that distinctness between the natural and the miraculous which theological authorities lay down.

Assuming, for argument's sake, the truth of Christianity, evidently the intention of its Author has not been to make the evidence for it so plain that its rejection would be the mark of intellectual incapacity. Conviction is not forced upon men as the knowledge that the government of England is constitutional, or that Paris is the capital of France, is forced upon all who choose to inquire into those subjects. The Christian system is one which puts on the strain, as it were, *every* faculty of man's higher nature, and the intellect is not (any more than we should *a priori* expect it to be) exempted from taking part in the

[1] Thus Professor Tyndall, in the *Pall Mall Gazette* of June 15, 1868, speaking of physical science, somewhat naïvely observes, "The *logical feebleness* of science is not sufficiently borne in mind. It keeps down the weed of superstition, not by logic, but by slowly rendering the mental soil unfit for its cultivation,"—*i.e.* by an *illogical* prejudice.

probationary action. A moral element enters into the acceptance of that system.

And so it is with natural religion, with those religious ideas—God, Creation, and Morality—which are anterior to revelation and repose upon reason. Here again it evidently has not been the intention of the Creator to make the evidence of His existence so plain that its non-recognition would be the mark of intellectual incapacity. Conviction, as to theism, is not forced upon men as is the conviction of the existence of the sun at noon-day.[1] A moral element enters also here, and the analogy which exists in this respect between Christianity and theism speaks eloquently of their primary derivation from one common author.[2]

Thus we might expect that it would be a vain task to seek anywhere in nature for evidence of Divine action, such that no one could sanely deny it. God will not allow Himself to be caught at the bottom of any man's crucible, or yield Himself to the experiments of gross-minded and irreverent inquirers. The natural, like the supernatural, revelation appeals to *the whole* of man's mental nature and not to the *reason alone.*[3]

None, therefore, need feel disappointed that evidence of

[1] By this it is not, of course, meant to deny that the existence of God can be demonstrated so as to demand the assent of the intellect taken, so to speak, by itself.

[2] It is reasonable to believe that, in matters of belief as well as of practice, God has not thought fit to annihilate the free will of man, but has permitted speculative difficulties to exist as the trial and the discipline of sharp and subtle intellects, as He has permitted moral temptations to form the trial and the discipline of strong and eager passions."—MANSEL, *Bampton Lectures*, 4th edition, p. 166.

[3] See some excellent remarks in the Rev. Dr. Newman's Parochial Sermons—the new edition (1869), vol. i. p. 211.

the direct action of the first cause in merely natural phenomena ever eludes our grasp; for assuredly those same phenomena will ever remain fundamentally inexplicable by physical science alone.

Enough has been said as to the distinction between absolute and derivative "creation." It remains to consider the successive "evolution" (Darwinian and other) of "specific forms," in a theological light.

As to what "evolution" is, we cannot of course hope to explain it completely, but we may define it as the manifestation to the intellect, by means of sensible impressions, of some ideal entity (power, principle, nature, or activity) which before that manifestation was in a latent, unrealized, and merely "potential" state—a state which is capable of becoming realized, actual, or manifest, when the requisite conditions are supplied.

"Specific forms," kinds or species, are (as was said in the introductory chapter) "peculiar congeries of characters or attributes, innate powers and qualities, and a certain nature realized in individuals."

Thus, then, the "evolution of specific forms" means the actual manifestation of special powers, or natures, which before were latent, in such a successive manner that there is in some way a genetic relation between posterior manifestations and those which preceded them.

On the special Darwinian hypothesis the manifestation of these forms is determined simply by the survival of the fittest of many indefinite variations.

On the hypothesis here advocated the manifestation is controlled and helped by such survival, but depends on some unknown internal laws which determine variation at special times and in special directions.

Professor Agassiz objects to the evolution theory, on the ground that "species, genera, families, &c., exist as thoughts, individuals as facts,"[1] and he offers the dilemma, "If species do not exist at all, as the supporters of the transmutation theory maintain, how can they vary? and if individuals alone exist, how can the differences which may be observed among them prove the variability of species?"

But the supporter of "evolution" need only maintain that the several "kinds" become manifested gradually by slight differences among the various individual embodiments of one specific idea. He might reply to the dilemma by saying, species do not exist *as species* in the sense in which they are said to vary (variation applying only to the concrete embodiments of the specific idea), and the evolution of species is demonstrated not by individuals *as individuals*, but as embodiments of different specific ideas.

Some persons seem to object to the term "creation" being applied to evolution, because evolution is an "exceedingly slow and gradual process." Now even if it were demonstrated that such is really the case, it may be asked, what is "slow and gradual"? The terms are simply relative, and the evolution of a specific form in ten thousand years would be instantaneous to a being whose days were as millions of millions of years.

There are others again who are inclined to deny the existence of species altogether, on the ground that their evolution is so gradual that if we could see all the stages it would be impossible to say *when* the manifestation of the old specific form ceased and that of the new one began. But surely it is no approach to a reason against the exist-

[1] *American Journal of Science*, July 1860, p. 143, quoted in Dr. Asa Gray's pamphlet, p. 47.

ence of a thing that we cannot determine the exact moment of its first manifestation. When watching "dissolving views," who can tell, whilst closely observing the gradual changes, exactly at what moment a new picture, say St. Mark's, Venice, can be said to have commenced its manifestation, or have begun to dominate a preceding representation of "Dotheboys' Hall"? That, however, is no reason for denying the complete difference between the two pictures and the ideas they respectively embody.

The notion of a special nature, a peculiar innate power and activity,—what the scholastics called a "substantial form,"—will be distasteful to many. The objection to the notion seems, however, to be a futile one, for it is absolutely impossible to altogether avoid such a conception and such an assumption. If we refuse it to the individuals which embody the species, we must admit it as regards their component parts—nay, even if we accept the hypothesis of pangenesis, we are nevertheless compelled to attribute to each gemmule that peculiar power of reproducing its own nature (its own "substantial form"), with its special activity, and that remarkable power of annexing itself to certain other well-defined gemmules the nature of which is also to plant themselves in a certain definite vicinity. So that in each individual, instead of one such peculiar power and activity dominating and controlling all the parts, you have an infinity of separate powers and activities limited to the several minute component gemmules.

It is possible that in some minds the notion may lurk that such powers are simpler and easier to understand, because the bodies they affect are so minute! This absurdity hardly bears stating. We can easily conceive a being so small that a gemmule would be to it as large as St. Paul's would be to us.

Admitting then the existence of species, and of their successive evolution, is there anything in these ideas hostile to Christian belief?

Writers such as Vogt and Buchner will of course contend that there is; but naturalists, generally, assume that God acts in and by the various laws of nature. And this is equivalent to admitting the doctrine of "derivative creation." With very few exceptions, none deny such Divine concurrence. Even "design" and "purpose" are recognized as quite compatible with evolution, and even with the special "nebular" and Darwinian forms of it. Professor Huxley well says,[1] "It is necessary to remark that there is a wider teleology, which is not touched by the doctrine of evolution, but is actually based upon the fundamental proposition of evolution." . . . . "The teleological and the mechanical views of nature are not necessarily mutually exclusive; on the contrary, the more purely a mechanist the speculator is, the more firmly does he assume a primordial molecular arrangement, of which all the phenomena of the universe are the consequences; and the more completely thereby is he at the mercy of the teleologist, who can always defy him to disprove that this primordial molecular arrangement was not intended to evolve the phenomena of the universe."[2]

Professor Owen says, that natural evolution through

[1] See *The Academy* for October 1869, No. 1, p. 13.

[2] Professor Huxley goes on to say that the mechanist may, in turn, demand of the teleologist how the latter knows it was so intended. To this it may be replied, he knows it as a necessary truth of reason deduced from his own primary intuitions, which intuitions cannot be questioned without *absolute* scepticism.

secondary causes, " by means of slow physical and organic operations through long ages, is not the less clearly recognizable as the act of all-adaptive Mind, because we have abandoned the old error of supposing it to be the result [1] of a primary, direct, and sudden act of creational construction." . . . . "The succession of species by continuously operating law is not necessarily a 'blind operation.' Such law, however designed in the properties and successions of natural objects, intimates, nevertheless, a preconceived progress. Organisms may be evolved in orderly succession, stage after stage, towards a foreseen goal, and the broad features of the course may still show the unmistakeable impress of Divine volition."

Mr. Wallace [2] declares that the opponents of evolution present a less elevated view of the Almighty. He says: "Why should we suppose the machine too complicated to have been designed by the Creator so complete that it would necessarily work out harmonious results? The theory of 'continual interference' is a limitation of the Creator's power. It assumes that He could not work by pure law in the organic, as He has done in the inorganic world." Thus, then, there is not only no necessary antagonism between the general theory of "evolution" and a Divine action, but the compatibility between the two is recognized by naturalists who cannot be suspected of any strong theological bias.[3]

[1] The Professor doubtless means the *direct* and *immediate* result. (See Trans. Zool. Soc. vol. v. p. 90.)

[2] "Natural Selection," p. 280.

[3] "That matter is governed by mind, that the contrivances and elaborations of the universe are the products of intelligence, are propositions which are quite unshaken, whether we regard these contrivances as the results of a single momentary exercise of the will, or of a slow, consistent,

The very same may be said as to the special Darwinian form of the theory of evolution.

It is true Mr. Darwin writes sometimes as if he thought that his theory militated against even *derivative creation.*[1] This, however, there is no doubt, was not really meant; and indeed, in the passage before quoted and criticised, the possibility of the Divine ordination of each variation is spoken of as a tenable view. He says ("Origin of Species," p. 569), "I see no good reason why the views given in this volume should shock the religious feelings of any one;" and he speaks of life "having been originally breathed by the Creator into a few forms or into one," which is *more* than the dogma of creation actually requires. We find then that no incompatibility is asserted (by any

and regulated evolution. The proofs of a pervading and developing intelligence, and the proofs of a co-ordinating and combining intelligence, are both untouched, nor can any conceivable progress of science in this direction destroy them. If the famous suggestion, that all animal and vegetable life results from a single vital germ, and that all the different animals and plants now existent were developed by a natural process of evolution from that germ, were a demonstrated truth, we should still be able to point to the evidences of intelligence displayed in the measured and progressive development, in those exquisite forms so different from what blind chance could produce." . . . . "The argument from design would indeed be changed; it would require to be stated in a new form, but it would be fully as cogent as before. Indeed it is, perhaps, not too much to say, that the more fully this conception of universal evolution is grasped, the more firmly a scientific doctrine of Providence will be established, and the stronger will be the presumption of a future progress."—LECKY's *History of Rationalism*, vol. i. p. 316.

[1] Dr. Asa Gray, *e.g.*, has thus understood Mr. Darwin. The Doctor says in his pamphlet, p. 38, "Mr. Darwin uses expressions which imply that the natural forms which surround us, because they have a history or natural sequence, could have been only generally, but not particularly designed,—a view at once superficial and contradictory; whereas his true line should be, that his hypothesis concerns the *order* and not the *cause*, the *how* and not the *why*, of the phenomena, and so leaves the question of design just where it was before."

scientific writers worthy of mention) between "evolution" and the co-operation of the Divine will; while the same "evolution" has been shown to be thoroughly acceptable to the most orthodox theologians who repudiate the intrusion of the supernatural into the domain of nature. A more complete harmony could scarcely be desired.

But if we may never hope to find in physical nature evidence of supernatural action, what sort of action might we expect to find there, looking at it from a theistic point of view? Surely an action the results of which harmonize with man's reason,[1] which is orderly, which disaccords with the action of blind chance and with the "fortuitous concourse of atoms" of Democritus; but at the same time an action which ever, in parts and in ultimate analysis, eludes our grasp, and the modes of which are different from those by which we should have attempted to accomplish such ends.

Now, this is just what we do find. The harmony, the beauty, and the order of the physical universe are the themes of continual panegyrics on the part of naturalists, and Mr. Darwin (as the Duke of Argyll remarks[2]) "exhausts every form of words and of illustration by which intention or mental purpose can be described,"[3] when speaking of the wonderfully complex adjustments to secure the fertilization of orchids. Also, we find co-existing with

[1] "All science is but the partial reflexion in the *reason of man*, of the great all-pervading *reason of the universe*. And the *unity* of science is the reflexion of the *unity* of nature and of the *unity* of that supreme reason and intelligence which pervades and rules over nature, and from whence all reason and all science is derived."—REV. BADEN POWELL, *Unity of the Sciences*, Essay i. § ii. p. 81.

[2] "The Reign of Law," p. 40.

[3] Though Mr. Darwin's epithets denoting design are metaphorical, his admiration of the result is unequivocal, nay, enthusiastic.

this harmony a mode of proceeding so different from that of man as (the direct supernatural action eluding us) to form a stumbling-block to many in the way of their recognition of Divine action at all: although nothing can be more inconsistent than to speak of the first cause as utterly inscrutable and incomprehensible, and at the same time to expect to find traces of a mode of action exactly similar to our own. It is surely enough if the results harmonize on the whole and preponderatingly with the rational, moral, and æsthetic instincts of man.

Mr. J. J. Murphy[1] has emphatically brought forward the evidence of "intelligence" throughout organic nature. He believes "that there is something in organic progress which mere Natural Selection among spontaneous variations will not account for," and that "this something is that organizing intelligence which guides the action of the inorganic forces, and forms structures which neither Natural Selection nor any other unintelligent agency could form."

This intelligence, however, Mr. Murphy considers may be unconscious, a conception which it is exceedingly difficult to understand, and which to many minds appears to be a contradiction in terms; the very first condition of an intelligence being that, if it knows anything, it should at least know its own existence.

Surely the evidence from physical facts agrees well with the overruling, concurrent action of God in the order of nature; which is no miraculous action, but the operation of laws which owe their foundation, institution, and maintenance to an omniscient Creator of whose intelligence our own is a feeble adumbration, inasmuch as it is created in the "image and likeness" of its Maker.

[1] See "Habit and Intelligence," vol. i. p. 348.

This leads to the final consideration, a difficulty by no means to be passed over in silence, namely, the ORIGIN OF MAN.[1] To the general theory of Evolution, and to the special Darwinian form of it, no exception, it has been shown, need be taken on the ground of orthodoxy. But in saying this, it has not been meant to include in the process of evolution the soul of man.

It is a generally received doctrine that the soul of every individual man is absolutely created in the strict and primary sense of the word, that it is produced by a direct or supernatural[2] act, and, of course, that by such an act the soul of the first man was similarly created. It is therefore important to inquire whether "evolution" conflicts with th doctrine.

Now the two beliefs are in fact perfectly compatible, and this is the case, either on the hypothesis—(1) that man's

1 Since the first edition of this work appeared, Mr. Darwin has published his "Descent of Man." Therein he shows elaborately the resemblances which exist both in structure and mode of development between man's body and the bodies of inferior forms. He also calls attention to similarity in diseases, parasites, the effects of medicines, stimulants, &c. All this, however, merely amounts to a proof of what no one denies, namely, that man *is* an animal; and consequently to the establishment of an *a priori* probability that *if* other animals have arisen by "Natural Selection," the animal man has also arisen in like manner, unless a valid objection can be raised from some other part of his nature. It is patent that an objection can be raised from his intellectual and moral faculties, and accordingly Mr. Darwin endeavours to show that there is no difference of *kind* between these faculties and the psychical powers of brutes. In this endeavour he fails utterly. The result is that Man (the totality of his being and not his anatomy only being considered) is seen, yet more clearly from this very failure, to differ from every other animal by a distinction far more profound than any which separates each irrational animal from every other.

2 The term, as before said, not being used in its ordinary theological sense, but to denote an immediate Divine action as distinguished from God's action through the powers conferred on the physical universe.

body was created in a manner different in kind from that by which the bodies of other animals were created; or (2) that it was created in a similar manner to theirs.

One of the authors of the Darwinian theory, indeed, contends that even as regards man's body, an action took place different from that by which brute forms were evolved. Mr. Wallace[1] considers that "Natural Selection" alone could not have produced so large a brain in the savage, in possessing which he is furnished with an organ beyond his needs. Also that it could not have produced that peculiar distribution of hair, especially the nakedness of the back, which is common to all races of men, nor the peculiar construction of the feet and hands. He says,[2] after speaking of the prehensile foot, common without a single exception to all the apes and lemurs, "it is difficult to see why the prehensile power should have been taken away" by the mere operation of Natural Selection. "It must certainly have been useful in climbing, and the case of the baboons shows that it is quite compatible with terrestrial locomotion. It may not be compatible with perfectly easy erect locomotion; but, then, how can we conceive that early man, *as an animal*, gained anything by purely erect locomotion? Again, the hand of man contains latent capacities and powers which are unused by savages, and must have been even less used by palæolithic man and his still ruder predecessors. It has all the appearance of an organ prepared for the use of civilized man, and one which was required to render civilization possible." Again, speaking of the "wonderful power, range, flexibility and sweetness of the musical sounds producible by the human larynx," he adds, "The habits of savages give no indication of how this

[1] See "Natural Selection," pp. 332 to 360. [2] Loc. cit., p. 349.

faculty could have been developed by Natural Selection; because it is never required or used by them. The singing of savages is a more or less monotonous howling, and the females seldom sing at all. Savages certainly never choose their wives for fine voices, but for rude health, and strength and physical beauty. Sexual selection could not therefore have developed this wonderful power, which only comes into play among civilized people. It seems as if the organ had been prepared in anticipation of the future progress of man, since it contains latent capacities which are useless to him in his earlier condition. The delicate correlations of structure that give it such marvellous powers could not therefore have been acquired by means of Natural Selection."

To this may be added the no less wonderful faculty in the ear of appreciating delicate musical tones, and the harmony of chords.

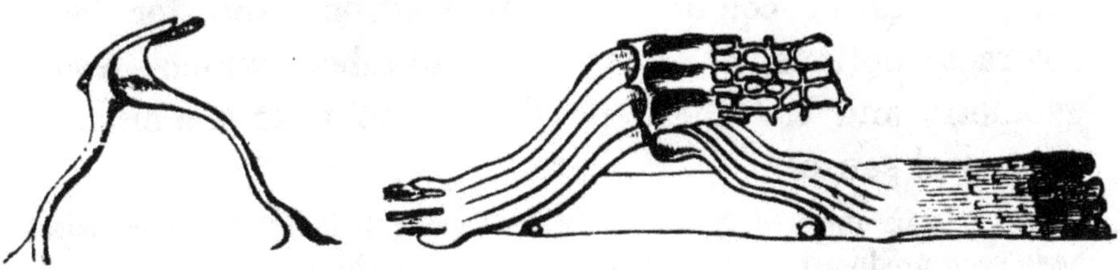

FIBRES OF CORTI.

It matters not what part of the organ subserves this function, but it has been supposed that it is ministered to by the fibres *of Corti.*[1] Now it can hardly be contended that the preservation of any race of men in the struggle for life could have depended on such an extreme delicacy and

[1] See Professor Huxley's "Lessons in Elementary Physiology," p. 218.

refinement of the internal ear,[1]—a perfection only fully exercised in the enjoyment and appreciation of the most exquisite musical performances.[2] Here, surely, we have an instance of an organ preformed, ready beforehand for such action as could never by itself have been the cause of its development,—the action having only been subsequent, not anterior. The author is not aware what may be the minute structure of the internal ear in the highest apes, but if (as from analogy is probable) it is much as in man, then *a fortiori* we have an instance of *anticipatory* development of a most marked and unmistakable kind. And this is not all. There is no reason to suppose that any animal besides man appreciates musical *harmony*. It is certain that no other one *produces* it.

Mr. Wallace also urges objections drawn from the origin of some of man's mental faculties, such as "the capacity to form ideal conceptions of space and time, of eternity and infinity—the capacity for intense artistic feelings of pleasure, in form, colour and composition—and for those abstract notions of form and number which render geometry and arithmetic possible," also from the origin of the moral sense.[3]

[1] It may be objected, perhaps, that excessive delicacy of the ear might have been produced by having to guard against the approach of enemies, some savages being remarkable for their keenness of hearing at great distances. But the perceptions of *intensity* and *quality* of sound are very different. Some persons who have an extremely acute ear for delicate sounds, and who are fond of music, have yet an incapacity for detecting whether an instrument is slightly out of tune.

[2] In his recent work on the "Descent of Man," vol. ii. p. 333, Mr. Darwin remarks: "As neither the enjoyment nor the capacity of producing musical notes are faculties of the least direct use to man in reference to his ordinary habits of life, they must be ranked amongst the most mysterious with which he is endowed."

[3] Loc. cit., pp. 351, 352.

The validity of these objections is fully conceded by the author of this book; but he would push them much further, and contend (as has been now repeatedly said), that another law, or other laws, than "Natural Selection" have determined the evolution of *all* organic forms and inorganic forms also. And Mr. Wallace, in order to be quite self-consistent, should arrive at the very same conclusion, inasmuch as he is inclined to trace all phenomena to the action of superhuman WILL. He says:[1] "If therefore we have traced one force, however minute, to an origin in our own WILL, while we have no knowledge of any other primary cause of force, it does not seem an improbable conclusion that all force may be will-force; and thus, that the whole universe is not merely dependent on, but actually *is*, the WILL of higher intelligences, or of one Supreme Intelligence."

If there is really evidence, as Mr. Wallace believes, of the action of an overruling intelligence in the evolution of the "human form divine;" if we may go so far as this, then surely an analogous action may well be traced in the production of the horse, the camel, or the dog, so largely identified with human wants and requirements. And if from other than physical considerations we may believe that such action, though undemonstrable, has taken and does take place; then (reflecting on sensible phenomena the theistic light derived from psychical facts) we may, in the language of Mr. Wallace, "see indications of that power in facts which, by themselves, would not serve to prove its existence."[2]

Mr. Murphy, as has been said before, finds it necessary to accept the wide-spread action of "intelligence" as the

[1] Loc. cit., p. 368. [2] Loc. cit., p. 350.

agent by which *all* organic forms have been called forth from the inorganic. But all science tends to unity, and this tendency makes it reasonable to attribute to all physical existences a mode of formation which we may have evidence for in any *one* of them. It therefore makes it reasonable to attribute, if possible, the very same agency which we find operating in the field of biology, also to the inorganic world. If on the grounds brought forward the action of intelligence may be affirmed in the production of man's bodily structure, it becomes probable *a priori* that it may also be predicated of the formative action by which has been produced the animals which minister to him, and all organic life whatsoever. Nay more, it is then congruous to expect analogous action in the development of crystalline and colloidal structures, and in chemical compositions, in geological evolutions, and the formation not only of this earth, but of the solar system and whole sidereal universe.

If such really be the direction in which physical science, philosophically considered, points; if intelligence may thus be seen to preside over the evolution of each system of worlds and the unfolding of every blade of grass—this grand result harmonizes indeed with the teachings of faith that, in the natural order, God acts and concurs with those laws of the material universe which were not only instituted by His will, but are sustained by His co-operation; and we are thus enabled to discern in the natural order, however darkly, the Divine Author of nature—Him in whom "we live, and move, and have our being."

But if this view is accepted, then it is no longer absolutely necessary to suppose that any action different in kind took place in the production of man's body, from that which took place in the production of the bodies of other animals, and of the whole material universe.

Of course if it *can* be demonstrated that that difference of which Mr. Wallace asserts the existence, does really exist, it is plain that we then have to do with facts not only harmonizing with religion, but, as it were, preaching and proclaiming it.

It is not, however, necessary for Christianity that any such view should prevail. Man, according to the old scholastic definition, is "a rational animal" (*animal rationale*), and his animality is distinct in nature from his rationality, though inseparably joined, during life, in one common personality. Man's animal body must have had a different source from that of the spiritual soul which informs it, owing to the distinctness of the two orders to which those two existences severally belong.

Scripture seems plainly to indicate this when it says: "God made man from the dust of the earth, and breathed into his nostrils the breath of life." This is a plain and direct statement that man's *body* was *not* created in the primary and absolute sense of the word, but was evolved from pre-existing material (symbolized by the term "dust of the earth"), and was therefore only *derivatively created*, i.e. by the operation of secondary laws. His *soul*, on the other hand, was created in quite a different way, not by any pre-existing means, external to God himself, but by the direct action of the Almighty, symbolized by the term "breathing:" the very form adopted by Christ, when conferring the *supernatural* powers and graces of the Christian dispensation, and a form still daily used in the rites and ceremonies of the Church.[1]

[1] Since the first edition of this work appeared, its author has had the satisfaction of meeting with the following passage:—"Man was made

That the first man should have had this double origin agrees with what we now experience. For supposing each human soul to be directly and immediately created, yet each human body is evolved by the ordinary operation of natural physical laws.

Professor Flower, in his Introductory Lecture[1] (p. 20) to his course of Hunterian Lectures for 1870, observes: "Whatever man's place may be either *in* or *out* of nature, whatever hopes or fears or feelings about himself or his race he may have, we all of us admit that these are quite uninfluenced by our knowledge of the fact that each individual man comes into the world by the ordinary processes of generation, according to the same laws which apply to the development of all organic beings whatever; that every part of him which can come under the scrutiny of the anatomist or naturalist has been evolved according to these regular laws from a simple minute ovum, indistinguishable to our senses from that of any of the inferior animals. If this be so—if man is what he is, notwithstanding the corporeal mode of origin of the individual man, so he will assuredly be neither less nor more than man, whatever may be shown regarding the corporeal origin of the whole race, whether this was from the dust of the earth, or by the modification of some pre-existing animal form."

Man is indeed compound, in him two distinct orders of being impinge and mingle; and with this composite nature

rational, after he was made corporeal. 'The Lord God formed man of the dust of the ground, and breathed into his nostrils the breath of life, and man *became* a living soul' (Gen. ii. 7). Here are two acts on the part of the Creator—the forming the dust, and the breathing the life." (See Sermons bearing on Subjects of the Day, by John Henry Newman, D.D.; New Edition. Rivingtons, 1869. Sermon viii. p. 101.)

[1] Published by John Churchill.

an origin from two concurrent modes of action is congruous, and might be expected *a priori*. At the same time as the "soul" is "the form of the body," the soul might be expected to modify the body into a structure of harmony and beauty standing alone in the organic world of nature. Also that, with the full perfection and beauty of that soul, attained by the concurrent action of "Nature" and "Grace," a character would be formed like nothing else which is visible in this world, and having a mode of action different from, inasmuch as complementary to, all inferior modes of action.

Something of this is evident even to those who approach the subject from the point of view of physical science only. Thus Mr. Wallace observes,[1] that according to his idea man is to be placed "apart, as not only the head and culminating point of the grand series of organic nature, but as in some degree *a new and distinct order of being.*[2] From those infinitely remote ages when the first rudiments of organic life appeared upon the earth, every plant and every animal has been subject to one great law of physical change. As the earth has gone through its grand cycles of geological, climatal, and organic progress, every form of life has been subject to its irresistible action, and has been continually but imperceptibly moulded into such new shapes as would preserve their harmony with the ever-changing universe. No living thing could escape this law of its being; none (except, perhaps, the simplest and most rudimentary organisms) could remain unchanged and live amid the universal change around it."

"At length, however, there came into existence a being in whom that subtle force we term *mind*, became of greater

[1] "Natural Selection," p. 324. [2] The italics are not Mr. Wallace's.

importance than his mere bodily structure. Though with a naked and unprotected body, *this* gave him clothing against the varying inclemencies of the seasons. Though unable to compete with the deer in swiftness, or with the wild bull in strength, *this* gave him weapons with which to capture or overcome both. Though less capable than most other animals of living on the herbs and the fruits that unaided nature supplies, this wonderful faculty taught him to govern and direct nature to his own benefit, and make her produce food for him when and where he pleased. From the moment when the first skin was used as a covering; when the first rude spear was formed to assist in the chase; when fire was first used to cook his food; when the first seed was sown or shoot planted, a grand revolution was effected in nature, a revolution which in all the previous ages of the earth's history had had no parallel, for a being had arisen who was no longer necessarily subject to change with the changing universe, a being who was in some degree superior to nature, inasmuch as he knew how to control and regulate her action, and could keep himself in harmony with her, not by a change in body, but by an advance in mind."

"On this view of his special attributes, we may admit 'that he is indeed a being apart.' Man has not only escaped 'Natural Selection' himself, but he is actually able to take away some of that power from nature which before his appearance she universally exercised. We can anticipate the time when the earth will produce only cultivated plants and domestic animals; when man's selection shall have supplanted 'Natural Selection;' and when the ocean will be the only domain in which that power can be exerted."

Baden Powell[1] observes on this subject: "The relation of the animal man to the intellectual, moral, and spiritual man, resembles that of a crystal slumbering in its native quarry to the same crystal mounted in the polarizing apparatus of the philosopher. The difference is not in physical nature, but in investing that nature with a new and higher application. Its continuity with the material world remains the same, but a new relation is developed in it, and it claims kindred with ethereal matter and with celestial light."

This well expresses the distinction between the merely physical and hyperphysical natures of man, and the subsumption of the former into the latter which dominates it.

The same author in speaking of man's moral and spiritual nature says:[2] "The assertion in its very essence refers wholly to a DIFFERENT ORDER OF THINGS, apart from and transcending any material ideas whatsoever." Again[3] he adds: "In proportion as man's *moral* superiority is held to consist in attributes *not* of a *material* or corporeal kind or origin, it can signify little how his *physical* nature may have originated."

Now physical science, as such, has nothing to do with the soul of man which is hyperphysical. That such an entity exists, that the correlated physical forces go through their Protean transformations, have their persistent ebb and flow outside of the world of WILL and SELF-CONSCIOUS MORAL BEING, are propositions the proofs of which have no place in the present work. This at least may however be confidently affirmed, that no reach of

[1] "Unity of Worlds," Essay ii. § ii. p. 247. [2] Ibid. Essay i. § ii. p. 76.
[3] Ibid. Essay iii. § iv. p. 466.

physical science in any coming century will ever approach to a demonstration that countless modes of being, as different from each other as are the force of gravitation and conscious maternal love, may not co-exist. Two such modes are made known to us by our natural faculties only: the physical, which includes the first of these examples; the hyperphysical, which embraces the other. For those who accept revelation, a third and a distinct mode of being and of action is also made known; namely, the direct and immediate or, in the sense here given to the term, the supernatural. An analogous relationship runs through and connects all these modes of being and of action. The higher mode in each case employs and makes use of the lower, the action of which it occasionally suspends or alters, as gravity is suspended by electro-magnetic action, or the living energy of an organic being restrains the inter-actions of the chemical affinities belonging to its various constituents.

Thus conscious will controls and directs the exercise of the vital functions according to desire, and moral consciousness tends to control desire in obedience to higher dictates.[1] The action of living organisms depends upon

[1] A good exposition of how an inferior action has to yield to one higher is given by Dr. Newman in his "Lectures on University Subjects," p. 372.

"What is true in one science, is dictated to us indeed according to that science, but not according to another science, or in another department. What is certain in the military art, has force in the military art, but not in statesmanship; and if statesmanship be a higher department of action than war, and enjoins the contrary, it has no force on our reception and obedience at all. And so what is true in medical science, might in all cases be carried out, *were* man a mere animal or brute without a soul; but since he is a rational, responsible being, a thing may be ever so true in medicine, yet may be unlawful in fact, in consequence of the *higher* law of morals and religion coming to some different conclusion."

and subsumes the laws of inorganic matter. Similarly the actions of animal life depend upon and subsume the laws of organic matter. In the same way the actions of a self-conscious moral agent, such as man, depend upon while they subsume the laws of animal life. When a part or the whole series of these natural actions is altered or suspended by the intervention of action of a still higher order, we have then a "miracle."

From the foregoing observations we seem to find a perfect harmony in the double nature of man, his rationality making use of and subsuming his animality; his soul arising from direct and immediate creation, and his body being formed at first (as now in each separate individual) by derivative or secondary creation, through natural laws. By such secondary creation, *i.e.* by natural laws, for the most part as yet unknown but aided by "Natural Selection," all the various kinds of animals and plants have been manifested on this planet. That Divine action has concurred and concurs in these laws we know by deductions from our primary intuitions; and physical science, if unable to demonstrate such action, is at least as impotent to disprove it. Disjoined from these deductions, the phenomena of the universe present an aspect devoid of all that appeals to the loftiest aspirations of man, all that stimulates his efforts after goodness, and presents consolations for unavoidable shortcomings. Conjoined with these same deductions, all the harmony of physical nature and the constancy of its laws are seen unimpaired, while the reason, the conscience, and the æsthetic instincts are alike gratified. We have thus a true reconciliation of science and religion, in which each gains and neither loses, one being complementary to the other.

Some apology is due to the reader for certain observations and arguments which have been here advanced, and which have little in the shape of novelty to recommend them. But, after all, novelty can hardly be predicated of the views here criticised and opposed. Some of these seem almost a return to the "fortuitous concourse of atoms" of Democritus, and even the very theory of "Natural Selection" itself—a "survival of the fittest"—was in part thought out not hundreds but *thousands* of years ago. Opponents of Aristotle maintained that by the accidental occurrence of combinations, organisms have been preserved and perpetuated such as final causes, did they exist, would have brought about, disadvantageous combinations or variations being speedily exterminated. "For when the very same combinations happened to be produced which the law of final causes would have called into being, those combinations which proved to be advantageous to the organism were preserved; while those which were not advantageous perished, and still perish, like the minotaurs and sphinxes of Empedocles."[1]

In conclusion, the author ventures to hope that this treatise may have contributed, however slightly, towards clearing the way for peace and conciliation and for a more ready perception of the harmony which exists between the deductions from our primary intuitions and the teachings of physical science, so far, that is, as concerns the evolution of organic forms—*the genesis of species.*

The aim has been to support the doctrine that these

[1] Quoted from the *Rambler* of March 1860, p. 364: "*Ὅπου μὲν οὖν ἅπαντα συνέβη ὥσπερ κἂν εἰ ἕνεκά του ἐγίνετο, ταῦτα μὲν ἐσώθη ἀπὸ τοῦ αὐτομάτου συστάντα ἐπιτηδείως, ὅσα δὲ μὴ οὕτως ἀπώλετο καὶ ἀπόλλυται, καθάπερ Ἐμπεδοκλῆς λέγει τὰ βουγενῆ καὶ ἀνδρόπρωρα.*"—ARIST. *Phys.* ii. c. 8.

species have been evolved by ordinary *natural laws* (for the most part unknown) aided by the *subordinate* action of "Natural Selection," and at the same time to remind some readers that there is and can be absolutely nothing in physical science which forbids them to regard those natural laws as acting with the Divine concurrence and in obedience to a creative fiat originally imposed on the primeval Cosmos, "in the beginning," by its Creator, its Upholder, and its Lord.

INDEX.

D.

E.

F.

G.

H.

I.

J.

K.

L.

M.

N.

Q.

R.

S.

T.

U.

V.

W.

Y.

Z.

R. CLAY, SONS, AND TAYLOR, PRINTERS, LONDON.

CPSIA information can be obtained
at www.ICGtesting.com
Printed in the USA
LVHW040728020323
740708LV00002B/133

9 783382 115234